BEEKMAN HILLS

KC ENDERS

ISBN-979-8-9911880-0-5

TROUBLES

BEEKMAN HILLS

Troubles
BEEKMAN HILLS

Dedication
*To my 'fiends'. There is no way this I could have done this
without the support of each of you.
Thank you!*

ONE

Orphan.

Origin: Late Middle English (noun)-Late Latin *orphanus*
destitute, without parents.

I'm an orphan.

It's an unofficial designation, but it fits. I'm broke as hell putting myself through college, and that's close enough to destitute.

The "without parents" part is tricky. They're both alive. They even live in the same small New York town as me; we just don't interact. At all—no phone calls, no dinners together.

Nothing.

Cutting them out of my life was not an easy choice until

it was. Cut ties, or let them drag me down. If I didn't have Gracyn as my roommate, I don't know what I'd do.

I scoop another handful of ice into the blender and hold the lid in place. Flipping the switch, I watch as the whiskey blends with the lemonade. When the ice is a slushed perfectly sassy pink, I pour the whiskey sours into tall glasses, adding straws and a couple whiskey-soaked cherries. My nana taught me to make these before I hit double digits. Told me it was her "secret" recipe. I don't know that it's any great secret, but it's perfect every damn time.

The sound of the blender is replaced by the whir of Gracyn's hairdryer as I take the handful of steps down the hall to our bathroom. I squeeze between where she's leaning against the vanity and the tub, knocking into her as I pass and hand her a whiskey sour hoping for a distraction.

I shove my arms up into the front of my new tee shirt and pull it away from my body, needing to stretch it out over my boobs a little. Gracyn bought us matching shirts for St. Patrick's Day and, of course, she bought a size smaller than I would have.

"What are you doing?" She slams her glass down and smacks at my hands. "That shirt fits you perfectly. Leave it alone."

"Gracyn," I whine, "we're just going to McBride's. Why do you feel the need to pour me into this tiny thing?" I'm not proud of the whining, but I feel way too exposed.

I prop my hands on my hips and face the mirror full-on. The thin green material stretches tight over *the girls* and the neckline scoops way lower than I'm comfortable with. Gracyn stares back at me, slurping from her glass.

It's fascinating, watching her brain freeze hit, twisting

and contorting her features. I try to push down the laughter that bubbles up, but it's not working.

"Lis, you need to stop hiding your curves—use them, show them off. And for the love of God, promise me you'll try and have fun tonight?"

I settle myself on the side of the tub in our tiny bathroom while she finishes her smoky cat-eye. "It's time for you to get back out there. Just a little bit. Maybe flirt a little—kiss someone tonight." Gracyn waves her hands up and down the script on her shirt, like she's presenting prizes on a game show. "Kiss me, I'm Irish-ish" is scrawled across our chests, highlighted with bright red kissy lips. The shirts are cute, but it would be so much better if the lips weren't perfectly centered over my left boob.

"There's not going to be anyone new there. I'm pretty sure I've kissed everyone I needed to in this town." It's mostly true. Beekman Hills is nothing but a sleepy little college town about an hour outside New York City. Gracyn and I grew up here and sadly never left.

MCBRIDE'S PUBLIC HOUSE is only a few blocks from our apartment and the walk down Main Street is cold. Our breaths trail behind us in white plumes. I pull my fleece tighter around me and pick up the pace. Most of the businesses along Main Street are closed for the night, but the scent of cinnamon and coffee still linger outside the coffee shop as we hurry past.

The line to get into the pub winds around the white clapboard building that's been here longer than I've been alive. College students and townies dressed in whatever green and plaid they could find—short skirts, ridiculous hats—and frat boys in kilts. All these people are in line, anxious to get their hands on cheap green beer and listen to a really bad Irish band.

Gracyn and I scoot around the back of the building and push through the door into the kitchen. Francie McBride's bright gaze peers up at us over an impossibly tall stack of plastic cups. He juts his cheek out around the tower precariously balanced in his hands for a quick kiss. "'Lo, love. Just gettin' in, are you?" His accent is extra thick tonight.

Gracyn and I have not had to wait in a line here for years. Francie busted me when I was nineteen trying to drink with a fake ID. He sat talking to me for hours instead of calling the cops, taking me under his wing and eventually bought me my first legal drink. He's been kind of a dad to me ever since. My own father couldn't be bothered finding his way out of the bottom of a bottle.

Gracyn pulls her jacket off over her head showing off her creation. "I bought us matching shirts for tonight and she didn't want to wear it. It took some time to convince her."

"No, it took whiskey to convince me." I pull my bottom lip between my teeth and shift uncomfortably.

Francie steps back to look at us as I drop my jacket on a stack of boxes, eyes crinkling above the scruffy beard he's had forever.

"Let me help you take those out to Finn," I say to try and move the conversation off my chest.

"I've got these. Go and have a pint. Off with you, then." Francie pushes past me, chuckling at our shirts, shaking his head. "Come on, then. I've a new lad at the bar tonight, make sure he treats you right, yeah?"

It's tight, but following close behind we get through the chaos pretty quickly. At the scarred, deep oak bar Francie bumps Finn and throws a nod in our direction. Finn turns, his wide smile about splits his face as he makes his way over to us, pouring drinks and collecting money as he goes. He hops up leaning over the bar and lays a kiss on me.

He thinks he's the Irish Casanova, but the boy is too sweet to pull it off.

"Finn, I need a pitcher and two cups," I shout to him slapping ten dollars down on the bar.

"And two shots of whiskey," Gracyn yells throwing down another ten.

Finn slides us our plastic cups before filling the pitcher. "Give us a kiss, Gracyn, and I'll get it for you." He's already reaching for the bottle and a couple of shot glasses.

Gracyn leans over the bar and Finn's eyes go wide with surprise, spilling whiskey as he pours. He thinks he has a chance, but she's a flirt, plain and simple, so the kiss Finn thinks he's getting? Nothing more than a peck on the cheek.

We down our shots and turn, taking in the crush of wall-to-wall bodies. There's a tiny bit of open space by the pool tables, so I grab the pitcher and start making my way through—turning sideways, trying hard not to brush up against strangers. I breathe a sigh of relief when we're through and fill our cups.

The band in the corner launches into their next set, filling the old bar with strains of violin and lilting voices bouncing around the room.

"Have you heard from them?" Gracyn leans in close, not so much for the noise level, but more to keep this conversation just between us.

I take a drink of the crappy beer and shake my head.

"Nothing? From any of them?"

I shake my head and sigh. "Nope. Not a word." I should be surprised, sad, something, but this is how my family is.

Gracyn walked in on my boyfriend—ex-boyfriend—bending my sister over the hood of my mom's car on Christmas Eve.

Nope, not going there—not tonight.

"I thought I'd hear from Rob when Francie kicked him and Maryse out last month, but, nothing," I say.

"Unreal. What a dickhead. *Hey—*" She lurches at me spilling beer down my front. It doesn't feel cold in the cup, but when it's running down my cleavage, it's frigid.

The icy sneering glare of Rob's best friend, Tyler, is worse. "Watch where you're going, bitch. You wouldn't want to get thrown out of McBride's." Tyler wasn't all that nice to me when I was dating Rob, but since we broke up, he's been an absolute dick.

Somehow, this is my fault. I feel eyes on me from all around. I hate being the center of attention, and with bodies pressing in from all sides, my skin feels hot and too tight. I blink at the ceiling trying desperately to stem the tears starting to form. There's no way I can make it through the tightly packed crowd before they spill and, God help me, the last thing I want is for it to get back to Rob that I'm still crying over him—because that's exactly the story this asshole will tell.

"Oi!" A low growl comes from Francie's new guy as he slices through the crowd like they're not even there. "None of that—apologize to her. Now." His voice, strong and thickly accented, carries over the band and bar noise, leaving no doubt that he's serious. He stands with his back to me, shielding me from the rest of the room.

Gracyn reaches for the bar towel in his hand and he nods to her.

"Not my fault she spilled her drink—looks good on her though." Tyler looks around the broad wall between us, leering at the way my shirt clings to my very obviously cold boobs.

The music has stopped, all attention is on me now and I just want to disappear.

Francie checks me with a quick look and a nod placing a warm hand on my shoulder. "Aidan, take her round back and fetch her a dry shirt from one o' the boxes back there. I'll take care of this one." With a firm hand, Francie collects Tyler's cup and chucks it in the trash. "Out, and ye'll not come back. Go drink wit' that bastard friend o' yours. Off with you, then."

The new guy, Aidan, takes the towel from Gracyn and pauses, his hand between us. He moves to try and blot at my shirt but stops, handing me the towel instead. "Erm, here."

I clutch the white towel to my chest, trying and failing miserably to hide my discomfort.

Grabbing my hand, he pulls me in close behind him leading me to the backroom. He rifles through some boxes pulling out a clean shirt that is huge—huge. "This should do, then."

"Thanks. You didn't have to do that, you know."

"Your shirt's soaked." He rests his hands on his hips, making a point to meet my gaze.

"I meant coming to my rescue. I'm used to his shit. I'd have been fine." I shake out the dry shirt pulling it over my head and wrap my arms around myself inside—hiding a little.

"Jesus, what are you doing?" Aidan turns on his heel, his broad back blocking the doorway. "Hang on, I'll just—" Muttering, he pulls the door shut behind him.

I change quickly, relieved to be dry and out of the cold, clingy shirt.

The door doesn't budge when I push at it. I knock, but the noise in the bar means the sound gets lost. Sighing, I turn to lean back against it, and pull out my phone hoping Gracyn will feel her phone vibrate, or come looking for me soon. Before I slide halfway to the floor, the door flies open and I tumble out, not at all gracefully.

Shit.

"That's twice, I've rescued you now." Aidan's lips quirk up on one side, like he's trying to suppress a smile as he helps me up off the floor. "Sorry, I was leaning on it—making sure no one walked in on you." His warm hand envelopes mine, squeezing before I slide it away.

"So, what does that mean, I have the luck of the Irish?" I can't believe that really just came out of my mouth. I close my eyes and take a deep breath, trying to push my complete awkwardness away with the exhale.

"You're Irish then?" His brow cocks up, disappearing under his black hair falling forward across his forehead. Dark blue eyes dance across my face as he pulls a curl from the collar of my new, way too big shirt.

"Absolutely." I'm not the least bit Irish. Not at all. "Everyone's Irish on St. Patrick's Day."

"Well, then. Let's get you a fresh beer and back to your

friend." His touch is hot, low on my back, guiding me away from the quiet and back out to the crowd.

Gracyn hands me a beer and looks up at Aidan. "Thank you."

"Think nothing of it." His eyes crinkle at the corners as he smiles down at me before sliding back behind the bar. His teeth gleaming white against the dark scruff along his jaw. It's perfect, warm and sweet, right down to the slightly crooked tooth, front and center. I miss the warmth of his hand as he falls right into the rhythm again, pouring drinks and smiling broadly at each person.

As we move across the room, my skin prickles again. Turning around, my gaze goes straight to Aidan—only to find him watching me. I smile and turn away feeling my stomach flip and flutter.

Gracyn finds some people we work with, people I know and feel comfortable with, but I feel eyes on me the whole time. That itchy, scratchy feeling that tells me I'm paranoid about Rob and his stupid friends. I know Francie threw those guys out, but I can't help scanning the room, and each time I do, my eyes fall on him instead.

Aidan.

He and Finn are in constant motion. Working the bar like they're dancing, playing to the crowd like nothing I've seen before. Aidan is older than me, for sure, but it shows more in his bearing, the way he moves—the way he commands attention, than anything else. Looking around the room, I see most of the girls are staring at him, or undressing him in their minds, I'm sure.

His green plaid button-down stretches across his broad

shoulders as he reaches for the next pitcher to fill. The buttons strain across his muscled chest a little when he takes a deep breath, pulling on the tap. And just a touch of his flat stomach shows as he reaches up to push his black hair back from his face as the green beer fills the plastic pitcher. He surveys the room, brows pinched together like he's searching for something.

I watch as he takes in every corner of the room—scanning the faces—until his gaze settles on mine and his features relax into a smile.

TWO

Aidan

In the past two weeks of working this pub, I thought I'd seen it busy. Not in the least. Right now, the place is packed wall-to-wall with university students and probably half the population of this small town—and the queue to get in still snakes around the building. If you'd asked me six months ago I would have thought I'd be spending the day in a pub with my brother, but plans changed and I needed to get out of Dublin.

Francie welcomed me with open arms and a cold pint when I showed up at his door. I'd known him most of my life. When he offered me a place to stay and a few shifts in his pub, I jumped at the chance to lose myself for a bit. I moved in with a couple of his bartenders and while it was nothing special—a loft space in their two-bedroom apartment—it was the distraction I needed; a good place to get my head together.

Tonight, though, McBride's is anything but quiet. No time to think—just pitcher after pitcher of green-tinted beer, and bad decisions being made all about me. Francie warned me that St. Patrick's Day is a bastardization of what it is in Dublin. Last week he painted the double lines on the road out front bright green. He's been paying a huge fine to the city for years for the stunt, but smiles while the police write him his summons and calls the whole thing good advertising.

He's a good man, Francie is, making sure one of his bartenders has the night off to celebrate—works his arse off to make up for the missing man, keeping supplies up and things under control with the patrons.

The stacks of cups coming from the storeroom grabs my attention well before I see Francie. At least people make space letting him through. Maybe it's the realization that if they don't, then the shite beer he's tinted green stops flowing.

I reach for a wad of bills and the next pitcher, chuckling at Finn laid out across the bar top giving a peck to a girl. I've seen her in here once before, the night I arrived and laid my heart out for Francie.

She laughs at Finn and his *moves*, comfortable with him —but maybe not entirely comfortable in her skin with the way she's tugging at her shirt. When her friend leans in—her lips puckered at Finn, I see him pause like a deer in the head-lights. He fancies himself a ladies' man, but generally can't hide the bit of surprise when his plans actually work.

Time passes in a blur of people and pitchers, flirting and laughing—until it doesn't. I don't see the lead up to it, but some knobhead just shoved some blond thing, spilling her beer down the front of her friend. The poor girl is soaked.

I am over the bar and plowing through people before things can escalate—or because I can't stand that shite and have to make him apologize for being an arse. It's not until I turn to check on the poor girl drenched in beer that I see it's *her*. And I'm about to mop the towel across her soaked chest. Thank Christ, I stop myself just before I have my hands on her gorgeous tits, overflowing from her tiny shirt.

She's fighting tears, looking absolutely miserable. My heart clenches and I want to protect her—give her some cover. So, I pull her in tight behind me as we make our way through to the back of the bar.

"WHAT D'YE DO, give her the biggest shirt ye could find?" Finn quips as I pass behind him getting back to work after helping *her*.

"It was the first one I grabbed. Thought it'd do fine." That's not at all true. Something about her being exposed after all of that bothered me. She didn't look particularly comfortable in the tight shirt she was in before it was plastered to her round, perfect tits. *Jesus*—I covered her up so no one would be thinking of her that way.

Reaching for the next pitcher, I get back into the rhythm of the bar. "What happened anyway? I didn't see."

Things have settled a bit and we're able to stand side by side and chat for a moment. Finn's cheeks go full red as I tell him what I saw and he starts cursing switching to Gaelic for the full effect. "—and Francie threw him out, yeah? Lissy's okay?" His jaw ticks and eyes dart around the room.

"He did—he's gone, mate." I follow his line of sight and see her smiling at her friend finally relaxing a bit. "What's her story? She's gorgeous."

"Don't. Just leave that alone. She's special." He makes a

good effort of puffing up his chest and trying to make sure I know he's serious.

"Right." No way I'm intimidated by this pup, but we're obviously done talking for now. Scanning the room, I can't help but to find her in the crowd—her pull magnetic.

She's beautiful—gorgeous, really. Auburn hair cascades in a mass of curls down her back. I think of the silky strand that passed through my fingers in the storeroom—and her deep green eyes.

I fill several more pitchers answering the same question I've heard all night long. *You're new here, right? So, are you really Irish?* The accent and a little bit of flirting can accomplish just about anything I need it to, and the girls here are drawn to it like flies to honey. My tip jar is full up again, and there's still hours yet to go.

The night feels like it'll never end. Pushing my hair back again and holding it there, I glance slowly around the room, hoping to see it starting to clear out. I'm completely disappointed to see it's just as packed as it has been since we opened today. My gaze bounces around the room until I find her.

Finn mentioned her name, but that was hours and hundreds of pitchers ago. I wonder about her story, trying to work it out in my mind as I think about the timid, self-conscious way she holds herself. The way Francie and Finn seem to wrap her up and look out for her. The photographer in me wants to capture her image. Tease out the sadness she holds in her eyes. This girl is absolutely gorgeous. Stunning. But she's seen some troubles.

She darts her gaze away from me, back to the conversation flowing around her. I can't help my smile and shake my head, chuckling under my breath. As much as I was working her out in my mind, I just busted her checking me out. And that's okay. I like that she was looking at me. The idea that maybe she's trying to figure out my story as well. *I don't want to think of that tonight.*

It's coming on four in the morning when Francie finally starts ushering the last of the people out the door. I head to the back and put the keg of Guinness back on tap and pour one for myself and Finn. There's no way I'm closing out this night without having at least one. Francie's shrill whistle hits me from where he's shuffling people out the front door. He nods at the tap with a little bit of longing in his eye, so I pull a pint for him as well.

Coming around the bar, with three pints in one hand and snagging a bag of rubbish with the other, I do a quick scan and see the last handful of people heading for the door. What I don't see is the blur of luscious curves coming out of the storage room. I have no time to move—barely time to brace myself—I drop the trash, and wrap my arm around the stumbling girl to keep her from falling.

Again.

"Ohmygod, shit. Ohmygod."

The minute I realize who I've got my arm wrapped around, I pull her a little closer, hold on a little tighter. "You're alright, then?" Her arms are trapped between us, one hand pressed flat to my chest. Everywhere we're pressed together, from hip to shoulder, tingles like there's some kind of current running between us.

Slowly, she tilts her head back and looks up at me, her eyes wide and sparkling. "I'm so sorry."

"That's three." I smile down at her, not quite ready to let

her go. Her brows pinch together as she purses her lips, confusion washing over her perfect features. "I've saved you three times tonight."

"You have." She straightens, pulling away from me. "Thank you...really. I...I—um, thank you, for everything." Her voice is soft and shy. I keep my arm wrapped round her a bit longer than I need to, because I *want* to. But when I finally let her go, I feel the loss of her body pressed up against me far more than I should. She steps back with an awkward smile quirking at her lips.

"G'night, then."

"Good night." She turns away, going straight to Finn and Francie, hugging them and gracing each with a kiss on the cheek. Her attention briefly lands on me as she and her friend trip out the door a little unsteady on their feet. Arms linked and heads tilted together like they're sharing a secret.

"Francie." I prop the door open with my shoulder, letting the early morning air sweep through the pub. I watch the two girls walk away, the streetlights spotlighting their path as they go. "They're alright walking home this late, yeah?"

He stands on the walkway out in front of his pub; his pint in one hand and the other stroking his beard as he narrows his eyes on the girls. Several blocks away now, she turns and waves before disappearing into the small apart-ment building. "She knows I've got her back." Francie fixes me with a pointed stare, brows pinched in earnest.

That message is delivered loud and clear.

THREE

Gracyn and I are completely holding each other up as we pick our way down the sidewalk to our apartment. We share a second-floor apartment in an old building just off the town square. "Holy shit, Gracyn. What even happened tonight?"

"Did you kiss him? Were you licking him in the storeroom?" She tries to hip bump me but misses, and I have to grab her so she doesn't fall. "You were so kissing him, right?"

"Nope." I sigh, but I really wanted to.

"Liiiissss," she draws my name way out dramatically, "but, did you see? Did you see how he rescued you? It was like a fairy tale." Gracyn's leaning all her weight into me, her head tilted—almost resting on my shoulder.

I did see it, and I can still feel the heat from his touch lingering on my back. Where our bodies were aligned from my hip all the way up to my chest. If I closed my eyes, I swear I can feel the hard planes of his chest against the palms of my hands. But if I do close them, I'm pretty sure the two of us will bust ass and I know Francie is watching from the doorway to make sure we get home safe.

"Which time?" I swing my still-wet shirt back and forth, trying to keep my mind from wandering back to Aidan. The feel of him. "He saved me more than once tonight, G." Rob never went out of his way to do anything for me. *He just broke my heart.*

Gracyn climbs the steps to unlock our door as I turn to wave at Francie. But Francie's not standing outside alone. Aidan is with him—leaning against the door drinking his pint. He raises his glass and nods to me before we each turn, disappearing into the warmth inside.

GRACYN PLOPS down on the couch with a bottle of water and a bagel, scrolling through her phone, her body swirling as though the world spins around her. I toss my wet shirt into the laundry basket and start peeling my beer-soaked bra off. "I'm gonna shower off before bed, you okay?" Gracyn doesn't even look up from her phone as she waves me off.

While the water heats up, I stare into the mirror, assessing myself. I take a deep breath and remind myself to stop focusing only on my faults. I try to see myself through someone else's eyes, but I end up falling into old habits, finding my eyes too wide, my boobs too big and my thighs too thick. I twist my hair up into a messy bun, not wanting to bother with drying it tonight.

I step under the spray and let the warm water fall over my shoulders, washing the stale beer away.

I knew something would happen eventually.

It's been some kind of a game to see who could humiliate

me more since we broke up. Can you even call it a breakup? Was I supposed to let Rob just have his fun with Maryse until they were done? Or wait until he picked the time most beneficial to him and his fucking political aspirations to publicly break up with me? I think not. Catching them in the act on Christmas Eve was all the humiliation I needed.

But this is the new me. One my family didn't expect, the me they didn't think I was capable of being. I walked as far away as I could in this little town, from the toxicity that is my family—the people who are supposed to love me unconditionally. Gracyn has a theory that Maryse is jealous of me but that thought is ridiculous. I can't help but laugh at that as I step out of the shower and make the usual comparisons. Height, hips, and hair—I've been told since forever that she is the standard and I fall short in every way. I'm still working on being okay with me just the way I am.

By the time I brush my teeth and fall into bed, the sun is ridiculously close to rising. I burrow down into my crisp sheets and close my eyes, thankful that I don't have to work until late in the afternoon. On the edge of asleep, I feel my bed dip and hear Gracyn mumble, "Not gonna talk about it?"

"Talk about what, G?"

"Any of it—all of it. Rob and Maryse. You think they asked Tyler to do that, to embarrass you at McBride's?"

"When did he change, Gracyn? When did he become this pompous asshole?" I know I missed all the signs. I was too busy working to pay my rent, buy my books—too wrapped up in keeping my own GPA up for my scholarship.

Rob's finishing up law school with a position already waiting for him in his father's law firm, Barrett & Barrett. It sounds far fancier than it is—that second Barrett in the title, that's Rob. When we started dating there wasn't any of this pretentiousness. He was just a normal guy who wanted more. Wanted to make his dad proud by following in his footsteps, make a difference in the world.

"Mmm...about the time he started dating your sister? All of those people are evil, Lis. You're better off without them." It seems simple enough when she says it, but knowing how little my mom and sister—let alone my dad—consider me hurts in a way that I can't just shrug off. "Even the most perfect little families have skeletons. At least yours are all out in the open."

The mattress bounces as Gracyn flops over to face me, her waggling eyebrows contrasting with her drunk, droopy eyelids. "Let's move on. Francie's new guy—you gonna tap that? It's time to move on."

"Jesus, Gracyn. Really?"

She falls onto the pillow and her breath evens out. She starts to snore, leaving me staring at the ceiling thinking back over the past couple months. How crushed I was. How my mother implied it was my fault that Rob cheated on me.

You're too independent, Lisbeth. If you had made yourself more available to Robert, been more interested in his goals like your sister is, he wouldn't have looked to spend time elsewhere.

After that, I really had nothing to say to her. Anna Rittenhouse has an unbelievable talent for rationalizing everything to suit her purpose. And her purpose once again, was to boost up her favorite daughter, Maryse.

Gracyn is the one who put me back together. She spent Christmas with me like we usually did, but instead of hanging out in our apartment after family dinner, laughing at Maryse and my mom, Gracyn consoled me. She sat with me on the floor handing me tissues until I ran out of tears. She filled my wine glass until we ran out of that too.

She went down to McBride's and made sure Francie knew what had happened. She also talked Finn out of finding Rob and *taking care of him* for me. They were my true family. These people who wrap me up in love and support that I've never felt from the ones who were related to me by blood.

I WAKE up with Gracyn's hair across my face and a desperate need for coffee and greasy food. "Unng—are you drooling on my pillow?" I whine, shoving myself out of bed to head for the kitchen.

"Coffee..." The morning drama with her is real. She's capable of little more than grumbling until she's had her caffeine.

"Go take a shower. You smell like the stale beer and we have to work—" I look at the clock on the microwave and groan. It's almost one o'clock. "—soon. We have to work soon." I start the coffee and drink down a full water bottle as fast as I can. I'm not hungover—I slept through that whole thing—but I'm thirsty, and tired, and a little sad.

Gracyn shuffles into the kitchen, her hair wet and her

eyes still half shut. "Are we going to the diner for food or straight to the bistro so Tony can cook for us?"

"Diner."

"Or should we go to McBride's and get food there? You can flirt some more with…" She looks at me over the top of her mug, searching her fuzzy memories for his name.

"Aidan. His name is Aidan. And no, I'm not going there, I've gotta get through the rest of this year, graduate and get a job that pays better." I turn away, looking for my car keys.

"Lissy, you've got to start dating again sometime. He's perfect—TDH, muscles for days, and probably only here for a minute."

"TDH?"

Gracyn shrugs like it should be obvious. "Tall, dark, and handsome, sweetie. He can be your rebound, no pressure." She's serious. How can she be serious about this?

"For the love of God, Gracyn. No. I'm fine."

FOUR

Aidan

It's been almost a week that I've been looking for her with every chime of the bell. Hoping to see her come back through the door of McBride's. I've worked every shift I could in that time, not wanting to chance missing her. Francie went all protective when I asked about her, and Finn's been useless for anything beyond her name and that I need to keep my distance. Jimmy, the other bartender who shares the flat, talks about her while we clean the bar and pour drinks.

He's told me she's at university, almost done with her program. That she works at Bistro Antonio across town—waiting tables and pouring cocktails. I went in there for lunch a couple days ago, hoping to see her, wanting to chat her up, but she wasn't working. I hung out as long as I could without bleeding over into the dinner rush, but she must have been to class and I had my shift at McBride's. I caught sight of her friend, the one Finn fancies, as I left, but no sign of Lisbeth.

Tuesday, I spend most of the day in New York City. I was able to arrange a meeting for a photo shoot. It's not the journalistic side that I'm used to, but I miss being behind my camera, and shooting a few weddings for the right people will get me back to doing what I love.

The train ride in to New York City is a little over an hour, giving me plenty of time to think about what's next for me. The rhythmic sway of the train lulls me deep into the introspection I've been trying to avoid lately. Tending bar has been a great mindless distraction, but with all the time I've taken off since Michael died, I probably need to focus a bit back on my career. After university, I fell into photojournalism and made excellent use of my cameras and passport. *Until I got the call home.*

If this meetup goes well, I'll be able to fill more of my hours doing what I'm really good at—and pad my wallet as well.

A flash of auburn hair on the platform brings my thoughts back to the pub. It's not her. I wouldn't be that lucky, but I want to see her again. Spend an evening chatting her up. There's something magnetic about her that draws me in. She's stunning, yeah, but there's something else—something more to it.

MCBRIDE'S CAR park is quite empty when I stop in on the way home from the train station for a pint and some dinner, and to plan for the photography job I just booked. I'm sure there's nothing to eat at our flat since it was Finn's turn to get food in.

Francie's chatting with a man at the bar and Finn, of course, is busy with yet another girl.

I head to the kitchen and drop my dinner in the fryer. It's just easier to do it myself than trying to get Finn's fucking attention. And after setting my chicken tenders and chips on the bar, I start my pint and take stock of the bar. Finn is truly useless when he's flirting, so I clean the glasses he's let pile up, stock the fruit trays and wipe down the bar before topping up my pint, adding a shamrock flourish in the foam just for the hell of it.

As I reach out to place the glass next to my dinner, I'm met with the most beautiful green eyes—an almost olive green with gold and brown twisting through them. And they belong to *her*.

Dear God, help a poor bastard like myself.

"Hiya. What can I get for you?"

She smiles brightly, plump pink lips spread wide, and gives my plate a little nod. "That looks perfect. Did you know I was on my way?"

I smile back and wink, grabbing a glass for her. "I was hoping...only hoping." She chuckles and points to the Guinness when I raise the glass and nod toward the taps. "Are you wanting some dinner as well, then?" I ask, leaving her pint to settle.

"Seriously, I'll have exactly that." Her eyes crinkle as she looks at my basket of food. "This guy's obviously got fantastic taste."

Chuckling, I place her pint in front of her and head to the kitchen dropping more food in the fryer. With a hard squeeze to his shoulder, I let Finn know to listen for the timer, grab the vinegar, and head 'round to settle in next to her at the bar.

"So, I've good taste, then? Here, take this one. Finn will bring mine out in a bit." I move my basket closer to her. "I've not seen you in since St. Paddy's."

She grabs a chip and pops it in her mouth. Is she humming? Yeah, she's fucking humming...and bouncing in her seat a bit. I can't help the smile that quirks up on one side of my face. "You are correct. I haven't been in since. I think I needed some time to process all that green beer." Her small frown and scrunched-up nose tell me there's something more.

"I never actually introduced myself, I'm Lisbeth. Lis, really." She wipes her fingers on her thigh before reaching out to shake my hand. Just then, Finn drops my food on the bar in front of her.

"Lissy. How are ye?" Finn leans in for a peck on the cheek. "You've met Aidan, then?"

She slides the basket across the bar to me.

"We were just getting to that." She thrusts her hand out again to shake.

The moment our fingers touch, that current runs through me again. Forgoing her hand, I grasp her wrist and pull her toward me. I press my lips together, intending only to brush a chaste kiss on her cheek, but she turns just then. Just a bit, but it's enough that my lips land on the corner of her mouth, and time stills. Her eyes go wide before fluttering shut and I want to stay there, right there for the rest of my life. But fucking Francie chooses that moment to slam his glass on the bar making Lisbeth jump away. I'm pretty sure that was his intent by the murderous look in his eye.

What is his fucking deal? I've seen Finn and Jimmy flirting plenty with patrons and taking kisses far more intimate than that across the bar. She's smiling shyly with her fingertips resting against her lips when I drag my eyes away from Francie. I give her all of my attention, pitching my voice low. "You didn't think I'd let Finn have a kiss and just be satisfied with a handshake for myself, did you?" I turn back to my dinner giving her a moment to think about it.

She takes a long draught from her pint and lets out a contented breath—I want that satisfaction to be because of me. "No. I don't suppose so," she whispers, meeting my eyes in the mirror behind the bar. Mhmm.

"Tell me what you do when you're not here, drinking pints with the help."

She pops her last chip in her mouth and tilts her head back and forth while she chews. "I'm either in school or mixing drinks, myself. But I'll be doing instruction hours in the hospital soon, too."

"All of that? When do you find time for fun?"

She shrugs her right shoulder and wipes her hands dropping her napkin in the empty basket. "I don't really have a lot of free time. I either collapse on the couch with a movie or a book, or I come here with Gracyn, my roommate. She was here with me the other night."

Finn turns resting against the bar and folds his arms across his chest glaring at me. "And where's your Gracyn tonight?"

"She's in Florida for spring break, but I need the hours so..." another shrug as she peers at me over the rim of her glass, "I'm sure she's having enough fun for both of us."

"You didn't want to go?" I take her glass and reach across

the bar to refill it. The idea of her lying on a beach, her creamy skin kissed by the sun has me tied in knots.

"I would love to be on the beach, are you kidding me? But I get to take everyone else's shifts this week so that helps a ton. I should be able to cover tuition for my summer classes by the end of this week." Lisbeth gives a quick nod, genuinely excited by this.

"Your parents don't help you?" Her beer becomes her sole focus as Finn's head shoots up from his phone and Francie glares daggers at me. What the fuck?

"No, I'm doing this on my own. Just me." She says that like it's not any big thing before she snarks, "Plus, I got to have dinner with the help, so..." She pulls out some cash and hands it across to Finn, but I'm not done. I'm not ready for her to go, for this to end.

I reach out taking her hand and turn it over in mine. "Can I take you to dinner? A real one, not bar food. Do you have a night free this week?" The inside of her wrist has the softest and silkiest skin. I brush my thumb along it and feel her pulse ramping up. Her breaths are shallow as she watches my thumb pause and take measure.

"I...um, I have to..." She lets out a soft sigh and looks up into my eyes. "I only have tonight and tomorrow night off. I..." After a quick glance to Francie, she eases her hand away from mine, breaking not only our contact but our connection. I feel the loss of her hand more than just physically.

"I'll be needing your address to pick you up, then." I grab a napkin, a fucking cocktail napkin—how cliché—and a pen from near the taps. I slide them toward her. "And I'll be needing your number as well." I study her profile while she writes out her information. Her skin is pure like porcelain, and her lips are all I'll be thinking about as I try to fall asleep later. The taste of them. The feel of them.

I reach out and let a silky lock of her hair fall through my fingers as she finishes up her mobile number. The smell of her shampoo washes over me and, suddenly, I want to grab a fist full of it and drag her toward me. I want to feel it brush across my chest. I want a lot of things that would earn me all kinds of looks from Francie.

I'll have to talk to Francie—find out what his problem with me is. And get Jimmy to take my shift tomorrow night.

Why does she not have any help from her parents? Where's her support? And why is Francie keeping such a close eye on me?

FIVE

Lis

I feel his gaze on me as I walk across the bar, searing into my back as I leave for home.

I can still feel the way his fingers danced across the inside of my wrist caressing—sending electric heat through my veins.

The way his voice washed over me as we talked of everything and nothing at all. Deep and a little smoky like a good bourbon, I want to drink it in. Talking with him tonight—his focus solely on me—was like I was the most interesting person he'd ever spoken to. Like I was important. I don't know the last time I felt that.

I slide my car up to the curb right in front of my building, grab my bag from the back seat and check for cars before getting out. There's not a lot I like about being all alone this week, but I'm not ever going to complain about padding my checking account or a good parking spot.

Normally Francie watches to make sure I get home safe but he was acting ten different kinds of twitchy and weird tonight. I pull out my phone as I pop up the steps to my apartment and dial the number for McBride's. "Hey, Finn. It's Lis, can I talk to Francie for a minute?"

"Have to wait your turn. He's having a go at Aidan just now." Finn's obviously enjoying not being on the receiving end of a tirade for a change. I love Finn, but that boy is a mess. "O' course, Aidan might like an interruption. Are you up for swooping in to save your man?"

"What? Why is... Just, yeah. Tell Francie I need to talk to him." I hear harsh words filtering through the noise in the background before Francie jumps Finn's shit for interrupting, tearing into him, until I hear...my name. They get freakishly quiet and my heart pounds against my ribs. The shuffling of the phone, the hiss of static as it changes hands, and muffled warnings make their way through to me.

"What can I do for you, love? You're safe home?" It's not normally awkward when I call Francie, but tonight this is for sure. His words are terse and distracted.

I stumble through telling him I'm fine—that I wasn't murdered in the few blocks home. It suddenly makes sense— the garbled phrases, the tone of what I heard.

I steel myself with a deep breath and launch into it. "I know you're looking out for me, and you know I appreciate it, but..."

"Lisbeth darlin', I'm setting the boy to rights. He'll not be bothering you again, love."

He full-named me.

This is serious.

"Francie, we're going out to dinner tomorrow night. He wasn't bothering me at all. Last week you asked for my thoughts on him, so…"

"No, you're not. No. He's a shift to work tomorrow night so he won't be available." Where the hell is this coming from?

"Is he married?"

"No."

"Is he a murderer?"

"No, Lisbeth." Francie huffs, obviously frustrated with me. "I'm looking out for you and…"

"Is it my heart in general or is Aidan the problem?" My phone pings with a message distracting me from Francie's assurances that it's me he's worried about.

Unknown #: I've switched shifts with Jimmy. Just ignore Francie.

L: Aidan?

Unknown #: Yeah. Just tell him you understand and let him go. I'll take the verbal lashing and see you tomorrow.

Unknown #: 7pm

I stare at my phone trying to think of a response, but I'm at a loss.

Unknown #: Sleep well, love.

I'm finally able to get off the phone after giving Francis the required, *yes, I understand.* With a freshly poured glass of wine, I head in for a long hot soak in the bath. The bubbles will relax me, or maybe the wine will, but there aren't many things that a hot steamy bubble bath won't make better. And while the tub fills with lavender-scented bubbles, I make sure to save Aidan's number to my contacts.

. . .

THE NIGHT BARTENDER was supposed to be here an hour and a half ago. His car trouble means I've done all the dinner shift prep, restocked the beer coolers, and I no longer have time to buy something new to wear tonight. With both blenders whirring, a blown keg that needs to be replaced, and the clock ticking down the minutes, I'm about to come unglued.

I'm not normally a bitch, but I just can't today. Can't even.

"Let's get caught up and then you can run." My boss, Jenna, slides behind the bar and grabs a stack of drink orders. "Dumbshit needs to know he can't take advantage of you like this."

I've been working for her since high school, bussing tables until she needed another server. When a spot opened behind the bar, she gave me the chance. I get the new keg tapped and pour out the daiquiris, moving on to the next order up.

A few minutes later, we're caught up and Jenna pushes me out from behind the bar. "Go—I've got this. Have fun, Lissy." She hands me my bag after upending my tip jar into it.

"Thanks, Jenna. You sure this is okay?" She's been so tired lately, I feel really bad leaving her like this.

"I'm good." She stares past me to tonight's bartender ambling through the front door looking like he just got out of bed. The sound of Jenna ripping into him follows as I hop down the stairs, fading as the door shuts behind me.

· · ·

I HAVEN'T HEARD much from Gracyn since she left for the beach and I need her desperately right now. She's posted a few pictures on her Instagram, but has been pretty quiet—for her. Something's up, but I have a feeling, it's gonna take a bottle of wine to figure it out when she gets back to town this weekend.

I text her really quick, hoping she's available now—Lord knows, she might decide in the middle of my dinner that she needs to talk to me.

> **L: Hey…you there? I need to borrow clothes.**
>
> **G: Sure. Whatcha got going?**
>
> **L: Dinner?**
>
> **G: Who with?**
>
> **L: Aidan. From McBride's. Chatted last night. He's sweet.**
>
> **G: Mhmmm. Make good choices. All of that…**
>
> **L: Thnx. Talk later?**

I check when I get home and again when I get out of the shower but she doesn't text back.

My plans for a glass of wine while I straighten my hair and YouTube makeup tutorials are replaced with half-dried wild waves spilling down my back and a quick swipe of mascara.

I send up a prayer that Gracyn didn't take her black knit swing dress with her as I rifle through her overflowing closet. I have no idea where we're going tonight, but that dress is my favorite and I can dress it up or down easily enough, depending on what Aidan has on.

Fuck, fuck, fuck.

He's going to be here soon.

Finally, in the very back of her closet, I find the dress and pull it over my head while running back to my room for shoes. Taupe ankle boots or spiky heels—I grab both and set them by the front door.

After another coat of mascara, a little blush, and some lip gloss, I step back, trying to see myself as Aidan will. I haven't been on a first date in more than four years, and my nerves are just kicking in to full riot mode. I nearly jump out of my skin when I hear a knock at the door.

I take a deep breath and let it out slowly, trying to calm myself, but my heart slams in my chest as I swing the door open.

Aidan's black hair is still damp from his shower or maybe he took the time to style it. The curve of his lips, the stormy night of his eyes. The scruff on his jaw. I want to stand here and admire him, commit everything to memory—and maybe mess him up just a little.

His crisp white shirt stretches across his shoulders, sleeves rolled up to his elbows, showing the pure strength of his forearms. My eyes travel down his body taking in the way his dress pants fit snugly to his hips and thighs. He's even polished his shoes—totally an odd thing to notice but *Rob would never have bothered with that. He'd have bought new ones.*

Aidan cares how he looks, more than just a change of clothes and spray of cologne.

I get caught staring and feel a hot blush searing my cheeks. I bite at my lip and meet his smiling glance as I try to cover this awkward feeling. "You look great." His smile crinkles the corner of his eyes calming my inner mess.

"Thanks. You're sure, then, or do you want to take another look before we go?" he teases and reaches for the jacket I threw over the back of the couch. I slide my feet into my heels and laugh.

As he helps me slip into my jacket, he runs his fingers lightly down my arms—leaving a trail of goose bumps—until his fingers find the inside of my wrists. His touch there sends tingles through my entire body; it takes everything I have not to shudder. "Shall we go?" he rasps out as he reaches for the door sliding his other hand to my lower back, guiding me out.

SIX

Aidan

I guide her down the stairs to the walkway in front of her building keeping a hand at her back as much as I can. "Are you okay to walk? It's just a few blocks." I'd made reservations at a café close to where she lives, but those shoes she put on—fuck me.

She smiles and nods, teetering as we start toward the restaurant. I reach for her hand to steady her and tuck it securely into the crook of my elbow. The need to touch her driving me, I clasp my other hand over the top of hers, holding her firmly in place. Her gaze meets mine, followed by a sweet smile and a squeeze to my arm.

She blatantly checked me out when she opened the door to her flat. Her gaze lit every inch of my body, lingering on what she obviously liked. She moves her hand to my bicep. I can't help but flex the muscle; I want to impress her. I want to feel her hands caress me the way her eyes did. She shudders almost imperceptibly as I move my hand to reach for that spot on her wrist again. I rub small circles there with the pad of my thumb, focusing entirely on her reaction, the hitch in her breath. The soft sigh she lets escape.

The café is fine. Dinner's lovely. But Lis? Lis is fucking brilliant.

With the table separating us, it's awkward to reach across to her, and I miss the contact.

"Tell me more, Lisbeth. Why nursing?" The more time I spend with her, the more I want to know what's in her head, her heart. What her dreams are.

"I like to take care of people, help them when they can't do things for themselves. I get to see life in all its forms—beginning through the end. There's something beautiful about that, reverent."

My breath catches in my throat and I roll my lips in between my teeth.

Her fork clatters to the table and she reaches for my hand. "Aidan, are you okay? I'm—did I say something?"

"Erm, no. You're fine." I shake my head, unable to form the words just yet. Do I want to share this? Open up my heart the way I've already asked Lis to do?

Her touch is warm when she reaches her hand to cover mine, soothing me—calming me. I look up and her lips are pressed tightly together, dipping down at the corners. This was supposed to be a nice dinner with a lovely distraction. How did I get to a place where I'm shoving down raw emotions at the same time that I'm wanting to bare my soul?

I clear my throat and stare at nothing across the room. "I'm fine, I just—my brother just passed away. That's...that's why I'm here. In the States, I mean. I had to get away." I blink back the sting in my eyes and force a tight smile to my lips.

"I'm so sorry. What—do you—I'm sorry." Lisbeth wraps her free hand around mine, grasping it between hers and for the first time since I watched Michael's coffin get lowered into the ground, I feel able to say the words.

"He died very suddenly, diagnosed and then gone in a matter of weeks." How can that be? I don't want to do this, have this huge heavy weight smothering us. "He was thirty-two—far too young to die, but he'd be pissed if he thought he were ruining our evening." It's true, actually. He'd be livid with me with how this is turning out.

The laughter comes out unbidden and Lis looks a little shocked. "He was a smart-arse; I'm sure that comes as a huge surprise." This is what Michael would want, how he would want to be remembered. "The night before he passed I was sitting with him and he said, 'it was hard and fast, and over way too quick' and then he cracked up laughing like a twelve-year-old boy."

Lis smiles broadly and nods her head. She seems to get it. The need to laugh and hold desperately the happy memories. I raise my glass to his honor and finish my whiskey.

"So, you ran away." It's not a question, she says it like a fact.

"I did. But I think I landed well."

We linger over coffee and dessert, conversation turning back to her school and my work—my photography. We share a dense, decadent chocolate cake, and thank fuck she's focused on that, because I can't take my eyes off her. The way her lips slide the gooey sweet chocolate off the fork. The way her tongue darts out to lick at every last bit. The way her eyes flutter closed, lost in the ecstasy of the moment. The moan that escapes her lips. *I want to put that look on her face. I want to own that.*

Christ, I have to calm this shit down or the walk to her door will kill me.

After settling the bill, I pull out her chair and guide her into the soft evening air. The walk back to her flat is leisurely and relaxed. This town is quaint—quiet and safe-feeling. The walkways are lined with trees and the business owners decorate their storefronts. Idyllic, really. The biggest danger to Lis right now is me. My thoughts are anything but pure and wholesome.

At her door, she turns to me. "Thank you. I...this was great. Thank you." Her lips—*fuck*—they soften and lift sweetly at the corners.

"It was my pleasure, Lisbeth. Thank you." I reach my hand up to cup her cheek and lean in for a good night kiss. Chaste. Respectful.

But all my good intentions ignite, the moment my lips touch hers. I slide my hand through her silky hair to the back of her head. She gasps in a breath and parts her lips.

That moment.

That. Right. There.

I slide my tongue along her lips and taste the sweet hint of chocolate. It's overwhelming but not nearly enough. I deepen the kiss, tasting her. Our tongues tangle and fight for control.

My senses return when I hear and feel her moan low in her throat. That noise—the one from the restaurant. The one that she gave the cake, but I wanted for myself. I stop. I have to. Placing a truly chaste kiss on her forehead, I take her keys, opening the door.

"Good night, love." I need to bang my head against the fucking wall and go before I get carried away. I turn and head down the stairs. To safety.

MY FLAT IS empty when I get there. I need time and a glass of whiskey to sort myself. Tonight's distraction became an emotional carnival ride.

She's beautiful, and intriguing, and I want nothing more than to spend ridiculous amounts of time with her. Learning her, knowing her. *Christ, the way I want to know her.* The taste of her lips, and the ways they move. Her curves just barely hinted at under that dress she wore tonight. My thoughts are sinful, at best.

Eyes closed, I lay my head back against the cushions of the sofa and let my mind go—just for a minute. I can't stop it. Her chest rising and falling. Her pulse thumping to match mine. The feel of her skin beneath my fingertips. The pale pink flush on her cheeks as it creeps down into the neckline of her dress caressing the tops of her breasts. The featherlight touch as she moves her hands up my chest to land on my shoulders.

Fuck.

The key scrapes in the lock and I reach for one of the throw pillows on the sofa, jamming it down across my crotch and rest my tumbler of whiskey on top. Looking fucking casual, if I do say so. Finn tumbles through the door with a tiny little blond thing. That's just what I need tonight; to hear them through the thin-as-shit walls. His "friend" is completely engrossed in him and hardly acknowledges me, but the laughing grin from Finn speaks volumes. Shoving the pillow aside now that I'm no longer going to embarrass myself, I grab my earbuds and glass, and head up to my loft bedroom.

The squeals and giggles floating up the stairs promise to make tonight unbearable. I need to invest in noise-canceling headphones. Doesn't matter how loud I crank the volume, I can still hear them, Finn and his pixie. I try my best to ignore them and just fall asleep, but I give up. Before I register what's happening, my hand slides down my stomach to the waistband of my boxer briefs. Between the noises coming from downstairs and my lingering thoughts of Lisbeth, I reach in and grip my cock, stroking firmly. The release is not nearly satisfying—not near as good as what I imagine with Lis.

FRANCIE MEETS me at the door of the bar the next morning ready to tear into me. He was either waiting by the window or heard my piece-of-shit car coming from a mile away.

"The fuck do you think you're doin'?" he bellows, throwing his hands in the air spilling coffee all over the floor. I should have expected this. Talking Jimmy into trading shifts with me had been no big deal, but I hadn't thought about how bad the fallout would be today. I've got to work a full double shift now, I'm stuck here until closing.

"Francie, I took her out to dinner. That's it." I try to speak calmly, like I'm trying to soothe a spooked horse. "I walked her to her door and used my manners—made sure she was safe home and tucked away for the night. What did you think I was going to do to her?" He's being ridiculous.

Huffing a big breath out through his nose, Francie glares. "I've already talked to Lissy. I am well aware that ye behaved the gentleman." *What the fuck?* "But that girl has been through enough. She doesn't need you to work her up, lead her on and break her heart, Aidan. She doesn't need that shite again." He looks devastated, fucking heartbroken for her.

"Francie, what happened with Lisbeth? I know her family is not involved, but something else must have happened to put you in this mode..." I move him toward the bar and grab his coffee cup to refill it for him while I grab some for myself.

We're going to settle this. I need to know what's got him so up in knots. *Fuck, I need to know what I'm dealing with in her.*

I'm clearly invested in this girl—but I'm not prepared for the shite I pull out of Francie over the next hour while I clean and prep McBride's for the busy Thursday night. It takes some prodding and a little Jameson in his coffee, but I think I get it. All of it. The whole shitty story of the fucking bastard that broke her heart.

Francie assures me that I'll not have to deal with the arse and Lisbeth's sister, but, God help me, if I don't feel my heart squeeze. I get it, now—Francie's protection over her, Finn and Jimmy's affection—she's family to them. They're family to her. Blood may be thicker than water, but love is thicker than anything.

SEVEN

That kiss. The sweet touches throughout the night simmered on the walk back to my apartment and then when he kissed me? I thought I was going to melt right there.

Francie has been blowing up my phone most of the night. I ignored it all through dinner, but when it rings as I lean my back against the door, I answer.

"Lisbeth, where've you been?" he fusses and just that quickly, I'm pulled from my happy little bubble. His voice sounds mildly panicked. "What are you doing, love? Tell me you've got your head on straight and you're not gettin' caught up in a boy." He sounds pissed.

"Francie, I'm fine. We had dinner and talked," I soothe, hoping I can calm him down a little. "Aidan walked me home and was an absolute gentleman." Surely that'll put his mind at ease—or not. I talk to him for a good twenty minutes over the background of a full McBride's. The last thing I want is for Aidan to get ripped apart for taking me out.

It's time for me to start dating again. I've been working so hard in school and life to move forward from the devastation that Maryse and Rob left me with.

Like Gracyn said, this might be the perfect distraction.

Aidan is nice, but this isn't where his life is. His family, his career, are all back in Dublin and this is just a temporary reprieve.

Francie finally calms and promises not to lay Aidan out in the morning.

Ending the call, my thoughts go straight back to that kiss. It's all I can think about while doing my thing and getting ready for bed. I return the dress to Gracyn's closet and grab my laptop as I hop into bed. I slide under the covers and get comfy, pulling up a new browser to Google Aidan Kearney. And his photography. I have no idea why he's working in a bar.

I scroll through images of children in third world countries. Images of major political players across the globe. Of celebrities and their families. I scroll through the seemingly endless photographs, stopping when my eyes start to blur. Aidan is not just talented, he might well be famous. The photos he's taken have been published, printed, and shared thousands of times over. He's had his work in every major news outlet, both print and digital.

Then there are pictures of him in a school uniform showing an adorable, much younger version of Aidan. His dark hair flops down over his forehead, but his eyes. His eyes are the same. They are an absolutely stunning clear dark blue like the evening sky as the moon chases the sun across it. There is a cute little girl sitting with him. Her blond piggy tails are lopsided, but her bright green eyes are all smiles for

Aidan. I don't even think when I crop her out and save the picture to my desktop.

I fall asleep thinking of him, about why a relationship with him won't work. We're in such different places looking for much different things.

WITH MOST OF the staff being on spring break, I've worked back-to-back shifts Thursday, Friday, and Saturday this week and I'm absolutely exhausted. But I made the rest of my tuition for summer session and a little extra.

I drag ass home after closing up the bistro late Saturday night. I need a shower so bad right now and then to just crawl into bed. I want to wash away the grease and sweat. And, I really, *really* want the hot water all to myself, just one last time before Gracyn gets back.

I thought she was getting home tomorrow, but the lights are on and the sound of water running hits me as I throw my keys on the table by the door. "G, you here?" Instead of waiting for an answer, I crack open a bottle of wine and pour us each a glass. I have a feeling we're going to need it to get the dirt from this past week out of Gracyn.

"Hey, is that you?" she yells as she slides into her room and shuts the door leaving a trail of wet footprints behind her. "Go shower—I know you feel gross. I'll open some wine for when you're done."

"Way ahead of you." It's like she knows that she has no choice but to spill her shit. I grab my shorts and a thermal tee, and pray for just a little hot water.

"Oh. I think I might have used all the hot water, so..."

And there it is, reason 4,852 that I need to graduate early and start making real money. Our place is so small and so old, we're never guaranteed enough hot water for both of us.

I rush through my tepid shower to find Gracyn curled up in the corner of the couch. "Why are you home early?" She looks up from refilling her glass with this look on her face that I can't quite place. Sad, maybe, but not quite. "Are you okay? I hardly heard from you this week." She's already shaking her head before I can finish the question.

"Let's talk about you. How was your date with…what's his name again? Tell me about your week." She's in full-on avoidance and I give her the squinty eyes as she downs half her glass of wine.

"Aidan." I'll give her a little space before I press. "It was great. We talked over beers Wednesday night and he…he pulled me in for that kiss you seemed to think I needed. Francie about lost his shit over that and then we talked about you being away and me having to stay here and work, and school and his—" I pause to take a breath from my crazy and Gracyn looks really sad. "G, talk to me. I'll give you every detail later, but, honey, you need to tell me what happened. Is it…? Do we need to call the police? Do I have to kick someone's ass?" She's staring into her glass with an intensity I rarely see on her. "Gracyn, talk to me. I'm really starting to worry."

With a huge sigh, she refills both of our glasses and finally looks up at me. "I…I met someone." I try to school my features, but I feel my eyes growing wide. Gracyn has sworn up and down that she will not get serious with anyone until after she graduates. She never really wants to talk about why, but she's stuck to it for the past two and a half years. I give her the go-ahead nod so she'll keep talking.

"He's in a band that was playing at one of the beach bars and," she forces a huff of air out through her nose, "it's just shitty timing. He's in a band, for God's sake, did I mention that? He's in a band." She goes back to staring down her wine and I struggle, not knowing what to say.

Gracyn's studying to be an accountant. She's supposed to take over her dad's accounting firm, so a guy in a band is pretty far outside her wheelhouse. This doesn't fit to Mr. George's ideals at all, but I feel like there's more to it.

"Tell me why this one is a big deal." She glares at me over the top of her wine glass and I shrug, deflecting her hard look. "What's he like?" I draw out the *he*, hoping she'll at least give me a name.

"His name's Gavin, and he's different, not like..." She shakes her head, seeming to need to pull herself together. "God, he's so interesting—well read, crazy smart..." She draws her brows together and gets lost inside her brain.

"Where's the bad part, G?" This girl has been my rock, and it kills me to see her struggling like this.

She pinches at her lower lip and blinks several times before continuing. "We spent hours upon days talking on the beach—arguing over books and getting to know all the crazy, stupid little things about each other. He hates pickles, and loves documentaries." She looks so far away from this place— this moment.

"And then I came home and he moved on to his next spring break gig with his band. The end."

"But you got his number, right?" The look on her face

tells me everything I don't want to hear. "G, you did, didn't you? Exchanged numbers—email? Facebook?"

"We deleted each other's contact info before I left. You know how this goes, the timing was shitty and that's the end of it." I can't believe her. "Now, tell me about Aidan."

EIGHT

Aidan

She comes in a couple hours after I open for the day. It's been weeks since we had dinner. Since I left her at her door with just that kiss. It's been playing on a loop in my fucking mind.

School is her priority, she was clear on that. Very clear. And I respect that and her need to devote time and energy to her studies. I waited a full week before I texted her, other than the one I sent the next morning telling her how much I enjoyed our evening. But she didn't respond. Since then, I've spent a lot of time talking myself out of pursuing her. A lot of really good reasons to let this thing go. I'm not long for this small town.

The photo shoots I've picked up over the past couple weeks have gotten me noticed again by the right people. Maybe it's too soon to get back to it? It's been less than six months since I stepped away from my camera, from my career. My family—Michael and his wife— were so much more important at the time, but if I wait any longer, it'll be that much harder to get back to it. I can't lose momentum again.

But, this girl.

She settles in at the corner of the bar, dropping her bag on the chair next to her. The push and pull of her is bloody confusing. I make my way over to her, wiping the bar as I go. "Wasn't sure I'd see you again. You weren't avoiding me, then, were you?" *Christ.* Where the fuck did that come from?

"Sorry. It's been crazy. I..." She sighs pointing to the Guinness tap, her head tilting to the left just a little. "I had tons of work this week and spent every last minute in the hospital. I'm exhausted. I don't know if I'm gonna make it."

Hospital? "Are you all right?" I reach across the bar for her wrist, my thumb automatically caressing the tender skin that I love. I've completely forgotten all about *letting things go.*

"No. I'm fine, it was for school. I had clinical hours I had to do, but they assigned me nights." She takes a long pull from her pint. "I know I'll have to work them when I start for real, but I don't know how I'll make it. My days and nights are so screwed up."

I watch a yawn roll over her and take control of her entire body. "And I have to work at the bar tonight." Her wrist slides from my hand as she pulls her shoulders back. She sweeps her hair up off her neck and arches her back, pushing her chest out toward me.

I can't think. All I can do is stand here staring at her, my eyes raking down the graceful line of her neck—across her delicate collarbone, to the swell of her tits straining under the confines of her top. *Jesus.* I want to trace that line with my tongue. I want to taste her skin—touch, feel, nip at every part of her. She has no idea what she does to me—making me want things I have no business wanting.

Bracing myself on the bar, knuckles white from gripping so hard, I dig deep to find some semblance of control. I clear my throat, interrupting the sensual show in front of me. Lis looks suddenly embarrassed, like she just now realizes her effect on me.

"How long does your crazy schedule last?" I ask. "Will it be like that for weeks? Months?" I don't like the idea of her so tired, so worn out. But really, I'm selfish—I want to know if I can see more of her.

She shivers as she pulls her computer out of her bag. "This rotation is done for now. I'll have to do another over the summer and again in the fall. I'm just so tired," she manages to get out as another yawn takes over—her skin pebbling up with chill bumps. "Sorry, I can't seem to stop that—is it cold in here? I'm freezing."

I grab a couple mugs and pour us each a cup of coffee. The sweet contented smile that spreads its way across her face as she wraps her hands around the porcelain is intoxicating. I could fucking get lost in that. "Lisbeth, what can I do for you? Can you not take the night off—sleep a little?" She just shakes her head, wrapping herself more tightly around the warm mug. The tension is starting to leave her body and she looks like she might fall asleep on the bar. "You need to go home and take a nap, love." God how I would love to join her, though she really needs to sleep and if I were there...

She flicks her eyes up to the clock above the bar and grimaces. "I have to submit my clinical notes by one o'clock. Do you mind if I do it here? And can I have some fries?" She's grabbing for her coffee more than her pint at this point.

I refill her mug and head to the kitchen to make her some lunch—she needs more than a basket of chips to keep her going.

There's not a lot I can do to help, but I can feed her, maybe keep her warm. She's stopped typing and is practically falling asleep with her cheek resting on the heal of her hand and her eyes glazing over. I slide her laptop out of the way, and set down her plate. I grab my jacket from behind the bar and gently place my hand between her shoulders. She mumbles, "...'m awake..." as she sits up and scrubs her hand up and down her face. She was clearly not awake.

I wrap her in my jacket, rubbing her arms to warm her up. "I thought you could use more than just a snack, love." Pulling her hair free of the collar, I caress the side of her neck, lingering just behind her ear. I don't know what's come over me, but I want to lose myself in this spot.

She stills, holding her breath a moment before releasing a shaky breath. But instead of leaning into me, she pulls away.

"Th-thank you."

Nodding, I step back behind the bar to give her some space. "Sure. Let me know what else I can get for you." Not what I wanted. I rattled her, and maybe even scared her off.

I busy myself stocking the bar for the evening, lost a little in my head. Is she pulling back because of that arsehole? The bastard that fucked her sister? It seems different, more than that. Maybe it's me.

I clear her plate and refill her coffee while she works. It's just been the two of us here this whole time, and it's been *fucking torture*. I spend as much time as I can in the kitchen and stockroom, cleaning counters that are already spotless.

Straightening liquor bottles that I've already alphabetized. Am I avoiding her? Hiding from this pull I feel?

I hear her putting her computer away, zipping up her bag. I need to do something, say something to make the awkwardness go away. "Are you finished, then?"

She meets my eyes, as she slides off the barstool. I dump her pint glass into the sink and wipe down the already clean bar. "I think so. I got everything sent to my professors so we'll see. What do I owe you?" she asks as she digs through her bag for her wallet.

"Not a thing." She moves both of her eyebrows up and opens her mouth to protest. "This one's on me." I chuck the bar rag over my shoulder and cross my arms over my chest, hoping I'm giving out that there's no room for negotiation. She blows a lock of hair out of her eyes and just stares. She really does not do well with others caring for her.

"I can't let you do that. I feel so much better than when I walked in here earlier. Please let me pay you, Aidan."

I glance at my watch and look her straight in the eye. I'm pushing this a little, probably more than necessary, but she's dead on her feet. The need to take care of her drives me. When she starts to fidget, I lean toward her. "Go home and rest. Let me just do this for you. We'll figure out a way for you to pay me back later."

Her wheels are spinning and I can see the battle she's waging inside. "Okay. Thank you." She pinches her brows together and screws her mouth up on one side. Another deep breath and she relaxes as she lets it go. She gives me a quick nod and turns to leave. I watch as she hefts her bag higher on her shoulder and heads out the door—still wrapped in my jacket.

NINE

Lis

I am so glad I stopped at McBride's on the way home. We have nothing beyond a bottle of wine and stale crackers in our kitchen. I half wish that Aidan wasn't there though. I've done a pretty good job of avoiding him. I know I got scared. Talking with Gracyn about her trip reminded me that I need to stay focused. I have so much riding on school. Graduating early. Making this work. But he took care of me. I don't really know what to do with that.

I learned really early on that depending on people leads to nothing but disappointment. My mom flaked out right after she divorced my dad. She needed to work on her—at least, that's what she claimed. Really, she was pretty much done with being an adult and even though I was only seventeen, she decided I was old enough to manage paying the bills, going to the grocery store, cooking and cleaning. After all, she had raised me. *Right.* My dad drank away all of his money and my mother just didn't have anything left for me after paying my sister's tuition. I was used to Maryse being the priority. It had been going on for as long as I could remember.

I know I'm not good at having people help me. I can give without batting an eye. Doesn't matter what it is, if someone needs help, I'm on it. Accepting it? Yeah, no. It had me rattled, or maybe falling asleep on a bar mid-day did that.

I move to take off my jacket and realize, it's not mine. It was warm when I left the house last night so I just had my scrubs on. This is all Aidan—spicy, masculine. I hang it on the back of my desk chair and head back in to take a shower and wash away the hospital. I love what I do, but there's a lot of gross stuff I deal with there and I do not want to bring it into my bed while napping.

The hot water feels amazing, soothing my sore and tired muscles. I fall into bed and wait. As tired as I am, I just feel restless and disconnected. Like I'm too exposed. I drag myself out of bed and put his jacket back on. I wrap it around me and crawl back under the covers surrounded by Aidan. After checking my alarm, I let sleep wash over me.

I COULD HAVE SLEPT for days, but by the time I get to work, I almost feel human. I dump my bag and Aidan's coat in the back room and check the bar stock. Filling napkins and straws. Cutting up fruit. Checking the kegs and listening to the hustle and buzz of the restaurant on a Friday night.

Jenna pulls out a chair and sits at the end of the bar. "Hey. How'd your hospital thing go this week?"

"It was good. I didn't love working nights. No...that's not true. I actually loved the quiet hush of the hospital at night, but my body and brain are so confused right now." Out of habit, I pour a glass of her favorite wine and set it in front of her. She eyes the deep crimson liquid and slides it back toward me, resting a hand on her belly. "But the people. Jenna, I love it. I love helping them and making sure they're comfortable and settled and the...all of it. I love all of it." I sigh and offer her a huge smile. She knows my dream—my nature—and how hard I've worked to get here.

"Sweetie, you will make the best nurse. The absolute best." She winks at me. "I'll let you change my bedpan any day." I love this woman. She and Tony just found out they are having a baby and if everything goes the way it's supposed to, I'll be graduated and waiting on the results of my boards by her due date in January. I would love to be there when she delivers.

I look at the wine I poured and it clicks that my pregnant boss can't enjoy her favorite drink for months yet. I really am tired. I grab a new glass and fill it with ice, a couple limes, a splash of cranberry juice, and soda water. Jenna laughs as she takes a long drink and looking longingly at the wine.

"I do miss a glass of wine. Tell me what else is going on. I feel like I haven't seen you in forever. You still seeing that guy?"

I pick at my words, trying to sort out how I feel. "We went out to dinner, that's all. I don't really have time. I need to get through this year and pass my boards. Then...I'll think about it." It's like I'm constantly trying to talk myself out of wanting to spend more time with Aidan.

She's looking past me, over my shoulder, smiling at a customer.

I paste on my smile and turn to greet...Aidan. How much

of that did he hear? "Hey. What are you doing here?" My heart skips erratically as I place a cocktail napkin on the bar in front of him.

"Thought I'd have you tend to my needs for a change." His smirk is ridiculously sexy. I feel flutters deep in my belly. "I'll have a whiskey, neat. And a menu." I hand him a menu and turn to get his drink. Jenna's having a full, silent conversation with me, one I'm trying desperately to ignore. I do catch the look she gives me when I grab for the house whiskey. She shakes her head, looks directly at the good stuff and nods, smiling her wicked little smile.

She and Gracyn have obviously talked about who I'm dating. Not dating—one date. And drinks and food at McBride's. And today—how he took care of me. Dammit. I grab the bottle of Basil Hayden's and a heavy crystal glass. Jenna gave me the go-ahead, whether she realizes it or not, so I pour him a generous glass. I fill a small pitcher with distilled water, placing it on a small plate with fresh lime wedges and mint. Jenna's quiet laugh barely reaches me as she grabs her drink and heads back to her office. There's no way in hell I'm getting away with avoiding the dating discussion with her now.

I place the tumbler in front of him and the small plate off to the side, turning it so the limes and mint are toward him. Presentation is everything—or maybe I'm putting way more thought and effort into this than is necessary—since I'm not interested, and I'm *so* focused on school. *Right*.

I take his dinner order and excuse myself to the kitchen to grab his salad and a breadboard. Tony yells as I'm on my way out, "Is this what Jenna ordered? Christ, she's killing me with these pregnant cravings. She's never had a rare steak in her life." I lose the rest of his rant to the flare of the grill and his mumbling.

"No. She went back to her office, that's for a..."

"For a special diner at the bar, Tony." Jenna elbows me as she scoots past to grab a bowl of soup. "Lis is trying to impress someone." She winks at me with a big goofy grin on her face. I just turn and walk away. Nothing I say is going to stop the inevitable teasing.

My heart flutters as I set Aidan's place at the bar and serve his salad and bread. "What are you doing here, for real? I...I'm sorry I left with your jacket earlier. I have it in the back, let me go grab it for you." I take a step back, but he reaches for my hand and stops me.

"Erm—don't worry about it. I'm away this weekend. I've got to go into the city for a meeting. Do you want to go with me?"

"I can't." I really want to. "I have to work and get ready for finals, I have a ton of studying to do." Why am I so disappointed? I have no problem telling everyone else that I'm not interested and I need to focus. I just can't seem to convince myself. "I'll be done in three weeks, maybe we could go then?" *What the fuck?* My mouth and my brain are so not communicating.

"Absolutely. We'll go when you're done." His gaze locks with mine and I feel those fluttery tingles again. It's like he can see deep into me. It's uncomfortable—I don't know if I like it.

I turn away to fill drink orders for the servers and a few other patrons at the bar, trying to give myself some space. I'm just so aware of him. I can feel his gaze on me. As I duck under the bar top to grab his dinner from the kitchen, I hit my damn head and muffle a curse. The soft laugh from Aidan doesn't escape me and my cheeks catch fire.

I set his plate in front of him, and clear away the others. "Is there anything else I can get for you? Another drink?"

He gives me a quiet *mhmmm* as he cuts into his steak.

"Does everything look okay?"

He watches as I pour him a fresh whiskey. "Things couldn't look any better."

I snap my attention up to meet his hooded gaze. My whole body heats up. Desire rushing through me. "I...uh... okay. I'll let the chef know."

He has me so off balance and flustered. I know I'm running away again, but I let the hostess know the bar is unattended for a bit, and run to the restroom. Bracing my hands on the counter, I stare at my reflection. For the love of God, I look panicked.

He's just being kind—I'm just a distraction. I wash my hands, letting the cool water run over my wrists hoping it'll help to calm me. He's getting to me.

My mini-breakdown lasts longer than it should and when I get back to the bar, he's gone.

Just gone. His glass is empty. Plates neatly stacked. Gone.

I fill the drink orders that have accumulated while I was busy falling apart in the bathroom for no reason, and check on the rest of the customers at the bar. When I clear Aidan's plates, I find a hundred-dollar bill and a note on a cocktail napkin. I clear his tab and tuck the ridiculous tip in my back pocket. No way in hell am I keeping that. With a quick glance to see that everyone at the bar's glasses are full, I lean against the register and focus on the note.

.   .   .

Lisbeth,

I enjoyed taking care of you this morning and wanted to see you again. I'm sorry I'm making you uncomfortable. That's not my intent. I'll leave you be for the remainder of your term so you can study and make grades. But I've let your boss know that you need the weekend after term end off work. Don't bother trying to change it—she agrees fully that you need a break. Study hard. Do well. And I'll see you in three weeks' time. Hang on to my jacket as long as you need.

xx

Aidan

TEN

Aidan

It's time. The last three weeks of her term are over and I've got our trip to NYC planned. Gracyn has been brilliant, feeding me details on when Lisbeth's last exam is, letting me know what time to be here. Waiting.

The day is gorgeous and it gets even better as I watch her walk toward her building. All her focus on her phone, brows pinched together and nose wrinkled. I want to photograph her. She is art in motion. And she's not paying attention at all to her surroundings, just about tripping over me sitting on her steps.

"Shit. You scared me." Her hand flies up to her chest as she startles. "What are you doing here?"

I can't help the grin that spreads across my face. "How was your exam?" I hand her a steaming cup of coffee and stand to let her by.

"Good. I'm done—for this semester." I watch as she rolls

her shoulders shaking off the stress of the term and adjusts her ruck. Every movement captivates me. She is stunning.

"Mmm…thank you for this. That final started way too early." She raises the coffee to her lips and inhales a long pull from the cup. "Oh my God, this is so good." She's wrapped around her coffee like it's going to save her life. The tension visibly leaves her body as the caffeine settles in.

Following her inside the flat, I take her bag and set it by the front door. "We have a few minutes, if you want to grab your bag. I think Gracyn put everything you'll need for the day in there." Her expression is beautifully confused.

She sets her coffee on the hall table and props a hand on her hip. "What do you mean?"

"Love, I told you weeks ago we were going to the city today to celebrate your term end. You're done now, yeah?" She nods tightly, like I'm an eejit since we just fucking discussed this. "Where's your confusion, then?" I step closer to her. "Grab what you need," I lean in and pluck the coffee from her hand, "and let's go." I look her straight in the eye as I take a drink from her cup, loving that my lips rest where hers were only minutes ago. I smile and turn, heading out the door—grabbing her keys on the way to make my point.

THE CITY IS HUMMING with activity, a drastic change from the quiet calm of the train ride in. We practically had the train car to ourselves and the solitude combined with the movement of the train and clack of the tracks lulled Lisbeth to sleep. Her head dipped to my shoulder as the car swayed on the rails. The scent of her hair enveloped and soothed me and I savored the feel of her body against mine. It was heaven.

As we exit Grand Central Station, I stop and grab a hot pretzel and a couple bottles of water. "Is there anything specific that you want to do today? Museums? Shops? A show?"

She shakes her head when I point to the mustard accompanying our paper-wrapped pretzel.

I hand Lisbeth a bottle of water, and place my hand at her back, guiding her down the crowded sidewalk.

"Nothing specific, I just really like it here. The people watching is out of this world—where else can you see Elmo, Cinderella, and the Naked Cowboy in the same place?" We head north toward Central Park, weaving through the throngs of people and sharing our pretzel.

"I have a friend from Dublin, here." I look to see her reaction. "He asked to meet for a drink a little later on, is that alright?"

"Of course, are you kidding me? I can hang out in the park, or whatever, take as much time as you need—I can just..." She's so sweet.

"Jimmy's down here too. He had to visit his gran this morning but said he'd meet us for dinner so you've someone to talk to while I catch up with Liam." I've waited far too long to spend this time with Lis, I don't want to spend even a single minute away from her.

We continue on along some of the smaller paths and come out at a small white gazebo and huge rock that juts out into the lake at the center of the park. There's a boathouse along here somewhere, but the view from this rock is gorgeous and we are remarkably alone.

It amazes me that in a city of this size, two people can find a private moment at all, let alone in such a public place. I watch as she scrambles up the rock. I should have gone ahead of her and helped her up, but the view from behind her is worth my breach of chivalry. I climb up after her and set myself down on the top of the rock.

Turning with a sweet smile over her shoulder, she lowers herself down next to me. "This is one of my all-time favorite places. I love it here." She practically whispers, "It's so serene. I saw a marriage proposal last time I was down here." She looks toward the arched bridge wistfully. "It was the most beautiful thing I've ever seen."

I run my hand down her back, unable to refrain from touching her. Grasping her hand, I pull her in close, her back to my front. Her body melting into mine. She untwines our hands, instead running her fingers lightly up and down my arm. "Tell me what was beautiful about it. Was there a rowboat? Champagne and great declarations of love? Tell me you heard him quoting Oscar Wilde."

"No. Nothing that elaborate. Just a simple proposal. At the center of that arched bridge." She nods off to our left. She's quiet a moment and obviously touched by the memory. "They weren't dressed up, they weren't doing anything fancy, just enjoying a day together completely alone, surrounded by a ton of people. He paused just shy of the top of the arch, pulled her around to face him, holding both her hands in his." She meets my stare and smirks. "No Wilde was harmed or abused in the overture. He just got down on one knee and asked." She looks back at the bridge—seeming lost in the memory. "She said '*yes,*' and he pulled a small box from his pocket. It was a normal, nothing day that became the start of their forever."

It hit me then how simple she is. Not simple. Uncomplicated in her wants and desires. I'm the one making things complicated for her.

I'd heard what she told her boss the night I had dinner at her bar. I got it the first time she told me she had a plan and needs to stick to it. I just can't stop myself from wanting to be with her. This is becoming more than a distraction to me—much more.

I hold her hand, touch her back, some kind of contact for our walk through Central Park and the little zoo that's there. The time passes far too quickly and we need to get on to meet up with Jimmy and Liam at McCoy's.

I need to talk to Liam. I need to know what's going on at home.

ELEVEN

Aidan's been touching me in some small way all day. And though I'm not used to being on the receiving end of so much attention, I don't hate it. I don't hate it at all. Weeks ago, it made me really self-conscious—exposed and on edge. But, now I think I like it.

It was reassuring, having his touch as we walked through Central Park and the zoo. It had been so much a part of our day that it totally takes me by surprise when he drops my hand and puts a little extra space between us as we walk into the pub where we're meeting Jimmy for dinner. I try not to bristle, but it just doesn't feel right.

"I'll be right back, I'm going to run to the restroom." I've felt off kilter since practically tripping over Aidan outside my building this morning.

What are we doing?

Aidan is at the bar, deep in conversation with someone but Jimmy's at a booth near the back of the pub. I move to slide into the seat across from him, but he pats the seat next to him. "Sit here. If he's gonna be a daft fool, we can work on making him realize it. Come 'ere."

I perch on the edge of my seat and reach for a menu. "What do you mean?"

"I saw him. Dropped your hand and took a step away. Fuckin' stupid arse..." I miss what he mumbles after that as the pub erupts in cheers at a game up on the screens around the bar. Jimmy snaps his focus to the game and launches into a tirade on Gaelic football and the team that just scored. "...it's like rugby but fewer rules, yeah? The players are tougher, harder—thicker skulls." I nod along, not really paying attention, my mind picking the day apart. "...played back in Dublin."

"Wait. What?" I drag my gaze from the screen to Aidan. This is not where my focus is. I can't see Aidan in the short shorts, no protective gear, with ruddy cheeks and sweaty hair fighting for an oversized football. "But he's a photographer. They would crush him." As fit as he is, Aidan is small compared to the guys in this game.

"Concerned for him?" Jimmy smirks. "He played for his school—he was the big one on the field then, yeah." He leans in sliding a pint glass toward me.

I push him back and taste what he ordered me. "What is this?"

"That, love, is a snakebite. Treat it with respect, or we'll be carrying you to the train." He laughs at me while checking to see where Aidan is. He's no longer at the bar, they've moved to a small table by the door. He looks pissed, really angry about something.

Jimmy tries to pull my attention away from what's

becoming a pretty heated discussion. He signals to the waitress and turns to me. "Are we celebrating tonight?"

"Celebrating what?" The waitress sets a couple shots on the table and waits while Jimmy orders some appetizers. I down the shot of Jameson and look back toward Aidan "What is he so upset about? Do you know?"

"Erm, you'll have to take that up with your man." Jimmy signals for another round of shots and puts his arm around me pulling me closer. The waitress unloads plates piled full of nachos and potato skins. Our table is ridiculously full with all the food, fresh pints, and more shots. Aidan looks over and his expression goes from curious to pissed when he takes in the drinks and empty shot glasses in front of us. Or maybe it's how close Jimmy's leaning in to me.

"Jimmy." Our faces are closer than I realized. "What are you doing?"

He reaches across me, enveloping me in his grasp as he grabs the ketchup. "I told you. We're going to show him what he's fuckin' with." He sits back and looks straight at Aidan with an eyebrow about lodged in his hairline. Challenging him.

I feel even more off balance than I did when we walked in here. The shots, the things coming out of Jimmy's mouth and the steely glare Aidan's throwing this way. I grab the two shots that were just deposited at our table and down them one after the other, immediately realizing my mistake.

The alcohol burns its way through my veins, making my head swim and my cheeks heat up. When Aidan finally tears his attention away from me, I feel like I can breathe again. I excuse myself to the restroom, needing some space to think.

I lock the door behind me and fall back against it. What

am I doing? The back and forth in my head is driving me insane. No matter how hard I try, no matter how busy I make myself with school and work, I end up thinking about him constantly. I crave him. His wit, the way he cares for me—his touch.

Rob is my benchmark. Ours is the only real relationship I've had and that was a mess. I've never done the casual hookup thing—can't imagine a one-night stand. Emotionally, it's not me, but adding in my clinical knowledge, makes it a hard no.

This thing with Aidan falls somewhere in the gray area. There's definitely an end point. He's here for an extended visit, not to make a life. I know I'm not ready to jump into dating or anything serious, the draw to him is very real. I can spend time with him—date him—knowing that it will end. It all makes perfect sense bumping through my whiskey-addled brain.

He can be my distraction.

The bumping turns to pounding and I realize it's not in my brain, but someone needing the restroom. The pub filled up while I was hiding out, and there's a line five people deep. And Aidan is at the table with Jimmy. Heads bent together in a heated discussion, mirroring the scene between Aidan and Lance? Lucas? before I escaped into the restroom.

The conversation blatantly dies as I return to the table. Jimmy's turned his back to the brick wall with his legs stretched across the seat, and nods toward the spot next to Aidan.

Aidan reaches for my hand, guiding me down to sit with him. "That took a lot longer than I thought it would. I'm sorry." His thumb rubs my inner wrist sending electric heat coursing through my body.

I'm at the tipping point, where I either should stop drinking and take a nap or just fully commit to feeling awful tomorrow. "We...we had some things to straighten out, Liam and I. I'm sorry for the time it took. But you and Jimmy—you were alright, yeah?" There's a spiky edge to his question, something else that I can't quite read.

"Yup." My rational thoughts blur into a fuzzy haze, my pulse speeding up under the lazy circles he's tracing on my wrist. I reach for Aidan's tumbler of whiskey and drain it in one gulp. I just shut my brain off, letting go of my tightly ordered thoughts and become a happy little mess.

Aidan

I got well and truly stuck in the conversation with Liam. I had agreed to meet him—really, he strong-armed me into it— while he was in town, but this is not at all where I want to be.

I left Dublin to get away from the drama and to try and grieve my brother's death. On my own. In my own way. Michael was too fucking young to die. And now his widow has more shite on her plate than anyone should.

Liam had gone 'round to check in on Lorna, and because burying her husband at twenty-six was not enough, she just learned she's fallen pregnant. The hits just keep on coming.

While I thought this would be a quick meetup, I've spent far longer with Liam than I had planned, watching as Jimmy and Lisbeth drink and laugh—watching him move closer to her. That shite's not okay.

I can feel my blood heating as I tense, staring daggers

through him. I'm not concerned he's making a move on her. I just wish it were me cozied up to her.

"Are you fuckin' listening to me?" Shite. I am—but not really. "Lorna's not okay. She's really struggling. I think you need to talk to her. Maybe come home."

"I'll talk to her. But Christ, Liam, I can't come home just now. I—"

He follows my line of sight and drops his pint glass to the table. "Yeah, mate. Sure." Liam huffs out a judgmental breath, shaking his head. "Aidan, have your fun here, yeah? But you've family at home that need you. She's having a baby. She just buried her husband. You were best fucking friends and the one helping her deal with all that and then you just fuckin' left—" Liam's good and hacked off at me for leaving Dublin just days after Michael's funeral. "She depended on you. And now she needs you more than ever— and you're over here, fuckin' about." He's practically spitting the words at me now and Lisbeth is watching us.

Fucking hell.

I lean in toward Liam, my voice calm and low. "I will talk to Lorna. I'll let you know when I've spoken with her. And what we're gonna do." I push back from the table and stand. "It was good to see you, Liam." I clap him on the back and turn, ready to put this all behind me for today and get back to Lis.

I watch Lis walk away as I move toward the table in the back. She seems to have this need to escape when things start to overwhelm her. Like she just needs to wrap her head around the situation on her own before she can face it.

I slide into the seat across from Jimmy, my thoughts swirling around in my head. I ran from the overwhelming emotion of losing my brother and left my best friend in the process, and now I'm not ready to go back. Eyes trained on the door of the loo, I swirl the whiskey 'round my glass wishing that my thoughts could order themselves the same way.

"Are you fuckin' listening to me?"

"What?" No. I've not heard a damn thing Jimmy has said.

"The fuck are you doin'? You're stupid—droppin' her hand and blowing her off. Francie saw that, he'd fuckin' lay you out..." Jimmy's ripping into me.

I lean in and make sure I've got his attention so I can catch him up on Lorna and the baby.

"Don't you fuckin' ruin shite with Lis, man. You need to come clean. You need to tell her what's goin' on." Jimmy emphasizes his point by pounding his shot glass on the tabletop.

"I know, just...let me talk to Lorna first, figure out what to do there. I...*chsssss*—" I break off mid rant as Lisbeth comes back to the table.

I don't want to do this now. I've wasted enough of the evening and I want to take it back, spend it with this girl—not thoughts of my brother's pregnant widow.

THE TRAIN RIDE back home was a mess and I feel nothing but relief that I have these two safely tucked away at McBride's. I tried—truly tried—to talk them into calling it a night but they're dead set on drinking each other under the table.

I end up helping Finn behind the bar since Jimmy's in no

shape to work his shift. It's not all that busy tonight, but that and his inebriation give me the leverage I need to swap shifts and have tomorrow free to spend with Lis.

She's going to feel like shite as it is, so I water down her drinks and try to get her to eat something. "What is it with you and food? We should just go have a picnic—that's totally what we should do." She slams both palms down on the bar to make her point. "We should go to...that place on the river... that mansion?" The place is beautiful. It's a historic mansion with gorgeous grounds and gardens. I drove through there a while back and have had it pegged as a place to go and shoot —to get creative with my photography.

"Maybe we should get you home soon so we can take advantage of..."

She cuts me off with another slam to the bar top. "There will be no taking advantage of m-me tonight. Nope. Sorry, not gonna happen." She's adorable and trying so hard to look offended and serious...and not off her tits.

"No feckin' takin' advantage of your girl. You treated 'er like shite today and you canna do tha...and ye nade ter be 'onest wit 'er..." Jimmy's far gone and making no fucking sense anymore. I can hardly understand his slurs—hopefully Lisbeth will miss what he's getting at, as well. But I slide him another pint to distract the bastard from spilling about Lorna.

Jesus, I need to call her first thing in the morning and talk with her.

"Love. We need to take advantage of the beautiful day tomorrow." Though, Christ, if I'm honest with myself, I'd love to take advantage of her. "Let's get you safe home and to bed, and we'll go on that picnic tomorrow." Jimmy glares at me, just now figuring out that I distracted him with a beer. I hold his stare and slide him another pint. "We'll talk later, yeah?"

As I help Lisbeth toward the door, I turn to Finn. "I'm taking her home now—and Jimmy's got my shift tomorrow. You good?"

Finn looks up from his phone. "I am. You taking Jimmy home wit' you?"

Shaking my head, I laugh and silently tell him *no*.

TWELVE

My head is a splitting, fuzzy mess. I cover my eyes to keep the bright sunlight from killing me, as I feel around for my phone. Why? Why did I do this to myself? Why did I drink so much? After rummaging through my sheets and blankets, I finally find my phone stuck to the back of my thigh—Jesus. I peel it off and swipe the screen awake squinting to check the time. Thank God, it's only ten o'clock. I close my eyes as gently as I can, not wanting to face the world yet.

I know Aidan brought me home and Gracyn helped him tuck me into bed, with a glass of water and a bottle of ibuprofen. Probably, I should feel worse than I do, but I pull my duvet up and snuggle in to sleep this misery away. *I'm never drinking again.* Who doesn't think that at a time like this? Just as I'm drifting off to sleep, my phone buzzes with a text.

> **A: I'll be there in an hour.**
> **L: Why would you do that?**
> **A: This was your idea.**

L: OK. What was?

A: Our picnic at the mansion. I'll bring the food. Drink your water and hop in the shower. You'll feel better.

L: I doubt it.

Reluctantly, I drag myself out of bed and have to sit right back down. Good God, just how much did I drink last night? *Way too much.* I take a couple sips of water and wait for my stomach to accept or reject what I'm putting in it. Somewhat satisfied that the water is not going to make a reappearance, I shuffle to the bathroom. I start the shower before even chancing a look at the mess in the mirror. Mhmmm—ratty auburn hair, raccoon eyes.

I strip out of my clothes and step into the steam, letting the hot water wash over me. My body shudders, actually shudders, in appreciation and I find a small bit of hope that I'll live and not resent the hell out of life today. I stay in the shower far longer than strictly necessary and come out feeling pretty close to human. Not human enough that I deal with blow drying my hair. Instead I lazily twist it into a loose braid, where it leaves a wet spot as it lies on my tank top. I swipe on a little mascara and brush my teeth twice.

Absently, I glance at my phone to check the time, and grab my sandals and the biggest, darkest pair of sunglasses I can find.

"Gracyn?" The sound of my knuckles against the wood sends a fresh flash of pain through my skull.

"Yeah? You feeling okay?" she rasps, her voice laced with either tears or sleep.

I scoff at her question as I crack her door open, holding up her sunglasses. "Not great, can I borrow these?" She is exactly where I want to be—in bed—in the dark, not headed out into the world with a hangover. "How am I going to do this? I don't know that I'm gonna make it today." My eyes close and I lean my head against the doorframe—the cool wood offering a touch of relief to my aching head.

"Lissy, you'll be fine. Go get another glass of water. You drank the one he left you last night, right?" This conversation is usually the other way around. Me taking care of her. I know the routine, I just don't want to move. "Go drink another, take something for your headache and pray he brings you something good to eat."

My feet make their way to the kitchen even though my head is still wishing it was soaking in the cool, smooth wood. In the kitchen, I move to fill a water bottle and take some ibuprofen. My phone buzzes just as I'm tipping the little brown pills into my hand. Of course, it makes me jump, spilling the perfectly round painkillers across the counter with each of them bobbling and tinkling as they spin around.

I lean my forehead on the cabinet in front of me and answer. "Hello?"

His voice is soft. "I'm here. Are you ready to go, or do you need a minute yet?"

"I'm ready. I..." I sigh and gather up the pills I dropped, popping a few of them in my mouth. "I just need to clean up my spill. Do I need to grab anything?" I swallow the pills just as they start to dissolve on my tongue with that acidic burn.

"Erm, yeah, actually. I forgot to grab a blanket. Do you have one we can use?" Bless him, his voice is still soft and low.

"I'll find something and be right out." I check my closet and grab the flat sheet from my extra set. It's just going to have to be good enough. "Bye, Gracyn. Thanks." There's no response, she's probably fallen back to sleep.

Sunglasses. Water bottle. Sheet. Keys. Deep, bracing breath and I head out to see Aidan leaning against the passenger side of his car. He looks at me with just a touch of pity and a beautiful smile.

"Good morning, love," he murmurs as he leans in and presses his lips to my cheek right by my ear. "You look beautiful. Let me take this." He puts the sheet in the back seat of his car and opens the passenger door for me.

AIDAN'S quiet while we walk toward the back side of the historic mansion. I've toured it tons of times and while the mansion is beautiful, the grounds are unreal. This place was built as a summer home for a railroad tycoon during the Golden Age with servants' quarters, a carriage house, and formal gardens. It's magical. My happy place.

In dire need of a little shade, I steer him toward my favorite spot. It's a little niche tucked into some trees—perfect for a hammock and a good book. Sadly, I'm pretty sure the park service would frown on my efforts if I tried to put one up. Instead, I spread the sheet out where the grass is soft and fewer people are around to spoil the peacefulness. And it's idyllic back here. Really perfect.

"This is lovely." Aidan squints toward the sun. "We'll be good here? I've Irish skin, yeah? I don't want to burn and freckle..." He turns his smirk to me and chuckles softly.

Now, I totally want to see his cheeks turn red. And I can't help but stare at the fine smattering of freckles high on his cheekbones and across the bridge of his nose. "No, I think your delicate complexion will be fine." I'm starting to feel a little icky again. "Can we eat? I think I have a bad case of..." I scrunch up my nose and shake my head a little reaching for my water bottle. I really should have known better.

Aidan sets the bag on the grass and pulls me down to the middle of the sheet. "Lisbeth, don't try out-drinking Jimmy again. Love, he's Irish..." God, I was an idiot to think I could hang with him. "And he's years of experience on you."

I groan as Aidan unpacks sandwiches and fruit, knowing I need to eat, but the lurch in my stomach from the leftover alcohol is a lot to handle right now. I grab my water and let the cool liquid roll down my throat, saying a silent prayer. "You learned your lesson, then? No more showing off—trying to prove yourself?"

I mumble a quiet *no* as he unwraps my sandwich and hands it to me. God, it's perfect. Aidan's amazing. He keeps doing these little things, taking care of me. Making sure I have what I need.

"What? Why are you laughing at me?" Food finally sounds like a good idea to me. He can laugh all he wants, this is the stuff that love is made of.

"Lisbeth. I don't think I've ever seen someone so thoroughly enjoy a fuckin' turkey sandwich. You've hearts in your eyes."

THIRTEEN

Aidan

I brush a lock of auburn hair back off Lis' cheek, tracing the soft lines of her lips. Her nose twitches and she reaches up to brush away the tickle. Christ, she's beautiful all rumpled from sleep. I can't help but smile softly at her as she comes awake.

"Did you sleep well?"

"Mmm… I fell asleep?" She rolls to her back and wipes at her eyes. I reach over and gently dust an eyelash away from her cheek.

"Love, you've been out for an hour or so. You drove everyone else away with your sweet snoring." Sitting up, she looks around us, eyes wide and darting around, pink staining her cheeks. Most of the others are gone, but it had nothing to do with her.

Only a handful of people are spread across the lawn. We pack up the trash and remnants of our food quietly. Watching a couple kids playing with their mum.

There's a path near where we're sitting leading away from the house. An older couple passes by, holding hands as they stroll toward the car park. Lis leans into me and quietly asks, "How long do you think they've been married?"

"What makes you think they're married?" I lean in closer. "Maybe they meet here for their weekly tryst." Her face—Jesus, the look on her is priceless.

She pulls away, and stares at me, her mouth forming that perfect little "O." "Aidan, they've got to be in their seventies—really? They're married and have kids and probably a ton of grandkids." She gets a good smack in on my arm and I grudgingly release my hold. She looks suddenly shy and a little unsure as she asks, "Do you...um, want to go see the gardens?" She looks around like she's trying to find a place to escape to.

We're going to have to talk about that.

We have a lot of shite we need to talk about, but not today. It can wait for another day. Lorna didn't answer my call this morning, so it's best if I wait to talk about that bit.

The path leads to terraced gardens. I catch the sweet heady scent of the flowers well before the riot of colors surround us. The gentle breeze carries the fragrance through the tunnel of the trees. I stop to pull my camera out of the case as Lis walks on ahead. The sunlight dapples through the trees casting her in the most beautiful green and golden glow.

"Lisbeth, will you stop a moment?" I snap several frames just as she turns to look back at me. Her smile soft and her eyes go from questioning to sparkling in a heartbeat.

Lis hops down the steps as she leads us deeper into the gardens. The color is breathtaking. I stutter to a stop when we round a corner—graced with the sight of a gazebo at the far end of a reflecting pool. The light. The sun dipping lower in the sky; we're coming up on the golden hour. The time when the sun's rays are pure magic. I live for light like this.

She glides along the edge of the pool toward the gazebo, arms out to the sides for balance. There's a statue of a woman at the far end. Grecian? Roman? It hardly matters. It's a beautiful day and I have a subject I can't wait to shoot.

She stops in front of the statue and gazes up at it, taking in its form.

Click click click

The shutter counts out quietly. Lis turns and grins at me. "Can you imitate her pose?" Her right arm goes up and bends so that her hand is just behind her head. Looking back at the statue, Lis mimes gathering flowing robes and pops her left foot back just a touch so her shoe rests on the toe. "Tilt your head—to the right. Look down a little, toward the center of the pool."

Click click click

This light. This is one of those moments. I don't usually do artistic portraits. I shoot the news, humanitarian pieces, photos that oftentimes evoke hard emotions. That's my career. But every now and then, God hands you a moment—a subject—that's too good to waste.

Click click click

I need my other camera. Digital is good. I love the instant feedback with a digital camera, but there is something undeniably magical about film. Old school. It's more of a challenge. Film forces you to focus on the subject as opposed to watching the screen. It's more of an art.

I stoop down to grab my old camera body and glance up at her as I affix the lens. The sheet she brought for our picnic catches my eye. Pulling it out of the satchel, I unfold it as I approach her. She drops her arms and shifts toward me.

"Do you think we can use this? Wrap it around you like her robes?" I ask her.

She takes the sheet from me and turns to study the statue. Gathering the material, draping it around one shoulder, and tucking it into place, she does a brilliant job imitating the look.

I adjust the sheet as it flows across her chest and bunches over her left arm. After coaxing her back into the statue's pose, I drag my hand down the underside of her raised arm. I tilt her chin, making minor adjustments as I hold her gaze. Scooping her hair forward over her shoulder, my fingers twisting through the silky burnished locks, I lean in so my lips graze her ear. "Breathe." She releases her breath and closes her eyes. She's as affected by this moment as I am.

I jog back to my spot, anxious to frame the shot. It's beautiful, but— "Can you push your top down your shoulders a bit? Just so it doesn't show around the sheet?"

Mesmerized, I watch as she does that thing girls do. That thing where they can slip out of a bra without exposing themselves? Yeah, that. She shimmies her tank top and bra off her shoulders. Fucking witchcraft. She holds my eyes as she raises her arm and gets back into position. *Christ, now I'm the one not breathing.*

Click click click

Click click click

We haven't seen anyone else since we've been in this part of the garden. The sky is turning the most beautiful soft golden color as the sun moves further west.

Click click click

"Erm...the sun's filtering through the sheet. It's...it's back-lighting your shorts. Really taking away from the stunning artistry of the shot." I smirk as she raises her eyebrow at me. I know I'm pushing my luck, but it really is taking away from what this shot could be.

She cocks her head and reaches into her "robes." God, how does she maneuver without dropping that thing? I can't move my eyes as I watch her unbutton her shorts and wiggle them down her legs.

Breathe.

Breathe.

Damn, I have to keep reminding myself to do that simple task.

Click click click

I shoot more film as she gets herself back into the pose.

Breathtaking. Absolutely, fucking breathtaking. The soft rays of the sun highlight her curves and set her auburn hair to flame. The effect is unreal. She looks like a goddess.

Click click click

I work my way through the rest of the film, capturing subtle shifts in her expression and changes in the light as it slowly fades. I don't know if she's listening for the shutter click—that's no longer there—or if she somehow senses that the moment has passed, but she raises her eyes to mine and time stands still.

I put down the camera and move toward her.

I can't stop myself.

My hand goes around the back of her neck, fingers weaving into her hair. Neither one of us takes a breath for that moment. That moment just before our lips brush, ghosting across each other. It's a split second that lasts for days. I press closer, kissing her again, suddenly all too aware of her lack of real clothing. Her lips are soft and yielding. She tastes faintly of strawberries and wine. The kiss is getting ready to take on a momentum of its own when I force myself to pull back just a bit.

"I should...we..." She shifts, and hugs the sheet closer to her body shivering a little. The sun is setting and the air is rapidly cooling. "The grounds close at dusk. We should probably get going."

I pull in a deep breath and step back while running my fingers through my hair. "Erm, yeah. Right. I'll, uh...pack up my cameras while you..." I wave my hands at her and the sheet, unable to find words that make any sense.

I HOLD her hand as we walk through the grounds back to the car park. I want to touch her. Maybe it's the intimacy of the moment. Maybe I don't want her to pull away again. Maybe I've become completely intoxicated by her, but the reflecting pool changed something in me. Maybe in her too.

I walk her around to the passenger side of the car and help her in, not letting go of her hand until I have to. What. The. Fuck? Lis shifts nervously, giving me the side eye as I settle in the driver's seat and turn down the radio. "So, are you going to let me see?"

"See what?" I want to hear her ask.

"The pictures. I want to see what you got. What I look like."

I sit and smirk at her for as long as it takes to make her a little uncomfortable. I think I like her a little rattled.

"What? Can I see them?"

"Well that's the thing. A moment like that needs to be treated special. Treated and captured in a way that sets it apart from all the rest."

She scrunches her nose up at me as I pull out onto the main road heading to her flat. "You'll have to wait for the proof sheet."

"What? Just give me the camera, I'll scroll through and scrap the shitty ones before you doctor them up with filters and magic." The scent of her hair floats around me as she turns, trying to reach the ruck in the back with my equipment. My skin tingles and raises chill bumps where the strands brush faintly across my arm.

"I switched cameras. This afternoon could only be done justice with film. I'll need to develop them at the dark room. I should have the proof sheet tomorrow—maybe later tonight."

Lis huffs out her frustration right there.

"Are you cranky, then? Need to get you home so you can take another nap, or go to bed early, yeah?"

"I have to work tonight." She drops her head back and closes her eyes. "Jenna texted me—the other bartender called in sick. Bastard is probably just hungover." This girl works hard. Too hard.

I pull up to her building and hop out to get her door. Not sure if I'm being a gentleman, full of shite, or just have to touch her again, but as she steps out of the car, I wrap my left hand around her neck and pull her to me. It's still there. That magic from earlier. I brush my lips across hers, hating that I have to let her go for the evening. "Be safe at work, yeah."

She nods, licks her lips, and makes her way inside.

I set off for the photo lab straight away.

FOURTEEN

Lis

"Hey, what time are you working tonight?" Gracyn really needs to get a handle on her volume control.

"Seven to close. You wanna shush a little?" Easing out a deep breath, I close my eyes willing myself to grab another water and some more ibuprofen. I'm definitely feeling better, but I need sleep.

"Still have a headache? You're looking all wobbly and woozy—sun too much for you today?" She's obviously feeling perkier than she was this morning, and there's no escaping her now. I shrug and shuffle down the hall to my room to change for my shift.

"Are you working tonight, too? You wanna ride in together?" *Please, please let her say yes.* If she drives, maybe I can catch a quick nap. And make it through the weekend without having to put more gas in my car.

No lie, this week is going to kill me. I have rent, books for my summer courses, and a million other bills to pay for. My tiny financial cushion from spring break is officially gone.

"I think I'll drive, though." She looks at me with her lips curled up in a smirk. "You still look like shit."

My phone buzzes while I put some makeup on and try to tame my windblown hair.

A: Hey-I got darkroom time tonight. I can come by when I'm done.

L: How long will it take to process all the photos?

A: Christ, far too long. I'll just get the thumbnails done. Come by for a drink.

I can't tonight. I just can't. The past two days have been some kind of crazy and intense. I need a minute to think about this afternoon. About what passed between us.

Pouring drinks and mixing cocktails will give me just the right amount of monotony to work through my thoughts and feelings without having to face them directly.

L: Can we meet up tomorrow? It's going to take every-thing I have to make it through tonight with my head still pounding.

A: Right. I'll try to get time in the morning. We can hook up whenever and then I can make some prints.

L: Is that a spectator sport?

A: ...?

L: Can I watch you work?

A: I'll text you a time.

His last response takes a lot longer than the others. I don't have time or energy to try and figure out why. Gracyn's pushing me out the door and I have to force my brain to switch gears to get through the night.

Sadly, my plan for work taking my mind off Aidan and the past couple days, totally backfires. It's really slow for a Saturday night and I have way too much time on my hands. He's all I can think about and Jenna's not even here to distract me. *Why the hell did I need to come in tonight?* My mind is spinning. I really like him. I have fun every time we're together and he's so sweet to me—opening doors and always making sure I'm okay—I should try to trust him. Give him a real chance. Maybe he won't let me down.

When the night is finally over, I shoot Gracyn a grin. "Nope, not drinking tonight. I'm going home, crawling into bed, and sleeping yesterday off."

"Yeah, I kinda figured," she chuckles. "So, you haven't told me anything about the past two days with Aidan. I mean, obviously you got shitty yesterday, but what's going on with you guys?"

We grab our bags and walk out the back door.

She's pushing for info. She's been really off since spring break and I haven't wanted to bug her. "I don't know. I'm scared." I hate admitting that, but my fear is honest.

"Lis, you have to try eventually. You know that, right?"

Of course, I know that. It's all I've thought about tonight. "I do. It's just..." God, this is hard. "...I can't do it again. My heart can't handle the idea of breaking again so soon." I try to hold my tears back, but they just have to break free. Swiping at my cheeks, I try to pull myself together. Getting emotional goes hand in hand with being tired and I'm so there.

Gracyn hands me a tissue along with the start of an epic pep talk. "Lissy, he's been nothing but kind and considerate. You need to give the boy a chance. He fought Francie, has taken you out, respects your commitment to school and took care of your drunk ass without taking advantage of you—because let me tell you—he so could have taken whatever he wanted last night. You asked him to, multiple times. But he tucked you into bed, made sure you took something for your headache and that you had water. You don't want to compare, and I get that, but Rob wouldn't have done any of that, even on his best day. Aidan's different." She's totally right. "Tell me about today. What did you guys do?"

Sighing, I stare out the window. "He took me to the mansion for a picnic. Packed the most amazing food, and…"

"What?"

"I swear he watched me sleep for a couple hours—not in a creepy way, but just really sweet. And then we went for a walk to the reflecting pool."

"Dude. That's your favorite place. Did he know?"

"I don't know. I think I was babbling about it last night at McBride's." I can't believe I'm spilling this. "And he brought his camera. He…he took pictures of me." I drop that on her as I get out of the car and pray she leaves it alone.

"He what?"

"He took some pictures of me in the garden. He's a photographer, so, you know. It's no big deal, just…" I shrug as I open our door. And my phone pings. "It was nothing. You can have the bathroom first, just hurry. I need to be done with today."

Gracyn does her thing and is out the door in record time. She seems like she's getting back to her normal self—her before-spring-break self. I don't know what changed with her today. I'm just relieved to hear the lock click and finally be alone.

I take the longest, hottest shower I can stand. I scrub my

hair, condition it twice, shave my legs and let the lavender scent calm and soothe me. The thick lotion I slather on after toweling off feels like heaven. Pulling on my shorts and tank, I hear my phone ping. Again. I totally forgot that I got a text earlier. And, evidently a couple more while I was in the shower.

A: I've got the proof sheet done. Want me to come by?

A: You still there?

A: The place looks dead. Did you close early?

A: Christ. Could you check your phone?

The dots start up again. He's getting a little cranky; I'm not the only one who needs a good night sleep.

L: Give me a sec. I just got out of the shower.

That was stupid. Why did I text him that?

A: Are you needing help?

L: Thanks for the offer. I'm good.

My phone starts vibrating as soon as I hit send. Shit. "Hello..."

"Well?" The smoky timber of his voice sends a shiver down my spine.

"Well, what?" My teeth dig into the side of my lower lip as I try to hide my physical response to just his words.

"Are you wanting me to come by or are you free tomorrow mornin'? I've the dark room at ten o'clock for a couple hours." I can hear bar noises muffled in the background.

"Um, I'm free tomorrow, all day. You sound like you're busy anyway. I'll just meet you there." I try to stifle my yawn, but am not at all successful.

"Yeah, I came to the bar to grab a bite to eat and ended

up working for Jimmy. You might've given him more of a run for his money than he let on. He's lookin' a bit peaked and asked me to stay for him." His chuckle is low and deep, rumbling straight through me. He definitely affects me more than I am ready to admit. "You sound like you're ready for sleep yourself? I'll text the address and see you in the morning, yeah?"

I yawn again. "Uh-huh. I'll see you tomorrow."

"Sleep well, love."

IT'S BEEN ages since the last time I was in this part of town. I pass the building three times before I text Aidan that I'm here. A steel door creaks open down the alley and Aidan steps out. The sun is behind him with rays streaming down around him, highlighting his silhouette. He is breathtaking.

I slide through between his body and the doorframe, brushing up against him slightly. "'Scuse me."

The whole building stinks like chemicals—rotten eggs. It does nothing to enhance the 1970s plastic and linoleum decor. I wrinkle up my nose taking in the room. "This is... nice... How'd you find this place?"

Aidan huffs out an amused chuckle and reaches for my hand. "I asked at the college—I hoped they would let me use theirs, but this'll do. Not many people have a need for the labs now. But I learned the old ways when I was in school."

I raise my eyebrow at him—he's not that much older than me, right?

"Come with me, I'll show you the 'magic.'"

It's kind of creepy moving through the empty building,

past offices, and storage rooms. We are very much alone in here. Aidan soothes me with his warm hand—stroking my fingers with his thumb and squeezing me a little as we enter the darkroom. I check my watch. "What time did you get here?" The red light is on and there are shallow trays lined up on the work surface. It's a crazy, organized chaos.

Aidan quietly closes the door behind us and leads me over to a table with a folder and a small box. "Just before you. I mixed up some chemicals and got things ready." He puts one hand on my shoulder and leans into me a little grabbing the box. "Do you want to look and see what we've got?"

The room feels almost cold after coming in from the glaring sun and I'm suddenly very aware of his warmth at my back. I shiver when he straightens, opening the box.

"It's cool in here. Are you okay?" His warm breath on my ear sends another shiver through me.

"Um...yeah. I'm good. Let me see." I grab at the proof sheet, again feeling Aidan lean into me. He slides the sheet out of my reach and holds it away from me.

"You're eager, then." He smirks. Pressing his left hand into my lower back, he slips around to my side. He holds his hand there for a beat longer than he needs to, but not nearly long enough. Something changes, and he shifts his eyes from mine. Pulling back from me, he mumbles, "Well, erm... Right. Let's just get this set." He starts moving around, putting distance between us. Slipping the proofs under some weird magnifying thing—adjusting knobs, and buttons, and lights.

Is he nervous? This man has been touching me in some small way since I got here and now he's stepping away, keeping clear of me. He was all flirty on the phone last night. He's...I don't know. Trying to give me space?

"Can I see now?" We've killed half an hour with this little dance. It's obvious Aidan is stuck in his head. Maybe he's nervous? Scared to show me the images.

He blows out a big breath pursing his lips, and steps back. "Erm—you can. Just look through at the contact sheet and, erm...let me know when you're ready for the next one. We'll just..."

I'm a little freaked by this viewing thing he's been messing with. It's intimidating, but the image that greets me is nothing short of amazing. "Wow. That's..." I'm completely speechless.

"They get better," Aidan whispers as he reaches over and adjusts the sheet so the next frame comes into view, his confidence coming back.

After a few awkward minutes of sliding the frames through slowly and clumsily, we start to fall into a rhythm, relaxing into each other. Aidan gets a little lost in his craft and forgets whatever it was that made him put distance between us earlier.

Each frame is better than the next. His artistic eye is seriously well developed. The light created a halo effect as it streamed through the arbor. Illuminating the subject's hair and the sheet that's wrapped and draped around her form. He's clearly decided which ones he wants to print. I want to see them all—it doesn't register that it's me in the pictures. It never even crosses my mind.

I move back a bit, just watching and listening. I could do this for hours, it's beautiful. I know I asked for the magic of making the prints, but I kind of get lost myself. It's dark and quiet. And as gorgeous as the shots are that we've looked at, Aidan in the flesh is a site worth appreciating. Maybe he would let me take some pictures of him.

I watch him fall into a kind of artistic abyss. He's lost in the poetry of his movements, and the lilting melody of his voice washes over me as he explains what he's doing. I'm absolutely captivated by him. I'm lost in him, lost to him.

FIFTEEN

Aidan

She's not paying attention to what I'm doing anymore. I can feel her gaze on me. I'm ready to dazzle her. *Christ.* Who thinks shite like that? It's like I was fluffing my feathers trying to impress her.

I don't know what the fuck made me so jittery earlier. I loved holding her hand, touching her when she first got here. When I pressed my body up against hers and her arse pressed back into me—her arse in that little skirt she's wearing—Jesus, Mary, and Joseph. I swear, I heard the fucking angels sing. Yeah. That's what did it. I can't be thinking of that here. Not the place for it. And space—I need to remember to give her some space.

I print the three photos we picked. No filters, no flair. Just the simplest process. She looks like I just presented her with the most amazing prize. Yeah—just fucking wait until she sees what I can do. I start the process over with the first photo. This one is my absolute favorite. I focus her image, fade, and blur around her. Highlight and exaggerate the beams of light streaming through the arbor. They point to her like a beacon, drawing your eye to her.

She's moving closer, intrigued. The magic—the fucking magic is working. I put the print through the final wash, giving her just a hint of what will be a beautiful piece hanging in my loft. I'll be spending a lot of time staring at this one. I hang it to dry, turned so she can't see the finished product. I want that moment to be one I can savor and I need to print a few others.

I take a deep breath as she approaches me, breathing in her sweet scent.

"Can you show me what you did with that? How...how did you blur the outside? How did you get it all focused like that?"

I feel her body pressed against me again. *Christ.* Is she moving fucking closer to me? I start the process for the next photo.

She's close.

Getting closer.

Asking me questions. I've got her attention again. And of course, I want to fucking take advantage of it.

The processing, I can do in my sleep. I go to autopilot and just get the prints done, murmuring the explanation as I go. She's excited, captivated, watching this happen. I hang this print next to the first to dry, turning, and she's right there. Right fucking there. "I'll be needin' to wash my hands. The chemicals, they're bad." I brush against her as I pass and wash up quickly. She's looking at the first print—staring at it. The wonder in her eyes stirs something deep inside me.

She makes this breathy sound as she moves from one

photo to the next. Fuck's sake, I can feel that sigh. I feel it deep within me tightening every single muscle. It's like I've lost control over my hands. They're in her hair before it registers what I'm doing. Her gaze lifts up to meet mine.

The light is low and she is stunning.

Time stands still as I move a hair's breadth closer to her. She blinks in slow motion, like we're muddling through the mire.

I feel her breath on my lips. Feel it feather across me. I lean in that last little bit until our lips brush and that spark is too much to resist. I don't want to stop.

I grasp the hair at the nape of her neck and drag her closer to me. My tongue sweeps out along her soft lips, back and forth until she opens for me, and I taste her.

God, she tastes sweeter than she did yesterday. Sweeter than I have words for.

Stepping in, I guide her, direct her, move her against the wall. This is a bad idea. *So bad.* This is not the time or place. Shifting to step away, I feel her move with me. She's almost dancing with me, giving in to me. I press her back into the wall, fingers twined through her hair as I run my other hand down her cheek, caressing her neck, stopping on the swell of her breast. Holding her there. Pressed between my body and the wall.

My head is telling me to stop.

My heart? My heart wants to hear nothing of it.

She slides her hands down my arms, and behind my back, grazing the waistband of my trousers—my skin tingling from the heat of her touch. Dragging my nose along her jawline, I plant small open mouth kisses from that spot by her ear—that spot—down her neck to where it meets her shoulder. I could get lost in the line of her collarbone. That delicate bone has to be one of the sexiest spots on a woman.

I run my hand around her waist skimming up under the bottom edge of her t-shirt. She gasps a sweet breath when I brush my fingers up the soft skin at her side. Spreading out my hand, my fingers wrap around her back and my thumb caresses the underside of her tit. I'm trying—but when she runs her hands up under my shirt and digs her fingers into my back, I lose what little grasp I have on my control. I make short work of her bra clasp and palm her left breast while I tug at her shirt to get that shite out of my way. Something clatters as it lands behind me—I couldn't care less what I just fucking spilled. I wrap my lips around her nipple and pull it between my teeth.

Her gasps and moans are music to my fucking ears. I need her lips, I need to taste her, I need to own every one of those sounds. Grabbing her arse, I lift her up, her legs wrapping around my hips. She grips me tightly as I carry her over to the work surface—clearing the solution trays to the floor, not giving a shit what's there. I don't think my cock can get any harder as she rakes her fingers through my hair, pulling on it as I grind into her. I lean in setting her down, a hand to her chest I push her to lie back. The low light casts shadows across her, accentuating her curves—her peaks and valleys. As much as I appreciate the art of the moment, I need to touch every inch of her.

"Aidan..." It comes out as a breathy moan. She tugs at my shirt as I reach behind me and drag it off—adding it to the pile of cast-off clothing behind me. She has me fucking captivated. The feel of her nails scraping across my shoulders and down my back has me shaking. "Please..."

I'll do anything for her. "Please what, love? What do you need?"

She practically purrs as I run my hands down her body, skimming over her curves to the sides of that flirty little skirt. This fucking thing has been driving me insane. I slide my hand down her knickers, teasing her as much as myself—light skimming touches. I want to draw this out. I want to explore every inch of her, worship her, make her mine. I run my thumb up and down her core feeling how her body reacts to my touch, caressing her and circling her clit through the fabric. My fingers slip under the fabric of her knickers. *Christ, she's wet.*

Sliding my thumb up to circle her bundle of nerves increasing pressure as her breathing picks up and she starts panting out my name.

"*Aidan...God, Aidan...*" One finger circles her, and dips in—two fingers. "*...Aidan...*" She is stunning like this. My left hand firmly holding her in place, my right pumping, stroking, driving her higher...closer. "*...Aidan...*" It's fucking amazing hearing my name on her breath. She bucks her hips with the first pass of my tongue. "*...Aidan...*" she keens with the second pass. And when I wrap my lips around her clit sucking hard, her back arches and she fucking comes apart—pulsing around my fingers, heels digging into my back, my other hand clutched to her chest.

She. Fucking. Comes. Undone.

I kiss along her inner thighs as she calms, sliding my fingers from her, and putting her knickers right. Her gaze meets mine as I stand and suck my fingers into my mouth, tasting her, licking them clean.

SIXTEEN

Lis

He drags his fingers from his mouth and I have to look away. *No one has ever...done that to me before.*

"Done what—which part?"

I snap my eyes back to his. They're dark and hooded.

"I didn't think I said that out loud. Sorry." I push myself up to sitting and smooth my skirt back down over my thighs. Aidan steps in. His erection straining against his zipper.

"Answer me, love. What has no one ever done to you? Licked you?" He pulls me to the edge of the table pressing his hard cock to me. I can't help the shudder—or the quick intake of breath. "Made you come?" Leaning even closer, he brushes his lips against me as his words rumble low in my ear, he presses me tightly to him. "Made you worship his name?" He's biting and sucking on my earlobe, distracting me. "Tell me." The shell of my ear is on fire as his tongue traces it.

"All of it." I can barely speak. Drawing in a deep breath,

his chest expands against mine and he dives for my mouth. Devouring me. *Oh. My. G*—Jerking his head back, Aidan holds me tightly—shielding me from the door at the other end of the room. "Someone's here?" Panic bleeds through.

"They won't come straight in. The light outside—whoever it is knows the darkroom's being used."

I'm panicking and he's cocking an eyebrow and smirking like this is funny.

"I'll see what they want. Maybe we should...fuck..." Grabbing his shirt and tugging it on, he hands me mine. Pausing at the door, he makes sure I'm dressed. He adjusts himself and takes in the mess of trays and negatives on the floor, "Don't touch anythin'. I'll be right back."

Murmurs float through the door, I can't make out what they are saying, but I hear Aidan's laugh and his hand on the doorknob. He slides back in smiling and shaking his head. "The darkroom's been double booked. I told the guy we had a chemical spill and needed to clean up—he, uh, wanted to share time. Not fuckin' gonna happen." Aidan throws away the ruined negatives, gathers the prints he made and hands me his bag. We clean up as quickly as we can and leave. Thank God, the other photographer is nowhere to be seen.

IT'S like a different world outside than when I got here. The sun that was beating down earlier has been replaced with clouds and the wind is whipping off the river. My hand slaps down to grab hold of my skirt trying to keep it in place. Aidan reaches out taking his bag from me. "Much as I'd love to have my hands on your arse again, I'll let you get hold of that. I don't want to think of anyone else seeing your knickers." He slings the bag over his shoulder and settles his hand on the small of my back. Well, really, it's on my ass. "What should we do with the rest of our day?"

The rumble from my stomach answers for me. "I guess I'm hungry. Want to go grab a bite to eat?"

The look he shoots me is full of mischief and satisfied pride.

"Already ate, love."

I'd smack him, but this skirt will be gone if I try.

"Hmmm...Aidan, I'm going to go to the bistro and get lunch. Would you like to join me there?" My voice is so sugary sweet and my smile is as plastic as it can be. Fumbling with my skirt and my keys, trying to stay decent, I struggle with unlocking my car door.

I feel his warmth behind me just as he reaches around to take my keys. As soon as I give them up, he presses me into the side of my car, pinning me there with his chest against my back, hips against my ass. Maybe, I don't really need lunch. My stomach rumbles again and I drop my chin to my chest laughing. Sex or starvation?

"I'll follow you there. We'd best get you fed—don't want your strength waning." He presses into me one last time before opening the door. Staying close, he shields me as I slip into my driver's seat. "Wait for me when you get there. I'll help keep your honor intact." With a wink, he closes my door and heads further down the street to his car.

Watching him, the way he moves, the way he carries himself makes my heart skip a beat. He's so full of confidence and grace. His khaki pants wrap his ass perfectly, and his t-shirt? That shirt is stretched tight across his broad shoulders and is clinging to his arms. There's a shadow, just barely hinted at beneath the fabric on the left side, high on his shoulder blade. I caught a glimpse of the tattoo in the darkroom—just that it was there. I can't imagine ever getting a tattoo. I don't know that there is anything I would want to permanently mark myself with, but I want to know what he has. And why he got it.

GRACYN DROPS the menus at our table with a basket of garlic bread and a couple glasses of water. "What have you guys been up to this morning? Anything exciting?" She bumps me with her hip and plops down in the booth next to me. Aidan huffs out a chuckle while I pull my lower lip between my teeth and cock my head to the side. Looking back and forth between us, her smile takes over her face. "I'm guessing there's a good story in there somewhere." Aidan's eyes sparkle, the skin crinkling at the corners. "And I guess I'll have to wait and get it from you later, Lis. What can I get for you today?"

"I'll have the chicken parmigiana sandwich. Fries, and seltzer with fruit. Please."

Gracyn looks up at Aidan, waiting for his order. "I'll have the same, with the fried mushrooms for an appetizer. Guess I'm still hungry, after all." He winks. He fucking winks at me with Gracyn right there.

"Got it. I'll put this in and be right back with your drinks."

My face flames red and I duck my head away rummaging through my purse for absolutely nothing. I could just die right now.

And, of course, my dear friend misses nothing. "We'll

talk later." She tickles my back as she skips away from our table.

After lunch, we grab a couple picture frames from the store and head to Aidan's apartment to look through the few pictures we were able to print before we got distracted.

SEVENTEEN

Aidan

Jesus. Having at Lis in the darkroom was not what I fucking planned, but I'll be damned if I'm going to feel bad about it. I just want her more now. Our weekend of no work ended with me taking on Finn's shift Sunday and Lis at home—not mine, hers. I want more.

My thoughts were that she'd have a lot more free time with her term having ended, but it's like her spring holiday all over again. Every available minute is spent working for the two solid weeks before Lis starts in with her summer term. I have never seen anyone so driven.

I pick up several photo shoots while she's working and manage to sell some of my journalistic pieces to a few news outlets in the city. My career is getting back on track, but I've spent far too little time with Lisbeth.

And I've not heard from Lorna—at all.

No texts. No calls.

Nothing.

I walk into Lis' bar and settle in an empty spot at the end. She's mixing drinks for tables in the dining room, while smiling and chatting up the people at the bar. It's busy enough in here to afford me the luxury of watching her. I take her in, every move, every smile.

Last time I was here, we were still just friends. Just an innocent thing. Now, I can't get her out of my mind. The look of her, the sounds she makes—the taste of her. Beyond that, I just like her. The little things. The corner of her lower lip between her teeth when she's concentrating. The way one eye all but closes when she smiles really big. Her quiet determination. She's amazing.

"Hey," she says with that smile. The one that pinches her eye shut. "What can I get you?"

I prop my elbows on the bar and speak quietly. "I'll have a whiskey, yeah?"

When she leans in to hear my words, I take hold of her hand and my thumb slides to her inner wrist. That spot calls to me. Her skin is so soft there—so smooth. And the smell of her perfume is fucking intoxicating. She sighs and leans just a little bit closer. Seeking a kiss. Just a quick one, but I'm over the moon that she does that.

"Do you want dinner too, or are you just here for the whiskey?"

"The whiskey is fine, a steak would be great, but I'm here for the company. I've missed you."

Another smile and she pulls away, fixing my drink, checking the others at the bar.

"How was your class today?" I ask when she comes back down to my end of the bar. We've not spoken much since she started her summer term three days ago—we've had maybe seven texts in the last three days.

Lisbeth's face totally shifts, her shoulders slumping, and her lower lip goes between her teeth. I want to be the one nibbling them. "We had a quiz today. I didn't do well at all." She pops down a bit to pull a pint for the old guy sitting a few seats over. "I might need to drop it and just graduate next May with everyone else." She tries to hide the stress and worry behind a weak smile.

"It's one quiz. You've got time to make your grades. Why are they giving exams two days in anyway?"

"The class is accelerated, like really accelerated. And it's Advanced Anatomy—a ton of memorization. I should probably drop before it's too late." She grabs a napkin rolled around utensils and places it in front of me with the salt and pepper shakers.

"If you drop this class, you have to push off your graduation?" She bites at her lip again and nods. "Why would it be easier in the fall? Why take it later?" She puts so much pressure on herself to do well. To do it on her own.

"The semester is longer, so I'd have more time to memorize the body systems—and I'd have my study group. They're all taking it then and we can quiz each other—flashcards, that kind of thing." She moves down the bar checking her patrons, filling drink orders for the dining room.

The smell of steak and mushroom risotto fills the air around me making my mouth water, and Gracyn slides a plate in front of me.

"How're you doing tonight? My girl there has been a bear the last couple weeks." She stares me down, hand propped on her hip, attitude in full effect. "You know anything about that?"

"Jesus, Gracyn. Lighten up. I told you it has nothing to do with Aidan." Lis' hands go to the long loose braid hanging over her shoulder, fingers twisting and twirling at the soft curl at the end.

"I'm tired and this class is going to kill me." Turning to me, Lis asks, "Is your steak cooked alright?"

"Fucking perfect." It's red in the center and perfectly seared on the outside. I cut a piece and scoop up some of the risotto, turning the fork to Lisbeth.

I'm awestruck watching her lips wrap around the fork, hearing that moan low in the back of her throat. She's fucking made that noise for me—beautiful. I adjust my cock and look up to find both girls' eyes on mine.

Gracyn raises her brow and points her finger in my face. "Don't you hurt my friend. Don't you dare...or you won't need to do that ever again." She waves a hand toward my crotch and walks away.

"So, your class...would it help to have someone quiz you on your facts?"

She tilts her head from side to side like she's thinking about it.

"Maybe?" And the lip again.

Between her teeth.

I reach up and pull it free with my thumb. "I would love to help you study. I'm fairly sure I'm capable of quizzing you. When is your next exam?"

With that, her whole demeanor changes.

"I have another quiz Friday. And I only have until the middle of next week to drop this class and get my money back. Aidan..." Elbows on the bar, she puts her face in her hands. The stress is rolling off of her. "What am I going to do? I've worked so hard. I need to graduate in December. I just need to be done. I'm exhausted. I'm gonna cry if I have to extend this whole thing another semester." Hands rub down her face as she looks up at me, worry pinching at the corners of her eyes.

"Lisbeth, let me help you, please? I want to help. What's your week look like?"

"I just talked to Jenna and took the rest of the week off. Gracyn's going to cover for me here, so other than my class, I'll be studying."

EIGHTEEN

Lis

I can't let this one stupid class set me back a whole semester. I've worked so hard and for far too long.

Last night, Jenna told me not to worry about my shifts for the rest of the week. She grabbed cash from the register and tried to give me a "summer bonus" to offset my lost income, but I tucked it back in the drawer with a quickly scribbled *Thank You* before I left for the night.

Aidan kept me company for most of the evening, talking between customers, sharing his dinner with me and trying to ease my worries over this class. I've got to make this work— got to pass this and then the next one in the series next month.

I used to love summer classes—being able to concentrate on one class at a time, immerse myself in the material and just get it done. In theory, it's great, but I may have to just suck it up and push off graduation.

I set my coffee on the corner of my desk making sure to pack away my notes and the review packet for Friday's test.

Aidan told Francie he needed the next couple of days off to help me study. Francie even pulled both Jimmy and Finn into work making sure the guys' apartment is quiet and I can concentrate.

The sun beats down on my shoulders replacing the chill from the classroom as I walk out to my car. I grabbed everything I need to spend the next several hours shoving as much information into my brain as I can. Aidan is really sweet offering to help me, but I fully expect him to get bored after a while. This way, I can go straight to the library or coffee shop and keep studying when he's had enough.

I pull up to his loft with my coffee refilled and the hot wind whipping through the car windows. After parking, I wrap my hair up in a messy bun high on the back of my head, and swap my sunglasses for real ones.

As I lean in the passenger side to grab my bag and coffee cup, my skin tingles and I feel his gaze on me. I should have taken the time to tie my hair back before the wind on the drive over made it such a mess. Should have put more effort into how I look. *I'm here to study. That's all.*

Straightening up, I reach to pull my bag higher on my shoulder but feel the weight lifted from me—literally and figuratively.

"Let me take that." Aidan grabs my leather tote bag and closes the car door. I'm backed up against the hot metal and pinned in place by him. "You ready to learn my body?"

"Wh-what?" The tingles I felt moments ago turn into a full riot of chills along my arms and neck.

"I figure you'll have to map the terms you're learnin',

yeah?" What is he doing to me? "It's anatomy we're study-ing?" I can barely manage a nod. "I'll let you use me anyway you need in order to get your grades. I'm at your mercy."

Holy hell.

Aidan steps back with that smirk on his face, the one that says he knows he's got my heart racing. He pulls me toward the steps and guides me inside.

My brain finally kicks into gear and I stop short. "You know I'm here to study, right? For a test?"

His low chuckle goes right through to my core. "Of course, love. Whatever you need." He drops my bag on the small table in the kitchen and grabs some sandwiches out of the fridge. "I thought you might like some lunch before we start, but we can get straight to it if you prefer."

Is he talking about studying or did he think this was going in a different direction? I'm so confused right now.

"I..." I'm not opposed to the idea of sleeping with Aidan —feeling more of what he gave me in the darkroom. I've thought about it a lot. A lot. "...Aidan, I have to study. I..." I've avoided his eyes through this whole exchange and need to take a deep breath before I chance it. Releasing it slowly, I lift my eyes to find him laughing at me?

"Lisbeth, I promised to help you study. Relax, eat and we'll make the flashcards and get your terms memorized."

"You're a shit," I huff out at him as he chuckles at me and grabs us a couple glasses of water. "It's just...this is really important and I...I..." I couldn't tell if he was serious, if he wants me, or just *that*.

But I can't say it. My heart squeezes a little at the thought of a relationship, of taking this further. I'm petrified of being cast aside.

Again.

"Lisbeth, stop. I'm sorry if I crossed a line." All joking is gone, his expression soft.

I hand him a stack of flashcards I made early this morning before class and he patiently quizzes me for the next several hours, but I can't help thinking about it. *That line.*

Eventually, we stop and grab some dinner close by. I need a break—out of his apartment. I'm starting to make mistakes and getting answers wrong.

After burgers and a couple beers we walk slowly back to Aidan's loft. The fresh air caressing my skin as it clears the fuzz from my brain. Since he's been quizzing me on muscle groups, I run through them as he trails the back of his fingers down my arm—*trapezius-spine of scapula-deltoid-brachialis-brachioradialis-flexor retinaculum.*

"Good on you." He's got that spot on my wrist again, rubbing soft circles with his thumb.

"Did I say those out loud?"

"You did, and you got them all perfect. I think the flexor retinaculum is one of my favorite spots on you." He raises my hand and places a sweet kiss on the inside of my wrist.

We make our way up the stairs to the door. Aidan unlocks it, but holds me there—pressing his front into my back. His hand slides across my belly, pulling me tight to him, his lips skating across the back of my neck. "Though, I'm fond of this spot as well."

My skin tightens with anticipation and desire. I've spent every one of the nights since the darkroom thinking about this. I was surprised, and kind of disappointed, that it seemed like a onetime thing. Aidan hadn't made any further attempts; didn't try at all.

We spent time together, but maybe we were always around other people. Gracyn at our place, Finn or Jimmy here.

"Let's go study, love. We've a lot left to cover."

And just like that, I'm back to confused and frustrated. Which has me answering questions wrong again and getting pissed.

"I think I'm getting dumber."

We're on the couch with the fucking flash cards and I can't seem to get anything correct. The flash of his camera snaps my attention from my puddle of self-doubt.

"What are you doing?"

"Getting creative with your studies. The curve of your trapezius wrapping 'round to your collarbone is gorgeous." Turning the camera, he shows me the image.

Captured in black and white, is my pale neck, exposed and open to him by the tilt of my head and the strap of my tank that's slipped down my arm.

"Maybe I should be taking pictures of you." His lips are right there when I turn my head. Right fucking there.

"Maybe you should use me like I offered earlier. Practical applications, yeah?" He's so close. And not smiling anymore. Heat and desire are flushing my chest and burning through me.

He leans forward placing his camera on the coffee table and I run my nail down the exposed muscles in his arm. He stills sucking in a breath.

Grabbing at something from the table, Aidan straightens and pierces me with his dark gaze. "Take this," he rasps as he hands me a pen and reaches behind his head. He pulls his shirt off, leaning back into the arm of the couch. "Mark me. Label the muscles." His voice is low and husky.

I shift closer. This is such a good idea—and such a bad one.

The pen cap pops as I pull it free. He's laid out for me, his breathing slow and deep. His eyes flash darkly from the pen in my hand to my eyes, to my lips. I know I'm biting the bottom one, trying so hard not to shake as I move the tip of the pen to the skin at the base of his neck. He's not a bulky gym rat, but he is well defined. *Really* well defined. He holds his breath as I drag the pen across his skin outlining the muscles of his chest. *Holy shit.* His nipples harden and his skin pebbles up.

"Lisbeth," my name rasps across his lips, "name them. Now."

Barely making contact, I feather my fingertips across his skin, naming each of the muscles, circling his nipple, scraping the skin there with my nails.

Heaving out a harsh breath, he grabs my wrist. Neither of us move. We're stuck here, searching, deciding, reading each other. I know he can feel my pulse is racing. With my hand held firmly in his grasp, he sits up and pulls me closer.

"Lisbeth." He breathes my name across my lips.

I full-on shiver as he pulls me so I'm straddling him.

With one hand wrapped around my wrist and the other on my hip, Aidan shifts me closer still. All thoughts I'd had that he didn't want me fly away as he moves his hips again, grinding his cock against me.

Finally—*finally*—our lips connect, his tongue sweeping along my bottom one. Pushing his way in, he licks my top lip and deepens the kiss, exploring me, devouring me. Ripping my breath away. He places my hands around his neck and grabs me by the backs of my thighs, standing like it's no effort at all.

His lips never leave mine as he carries me up the stairs to his loft bedroom.

Turning, he sits on the bed, pulling me with him. He slides his hands up my sides, taking my shirt with them, pushing my arms over my head as he launches my tank to the floor. His hands land on my hips and squeeze—just a little—before trailing heat back up my sides to my breasts. They tighten and tingle as his thumbs caress the sides driving me crazy with need before his fingers trail up, pulling the straps of my bra down my arms—pinning them to my sides. Not really trapped, but Aidan stops, holding me there.

"Lisbeth? This okay?" My name rasping across his lips steals my breath away.

All I can do is nod, my fingers tremble as they seek out his plump lower lip. I want this. I'm scared, but I want this.

Reaching behind me, Aidan unhooks my bra and adds it to my tank on the floor. He leans in, whispering, "Gorgeous," against my skin. I barely catch the word as he kisses across my breast—licking, scraping his teeth along my skin— pebbling my nipples to hard almost painful peaks. Twining my hands in his silky black hair, I gasp at the scrape of his stubble on my sensitive skin.

He pulls back checking my eyes. Okay with what he sees, he slides his hands around to unbutton my shorts, his fingertips trailing along the top of my panties.

I'm surprised, shocked, when he pushes me off him, my feet landing on the floor. I barely keep my balance as I reach for the button, certain he's changed his mind. Pushing my hands away, he hooks his inside the waistband of my shorts.

"Do you want me to stop? 'Cause I don't want to, not in the least," he rasps as he presses open-mouthed kisses from one hip to the other.

"Don't." I squirm, his kisses tickle as they fuel the need and desire coursing through me. He starts to pull away. "No, Aidan. Don't stop." The words come out on a breath, and I press my hands to his shoulders.

His thumbs dig into the waist of my panties, shoving them and my shorts over my hips until they fall to the floor. Pulling me with him, he moves back to the middle of his bed. His lips gliding up my torso to the underside of my boobs.

I feel exposed as he lies back, his gaze taking in all of me before he meets my eyes again.

"Lisbeth, this is all you. This goes at your pace, love. As fast or slow as you want—or stop when you say."

My heart skips a beat. He knows me and how much this means to me. He has been so considerate of me. Telling me I have control, when I know deep inside who's really in charge —and that's okay with me.

I drag my fingers down his torso and reach between us. Popping the button on his shorts, the zipper spreading wide, I run a fingertip along his boxer briefs, circling the dot of moisture at the tip of his cock. He's hard—really fucking hard.

Gasping, I fall forward as he bucks his hips, my hands landing hard on his chest. He shoves his shorts and briefs down, his cock exposed. Thumbs press in at my knees, spreading them wider before sliding up the inside of my thighs.

Once again, he pauses silently asking permission—waiting for the dip of my chin before touching me. He slides his thumb from my opening to my peak, spreading my arousal. Circling my clit changing the pressure as he does, bringing me right to the edge. Heart racing, my eyes wide.

He stretches to the side, grabbing a condom from the drawer next to his bed, ripping the package open with his teeth. I whimper when he takes his hand away from me to roll it down his length. The whimper turns to a gasp as he grabs my hips and slides me back and forth over the hard length of his dick. He had me so close before, it takes nothing to set me on edge again.

Aidan relaxes his grip on my hips, giving control back over to me. Letting me make the next move.

Leaning forward, I lift my hips and reach between us, positioning his cock and sliding slowly down his length. I rest my hands heavily on his chest, his wrap around my hips—fingers pressing into my flesh—supporting me, holding me.

His jaw clenches, muscles ticking. Neither of us move, savoring the moment, allowing us both to adjust. *Holy shit.* I release a trembling breath through pursed lips, closing my eyes and feeling all of him.

"Look at me, Lisbeth. Open your eyes—I need to see you."

He holds himself back until my eyes, soft and glassy, drift open to meet his heated gaze. Only then, when he's got that contact, does he start to move—sliding out and thrusting in, the drag of his cock pushes me again. Pushes me back to the edge I've already been on too many times. It takes nothing for me to get close—close, but not quite.

He whispers, murmurs, tells me he's got me. "That's it,

love. Let go..." I'm so close. I can feel my pussy grip him—tightening, squeezing his cock. I just can't quite get there. I don't know what to do, how to move, how to make this happen.

"Help me, Aidan. I...can't...please..." My heart slams in my chest, on the edge of exploding

He pulls me down to him—chest to chest—moving me, taking the control he had the whole time. The change is all that I need—the change gives me the pressure, the friction I need.

To. Come. Undone.

NINETEEN

Aidan

And there it is.

The look on her face, the sounds that she makes, the moment she falls apart, it's all I'll ever need again. And I follow her. Every muscle in my body tightens, contracts, and then relaxes as we both shudder, panting to catch our breath.

After tossing the condom into the bin, I slide back in bed and wrap myself around her. Her hand in mine, both of them pressed firmly to my heart. This feels like more.

More than a shag, more than a fling.

Just more.

The moment she gave herself over to me, needed me and asked for, pleaded for my help, something changed. Lisbeth has been burned and burned badly, but in that moment of putting her needs and desires first, something shifted.

She trusted me.

And I want to cherish and honor this.

Feeling her heart beat and listening to her soft, even

breaths, I lose myself to a sleep I've not slept since arriving in Beekman Hills.

Several hours later, I only just register the sounds of the boys coming home from the pub. I can hear everything in this fucking loft and usually they're louder than a pack of wild dogs when they come in after work.

Lis' things strewn about, and my fucking shirt on the floor down there must not be lost on Finn and Jimmy. The volume drops and other than a few whispers and a quiet chuckle, I hear little else.

The thought crosses my mind, with her body pressed up against me, to wake her and have her. Have her again. But as much as I can hear them downstairs, they can hear every move I make up here. This thing we have between us is not something I'm willing to share. I won't do that to her, she's mine.

Trust.

I WAKE with Lisbeth's head in the crook of my shoulder and a hand on her hip. My other hand, though. It's resting on my chest—with hers pressed firmly between it and my heart. Like she owns it. Like it's hers. I lie there relishing this for as long as I can. My body screaming for another go. To explore every curve, hear every sigh, every moan. And like a bucket of cold water, those thoughts are washed away. Those sounds are just for me. Mine. I'll not take advantage and share that with anyone, especially the two arseholes sleeping below us.

Sliding from the warmth of her body, I grab my jeans and head downstairs for coffee. As it brews, I look through the fridge taking note that there's still bacon and eggs. I'll make

Lis breakfast when she wakes and then dive right in—to studying, helping her.

I grab my phone and steaming cuppa, stepping out onto our minuscule deck. Three texts and a missed call. Mostly work—photography inquiries, but there's one from Lorna.

Lorna: Hey. Sorry for not getting back to you before now. Can we talk? Soon? xx

Aidan: Yeah. I'm committed to something for a couple days...I'll call.

Aidan: Sunday?

Lorna: Yeah. Good.

She's yet to tell me about the baby. We're going to need more than a quick chat for this.

Liam's seen her a couple times since we talked, but I can't figure why she's been avoiding me. It's got to be tearing her up. They had been trying for a family before my brother's diagnosis. Jesus. I still can't believe how quickly he went. Fucking cancer.

"You look like you have the weight of the world on your shoulders." Her soft voice washes over me as Lis ghosts her fingers lightly down my spine, a trail of goose bumps showing in its wake. She presses a small kiss to the Celtic cross on my shoulder. I reach behind me, grabbing her hand from where it rests low on my back and pull her into my arms.

"Hmmm... Just thinking of some things going on in Dublin." This moment doesn't need to be ruined by my brother's death. I'll tell her later, when she's not worried about her studies. Leaning in and taking the kiss I want—need—the topic is laid to rest.

"Coffee's ready. We can get back to your studies after

breakfast," I murmur, bringing her hand to my lips to press a soft kiss to her knuckles.

Inside the kitchen, I push her up against the counter, trapping her. Molding my body to hers, as close as I can, feeling every curve. I take a final kiss and tear myself away from her to hide adjusting my cock. The last thing I want is for her to think that's all I'm after.

The moment I turn to hand her a cup of coffee, she meets me with a warm cloth, rubbing away the ink trails from my shoulder and chest. She's so gentle with me. Trading coffee for the cloth, I rub at the marks and have them just about taken care of when Jimmy stumbles out of his room to plop down at the table. In his fucking boxers.

"Making the eggs? There tea or just feckin' coffee?" I want to smack him upside the head, but he at least gets us back on track. "Mornin', Lis."

And, of course—fucking of course—Finn shows his face only when the smell of bacon fills the flat. Grabbing his plate, he pulls a chair up next to Lis. "You the reason I couldn't sleep?"

"What? No..." Lisbeth stutters as her neck flushes pink.

"Thought that was you I heard screamin' all night." Finn winks, thinking he's being funny, but Lis is uncomfortable and I'll be kickin' his arse soon. I'll kill him.

"Finn." Jimmy lifts his head from the table, shooting him a warning.

"I'm going to go...um..." Her words get lost in the embarrassment swirling around her as she escapes up to my loft.

"Christ, Finn. Are you fuckin' stupid? Why would you do that?" I growl, hands clenched, muscles quivering. "She —*fuck*—no fuckin' class. Might want to look at yourself—

see why you're not near as slick with the girls as you think you are. Fuckin' arsehole." I pace the length of the small kitchen trying to keep calm. "Out. I need you out of the flat today."

"Jimmy's on at the bar, I've all day to hang out wit' you." Finn grins, oblivious of just how close I am to throwing him out of the flat right now.

"No. Out," I grit out as I turn my back to them. "Get the fuck out, and don't come back 'til tomorrow. Fuckin' bastard. Don't think I won't kick your sorry arse." Their grumbles follow me as I launch my body up the stairs, taking them two at a time. Finn will feel bad and apologize once Jimmy gets it through his thick skull what he did to fuck up, but for now, I can't be near him.

Crawling across the bed to her, I wrap my fingers around her wrists and I settle myself in front of her. "Lisbeth. Don't let him..."

"It's fine. I'm fine. Maybe I should just go. Study at my place."

"He's goin'." I rub circles with my thumbs—caressing that spot—bring one wrist and then the other to my lips, planting a soft kiss on each. "He'll be gone all day. Stay. Please. Jimmy's goin' to work. We'll study and get you sorted. Please —let me do this. Let me help you."

"Your accent changes depending on what's happening." The smile creeps up her lips.

"What?"

"It does. When you're mad," she leans in, "when you're drinking," her warm hands slide up my legs, "and when you're..." She squeezes high on my thighs, her thumbs pressing in right by my cock.

"When I'm what?" Every time she moves, the subtle scent of her perfume teases me.

"When..." Her eyes go straight for my crotch, making my cock twitch.

"When I fuck ye?" I want to push her back and bury myself in her for the rest of the day. I want to hear my name on her lips. I want to make her scream, the way Finn was talking about. I want her to forget he said that shit. "They're still downstairs, love. Much as I want to, I don't want to share you. Not with them here to listen."

We're wrapped up in each other's breaths, hands twined through her hair, pulling her in. My lips sweep across hers; she darts her tongue out, licking my bottom one. Fuck. Her name comes out on a groan as she palms my cock, and rakes her teeth across my lip. Biting me. Squeezing me. She's pushing this. She knows we're not totally alone and she's still going. Working me up, making me hard.

The sound of the shower starting fills the loft as the front door slams. I pitch forward, shoving her into the mattress, silently pulling at her clothes and we spend the rest of the day completely wrapped up in each other. Finn stays away and Jimmy must find someone to go home from the bar with.

The flat is ours alone.

We spend hours studying for her exam until she knows her material inside and out. When Lis finishes packing away her books and papers late in the evening, I set her bag by the front door.

I grasp her hand and lead her back up to my room and study the subject I've been yearning for all day. *Her.* What makes her sigh, gasp, and tremble. What makes her blush and beg for more.

. . .

HER TEST IS early Friday and I wake to the mattress shifting as she tries to leave. Wrapping my hand around her hip, I pull her back to me. "Aidan, I need to go." God, I don't like the feeling of her leaving my bed.

"Just five more minutes." I drag her so she's lying almost on top of me, her heart aligned perfectly with mine—beating with mine.

"I have to go home and clean up—change before my test," she murmurs into my chest dragging her fingers across my stomach. "And I don't want the weirdness from yesterday, again. I didn't mean to spend the night—"

"They didn't come back, either of them. Take a shower here. I'll get you coffee and something to eat on your way." Squeezing her tight to me, pressing a kiss to the top of her head, I untangle us and leave the only place I want to spend my day.

After Lis leaves with a bagel in one hand and her coffee in the other, I try calling Lorna but get nothing. No answer. Nothing Saturday. Nothing Sunday. Late in the day Monday, just as I catch Lis' eye through the window of the bistro, Lorna phones. The tears are heavy in her voice and there is no way—no way—I can have this conversation in a bar. Closing my eyes, I back away just barely registering Lis' expression as I turn and head to my car for what can only be a heart-wrenchingly emotional conversation.

"Aidan—please come home."

TWENTY

Lis

I walk out of my test exhausted and emotionally spent. I feel really good about the test itself, but I'm wiped out and I have to work all weekend to make up for the days I spent studying. Maybe, though. Maybe I'll get through this.

Maybe.

The weekend passes in a blur of sleep and hours upon hours spent mixing drinks. Aidan left for a shoot and will be away for a few days. It's built-in space. The space I usually crave to get my head on straight and in the right place. And I don't want it. Sex changes everything, but I'm feeling like it's a good change and I find myself wishing time away.

Grades for Friday's test won't be posted until tonight, but I still feel really confident that I did well. Anything above a B and I'll stick it out for the summer session. The bistro is slow and I settle in to study. Aidan is meeting me here for dinner and then, who knows. I know this is scary territory. I've opened my heart to him. I've let him in.

Jenna pulls me out of my textbook. "Lis." She nods toward the front window. "You waiting for someone?"

"Who is Lissy waiting for?" It's so slow in here tonight that Tony's left the kitchen to his sous chef and is having dinner with Jenna. I don't know if it counts as a date if you own the restaurant and cooked your own entrees, but that's what they're doing.

I bring Tony another beer and look out the window watching Aidan cross the street toward the bistro. Toward me. "Who's that?" Tony's gaze going from me to the man who's wiggled his way past my barriers. The man who takes days off from work to help me. The man who's made me feel important.

My smile spreads across my face, when he finally looks up and his eyes meet mine. I lean my body toward the window—feeling the pull to him—when his steps falter. Pulling his phone from his pocket, he stares at the screen for a beat. That same look he had last week washes over his features. The look like he's holding things together, but just barely. His shoulders rise with tension as he stops and puts the phone to his ear. Closing his eyes, he pushes the air from his body like he can push whatever news he's getting away with it.

My stomach twisting, I slink into a chair at Jenna and Tony's table and watch as Aidan pivots on his heel, turning back to cross the street. With nothing more than a small wave thrown my way, he disappears around the corner.

Aidan

"Aidan, I'm...I'm pregnant." Even knowing the words are coming doesn't prepare me for the level of devastation in her voice. "I'm... I don't know what to do." Lorna's words are nearly drowned out by her tears.

"Lorna, love, shhh...it's okay." It's okay. It's good, really.

Weaving through people, I make my way back to my car and lean up against the side, clinging to the hope that I can sort this quickly and get back to Lis.

"It's not, Aidan. I can't do this alone. This was supposed to happen with Michael, not by myself. I'm all alone." She's sobbing, now. Unable to catch her breath, she hiccups through the miles and my heart breaks all over again.

Resigning myself to the fact that I'm not spending my time with Lis tonight, I get in the car and head home, hoping the flat is empty or at least quiet. It might be time to think about getting my own place.

"Lorna, you're not alone. You've your parents and mine. You've family and people who love you within arm's reach. And now—now you have a piece of Mick too. This is what you wanted. What you both hoped and prayed for. Shhh... you're alright." Hearing her devastation through the phone and not being there to make her a cup of tea, hold her hand while she cries, is so much harder than I thought it would be.

We'd spent the two weeks from Michael's diagnosis to his death in a shocked version of that. Holding on while letting go. I'd been scheduled to leave on assignment when he'd called and asked me to come over. The whole thing was unreal. Cancer sucks.

"Lorna...Lorna," Not sure she can even hear me through her tears, I call to her softly, trying to soothe her, trying to calm her. It's late in Dublin. There's a good possibility she'll end up crying herself to sleep. And then what? *Christ.*

I'd needed the space, distance, from his death to get over the shock. To grieve. But I'd not thought or planned for this. This may well be too much to talk through on the phone.

Heading straight through the flat to the kitchen, I pause to stare out the window. The neighbor's kids play in their garden. Heart heavy in my chest, I reach for a beer, opt for a whiskey, and go sit out on the deck. The warm humid air even feels sad wrapped around me.

"Will you talk to me? I need you to talk to me, just like before, like we did a couple months ago. Teacht anois." *Come now.*

"...I miss him so much..." There. We're making progress. "Aidan, what am I going to do?"

"Lorna, you're going to have a baby. A piece of Michael, a piece of his heart to hold close to you for the rest of your life. You don't ever have to give him up, now." Lord, don't let that compound the sadness. "Tell me the good stuff. You've been to the doctor, yeah?"

My hand goes to the back of my neck, squeezing as I wait for her to say yes. To let me know she's at least done this— Christ, she's got to be four? Five months along? I don't know.

"When are you due?"

Lorna sighs. "November...the end of the month." She sniffs, but her voice is starting to sound stronger. "I heard the baby's heartbeat, and all I could think is that Michael should be with me. God, he'd be beside himself."

It feels like hours that we talk. About everything, about

nothing, about my brother's baby and how she's going to be just fine. She needs to talk to both sets of grandparents—I can't believe she's not told them yet.

"Lorna, you need to take care of yourself. Think about how excited they'll be."

"I know. I think maybe...I wasn't ready for the excitement part? I don't want to be sad about such an amazing gift, but...it's bittersweet, yeah? And I'm surrounded by him, but he's not here. It's...I don't know. Maybe I need to move."

She is surrounded by him. I tried to help her clear some of his things away after the funeral, but it was too soon. I didn't make it a week before leaving Dublin. Trying to run from the grief.

"You need a holiday, maybe. Go shopping in London. Spend a few days at the beach. Visit a spa. Is that kind of thing okay for you to do?"

Finally, she lets out a laugh. It's small and sad, but it's a move in the right direction. "Yeah. I can do those things. I just feel like I should save every penny—I don't know. And alone? That kind of thing's not fun alone, Aidan."

"Don't worry about the money. I'll send it to you. Take a girlfriend. Take one of our sisters—Christ, there's enough of them to choose from."

We were both from big families, but Lorna and I had been close. Close in age, growing up together we were always running about. At their wedding, I was both the best man and the man of honor.

The last of my whiskey slides down my throat as my thoughts turn to my niece or nephew. "Will you find out whether it's a boy or a girl?"

"I will. Next month, I think. You could...you could go

with me? I miss you, Aidan. Are...are you coming home soon?"

No. Maybe.

Her question asks for answers that I can't give her right now.

"I don't know. I'm doing well here. I'm settled." Torn. I'm absolutely torn. I ran away from Dublin and now—now there's a reason for me to stay here. "I'll send you some money. Go somewhere—take care of you and we'll talk soon, yeah?"

Fucking hell.

I log on to my bank account and send a good chunk of money to Lorna. Enough for a holiday and some extra to help ease the expense of setting up for a baby—or to help ease my conscience. I want to stay. I want to see what this is with Lisbeth. I want a chance at the happiness my brother and Lorna had—just no tragic ending.

Jimmy eases out the door and joins me with the bottle of whiskey resting at his side. "Was that Lorna, then?" He pours a good measure for each of us. "She tell you, finally?"

"She did."

The street light illuminates the amber liquid as I swirl it around my glass. Legs stretched out in front of me, I lean my head back against the side of the building and close my eyes. Jimmy lowers himself down next to me and waits. Patiently. He nods and sips his whiskey as I fill him in on all that Lorna and I talked about.

"What are you goin' to do?" He shifts his eyes from the faint smattering of stars barely visible above us to my face. Gaging where my head is. "Are you leaving? Goin' back home?"

The question sucks just as bad the second time I'm asked it tonight. "I don't know."

Aidan

"Aidan, I'm...I'm pregnant." Even knowing the words are coming doesn't prepare me for the level of devastation in her voice. "I'm... I don't know what to do." Lorna's words are nearly drowned out by her tears.

"Lorna, love, shhh...it's okay." It's okay. It's good, really.

Weaving through people, I make my way back to my car and lean up against the side, clinging to the hope that I can sort this quickly and get back to Lis.

"It's not, Aidan. I can't do this alone. This was supposed to happen with Michael, not by myself. I'm all alone." She's sobbing, now. Unable to catch her breath, she hiccups through the miles and my heart breaks all over again.

Resigning myself to the fact that I'm not spending my time with Lis tonight, I get in the car and head home, hoping the flat is empty or at least quiet. It might be time to think about getting my own place.

"Lorna, you're not alone. You've your parents and mine. You've family and people who love you within arm's reach. And now—now you have a piece of Mick too. This is what you wanted. What you both hoped and prayed for. Shhh... you're alright." Hearing her devastation through the phone and not being there to make her a cup of tea, hold her hand while she cries, is so much harder than I thought it would be.

We'd spent the two weeks from Michael's diagnosis to his death in a shocked version of that. Holding on while letting go. I'd been scheduled to leave on assignment when he'd called and asked me to come over. The whole thing was unreal. Cancer sucks.

"Lorna...Lorna," Not sure she can even hear me through her tears, I call to her softly, trying to soothe her, trying to calm her. It's late in Dublin. There's a good possibility she'll end up crying herself to sleep. And then what? *Christ*.

I'd needed the space, distance, from his death to get over the shock. To grieve. But I'd not thought or planned for this. This may well be too much to talk through on the phone.

Heading straight through the flat to the kitchen, I pause to stare out the window. The neighbor's kids play in their garden. Heart heavy in my chest, I reach for a beer, opt for a whiskey, and go sit out on the deck. The warm humid air even feels sad wrapped around me.

"Will you talk to me? I need you to talk to me, just like before, like we did a couple months ago. Teacht anois." *Come now*.

"...I miss him so much..." There. We're making progress. "Aidan, what am I going to do?"

"Lorna, you're going to have a baby. A piece of Michael, a piece of his heart to hold close to you for the rest of your life. You don't ever have to give him up, now." Lord, don't let that compound the sadness. "Tell me the good stuff. You've been to the doctor, yeah?"

My hand goes to the back of my neck, squeezing as I wait for her to say yes. To let me know she's at least done this— Christ, she's got to be four? Five months along? I don't know.

"When are you due?"

Lorna sighs. "November...the end of the month." She sniffs, but her voice is starting to sound stronger. "I heard the baby's heartbeat, and all I could think is that Michael should be with me. God, he'd be beside himself."

It feels like hours that we talk. About everything, about nothing, about my brother's baby and how she's going to be just fine. She needs to talk to both sets of grandparents—I can't believe she's not told them yet.

"Lorna, you need to take care of yourself. Think about how excited they'll be."

"I know. I think maybe...I wasn't ready for the excitement part? I don't want to be sad about such an amazing gift, but...it's bittersweet, yeah? And I'm surrounded by him, but he's not here. It's...I don't know. Maybe I need to move."

She is surrounded by him. I tried to help her clear some of his things away after the funeral, but it was too soon. I didn't make it a week before leaving Dublin. Trying to run from the grief.

"You need a holiday, maybe. Go shopping in London. Spend a few days at the beach. Visit a spa. Is that kind of thing okay for you to do?"

Finally, she lets out a laugh. It's small and sad, but it's a move in the right direction. "Yeah. I can do those things. I just feel like I should save every penny—I don't know. And alone? That kind of thing's not fun alone, Aidan."

"Don't worry about the money. I'll send it to you. Take a girlfriend. Take one of our sisters—Christ, there's enough of them to choose from."

We were both from big families, but Lorna and I had been close. Close in age, growing up together we were always running about. At their wedding, I was both the best man and the man of honor.

The last of my whiskey slides down my throat as my thoughts turn to my niece or nephew. "Will you find out whether it's a boy or a girl?"

"I will. Next month, I think. You could...you could go with me? I miss you, Aidan. Are...are you coming home soon?"

No. Maybe.

Her question asks for answers that I can't give her right now.

"I don't know. I'm doing well here. I'm settled." Torn. I'm absolutely torn. I ran away from Dublin and now—now there's a reason for me to stay here. "I'll send you some money. Go somewhere—take care of you and we'll talk soon, yeah?"

Fucking hell.

I log on to my bank account and send a good chunk of money to Lorna. Enough for a holiday and some extra to help ease the expense of setting up for a baby—or to help ease my conscience. I want to stay. I want to see what this is with Lisbeth. I want a chance at the happiness my brother and Lorna had—just no tragic ending.

Jimmy eases out the door and joins me with the bottle of whiskey resting at his side. "Was that Lorna, then?" He pours a good measure for each of us. "She tell you, finally?"

"She did."

The street light illuminates the amber liquid as I swirl it around my glass. Legs stretched out in front of me, I lean my head back against the side of the building and close my eyes. Jimmy lowers himself down next to me and waits. Patiently. He nods and sips his whiskey as I fill him in on all that Lorna and I talked about.

"What are you goin' to do?" He shifts his eyes from the faint smattering of stars barely visible above us to my face. Gaging where my head is. "Are you leaving? Goin' back home?"

The question sucks just as bad the second time I'm asked it tonight. "I don't know."

TWENTY-ONE

Lis

Gracyn is burrowed into the end of the couch with a glass of wine watching shit TV when I get home. "Hey. How'd it go today?"

"Not yet. Give me a minute?" I go straight to my room and ditch my clothes for jammies. Wrapping my hair in the messiest of all buns, I make a beeline for the glasses and bring the rest of the open bottle of wine to the living room. "Okay. I'm ready."

"You get the grade on your test yet?" Gracyn peers at me over the top of her glass.

"Nope. Hand me your laptop." The look on Aidan's face as he answered his phone earlier is replaced with the memories of ink marking his skin and the look in his eyes as he broke through my barriers. I log into my university account and take a big gulp of wine. "Ready?"

"Yeah. Go." Gracyn buzzes, almost as tense over my

grades as she is over hers. "What do you need to stick with it this summer?" She's practically bouncing with nerves.

"Anything over a B, and I should be okay. I just..." Gracyn jumps and almost spills her wine when I screech. *Almost.* "I got an A—holy shit." I bite my lip trying to suppress the huge smile that wants to take over my face. "G, I'm gonna make it. Oh my God, I'm gonna do this." Eyes huge, I split the rest of the bottle between our glasses.

"Yeah, you are. I never doubted you," she says with all the sincerity in the world. I'm the one with all the doubts and fears of failure.

I set her laptop on the coffee table and let out a huge sigh of relief, nestling myself into the arm of the couch and shoving my feet under the throw blanket she's got wrapped around her.

"And what about Aidan? Things are good there?"

The first thing that pops into my mind is the call he got— the frustration and concern etched across his face. He hasn't responded to my text, yet.

"I think, yeah. I haven't seen him since Friday, but yeah. He was incredible helping me...study?" I didn't mean for that to come out as a question. "He takes care of me. Makes me feel like I'm a priority to him. I think my trust—my comfort? —is important to him."

I grab my phone from the table and send him another message before dropping my phone in my lap.

"Yeah?" I know for sure that she's concerned for me, but her questioning it makes my glass pause on my lips. "What's the plan there? Is he staying, Lis? In the States? Or is he going back to Ireland?"

I check my phone for a message I know isn't there, lower my glass, my gaze falling to the loose thread in the blanket.

"I don't know. We haven't really talked about that. It's been all about me—my needs—my..."

"Don't you think you should find out—before it's too late?"

Deep breath in, I tilt my head back against the side of the couch.

"Lis?"

The air rushes out of my lungs. Thoughts are racing through my head. Pinging around inside my brain. "This is just a distraction, remember? It was your idea," I whisper.

"I...just don't want you to get hurt. Talk to him. Don't set yourself up for heartache again."

My eyes drop from the ceiling meeting hers in an intense stare.

Gracyn raises her hand, palm out while she rationalizes. "Not that I think for a minute he's going to go fuck Maryse behind your back, but what's he doing here? Where is his head? You need to talk to him. Soon."

"Yeah, I know." Not much about tonight's sitting well with me. "What about you, G? You gonna sit there and tell me I need to protect my heart, when..."

She cuts me off with a snort. "Dude, really? I've got your fucking back—I'm just looking out for you."

"When you've been *off* since spring break, Gracyn." Not good. I don't want to do this with her. I hate fighting. "What's up with your shit?" Trading my wine glass for her laptop, I open Facebook and search her timeline.

"What are you doing? Stop, Lis." Her feet push at me

and I have to grab at the computer to stop it from hitting the floor.

"Look Gavin up, do a search. Have you looked for him at all?" The heat rolling off her glare is scorching. "I love you, and you know I appreciate you looking out for me, but what about you? For the love of God, G—what's the deal? It's been months and I still find you staring at his picture on your phone, but you won't look for him? Contact him?" It's totally ridiculous that I'm getting this pissed.

Deflecting? Probably, yes.

"What if he's in the area? What if he's thinking about you as much as you're thinking about him?" She's blinking way too fast for that to be anything other than tears she's fighting. "Gracyn. What's the name of his band?"

"*The UnBroken*." She practically whispers it. "But I don't want to know. The timing's bad."

"The timing is only bad because you won't let it be anything else. I care about you too, you know. And you've been moping for months." There are a ton of posts on Facebook for the band—they're tagged all over Instagram—all over. "G, they were just here last week. They were the band that played the college summer series. Did you know?" She refuses to make eye contact with me. She absolutely knew. "You knew he was here and you took all my hours last week."

"You needed the time off to study. This class is important to you." I don't know what to even say to that.

"Don't you dare twist this and make it about me. You know someone else could've worked the bar. Using me as an excuse makes you sound like my mom—and you don't want that—I know you don't." My mother has been manipulating shit my entire life. Anything to make Maryse look good.

"Gracyn, I love you, but that's just wrong. I'm…I'm going to bed. I can't…forget it." The air in the apartment seems to have shifted. The tension is high and I'm pissed.

Of all the fucking things to do, twisting my needs to suit her wants and fears is too much. And she knows it. She's seen my mom pull that shit and Gracyn's been the one to scrape me off the floor from the aftermath. Literally.

Done with today. I'm done with it. The morning hasn't improved my mood. The fight with my friend reminded me why I'm not good at accepting help. I never thought this shit would happen with Gracyn.

Never.

"Lis, I'm sorry, okay? What…what do I need to do? How can I apologize?" She knows. She fucking knows that she can't twist things and use me as an excuse to get what she wants—or avoid what she thinks she doesn't.

I've got Gavin's tour schedule saved to my phone. They come anywhere close to this area again and I'm dragging her ass to the show. That'll help.

"Dammit, Lis, stop. Just…I knew I would end up there if I didn't have somewhere else I had to be." Her voice drops and she slumps into a seat at the kitchen table. "I needed to work that night as much as you needed the time off."

"Why not talk to me, though? What the hell? I don't understand." I throw my hands up in the air, before letting them fall to my sides.

"I know. I…you have so much going on and…listen to me, just for a minute." Her fingers twist through her hair, frustration rolling off her in waves. "If anyone gets how important this class is for you, staying on schedule to graduate early, it's me. I know. I get it—I've been with you through all of your family shit. I'm sorry I didn't tell you he was here and that I needed to be busy. I just...I will. Okay? Next time, I will." She finally raises her head and looks at me. "I just need some time."

"Gracyn, you're scaring me. Tell me what happened?"

"Not yet. Not now, but I promise to tell you everything. Soon." And with that, she leaves. No makeup, not put together. Just grabs her keys and leaves. Tears already streaming down her face.

This is so not right. It seems like every time things start looking like they're all going to line up and life is going to move forward without drama, something shakes loose. We'll be okay. It just goes to show that disappointment is lurking.

This is the most we've talked in weeks. We just haven't crossed paths—which is odd. I can honestly say I've not been avoiding her. I really hate conflict and the shitty feelings that never seem to dissipate, and talking is the only way I know to make things better. But she's been steering clear of me.

I dump the rest of the coffee into my go-cup and grab my bags. I'm going straight from class to work today, like I have been for most of the summer, and then hopefully to Aidan's.

Things have been going really well, other than with my dear sweet friend, and it scares the shit out of me. I don't want to think about the next thing to go wrong, but I feel like the snowball has started down the mountain.

MY KNUCKLES barely land on the door, when it flies open and Aidan steps into me. He wraps his hands around my cheeks pulling me in close and kisses me like he hasn't seen me in ages. I'm completely consumed by him as he kisses my breath away.

He pulls back and with his lips ghosting over mine, he whispers, "Christ, I missed you. What are you doing to me?" Aidan's forehead rests against mine as I breathe in the faint scent of stale beer, sweat and him.

"Come in, then. I was just waiting to take a shower until you got here."

He scoops my bag off my shoulder and pulls me through the door.

"Pretty presumptuous," I laugh when he turns to look at me, cheeks flushed and brows pinned to his hairline.

"Not what I meant, but if you're offerin', I won't deny you." His sparkling eyes contrast with the low, gravelly timbre of his voice.

Before a response has a chance to form in my head, the door swings open again, narrowly missing my backside. Finn and a couple guys from the pub stumble in, smirk hitching up on the left side of his mouth.

"Am I intererruptin'?" He looks back and forth between us knowing full and well that he might be.

"Nope. I just got here." I take my bag from Aidan's hand and stalk to the stairs. "Aidan, why don't you shower first? I'll go after you." And up the stairs I trot to the sound of snickering and mumbles.

FRESHLY SHOWERED, damp hair piled on my head, I walk through the apartment quickly, avoiding the furtive looks from the guys sprawled across the couch. Aidan is out on the small deck with a couple icy glasses of water for us and the noise blissfully dies as I pull the door shut behind me.

"Guess we're not watching a movie?"

Aidan huffs out a laugh and hands me a glass. "We're not. Sorry, it's pretty crowded here at times." He's leaning against the railing, arms crossed over his bare chest, shorts slung low on his hips. His gaze settles the four, loud man-children who took over the couch and TV.

With a decisive nod, Aidan straightens up and ducks inside grabbing a pillow and a light blanket from the basket by the couch. "Here, take my glass—" He leans over the railing and chucks the stuff he grabbed to the deck of the apartment below us.

"What are you doing?" I snort out a laugh and watch him scale down the ladder that runs down the side of the deck. "Aidan?"

"Hand down the glasses and come on." He reaches up and takes our drinks.

Shimmying down the ladder, I step onto his neighbor's deck. Aidan throws the pillow on a hammock spread between the deck supports. "Aidan, we can't just use his hammock," I laugh. The guy who lives here is nice, but this is a bit presumptuous.

"Help me with this. We'll spread this out and lie on top of it." He hands me the blanket and opens up the netting. "He's out of town this weekend. Asked me to watch for a package delivery." He climbs into the hammock and reaches for me, pulling me in. I yelp as it sways from my weight dropping in. Aidan chuckles, adjusting me so I'm half on top of him.

"He told me I was welcome to use his deck if I needed to

get away from the boys. They get to be a bit much sometimes. And you're the one I want to spend my alone time with." He trails his fingers down my arm as the breeze blows gently across us.

"This is perfect." I yawn, resting my hand over his heart. "Tell me about your tattoo—the cross." I've wondered since catching a glimpse of it in the darkroom. I've seen it plenty since. Traced it with my fingertip. Studied the intricate knots, the heart, and hands. The crown.

"I got it in honor of Michael." He places his hand over mine and slides it down so his thumb finds the inside of my wrist. "His passing."

The shift is subtle, but it's there. I can feel the tension, like there's more to say, but he's not quite ready. I get it.

"I'm sorry. So sorry." I place a soft kiss to his warm lips and press my hand to his heart, and the tension eases away. My eyes are heavy and everything about this moment feels right. I feel a connection to him that I haven't truly known before. Our breaths match—our heartbeats in sync.

As I drift off, I hear Aidan murmur, "*Codladh sahm*— sleep well."

TWENTY-TWO

Aidan

I lie here in the hammock with Lis' hand pressed to my heart once again. It's fitting, her hand resting there. She owns me.

I've been waiting for the question about my cross—she's spent a fair amount of time staring at it, tracing it. And it hits me. Right now—in this moment—my heart is cocooned safely between Michael's memory and Lisbeth's presence. The beats evenly match up to the rhythm of hers.

As exposed as we are, swinging in a hammock on my neighbor's deck, I can't imagine feeling closer to her—more in tune to her. It feels a lot like love, and I want to stay here. Not just here in this moment, but here—in the States. Thoughts of what I need to do in order to stay here start swirling through my brain. I'll need to sort my visa to start, an apartment of my own. To talk to Lis and tell her the rest the story. I just don't know how.

The hammock is a romantic idea, and certainly better than the sauna of my room, but I want more. I need to have a space for just us. For us to be together, maybe live together. The thought washes over me as the soft breeze ruffles her hair, blowing wisps of it across my chest and I relax into sleep, feeling like I have a plan, a purpose, and someone to share it with. Not someone, Lisbeth.

MORNING COMES WAY TOO EARLY, the sun streaming through the trees barely filtering it before it hits my eyes. This is how I want to wake up on the regular. Wrapped up in this woman, feels like the definition of *home*.

There's no way I can pull myself out of this thing without waking her. Instead, I squeeze her and tickle my hand from her hip, up to her waist and back down until she starts squirming.

"Why? Why would you wake a person like that?" she grumbles while planting her hands on my chest and pushing up. Her hair is a wild mess, her cheek is red where it was pressed against my skin all night, and she couldn't be more beautiful.

"I couldn't wait to see you. It was selfish." My smile stretches wide across my face as I slide my hand up her arm and try to tame her wild hair away from her face.

Much as I love this moment, I need to get things moving. "Come on, love. Let's go back upstairs." I swat her arse and try to sit up, but the hammock sucks me back in. The motion making us swing way too hard, the ropes creaking as we rock.

After another failed attempt and both of us almost falling out on our heads, we're out of the damn thing and back up on my deck.

"What's the plan today?"

"Go get dressed, we're going to get you some coffee and breakfast. I like you better when you're fed and properly caffeinated." I drop a kiss on her forehead and head up to my loft to grab my laptop and get ready for the day.

Lis

We round the corner to the diner, the bell jingling, and find a booth toward the back. I slide in and Aidan scoots in next to me. "Uh... What are you doing? Something wrong with that side over there?" I smile and nod at the other side of the table. "You know Gracyn and I make fun of people for doing this at the bistro. Right?"

"I do. You've both shared that with me many times, but we have to work on our to-do list, for today, yeah?" He pulls his laptop from his bag as the waitress comes to the table, coffee pot in hand. Bless her. I flip my cup on its saucer and push it toward her eagerly.

"What can I getcha?"

I dump in a dollop of creamer and inhale a healthy dose of the life-giving liquid. I look up to order and both the waitress and Aidan are staring at me. I might have groaned as I drank half my cup down. The waitress refills my cup for me while we order a mountain of food and Aidan pulls up a website for apartments in the area. "So, your plan?"

"Right. It's time for me to look at a different living arrangement. And I would love for you to help me. Would you look with me?" He turns his very serious eyes to mine and holds his breath.

"Okay. I can tag along. Do you know where you want to look?" I lean into his shoulder and wrap my free hand around his arm, for a better view of the screen. Yup, *just* for a better view of the screen.

"What do you think? You've lived here longer, I'll trust your guidance."

"Okay." We haven't really had the talk yet about how long he's staying. I bite my bottom lip and lean back to get a better look at his face. I'm taking Gracyn's words to heart and much as it makes me feel squishy, I ask, "Are you looking for something short term? Month-to-month?"

The air stills as I wait, searching his face. I want him to say he's staying. I do. I really do, but this is scary as shit. There's no way I could ever ask him to stay, so feeling him out is the safest for my heart. With the rest of his family still in Dublin, he has no reason to stay.

"Erm. Maybe three months to start. Just to make sure the location works." That tells me nothing. "Or maybe an Airbnb. That would make more sense since they're already furnished."

I pull back, dropping my hands to my lap, wiping sweaty palms on my shorts.

"So, just for an extended vacation, or...?"

"Lisbeth. Truly, I don't have any furniture, it would be smart to move into something furnished."

Our food arrives and we scroll through the site between bites. This is so far out of my comfort zone. Asking questions of someone, trusting them not to hurt me. And true to everything he has shown me, Aidan senses it, my nerves.

By the time we're done, we have forty minutes to make it to the first appointment.

Aidan

We spend most of the day trekking around town looking at different flats. Nice ones with no furniture, crappy ones with too much furniture and the stink of cats that will last far longer than the building will be standing. And a few that would be just about perfect.

Lis points out the things she likes and doesn't in each of them and I file that information away as quite important. I want her to like the place I get. I want her with me.

"I have a test to study for, again. It's the last one before my final and then I have like three weeks off before clinical rotations start. Do you want to order food and come hang out with me? And watch me study?"

"Much as I would love to watch—or help you study," God I love the blush that creeps up her neck at that, "I have some calls to return for work, for photography. And, I don't want to distract you." Her thoughts have gone straight to our first study session.

I park behind her car, really not wanting to let her go, but knowing I have to. Much as I would love to spend the evening with her, with nowhere to go and nothing to do but watch her work, I know I need to say no.

I press my lips tight together and step out of the car, rounding the front to open her door.

"So, you don't want to come over?" She leans into me wrapping her arms around my waist and tilts her head up. Her wide eyes bouncing back and forth between mine.

"I want nothing more than to come over—and over, and over." I push my smile as wide as I can while running my mind through all things I'd love to do with her—to her.

She smacks my chest, laughing while pushing away from me. I open the door to her car and tuck her inside. "I know this—school— takes priority right now. Your test is tomorrow?"

"Yeah, and my final Wednesday. But, then I have time. I can breathe for a bit—I can be all yours." Her hand hovers above her eyes, blocking the few rays of sun as I angle my body to shield her. It's the smile that squinches her eye almost closed.

"Can we do dinner after your final? Maybe make some plans for that *all mine* idea?" I'm already making plans and lists and more plans.

"Yup. That'll give me something to look forward to. Is there an incentive for grades? A sliding scale, maybe, better rewards for better grades?" It takes nothing for her to wink since her eye is about shut already, but it's adorable when she does it. She darts her gaze to the sky, mentally running through her schedule. "Wednesday?"

"That works. Study hard and I'll check in with you." I lean in her open window for the kiss that will have to get me through the longest stretch we've spent apart in weeks. Hands wrapped in her hair as she strains to get closer to me. It's not near enough, but I let her go. And bound up to my flat to put my plans in motion.

TWENTY-THREE

Relief washes over me as I walk my final exam to the front of the classroom. I'm almost done. I made it through this set of classes and it starts to settle in just how close I am to graduating. Oh. My. God.

My drive home is full of windblown, wild hair and blaring music. This feeling, there's not much better. I drop my bag under the table by the door and chuck my keys into the dish. I'm exhausted.

Gracyn promised to help me get ready for dinner tonight, but I can't resist crawling into my bed for a little bit. I close my eyes and commit to this nap.

"Hey. You need to wake up, Lis." Gracyn jolts me from a dead sleep. I sit up, throwing the covers off and rub the sleep from my eyes.

"What time is it?" My phone lights up with a couple missed calls and a voicemail.

"Yeah, I tried calling to let you know I'd be a little late, but you didn't answer. Go, jump in the shower and hurry." There's no point in arguing or pointing out that there's plenty of time. Gracyn has a look in mind, and I am at her mercy.

This thing with Aidan has grown, changed. He's found his way into my heart as much as that scares me. This date tonight is different. It doesn't just feel like a simple dinner out, it feels like more.

As soon as the shower is warm enough, I get to it. Our hot water situation has gotten worse over the past couple months and I have a very limited amount of time before I freeze. Shampoo, shave, shower gel. It doesn't take long for the water to cool, so I wrap up and think about moving to a nicer place once I graduate.

"You ready for me?"

"Does it matter? You're coming in regardless." Gracyn lost all modesty living in the dorms her first year of college. Sharing a community bathroom with fifty girls gave her that as well as the desire to move out as soon as the semester was done. I, however, had put up with digs from my mom and Maryse about my ass that was too big, my boobs being too much—my mom even suggested liposuction. So, I'm used to covering up as much as possible. I grab my robe and throw my towel around my hair.

Once my hair is dry, my body is moisturized and my toes are painted, Gracyn pushes me out to her room. "Tonight's big? This date?"

"It feels that way. I mean, we're celebrating the end of my summer classes. G, I'm gonna make it. I'm going to graduate; the hospital wants me. I'm gonna be okay. I won't have to struggle anymore. We can move to an apartment with two bathrooms, and hot water."

"What about Aidan? Didn't you guys look at places over the weekend?" Gracyn still hasn't talked to me about Gavin, and we've been kind of dancing around each other. Her helping me get ready for a date would have been nothing before, but now it feels like a big deal "Close your eyes, Lis— thanks. So, you talked to him, right? About what this is, how long he's staying?"

"A little? Not really. We looked at some furnished places, three-month leases, that kind of thing, so he'll be here into the fall." I shrug, not wanting to give this more weight than it already has. "But his whole family is in Dublin, G. His parents and his brothers and sisters. He's got nieces and nephews there. This, I mean, I don't know. I think I'm falling in love with him, but what if I do? What if I fall completely, head over heels, can't live without him in love and he goes home? What if he decides I'm not enough and he leaves me too? I don't know that I'll survive." It feels safe talking about all of this with my eyes closed, like I'm in my own little bubble.

"Lis," Gracyn sighs as she pulls my hair back over my shoulders, curling it as she goes, "look at me. You can't go through life so guarded. Rob, your sister, even your parents have been shit, but that doesn't mean you stop trying. And it sure as hell doesn't mean that Aidan is like them. Ask him tonight, just ask him. You're not making demands, but if you're worried about your heart, and you have every fucking right to be, then ask the question. Knowing where things stand is the only way, you can't *ostrich* this anymore."

"God, you're right. I hate it."

A few curls tumble down the side of my neck as she works her way through the rest, pinning my hair low at the back of my head.

"I don't hate it that you're right, I hate that I'm so stupidly scared of getting cast off again, that I get all tongue tied and nervous."

I reach up to pull at one of the loose curls, but Gracyn takes my hand, squeezing it gently. Her voice going soft. "You have nothing to worry about. Have you seen how he looks at you? Have you seen the fire in those stormy blues? That boy has it bad for you, Lis. Do what you have to do, ask what you need to ask and know that you are enough. You really are.

"Okay, let's get you dressed now." Gracyn pushes me out of the chair toward my room. "So he can think of undressing you all through dinner."

The dress she has laid out for me is unreal. "Where did you get this, Gracyn?" I know this dress.

"Do you remember trying it on? When we went shopping for the party at my dad's firm, and you were trying for funsies? I went back a couple weeks ago and it was still there." She's waiting for me to blow up, because this dress cost almost half of my rent. "Just stop. It was the only one left and on the clearance rack. Obviously, this was meant to be so just put it on."

I slip into the navy fabric, settling it just off my shoulders. It takes a little wiggle to get it over my hips, but once I do, the side zips right up.

With a deep breath, and tears threatening, I look up blinking. "Gracyn, what..."

"I said stop. It's not that big a deal. Here, put your shoes on." She hands me my maroon patent leather peep toe heels and drops my phone, keys, and lip gloss into her clutch. "You look amazing. Lis. Absolutely amazing." She's like my very own fairy godmother.

"I don't know what to say, Gracyn. Thank you..." Three knocks at the door and my head whips around.

"Go get him, Lis." I turn to open the door and hear her mumble something that sounds a lot like, *we'll see if he can leave the fucking country after he sees this.*

Aidan

The door opens and my heart stops. It stops and I can't breathe. I brace my hand on the doorjamb, and pray that I remember how to breathe before I pass out.

More than beautiful—far beyond gorgeous. She is devastating in her navy dress hugging every one of her luscious curves like they're a fucking gift just for me. With her hair pinned up, I trace the line of her neck to her bared shoulders and suck in a lungful of air. The dress wraps around her— caressing her chest, accentuating her narrow waist, molding to her hips. Just her calves peek out from below, but her shoes. Sexy-as-fuck dark red heels that I want to feel on my back with her legs wrapped tightly around my hips. *Dear God.*

Before I can find appropriate words to compliment Lisbeth, Gracyn pops her head around the corner.

"That's the reaction I was going for." She hands Lis a small purse and whispers in her ear. Her smile and the blush that runs up her neck is almost too much for me. "Have fun, kids. Make good choices."

I hope. I hope she chooses *Yes*.

TWENTY-FOUR

Aidan

The candlelight plays with the few tendrils of auburn curls that have escaped her pins. I can't take my eyes off the exposed slope of her neck. It's absolute poetry. As she studies the menu, I take my time studying her. Her eyes look brighter than usual against the dark makeup; her lips are a bold red, the bottom one caught between her teeth as if this is her biggest decision of the night.

Maybe it is.

Maybe she won't have to think about the answer at all when I ask her to live with me.

She lowers her menu and takes a sip of her wine. I reach for her free hand and pull it closer to me. My thumb over her knuckles, finger rubbing light circles on her wrist. "You look truly beautiful, Lisbeth."

She smiles sweetly over the rim of her wine glass. "Thank you." The waiter comes, takes our orders, and clears the menus, granting me the space to grasp both of her hands between us. "Is everything okay?" Her brows pinch together when she asks.

Jesus, I'm nervous. "It is. Just about perfect, yeah. Your classes went well so you're set to graduate and be done after this term?" It's taking everything I have in me not to blurt it out, and to wait for after dinner. I want to do this right—make sure she knows how much she means to me. Because she means so much.

"God, yeah. I can't believe I'm almost there, almost done. It finally feels real, you know? Thank you for everything you've done to help me. I know we got side-tracked a couple times, but in all seriousness, I would never have made it through these two classes without you." The flickering candle dances in her eyes. I could get lost in their depths. Jesus, they're beautiful.

"Anything you need, love. I told you that." The words want to spill off my tongue. "Lisbeth, I—"

The waiter brings our food just then and the interruption gives me the break I need to find the strength, the resolve to hold off from acting a fool. I want to ask when we're alone—in case she says *no*.

Lis thanks the waiter and waits a beat. Just a moment until he's clear of our table. "You what? What were you going to say?" I've lost all ability to focus on my answer as I watch the fork slide through her lips. My God, this woman. "Aidan? What were you saying?"

"Tell me. Which was your favorite flat of the ones we looked at?" I know I'm stalling, but I have to know that I made the right decision.

"Uh...not the cat place." She wrinkles her nose adorably.

"No," I chuckle. "Not that bloody flat. Not at all." I'm

fidgety, and I know it. I want her in my life, every single day. "Tell me your favorite. The one you liked best."

"Why do you want to know, Aidan?" I love that she's asking. I love the challenge that bleeds through her question. She sets her fork down and clasps her hands together on the edge of the table, leaning toward me, and I decide this is the moment.

"Lisbeth, love. I want you to like where I live. I want you to want to be there. With me." I don't put my fork down. Instead, I turn it toward her and watch as she parts her lips for me. I watch as she wraps them around what I've offered her.

Locking my gaze on her, I wait. Wait for the questions, the answers—wait for what will either make my heart sing or weep.

I had a speech prepared—flowery, lovely words—but patience is not in my arsenal tonight. The small box in my pocket becomes an unbearable weight. And knowing full and well that she's going to freak out, I pull it out and take the ring from its velvet nest.

Her eyes go wide and her fingers shake as she lifts them to her lips. Those lips that I want to capture. "Aidan...I...we..." Pink is tingeing her cheeks; her pulse looks like it's beating frantically at her throat.

"Lisbeth, I would love nothing more than to wake up to you every day. I want you to help me choose a place to live because I want you there with me." Her gaze bounces between mine and the ring in my hand.

"Aidan, I..."

"Do you know what this is? Do you know the significance of the Claddagh?" Slowly, she shakes her head. "Love, loyalty, and friendship. 'With these hands, I give you my heart, and crown it with love.'" My words whisper their way out, quietly enough that she leans closer to me. I reach my left hand across the table with my palm facing up.

"Where and how it's worn shows the true significance. Can I have your hand?" So slowly, she places her right hand in my palm. "On your right hand, with the point of the heart pointing toward your own means you're in a relationship—a committed relationship. It lets the world know that your heart belongs to someone. Will you wear it that way?"

She swallows and nods her head with a barely audible *yes*. "Are you...does this mean you're staying?" The fact that she questions that kills me.

"I plan to, yes. Lisbeth, I would love nothing more than to move you in with me and switch that ring to your other hand." I place a kiss over the ring where it sits on her right hand, and then press my lips to the empty ring finger of her left hand. "I know that this is big. I know that I'm asking a lot of you and I'm asking it quickly. It scares the shite out of me that we've only known each other four months, but I love you, Lis. I don't want to let you go. I want you with me."

I hold my breath, waiting.

I can't let the silence be. She hasn't said anything yet, hasn't responded, hasn't made a noise at all.

"It's down to two places. The smaller flat that overlooks the river is plenty big for me. But I feel like you were drawn to the townhouse closer to town—with the funky kitchen and the garden in the back. There's room for a hammock."

I glance up at her hoping for a sign, some indication of what she's thinking.

"The one with the claw foot tub? The brick walls and

wood floors?" Is it a good thing that her eyes are shining like that? I want to believe that it is.

"Yes, that one. Both are available right away. I can move next week, as soon as I get back from the city. The townhouse is just a three-month lease, but the flat is available for longer."

"Which one do you want?" she asks.

"Lis, I don't know how to say it any clearer. It doesn't matter to me. I'll have space, separation from the boys in either place. They're good guys, I appreciate them letting me crash with them, but I'm ready to get out of there. The only thing that matters to me is that you want to be there."

Her breath comes out in a trembling whoosh. Not at all what I was hoping for. "Can—can I think on it?" *Fuck.*

I clench my jaw, grinding my molars against each other. Nodding my head, accepting the utter disappointment at her reaction, I force a smile to my lips. It's fake as shite, but I hope it at least comes across as something better than a grimace.

"Of course."

"It's not *no*. I just, this is big. It's really big. I was with Rob for four years and living together never came up. It just..."

"Lisbeth, don't. Don't put me in the same category as that —as him. That's not fair or right."

Her gaze jumps to finally meet mine.

"I'm not. I'm just, God this is—I don't know." My heart has done its time on the amusement park rides tonight—up and down. Slowed to almost stillness and then thumping through my chest. "Let me try again, I'm not explaining this well," she starts. "I have stuck to a really strict, disciplined plan for the past three years. The only reason I'm here, within sight of graduating early is because of that plan. Focus and a handful of people who, for some reason, believe in me and support me when my own family can't be bothered, have gotten me here."

I know all of these things. I do.

"And I have to talk to Gracyn."

What the hell? I fight not to bristle at her rejection, devastated that she needs her friend to help her with this decision.

"Surely, she likes me enough, yeah?" I huff out a small laugh as I push my hair away from my face. I lean back in my seat searching for some sign that this isn't over.

Did I read too much into this? Maybe.

Lis

"Aidan, I'm not looking for anyone's approval or permission to do this. Yes, it's a big deal and I guess I wasn't sure about us." The hurt pinches his face and mars his features.

"I'm sorry. I shouldn't have pushed for this. It's too soon." His cheeks are flushed and his eyes are glistening as he looks away.

"Please just listen to me. Please?" A slow nod lets me know he's listening. I wait for him to turn back to me before continuing. "I wasn't sure about you—about whether you would stay. I've been petrified, wanting to ask you, but so afraid of the answer. So afraid that this is more to me than it is to you." My hand flutters back and forth between us, but settles over my heart.

"Lisbeth, I will love you regardless of whether you choose to move in with me. That's not going to change."

"You're giving up a lot if you stay here, and..."

"Lis, there is no place I'd rather be. I want to be here, with you. Or somewhere else, but only if you're there too." He leans across the table, reaching for my hand.

"Your family is all in Dublin. What about them? What about your parents and siblings? What about your nieces and nephews? You're willing to give up seeing them whenever you want? You're willing to give that up for me?"

"I'm not giving anyone up. I will see them plenty; every time I travel to the UK for an assignment, and I can't wait for them to meet you, Lis. I want you in my life, and your life is here." His voice drops to almost a whisper. "What else is holding you back? What does Gracyn have to do with this?"

No matter how I say this now, it's going to sound ridiculous. After that huge declaration, I feel completely foolish.

"I can't just leave her without a roommate. I need to give her time, help her find a new roommate or something. We've lived together for more than two years. I can't just run off and dump the other half of our rent on her. She's done too much for me to ever treat her like that. Can I say *yes, soon?*"

He stares at me for what feels like an eternity. I'm not sure Aidan has any idea how much it just took for me to do that, to stand up for myself. To open myself up and argue— push for what *I* need.

The relief is overwhelming as he nods. "Yeah. Yeah, I can do *soon.*" He settles our bill and we leave the restaurant hand in hand.

I don't think either of us expected the evening to end this way.

TWENTY-FIVE

Aidan

The bed is far too big to be mine. The air is too cool and quiet to be my flat. And the throbbing in my head is far too severe to be just the drinks I had at dinner last night.

The restaurant.

I peel my eyes open and try to take stock. Not in my flat. I rub my hands down my face and reach deep for the memories. I know for sure I had not planned on waking here alone.

Dinner.

My phone pings somewhere nearby, and the sound rips through my head. I look around again and see it on the floor. It's halfway across the room, past the jumbled pile of my clothes. Christ, what the fuck happened last night?

Lisbeth.

Maybe the whole fucking thing was nothing but a bad dream. Maybe she's decided. Maybe she's ready.

My stomach churns as I push myself up and sit at the edge of the bed. With elbows on my knees, I take deep breaths until the waves calm. I stumble to the loo, not sure whether to pray that I purge this shit or not. I splash cold water on my face and then rest my hand on the back of my neck.

I rifle through my clothes and pull on my briefs and trousers. Slow steady movements, nothing jerky to upset my tenuous hold on the situation. Hope crinkles at the edge of my heart as I grab my phone. The screen is cracked and there are glass chips on the carpet from an empty whiskey bottle. No wonder I feel like shite.

Nausea and disappointment roll through me. My plan was to wake wrapped up in the woman I love. To finally have some true privacy with her. To celebrate taking our relationship to the next level, moving in together. To touch and talk and kiss and love her.

I toss my fucked phone on the mattress and pull on the rest of my clothes. Throw the evidence of my misery away. I probably should have left the bottle on the floor with the shards of glass, but I can't. Instead, I clean up as best as I can and leave.

THE AIR in the flat is enough to drive me back out into the world. I couldn't stay at the hotel—that was to be with Lisbeth.

I sure as shit can't stand to be here. It's just another reminder of how much I want to move out.

I shed my clothes and step into the shower. I let the scorching spray rain down on me for as long as I can stand it. Sadly, it does little to improve my mood.

The hell with this. I can't hang around here. I need to

move, do something. Be somewhere else. It's not yet ten o'clock, but I throw on shorts and a t-shirt.

As I pound on Finn's door, I run a hand through my hair. "Hey, you awake?" I hear the faint sound of bed springs creaking and moans coming through the door. Jesus. "Right. I've got the bar today. You—you just carry on." The words fade as they leave my mouth. That should be me. My reality this morning. Instead, my heart hurts, my head is pounding and I'm heading to work.

It's ridiculous that I'm actually glad the pub is a fucking mess from last night. I lock the door behind me and flip on lights, just illuminating the bar. Only the bare minimum I need to see. I've spent far too much time in my head this morning and need a fucking escape.

As the mop bucket fills, I put all the chairs up on tables, stools up on the bar and crank the music. And pop some ibuprofen and pour myself a pint.

TO SAY I'm focused on the shit task of scrubbing the floor would be an understatement. Scrubbing, mopping, changing out the water. I'm washing up the last section when I see the back door open.

"I thought Finn was openin' today. Didn't you switch wit' him? Take today off?" Francie yells above the music as he takes in the state of the pub. "Jesus, would you turn that down, I can't think wit' it goin' like that."

"That's the point." I reach past the taps and lower the volume to a workable level. I finish up the floor, ignoring the rest of the shite he's asked me. "You wanna start putting the chairs down and I'll get the tables wiped before you unlock the door." I heft the bucket and head out back to dump it. I decide to wash the bucket and thoroughly clean the mop while I'm out there. *Shite should be done right the first time.*

"Yeah, it should but why don't you leave the poor mop alone and come inside. 'Ave a pint wit' me and tell me what's troubling you." Again, I'm so far in my head, I never heard Francie come out. "Come on, Aidan."

He nods to a barstool and slides me a fresh pint. "You took Lissy out last night, yeah?"

"Yeah."

He stands there, like the barman he is, folded arms resting on his belly, hip against the bar. He's had years of practice and will wait me out. I plant my elbows on the bar and scrub my hands over my face. Somehow with the music at a normal volume, my head hurts worse than it did before.

I take a long pull from my glass and heave the breath I'm holding out my nose. The longer I keep my mouth shut, the better. I don't want to deal with what I'm feeling, let alone talk about.

"Out wit' it, lad. Let's go. Did you fuck things up wit' my Lissy? I told you, you weren't to get involved if you were just goin' to mess around." He's all arsed up now.

"I didn't fuck it up. I don't think."

It's under his breath, but I catch something that sounds a lot like *and that's the fucking problem.*

"I can't do this. I'm a cliché, sitting here." I shove my barstool back catching it just before it hits the floor. "You sit, old man, and I'll prep the bar."

I grab a clean rag and attack the bar top. I scrub at nothing, moving just for the sake of moving. Tension is thick in the air. Francie watching me, waiting for me to stop muttering to myself. He moves 'round the bar meticulously straightening all the barstools

"Son, you're going to wipe the varnish off the thing." His voice is much softer this go around and that's what does me in. Bracing myself against the bar, arms wide, I drop my head and suck in a big breath.

"I don't know where I went wrong."

"Did you have a row? Have things gone arseways wit' the pair of you?"

"No, we didn't fight. I told her I loved her and asked her to move in with me." The words physically hurt to speak. Hearing myself say them out loud makes it all too real. I grab my glass and drain it in one go. And because this day can't go any further into the jacks, the keg blows as I'm refilling my pint, spraying the dark sticky beer all over me.

"Fuck." I slap the tap shut with a lot more force than it deserves. I rip the empty keg out like the whole thing is personal. And of course, the fresh keg I need is buried in the cooler under cases of bottled beer and other shite.

I tear through the cooler, stacking cases of beer, boxes of mixers, and bottles of liquor. I know I'm just a hair shy of breaking everything I touch. When I finally get a path cleared, I heft the fresh keg onto my shoulder landing it a lot harder than is necessary. The bruise will be a great reminder of this day I'd love to forget.

"I heard you back there, Aidan. Take a breath—think before ye go throwing that keg around, now."

"FRANCIE, I...Jesus, this is hard. I love her. I want to stay here—be with her—build a life. I thought I was doing that."

Now that I've opened my mouth, there's no stopping the tide that comes spilling out.

"We went together, last weekend. Looked at a million bloody flats. I appreciate the loft." I give him a pointed look, making sure he knows I mean it. "But I need some space. I need some privacy and some fucking sleep. Do you have any idea how loud those two are? Finn with his flavor of the week, and Jimmy...Jimmy's just fucking loud when he's—"

Francie cuts me off with a sharp slap of the bar. Pointing his finger at me. "I don't want to know any of that, yeah?"

"Yeah, and neither do I. I've got a good five years on them and I'm past that, done with it." Francie chuckles and shakes his head. "What?"

He leans forward on the bar, emphasizing his point. "Sure you're older than them. Those boys are the same age as Lisbeth."

I stop dead in my tracks. Paralyzed by that bit of information. I think I already knew it on some subconscious level, but she seems so much older, more mature than them. "Christ, I...it's easy to forget that. She's got her shit so together, so capable. I forget she's that young." Maybe I did fuck this up.

"So. You asked her to live wit' you and she said no?"

"She said she needed time. Needed to think about it and talk to Gracyn." I lift the keg into position and tap it, standing back as I purge the line. I fill Francie's pint, flip on the rest of the lights, and unlock the door.

He watches me, lips screwed up in a half smile, nodding his head. "That's not no, then." As hard as he's pushed me away from her, Francie seems almost hopeful. The door opens and the noise of the street trickles in, glancing up I toss a *hiya* at the couple, waiting for the rest of Francie's thoughts on this. "Our Lissy's a smart girl. One of the best. She'll take her time, yeah, but make the right decision—the right one for both of you."

The guy that just came in huffs out a disgusted snort as the girl he's with moves toward Francie. "So, where is my little sister? She's not answering my calls."

TWENTY-SIX

I feel like I didn't sleep at all last night. There were too many thoughts racing through my head for me to relax and fall asleep. I sat for a long time looking at the ring he'd given me. It looks nothing like the Claddagh that Francie's worn for as long as I've known him. This is so much more.

I twist it around my finger—around and around—sliding it off.

"Hey, you up?" The smell of fresh coffee wafts into my room as Gracyn knocks and cracks the door. "I didn't expect to see you back here this morning. Everything okay?"

I slide up toward the headboard as she hands me a mug and settles in next to me. "I'm okay." I fumble with the mug and trying to get my ring back on before I drop it in my covers.

"What the hell is that?" Gracyn grabs my hand and pulls me toward her, spilling coffee on my white duvet. It's not a typical Claddagh—not like any that I've seen before. There's a red stone in the shape of a heart, my birthstone maybe. And the silvery blackish metal that makes up the rest of the ring has small diamonds set in the crown. "Lis—"

"I know. I kind of freaked out a little when he gave it to me. But it's not an engagement ring, obviously." I can't take my eyes off of it.

"But it could be, right? It means different things on different hands and which way the crown faces? God, it's gorgeous." She pulls it closer and spins it around my finger sliding it off again. The sun streaming through the window hits the stones, scattering dots of light and color across the wall. "So why? Why are you here? Why did this date end with me drinking coffee in bed with you? Instead of eating a bowl of cold cereal on the couch by myself?"

I set my cup down on the table next to my bed and take my ring from Gracyn, turning it over in my hand. I have been all over the place thinking about last night. Thinking about what Aidan said, what he asked. That he's staying for me—for us.

As the words tumble out of my mouth, I run my feet up and down the sheets. "He asked me to move in with him. He said he's staying and he loves me. He asked me to move in with him." My nose scrunches up as I grit my teeth waiting for her reaction. Really, I want to not lose my shit.

Saying it out loud feels different. It makes my heart flutter and I can't sit still. My knee starts bouncing and I chance a peek at her face.

"Oh, Lissy, that's good, right? Are you gonna do it? Move?" Her wide eyes search my face.

"I told him I'd say *yes* soon."

"Not an appropriate answer to that question, Lis. Why didn't you just say yes? Not because of Rob?"

I bop my head back and forth. "Yes and no. But mostly because of you?"

"Nope. Nuh uh, not okay. Did we not just have a big thing about me not using you as an excuse to avoid life? You can't use me that way either, Lis."

"So not the same thing. I just—you've done so much for me, G. I can't just walk away and leave you here alone. Dump the rest of the rent on you, that's not fair. I told him I needed to talk to you and make a plan. That's what we do, right? We make plans and stick to them?" I pin her with a glare. "Isn't that why you walked away from Gavin? Because of plans and rules?"

"Not now." The edge in her voice cuts right into me. "We'll deal with that another day."

"Because it's not in the plan?" Snotty comebacks, I can do with Gracyn. Only Gracyn. "When are you going to talk to me about him?"

"Not today." End of story. She climbs off my bed and that subject is closed. "So, I start looking for another room-mate. No big deal." Those last three words, she tosses over her shoulder as she walks out of my room.

"Are you mad? I don't have to move in with him yet..." I grab my cup and follow her out to the kitchen.

"Yeah, I am." She slams the milk carton on the counter and stares at me. Her shoulders droop as she releases a tense sigh. "Lis, be selfish, just this once. What does your heart tell you? What do you want? Because it looked a hell of a lot like excitement right when you told me. But you're holding yourself back. Is it for you—because you're not sure—or because of something else?"

"I am excited. I don't think I realized how much, though, until I heard myself say the words. It's scary, and exciting and not at all what was in my plan book. You know—*you know*—I have to take a step back and think. I can't make decisions on the spot, not big ones. And this is big—really fucking big." I drop down into a seat at the counter. "I want to. It's crazy and probably wrong and absolutely one of the scariest things I can think of, but I want to do this. I love him and I want to wake up with him, every day. But that doesn't change us, and I'm not leaving you hanging."

My heart flutters when I realize what I just said. What I just admitted to myself for the first time.

Slowly Gracyn's lips lift and spread into a big snarky smile. "Well, then. I'm going to go start looking for a new roommate and you should get dressed and tell Aidan it's happening." She shoves me toward the hall. "Just know, you're not going to look near as hot as you did last night. I bet he's devastated thinking about those heels and where he wanted them last night."

THE VOLUME of voices coming through the door doesn't match the lack of crowd. It's still early and there's only a handful, a really small one, of cars parked outside McBride's. But the voice booming from the bar, nearly explodes as I step inside. And crash into Rob's chest.

"The fuck, Lis? Watch it—you practically ran over me." I step to my right and try to make sense of what's happening. Aidan's hand is planted firmly in the center of Francie's chest. Pushing him back from Rob and...Maryse? Everyone stops—talking, yelling, moving. Or it just seems that way to me. I don't know.

"Sorry. I-I didn't mean to—"

"Swear to God, felt like I got hit by a fucking linebacker." Rob rubs at his chest. I didn't even hit him that hard. And Maryse wraps herself around him and giggles. She giggles. Fucking giggles.

It's only seconds—seconds that feel like they drag on forever—before I shift my eyes to Aidan. His expression is fierce, fists clenched and veins popping on his forearms.

Where Rob is all loud blustery bravado, Aidan moves with a quiet purpose. Each determined step hints at the promise of barely held restraint.

"It's time for you to go. Now." His voice is a low growl that raises goose bumps on my skin.

I glance at my sister and ex-boyfriend. They're stunned silent, like deer caught in the headlights of a truck.

Rob rips the door open and practically runs out, leaving Maryse behind.

"I called you, left you a voicemail and you didn't call back." Her eyes flick toward Aidan as she settles her hand on the push plate of the door. "I came looking for you. I don't appreciate the way my fiancé and I were treated by your friends."

Her bitch factor is off the charts as she sweeps a diamond-crusted hand game show-style. "Our wedding is next month. See if you can lose a few pounds, I'm not sure your ass'll fit in the dress I picked for you."

And she's gone.

The bright sun flares in my eyes momentarily blinding

me when the door closes, throwing the room into a cool darkness. I don't know what just happened. The only thing I can do is laugh—high, thready and shrill. Aidan's hands wrap around my shoulders and he dips down, eyes darting back and forth between mine.

"So, that was my sister." Oh. My. God. "And her fiancé."

"Are you alright? Come, sit down a minute." He slides his hand around my back, pulling me in close.

The twenty feet between the entrance and the bar is all it takes for me to push the shock aside. Most of the shock. Aidan ushers me to a barstool and Francie sets a pint in front of me. With a nod toward the glass, he apologizes. "They weren't to ever be here again. I made that bloody clear to both of them way back."

"I know." Elbows on the bar, I rub my fingers at my temples. "Can I have a whiskey?" Francie sets the bottle on the bar with a couple of glasses, pouring for each of us. "That was not what I was expecting. Not in the least."

"Sláinte." The whiskey burns its way down burning off the rest of the ick from Maryse. Francie checks his watch as he comes around to me. He pulls me into a hug and plants a kiss on the top of my head, squeezing me tight. "I'll leave you, then. Lock the door 'til later if you need." That sends shivers through my already tense body.

I pour myself another shot and down it before pouring one for each of us. Aidan pulls me around to face him, my knees tucked up between his. Hands on the side of my thighs. "I don't know whether I want to pity him or kill him."

Aidan

I know what I want to do—exactly what I want to do. I want to kill the bastard and her sister too. Hearing the stories about her family was bad, but this? Seeing how they treat her. Tossing out insults like she doesn't matter.

This girl fucking matters.

It comes out on a huff, a sad little laugh, mostly through her nose. "What happened?"

I try to get some control over the anger simmering in my belly. It's making my skin itch. "Lisbeth—"

"Seriously, why were they here? Why can't they just leave me alone?" Her cheeks are flushed and her eyes are dark. Really dark.

"Francie told them never to come here. I'm allowed—I can make the choice to screen my calls. Avoid people who treat me like shit. I don't owe her anything. Not a fucking thing." She pulls her phone out and taps at it until her sister's voice starts in.

Lis, you need to call me. Rob and I have exciting news...

The high-pitched nasally whine is too much. I reach over and hit the bin icon and delete the message. "We know what she had to say. There's no reason to have to listen to that again."

"And a dress? She picked out a dress for me? Does she think, for a minute, I'm going to be a part of that three-ring shit show? I'm not sure I'm even going to it—why should I? God—if I go it's only to get in on the betting action on how long it'll take before one of them cheats on the other. Holy shit."

The words are just pouring from her. Spilling like there's

no containing them. I want to lock the doors so no one stumbles in on this. I want to let her punch and hit and throw things until she gets it all out. I want to pull her to me and make it go away. Because what I see, what I watch helplessly, is Lis start to crumble.

Tears shine in her eyes as she curls into herself. Her shoulders fold in, her arms tight across her chest. Hair swings forward like a curtain, a protective shield around her face. She's hiding, this is her retreat. "I—excuse me a minute. I just need—"

I hold tight to her hips as she tries to wiggle away. "No. No more running. You have your separation from that arsehole and sister. They're gone. You want to cry? Hide your beautiful face, you do that here—with me." Sliding out of my seat, I pull her into my chest and wrap her up in my arms.

I hold her. Just hold her as she falls apart. Her body melting from a tense ball of stress to mold perfectly fitting against mine. When she finally weaves her arms around me, gripping the back of my shirt, I feel fucking accomplished. The talking we've done, all the touching and loving over the past few months, and this is the moment. She let me in.

And I'm not letting her go.

TWENTY-SEVEN

Aidan

"Thank you." The sound is small and a little sad. She's tucked up under my chin and I feel her words against my chest more than I hear them.

"Of course. I told you last night I'll do anything for you." I pull back and wipe at her tears with my thumb. "Anything at all, Lisbeth. I hate that you're sad, that you're hurting. But I will drop everything to hold you. To help you through whatever it is."

With a finger under her chin I tilt her face up to mine. I need to know that she understands this.

"You own my heart." I kiss her lips, swollen from crying, red from chafing against my shirt.

"If I promise that I'm not running or hiding, can I go to the restroom?" Little by little she unwraps herself from me. Running her hands from my back and up my chest, pushing away. "I just want to splash cold water on my face. God, I got tears all over you." She sniffles as she runs her hand over the tear stains on my shirt. "I'm sorry—"

"You have nothing to apologize for." I watch her go and pull out my phone and ring Finn. I scrub at a thoroughly clean spot on the bar, waiting for him to answer.

"What d'you want, Aidan? I thought you were taking my shift."

"I was—I did—but I need you to come in. Take it back."

"Mmm. I don't think so. Pretty happy wit' where I am right now." I hear the sheets rustle and what sounds like a sharp slap and a yelp.

"Christ, Finn. Just fucking get here. I need to go. I'll take whatever shift you want next week, but just fucking get here."

I toss my phone to the bar as Lis comes out of the loo. Her face shiny and free of makeup. She looks absolutely perfect.

"Oh my God, Aidan. I don't have a choice, do I? I have to go to my sister's wedding. And that dress—I really am going to have to squeeze my fat ass into it."

She looks to her untouched pint still sitting on the bar. Her shoulders droop again as she pushes it away.

"Lisbeth, there's not a thing you have to do. Nothing. But whatever you decide to do, that you want to do, I'll be there with ye. If ye need a reason to be out of town, we'll go. Anywhere you want. If you decide to go, I'll go too—if you want me there."

My hands slide down past her hips, gripping tight, I pull her close. "And you're perfect, love. Fucking perfect. Not another word about your arse. I love you the way you are, and wouldn't want you to change a thing."

She slides her hands around to the back of my neck, scraping her fingers through my scalp, pulling me down to meet her lips. "Thank you."

This time the words are spoken against my lips and become a sweet kiss. Until I feel her teeth nip at my bottom one, driving me insane.

I grip her tighter, spinning so her back is to the bar. I have her caged in, just arching her back over the bar. Every inch in contact from our thighs to our lips, holding her, taking the kiss deeper. The groan that escapes me, and the press of our bodies leaves no doubt that I need Lis.

I need to be alone with her.

Finn needs to fucking get here in a hurry.

"Hate how we left things last night. I wanted to wake up with you this morning." I press my hips into her as I trail kisses from behind her ear, down to her delicate collarbone. "Want to wake up with you every day, love. But I'll wait, if that's what you want. I'll wait for you as long as it fucking takes for you to be ready."

The scent of her lotion is intoxicating. The feel of her curves, electrifying. But the sound of her gasps and sighs and moans whispering across my ear is absolutely dangerous. I'm lost in her, absolutely consumed.

"Is this why you wanted me here so fast?"

Finn is leaning on the doorframe, arms crossed over his chest, watching us. The shitty smirk on his face says he's been here longer than I thought.

I grab Lis' hand and pull her out into the bright sun. We stand there for a beat, my thumb drawn to her wrist. While I'm looking around, deciding where to go, Lisbeth steps in front of me, sliding her hands up my chest, resting her forehead between them.

"Are you done here? Is Finn—"

"Finn was supposed to be here anyway, I just couldn't be still this morning, so I opened the bar. I took a couple days off—planned on spending them with you." My words come out low and gravelly.

She tugs me down the street toward her flat. "Come on. Gracyn is home, but we need to talk. She's—I talked with her this morning. God—that's why I came to the pub. I was going to grab us some donuts and then come find you. Your car was there, so—And then Rob and Maryse—"

She starts and hops through her thoughts too many times for it to make any sense. I pause at the steps leading to her door. Lis turns, up one step to face me. It's just enough height on her that I have to lift my chin to meet her eyes.

"Why did you come to find me?" She pulls on my hand trying to move me up the steps looking back and forth between my face and the door. I shake my head slowly. "Tell me, Lis. Why were you coming to me?"

"Yes. I wanted to tell you yes." She shifts closer to me, her cool palms on either side of my neck, her thumbs barely brushing my ears. It takes a minute, but then, with a whoosh of relief the tension that's been with me since last night, drains out of my shoulders.

I pull her body flush against mine and kiss her deeply. "You mean that? Truly?"

"Yes, I need to help Gracyn find a roommate, but I want to do this—I want to be with you."

With my hands on her hips, I squeeze, digging my fingers into the sides of her arse. "Go pack a bag, not a lot, just for a day or two. I'm taking you away—stealing you and keeping you with me always."

I fight with myself to let her go for even a minute. She said yes and God help me, I'm afraid it's a dream.

"I'll be back in an hour. You'll be ready, then?" My mind is whirring through the things I need to do—through the places I can take her. Much as I love the vibe and pulse of New York City, I want something quieter, more intimate. I nip at her bottom lip, the one she bites when she's thinking hard about something, and I back away.

"Where are we going? What do I need to bring?"

Nothing. You don't need to bring a fucking thing. "Beach, whatever you need for the beach." I take two steps back to her and kiss her like I can't stand the idea of being apart. Because I can't.

Her laughter follows me as I run back to the pub to grab my car. I add finding a nicer vehicle to my list of things to do. Not for today. I only have an hour, less than that really.

On the way to my flat, I call a client from a couple weeks ago. He'd told me of a quiet little beach town on the Connecticut coast. He offers to have his assistant book us in for the next two nights. The confirmation for the Madison Beach Hotel pings through on my phone as I log in to my Airbnb account to take care of renting the townhouse Lisbeth likes.

I shove clothes in my bag—shorts, swim trunks, a couple t-shirts. My phone pings with an email as I debate bringing my trousers and a nice shirt. Just in case. Christ, we really don't need to bring a fucking thing. Room service is all we need.

. . .

I TAKE THE STEPS TO LIS' flat two at a time, reading my email as I go. Three sharp knocks to the door, and I wait. And wait. Gracyn's voice filters through the door, "Lis—can you get that?"

As soon as the door opens, I stalk in. Hands weaving through her hair as I push her up against the wall. Her hands come up underneath my arms, gripping tightly. The kiss is hungry, desperate, and full of how much I missed her in the past hour.

"Aidan. Oh my God." She's breathing me in, just as much as I am her. When I'm sure I don't care that her roommate is here, Lis pushes at my chest. I pull back just enough for her to speak. "Let me grab my bag." I pull her in, kissing her again before I release her.

But I don't really let her go. Hands firmly on her hips, I follow her to her room. Gracyn steps out of Lis' room, looking like she's holding tight to a secret.

I drag my hands from Lis, not wanting to let her go. "I owe you a lifetime of gratitude. I promise to take good care of her and always put her first."

Gracyn looks me up and down, trying hard to look parental. Hands on her hips, toe doing a little tap-tap-tap on the floor. "I warned you months ago what will happen if you don't. Just keep that in mind, and treat my girl right."

With a kiss on her cheek and a wink, her smile peeks through.

"Love, before we go, can I use your printer? I want to sign and send the contract for the flat back." I flip open her laptop and see a familiar picture saved in the lower right-hand corner.

I print the contract and sign it. While it scans through and into my email, I click on the image. It's me. My school photo from primary.

"Were you stalking me?" I tap at the screen eyebrow cocked, smirking at Lis over my shoulder. "I'm flattered."

"I Googled you—God, ages ago. I thought you were adorable and saved it. I might have cropped out one of your school friends, though." Nose wrinkled and her eye-closing smile takes over her face. "I guess that is kind of stalkerish. Do you mind? Want to email, canceling that contract?"

"Hmmmm—I don't. I want to take you away. I want to spend every minute with you—loving you." I grab her hand and her bag, pulling her along behind me.

Lis

Tension hangs heavy in the car. The two-hour drive through Connecticut is an exercise in patience and self-control. One that I'm not prepared for. One that I'm failing miserably at.

"So, you're not going to tell me where we're going?"

"I'm not. You'll have to wait and see," he quips like he knows what I'm thinking—that I have no patience.

"I really suck at surprises. Maybe you should give me a hint?" I turn in my seat and lean toward him. I absolutely hate the car's console right now; I feel like it's separating us by miles.

The scruff on his jaw rasps as he runs his hand up and down. "I don't know. I planned this trip, packed for it, and secured our flat in less than an hour. I think you should let it be a surprise. Maybe let me take care of things. Maybe let me treat you to a few days away, where you don't have to worry about a thing." He struggles to hold a serious look on his face, and his cheeks start rising in a smirk. "Maybe, you should just lean back, enjoy yourself, and thank me for wanting to treat you to something special."

"Maybe." It rolls off my tongue as I sit back and watch this man. How am I this lucky?

Before I can reach into the back seat to grab my bag, Aidan's pulled it out on his side of the car. The strap resting across his chest pulls at his t-shirt highlighting all the peaks and valleys. The lines and the muscles I know by heart.

I didn't know that men like him existed in real life. Kind and protective, a gentleman—but not spineless or weak. He ushers me into the lobby and checks us in.

The concierge explains the hotel's amenities as she clicks away at her keyboard. The beach, the restaurant, complimentary cocktail hour.

I hear her talking, trying to pull Aidan into conversation, hanging on his responses. He's polite, but short, clipped almost, trying to move things along.

"Thank you." He tucks the plastic room keys between his teeth while shoving his wallet back in his pocket with one hand, pulling me toward the elevator with the other.

When the doors are closed, Aidan hits the button for the fourth floor. And all politeness is suddenly gone. He crowds me into the corner, hands on the walls on either side of me. Caging me in.

"Lisbeth, we're not goin' to make that cocktail hour. Ye okay wit' that?" His eyes are dark, his voice is darker, accent thicker.

He steps back as the doors open at our floor. I smile at a

couple with a toddler and baby, loaded down with beach bags and a cooler as we exchange places.

"Probably a good thing they're headed out. Nap time would definitely be ruined," he mutters as he pulls me down the hall.

Stunned, a little off kilter, I look from the elevator to Aidan and back again. The woman hands her toddler a shovel from their beach bag and winks at me as the doors slide shut.

TWENTY-EIGHT

Lis

Our room faces the ocean and the view is breathtaking. I gaze at it briefly before hearing the thud of our bags hitting the floor.

I turn just as Aidan reaches me and backs me up against the glass door. His arms are braced on the glass by my head, his body pressing mine into the glass. "I want to do this right. Last night didn't go how I hoped, but I don't want to wait to have you." His eyes are dark, like the sky at midnight. They bounce between mine. "I will take you to dinner to celebrate. I will show you off to the world, but I need you, love."

It takes a moment, a heartbeat more, for my brain to catch up with his body, but when his lips crash against mine, nothing else matters. Not a thing. I wrap my hands around his back, pushing his shirt up. His muscles shift and flex as he slides a hand behind my neck. He palms the back of my head before tangling his fingers in my hair. Gripping it tightly, he tilts my head back holding me just where he wants me, deepening the kiss. And my need for him takes over.

His shirt is tight to his body and I struggle getting it out of my way. Aidan reaches back and pulls it off, breaking away only long enough to pull it past our lips.

"Jesus, Lisbeth, I can't get you close enough." He dances his finger across my skin, popping open my bra as he kisses from my jaw down my neck to the crook of my shoulder. And just like that, my shirt and bra are gone and his huge hands are palming my breasts. Pushing them up and together, he sucks a nipple into his mouth. Sucks hard and bites down sending a zing of pleasure and pain straight through my core.

I arch my back and slide down the glass, caught up in the exquisite things Aidan is doing to me. My nipple releases with a pop from his lips as he reaches down, wrapping his hands around the back of my thighs, lifting and turning me toward the wall.

"No fucking way anyone gets to see you, only me ever again. Lisbeth, you're mine now, yeah? Only mine." His growled words send shivers down my spine.

I wrap my fingers into the front of his waistband, pulling him to me while pushing him away at the same time. He groans into my mouth as my fingers brush against his cock. His skin hot to my touch. I pop the button and zipper, shoving at his shorts.

"Need these gone, please." My voice is husky with lust. This passion, desire, is not something I have ever felt before. I can't get him in me fast enough. It's almost desperation.

With his hips pinning me to the wall, he pushes at his shorts until they're gone. Kicked to the side with his shoes. He sets me on my feet, flicking the button on my shorts and slides his hands around my hips, pushing, gliding along my skin. As the last of my clothing slides down my legs, Aidan grips tightly to my hips, fingers stretching across my ass. My breath hitches as even his big hands can't span that far. This is so not the time for my doubt to show itself. I try to fight it, but I know I tense.

"Don't you dare get self-conscious on me, Lisbeth. I love every-fucking-thing about you."

He wraps my legs around him again, lifting me up against the wall. After tearing at each other's clothes it's a relief to feel his skin on mine, feel the head of his cock drag across my clit as he tilts his hips. Slow, crazy friction makes me pant in anticipation.

"Aidan, please..." I beg, "...Oh God, please... I need you, I need..." My words cut off as he fills me with one thrust. My mouth falls open, my gasp brushing across his neck.

My world is centered here, in this moment. There is nothing but heat and desire. Full to the brim with Aidan and need and love.

He pauses, for a fraction of a moment, giving me time to adjust. Getting himself under control. It doesn't last more than a heartbeat and he flexes his hips, pulling and pushing, each thrust punctuated with a groan and a gasp. Building and climbing, each of us desperate for the other.

All the pent-up frustration from last night, from the long drive, erupts with a snap of his hips and I fall apart. I gasp as I try to pull in a breath, shuddering around him, pulsing and trembling. Clinging to him with all that I have. Aidan draws out my orgasm, thrusting, chasing his own. With his face buried in my neck, panting and gasping, I feel his cock swell even more. His movements erratic, fingers digging into my flesh, he groans as he shudders and spills deep inside me.

My hands grip at the muscles of his shoulder and the back of his head, holding this man as tightly to me as I can. Oh my God.

"Jesus, love." His words vibrate against my ear sending another wave of shivers through my whole body.

Pulling his face from my neck, Aidan leans back to meet my eyes.

"Do—do you need to put me down?" I start to squirm, but end up moaning as his dick twitches inside me.

Aidan chuckles and does it again—the twitching thing—and gets rewarded with another moan from me.

"I don't. You need to quit that shite, Lis. You're gorgeous, so just leave it, yeah? Hold tight." As I brace my arms around his neck, he pulls us back from the wall and heads to the bathroom, carrying me like it's no big deal.

He sets me down on the cold countertop and pulls his cock out of me. His hands are heavy on my thighs as he leans back to watch. "Fuck, Lisbeth. I—we didn't—" The realization crashes into him. We've always used a condom before. His wide eyes snap up to mine, panic evident all over his features.

"It's okay, Aidan. Stop." My hands on either side of his neck, thumbs caressing his cheeks trying to soothe his worry. "I have an IUD. We're okay—it's okay." I guess we've not talked about this. We just have always, religiously, used a condom. His eyes bounce back and forth between mine, searching—almost pleading. "I promise, it's okay."

The relief whooshes out of him in the breath he was holding. "I promised you I would take care of you, always. I shouldn't have done that. I've always used protection. Always. You put your trust in me and I—Christ." His words still carry the sharp edge of panic.

"Stop. Trust *me*, Aidan. I would have stopped you if it wasn't okay. Please let it go, we have to trust each other, it's not just you proving yourself to me."

I pepper his lips with small kisses, willing him to relent and relax into me. But he's not done.

"I do—I trust you with everything I am, but you have to know. You *have* to know that I would never do anything to fuck with your dreams. Everything you've worked for—that's what matters." His words go straight to my heart. He's so intent on putting me first, making sure I'm okay. That I'm taken care of.

"I know." I pull him to me and quiet him with a kiss, sweeping my tongue along the seam of his lips. Wanting to show him we're good, begging him to open up to me and let this go.

Finally, *finally* he returns my kisses—letting me in with a groan. Our tongues tangle, the kiss growing in intensity.

He hikes my leg higher, my calf over the top of his ass. He keeps his hand on my leg, the other winding around my back. Fingers skate upward tracing designs I can't quite figure out with the way he's kissing me. I can't think about anything other than the way he's holding me, wrapping me up in him. I don't need anything else, just this. Just Aidan.

He angles his hips, hard again, his cock sliding through my slick center. Teasing me, getting closer and closer. Closer to where I want him with each pass, but not quite there.

I squeeze my hand between us, running my palm down my belly. He rocks back, dragging the head of his cock down, teasing, driving me mad. A gasp escapes me as my thumb circles my clit, rubbing in lazy circles. I'm waiting, waiting for that moment when he moves to drag his dick back to my clit. As he drives up again, I push down with my fingers guiding him where I want him. Where I need to feel him.

"Christ, Lisbeth. You feel like heaven. You're sure this is okay? I don't ever want anything between us again, but Jesus, Mary and Joseph..." He starts rocking gently, small concentrated movements, but with the way he's locked his arms around me I can't move. He's got complete control.

The teasing, the buildup, the rock of his hips—where his cock is hitting me.

"Yes...yes...oh God, Aidan...please..." I beg for him—to do what, I don't know, but I'm breathless and needy. And I feel myself coming apart all around him. Pulsing and panting, I come undone.

With my legs wobbly like jelly, I step under the hot steamy water. Aidan keeps hold of me, knowing I could melt into a puddle of goo at any moment. How did I get so lucky?

It's still so hard for me to believe this is all real. Aidan's soapy hands glide over my shoulders and knead at the muscles of my back before skimming down my sides. I yelp as he tickles me, grabbing tightly to him so I don't slip and fall.

"Hmmm—this is a waste of time. I'm just going to spend the rest of the night getting you dirty all over again." His hands are all over me, running up and down me, around my ass and down the backs of my thighs as he lowers to his knees. My fingers tangle in his hair as he presses hungry kisses to my belly, his fingers sliding in toward my center.

I feel it before it happens and there is nothing I can do

about it. My muscles stiffen and Aidan looks up searching my face for the problem. I don't know whether to laugh or cry when my stomach chooses this totally sexy moment to growl—loud.

Aidan's eyes crinkle and the laugh that launches from him echoes through the shower. I could die of embarrassment —just die right here.

"I'll be quick, love. And then we'll get you fed." He mumbles something more but it doesn't matter as he licks and nips his way to my pussy. I'm so sensitive, it takes no time for my orgasm to rip through me. He slides his body up mine as he stands, holding me tight the entire time. "You ready for dinner now?"

WRAPPED in a towel and brain still fuzzy from orgasms, I open my bag to grab panties and a t-shirt. Sitting on the top of the things I packed, are a cute dress and my maroon shoes.

"What do you want me to order for you?" Aidan calls from the other side of the room.

There's a piece of paper tucked into one of the shoes. I close my bag, biting my lip to hide the smile I know will scrunch up my eyes.

"Lis, what do you want for dinner?" Bag in tow, I head for the bathroom to get ready.

"I thought you were taking me out tonight. Showing me off to the world?"

His head whips up just as the door slams shut behind me.

TWENTY-NINE

Aidan

The restaurant takes my reservation, though at this hour, I probably don't need one. I'd have been more than happy to stay in, wrapped up in Lis and order room service. But when she opened her bag, and closed it as fast as she could, she asked if we were still going out to dinner.

Yes, I'd told her I couldn't wait to take her out and show her off to the world. I meant that, but tonight I just want to be with her. And love her.

I do—I love her. But I'm afraid that telling her will spook her again.

I check my watch and push myself out of the chair. "Are ye ready, love? They've a table for us, we should go soon."

Not a fucking thing could prepare me for the sight of her walking out of the bathroom. There is nothing revealing about the black dress she's wearing—high neck, sleeves to her elbows, full skirt to her knees. But it hugs her tits, cinching in at her tiny waist, flaring over her hips and arse. Sweet Jesus.

My eyes blaze a trail down her body, lingering on every delicious curve, but the best part? She's wearing those fucking shoes. The dark red ones from last night. The ones I couldn't get out of my head.

Licking my lips, I drag my lascivious gaze back up over every one of those bloody curves until she extends her arm, a slip of paper in her hand.

"Not sure if this is for you or me, but it's from Gracyn." She's got a brow cocked and the smirk on her blood-red lips is distracting as all hell.

I'm rooted to where I stand, knowing that if I move, it'll be to scoop her up and take her back to bed. Fuck the dinner reservations.

The sway of her hips as she saunters toward me, skirt swishing back and forth, toes peeping out of those sexy-as-fuck shoes. By the grace of God, I get myself together enough to take the paper from her delicate fingers.

You're Welcome!

My chuckle is low and husky, I wrap a hand around her waist and pull her to me.

"I'll be sure to thank her, but if we don't go right now, we're not going anywhere." I lean all the way in and kiss her cheek, just below her ear. I've time to taste her red lips later.

HAND IN HAND, we walk the few blocks to the restaurant. The soft evening air, salty from the breeze off the water, swirls Lis' skirt around her legs. Sailboats bob and sway in the moonlight, the rigging whispers and sighs across the night.

Every head turns as we walk through the restaurant. She's that stunning.

As I requested, we're shown to a table that looks out over the water. The room is intimate despite the full tables. The lights are low, and with very little effort, it feels like we're alone.

The waitress delivers our drinks—whiskey for each of us. They don't serve it nearly as elaborately as Lisbeth does, but the amber liquid fuels the fire in me as it slides down my throat. Christ, the fact that she doesn't order a fussy, frilly drink, but whiskey on the rocks, is another plus for her.

"Thank you, again, Aidan. This—this is amazing." I watch as she brings the tumbler to her perfect red lips, and I'm fucking jealous. Jealous of the glassware. *Jesus.*

Last night, I was consumed by nerves, terrified of the outcome of our dinner. It seems impossible that it was just yesterday. Tonight though, I'm much more relaxed. Leaning back in my chair, I sip my whiskey across from the woman I'm moving in with me. My ring sparkles on her hand as she swirls her drink around in her glass. The diamonds catch the light with each small movement. The stone in the heart, her lips, those bloody shoes—Christ, I can't get them out of my mind—are all the same deep sultry red.

"No one has ever done anything like this for me before, thank you." Her eyes wide and her face open and full of —love?

God, I hope.

"Lisbeth, anything—absolutely anything for you. Anything at all, love." That shoe peeks out from under the table with each bounce of her foot as we wait for our dinners. It's distracting as hell.

"So tomorrow, what's the plan? Are we spending the day?" I nod, watching as she swipes a drop of whiskey from the rim of her glass.

My nod turns to a slow shake as she sucks the amber liquid off the tip of her finger. I don't even think she's doing it intentionally—driving me crazy. That's part of what makes her so alluring. None of it is contrived—it's just the way she is. Fucking perfect.

"We can take a boat out. I think there are a ton of little islands off the coast—hundreds, if the tide is out. Or hike? Maybe go to a brew house. I think there's a good one in the next town over," she suggests.

"We're booked here through tomorrow night, so we can do whatever you want."

The server tucks our plates in front of us, checking to see if everything looks okay. Lisbeth moans as she takes her first bite and the rest of the meal becomes a battle to control myself. And to make that struggle worse, she picks the same dessert from our very first date. Her lips wrapping around the chocolate cake, sliding it into her mouth is all I can focus on. I'm completely captivated. Until I feel a ghost of a touch on the back of my calf. She's staring out at the water, her expression neutral.

I think maybe I imagined it, but when it happens again, she smirks and sets her fork down, dabbing lightly at the corner of her lips.

"Maybe we should just get the check?" *Fuck, yes.*

Tonight, I want to feel those shoes on my arse when I wrap her legs around me.

. . .

THIS GIRL IS BRILLIANT. She drinks whiskey neat and can keep up with me through the restaurant and the few blocks back to the hotel, all while wearing those fuck-me heels. She's perfect.

We practically run through the lobby. Our laughter filling the small alcove by the lifts as I skid to a halt. Lis' skirt spins out around her, showing more of her gorgeous legs than I want to share with the men sitting at the hotel bar. Of course, she catches me staring them down over her shoulder.

"You going a little caveman on me?" she teases, winding her arms up around my neck. And my heart swells—amongst other things.

"Would that bother you? The last thing I want is to scare you away now that I have you." I'm only half joking. Getting to this point was a hard-won victory.

I grip her hips, guiding her backward into the open lift, set to take advantage of our ride up when a hand slides between the closing doors. They bounce back open and two other couples step in. Since the tension and desire isn't nearly thick enough between us, Lis tortures me by slowly swiping a fresh coat of gloss on her deep red lips.

It takes far too long to get to our floor.

Lis

Aidan climbs back in bed and pulls me tight to his side covering us with the crisp white duvet. The cool air in the room feels almost cold as it chills the fine sheen of sweat clinging to my skin. I nuzzle his chest painting it with kisses, and he settles my hand above his heart.

The past couple of days have been a roller coaster of

emotions. My insecurities have more than gotten the best of me and I know I need to get them under control before they ruin this thing between Aidan and me. I'm getting better, stronger, and that can all be attributed to Aidan and his patience.

Never—never before—would I have been confident enough to flirt the way I did at the restaurant tonight. Licking whiskey off my finger, running my foot up and down his leg. I sure as hell did not need an extra layer of gloss on my lips in the elevator. That was all for him. For Aidan.

He has checked all the boxes. Every one of them would have a big old red check, if I had a list of things that a guy needed to do, to show, to complete in order to own my heart. He's done them all. He has made me a priority at every turn. Always making sure that I'm okay, that I have what I need and then some.

Maybe he feels my brain working overtime, I don't know. But he presses my hand firmly to his chest, the other hand twisting and sifting through my hair. Lulling me to sleep.

THIRTY

Lis

The smell of rich dark coffee pulls me from the kind of sleep I never knew existed. I stretch, feeling the twist of muscles I didn't know I had.

"That's an image I want framed on our wall." Aidan's propped against the wall, shorts slung low on his hips. I should be embarrassed by that comment—I would have been before him. But the first thought that pops into my head is that he said *our*.

Our wall.

We're going to have our own walls, our own apartment. I pull the fluffy duvet over my head and wiggle further down in bed laughing like a fool.

The bed bounces as Aidan climbs over me pinning me right there with the covers I wrapped myself in.

"What are you doing, love?" The smile I hear in his voice consumes me when he pulls the duvet down, just uncovering my face. Squirming does nothing to budge him off me, not that I want him gone. The weight of him on me, being completely at his mercy, I like it—love it. "You're hiding from me? How long do you think you'll be able to get away with that?"

"Uh, probably just for a few more days? When do you get the keys?"

"*We* get the keys next week." My heart. He has been so patient with me. So understanding of my hesitancy. And he's still here, taking care of me, putting me first—loving me. "I ordered breakfast, hope that's okay."

He brushes a kiss across my lips, lulling me into that sweet sense of security. "You're very vulnerable here."

"I am. I'm at your mercy." Sweet kisses rain down the side of my neck. I tilt my head, granting him more access. My body reacting to his, desire fluttering through me. I feel absolutely wrapped up in him.

"It would be a crime to let breakfast get cold, though. Why don't you get comfortable and I'll serve you?"

He hops off me with a smirk, and he throws me his shirt. *Wait, what?*

"I was perfectly comfortable."

Aidan adjusts himself as he crosses to the tray. At least I'm not the only one who thought this was going in a different direction. I tug his shirt on while he lifts the silver dome, I all but forget my disappointment.

The room fills with the sweet savory smells of French toast and bacon. This is the last little snowflake that causes the avalanche.

Tears well up in my eyes watching him fix my coffee with the perfect amount of creamer. They start to fall as he adjusts the silverware on the tray. And I blink at them, smiling when he places the tray across my lap.

"You alright?"

"I couldn't be any better." I try to rein the emotion in and fail spectacularly. "You are so incredibly good to me, Aidan. I—I can't begin to imagine what it is that you see in me. You keep breaking down my walls. I never thought—wasn't looking for this—any of this. I think, I've tried to push you away more than once, but you stuck with me anyway.

"And you know all my favorite things—how did you know this was my most favorite breakfast? I've had it once, maybe, when we've been out. You picked my favorite apartment to rent, everything we do, everywhere we go—they're all the things I love. You've done every little thing to take care of me." I sniff hard and let the breath out, lifting my eyes to meet his. "I tried to fight it, but I love you. I tried to keep you out, but I can't—I don't want to. For the love of God, I'm ruining the sweetest moment ever." The tray rattles on my lap as I press my shaky fingers to my lips. "I'm sorry."

Aidan beams at me and swipes at the tears that have escaped my lashes. "Lisbeth." He pulls my hand from my mouth, rubbing circles on my wrist. "I love you. That's the answer to every question you have. Because I love you. You make my life better in every way possible. I sure as hell was not looking for love when I came to the States. I came to escape something that came out of nowhere—something I never dreamed I'd have to deal with yet. My brother was my best mate, and I didn't think I'd ever get that back. You've given me so much more. I want you to let me love you, to show you every day that you're the most important thing in the world to me. And you have nothing to be sorry for—nothing." Careful not to topple the tray full of food, he presses the sweetest, most loving kiss to my swollen lips. "Just let me love you, yeah?"

All I can do is sniff and nod. I have no more words.

Breakfast is perfect. Aidan is perfect. Everything is perfect.

I know—*know*—there is no such thing as perfect, but all of this is as close to perfect as anything can get.

We spend the day walking through the little town of Madison, visiting shops, walking through galleries showcasing local artists and browsing through a book store. An actual real live bookstore. One that just sells books—no Starbucks, just books. Our pace is unhurried. There is nothing we have to do, nowhere we have to be, no school or work, no roommates. Just us.

There's no time that we're not touching in some small way. Holding hands, stealing kisses, wrapped up in each other. *I love yous* whispered against each other's lips, making up for all the time I spent trying to protect my heart.

There was no need, he owns it. And after all the ways he's shown me he loves me, I trust him with it completely.

After a light dinner on the deck of the hotel, we walk along the beach. Sand between our toes, collecting shells and smooth stones. Away from the lights of the hotel, Aidan pulls me to a stop and sits in the sand.

"Come 'ere, sit with me." He pulls me down, nestling my ass between his thighs and wraps his arms around me. "I don't want to leave tomorrow. I want to stay until we get the keys to our flat. I don't want to spend another night without you in my arms." His words are soft, just loud enough for me to hear over the sound of the waves.

I pull his hands around me, literally wrapping myself up in him. "I don't want to go either."

My life has changed so much over the past six months. Feeling Aidan all around me, there's not a thing I would change. Not one thing.

I lean and twist just so my lips meet the scruff at the underside of his jaw. I breathe him in, bergamot and vetiver, spicy and rich, warmth spreading through me. "Love you more than anything."

"Hmmm...I love you too, so much."

The stars glitter across the sky, the constant shush of the waves and the warm body around me, lull me to the edge of sleep.

"Come on, love. Let's get you to bed."

The walk to the hotel, the ride to our floor, as we get ready for bed. All of it quiet and peaceful—perfectly in love, peaceful. Up to the moment that I crawl between the sheets and settle in next to Aidan. He rolls to his side, the simple kiss not quite enough. His teeth nip along my lower lip, sending electric desire through my core. And just like that, clothes are peeled away ending up in a heap on the floor.

As frantic as we are to get to each other, skin to skin, nipples brushing his chest, we go slow. So slow. An inch at a time, he enters me, infuriatingly, deliciously, slowly.

When Aidan's hips meet my thighs, he stops, pauses. This is different, so different. Our confessions this morning impact every move, every action. Every little thing holds all the meaning we've not put voice to yet.

I rock my hips slowly, staring into his dark blue eyes. Seeing myself reflected there, I hope, pray, he sees himself in mine. Sees how he has invaded my soul.

He keeps his thrusts slow and deep. Every single move intentional.

I feel the build in the tightness of my muscles, in the soft grunts he makes as he exhales. The thump of his heart against the palm of my hand, like it's beating just for me. My eyes drift closed, lost in the ecstasy of this moment.

"Lisbeth, look at me. Please, love, look in my eyes."

I only just get them open, meeting his gaze when the slow, beautiful burn of my orgasm rolls through me. I gasp, whispering his name like a prayer. He draws it out as long as he can, jaw tense, arms bracketing me in, holding me like I'm a precious delicate thing. And when he comes, it's with my name on his breath and my heart fully his.

Aidan

These two days, with just the two of us, have been everything I hoped they would be. I fell asleep with her tucked in at my side. Her head on my shoulder, hand pressed to my heart, legs twined together, her breath fanning across my skin.

I wake up to the featherlight designs she's tracing on my chest and her lips pressed to my neck. It doesn't get any fucking better than this.

"Mornin'." I pull her tighter to me, planning to take full advantage of the time we have before we need to check out.

"Good morning. I didn't mean to wake you. Just needed to kiss you." Lis shifts so she's straddling me, her lips on a slow, lazy path across my chest. Tongue darting out to circle my nipple just before she bites down. No wonder she arches her back and fucking moans when I do that to her. Christ.

What started out as a sweet wakeup becomes a feverish, frenzied need for each other. She takes complete control and uses me, riding me, making me feel like a bloody king.

She was so shy, so tentative the first time we fucked. Afraid to ask for what she wanted, to demand what she needed. My girl has come so far. Gripping my cock as she slides up and down, taking what she needs. The sight of her, the feel of her—this. It doesn't get any better than *this*.

I HATE PACKING up our things to go back to Beekman Hills and draw the trip home out as much as I can. Instead of the highway, I take the back roads, winding through every small Connecticut town I can. We stop often, acting like tourists taking in the shops, and farmer's markets along the way. Neither one of us want to go back to the real world quite yet. I want to fast forward to waking up with Lisbeth every fucking day.

THIRTY-ONE

Aidan

I plug the address into my phone's GPS and yell across the bar, "I'll be back in a couple hours, yeah?"

Finn tosses me an *up-yours* over his shoulder. He's been pissy since I let him and Jimmy know that I was moving out. Not at all happy about his rent change with one less person to split the cost. I, on the other hand, couldn't be happier. I got an email on Airbnb that my new landlord had to leave town suddenly and wanted to hand over the keys three days early.

I take the steps up to the flat two at a time and rap at the door.

"Hey, yeah, so thanks for doing this, man. Pisses me off, I had no warning that this trip got moved up and I, ya know, just wanted to make sure that everything was all taken care of and shit. Cleaning crew just left, so here're the keys, you've got my email, right? Okay, and if you have any problems, um just, yeah, email me and whatever. Might be gone longer than I thought? So if you want it longer, um, just let me know, email, whatever, okay. Yeah. I gotta go, so um it's yours."

I swear the guy didn't breathe through his entire speech. But he shoves the keys to the flat in my hand and takes off out the door in a complete panic. I walk through quickly to make sure everything's in order before heading to grab my stuff from the loft.

I SHOWED up on Francie's doorstep almost six months ago with just my rucksack and a case full of clothes. It takes me a couple hours and two full trips to move all the shit I've acquired in that time, over to my new flat. Mine and Lis' new flat.

I shouldn't be this fucking excited. Shaking and nervous like a teenager with his first crush. I'm a couple years away from thirty, lived with a girl after college. But this is different. Lis is different. She means the fucking world to me and I can't wait.

Quickly putting my stuff away, I make sure to leave plenty of room for Lisbeth's things. Room for her clothes in the closet, empty drawers in the dresser, plenty of space in the bathroom for her shampoo and lotions.

My gaze falls to the claw foot tub. She went a little crazy over that tub—more than a little. And all I can imagine is her hair pinned on the top of her head, a glass of wine in her hand and bubbles hiding her curves from view.

Everywhere I look, I see some glimpse of our future. Side by side making dinner, working, or watching movies snuggled on the couch. Sliding into bed with her at night and tangled up in the sheets together every morning.

As soon as my things are all sorted, I send Lis a text. I have to work until the bar closes tonight, but I have to see her. I want to place her keys in her hand so she knows that this is us now.

A: Where are you?

L: Work.

A: Come to McBride's when you're done?

L: Hmm…miss me?

A: Always…see you later.

I shove my phone back in my pocket and with a last check to see that everything looks good, I head back to McBride's.

AS BUSY AS the bar is, time just doesn't seem to move at all. How many times can I look at the clock in an hour for the hands to only show the passing of minutes? At half past eleven, the air changes. I know she's here before I see her and palm the keys in my pocket in anticipation. I can't help the thump of my heart as I turn to take her in.

"Hey, handsome. That for me?" She nods at the pint in my hand, hopping up on the barstool I've saved for her.

"It is." I lean over the bar to steal a kiss as I set her glass and the keys in front of her, whispering, "And these are too." Her smile stretches wide, scrunching up her eyes.

"What? I thought we weren't getting in until Friday." She wraps one hand around the keys and the other rests on my chest, covering my heart. "I haven't finished packing, yet." Her eyes fucking sparkle as her lips brush across mine.

"Yeah, I got an email from the guy. His project date got pushed up and he had to leave early. I met him, Christ, almost twelve hours ago? Sorted my stuff before coming back here, so..."

"You're already moved in?"

"I am. So, I can help you tomorrow."

"THIS IS THE LAST BOX. What about your furniture?" I set the box on the island counter and press up against Lisbeth's back. Nuzzling at her neck.

It's cool and blissfully quiet in the flat. No roommates, just us. Pushing her hair aside I trail kisses down the back of her neck. Her gasp turns to a full-on laugh when my phone vibrates in my pocket—right up against her arse.

"I scheduled that call just for your pleasure."

Looking over her shoulder, she notes the name of my caller. "You asked your—mother to call? So I'd get a little thrill from your phone? Smooth." She turns and pushes at my chest. "Go talk to your mom."

And to add to our newfound domesticated bliss, she swats my arse with a kitchen towel. Flashes of payback, run through my mind as I swipe at my phone.

"Hey, Mum. How are you?"

"Aidan, love, how are you?" Mum tends to talk quite loud when she calls, as if her yelling into the phone will make up for the miles separating us.

I hear Lis snicker behind me and meet her gaze with a wink. *Eye-din.* She mimics my mum's pronunciation of my name, her big smile spreading across her features. "Am I interrupting your dinner? D'ye have a friend over? I can call you tomorrow, love."

"Mum, it's fine. Yes, Lisbeth is here, but we're fine to chat." I kiss Lis' cheek and head out the back door, so she doesn't have to listen to my mother yelling through the phone to me. "What's going on? How's everyone there?"

"Good. Everyone's fine. And you? We saw Lorna last week, poor soul. She's looking a bit better, though. Taking care of herself, now. Said she was planning a holiday before the baby comes."

"Good. I'm glad. She needs that. A spa day, then? A beach holiday?"

"I don't know. I don't think she said—I'll have to ring her mum and see if she knows. But thank you for helping her with it. It was lovely of you to send her some money for that." We catch up on all the family stuff and I prepare for what I hear at the end of every conversation.

"When are you coming home, Aidan?" We've talked about Lis, about my life here, but I'm daft for having not broached this yet.

"Mum, I—I'm not sure. I'm working on switching up my visa, planning on staying in the States." I wait for the explosion, for the tears and pleading. All my siblings live close enough for Sunday dinner, and I'm not just telling her I'm moving out of Dublin. I'm telling her I'm moving an ocean away.

And like only she can do, my mum takes me by complete surprise responding, "I hope I get to meet her soon. She must be very special."

"She is, Mum. She truly is."

Lis

Aidan's mom is adorable. I roll her pronunciation of his name around in my brain as I watch him talking to her outside. *Eye-din.*

His face lights up when he talks to her, smiling and laughing at the things they're talking about. And it hits me just how much he's giving up to live here—with me.

Because of me.

With a glass of wine in hand, I walk to the bathroom. While the tub fills, I dig through another box for my bath stuff and candles. The tub is huge—giving me plenty of time to arrange all my pretty bottles and candles on the windowsill.

I add my favorite scent under the stream of water and peel off my clothes as the churning water makes a mountain of bubbles. I turn off the lights and light a candle that I found on our trip. It smells like Aidan, filling the air around me with a mixture of our scents. The steamy water swirls around my ankles as I step in and sink down, letting the hot, gloriously hot, water surround and soothe me.

I stretch out as far as I can and turn the water off with my toe. The air is thick and quiet, the setting sun throwing cloud-filtered light through the bottles on the windowsill.

The colors dance across the bubbles and as I scoop them up and make piles on the surface of the water, my mind drifts to my family. My fucked-up, stupid little family. Their selfishness knows no bounds, and it would be so easy to stoop to their level and refuse to go to Maryse's wedding. It's the last thing I want to do, and they sure as hell don't deserve a thing from me. Not one person who knows the real them would think badly of me for not going.

I used to wish that Maryse and I had the type of relationship that I do with Gracyn. Where we can talk about things, ask the hard questions, get mad at each other but still know that the other person loves you and everything will be okay. We have never had that.

Gracyn's told me that Maryse is jealous of me, that she always has been. And my mom, too. That that's the reason they're so hateful. I'm not sure they know how to be happy. That they know how to think kindly of people and not put them down. That by putting others down, they are not actually lifted up and made better.

I have been so busy trying to survive them and their hatred, my whole life, I've never really taken the time to think how sad it really is. I swirl my glass and take a sip.

Aidan has a bunch of siblings, but when Michael got sick, Aidan dropped everything and went to be with him. I have one sister. One. I have to go to her wedding, be gracious and mature. I have to face my ex-boyfriend's parents and congratulate them on their new daughter-in-law.

As the last of my wine slides down my throat, the door cracks open and Aidan steps in with the bottle of wine and his camera.

"Fucking gorgeous." He kisses my lips and fills my wine, setting the bottle on the floor next to the tub. Pulling a lock of hair out of the pile pinned on top of my head, he drapes it over my shoulder, his fingers leaving a trail of goose bumps in their wake. "Look toward your glass, love. Let your eyes drift off though—yes—that, right there. Don't move."

His camera clicks as he takes shot after shot. Moving

around the room, murmuring thoughts and directions the entire time. When it finally hits me that the camera shutter is silent, I look up to see Aidan step out of his shorts. As he stalks toward me, I slide forward making room for him to step in behind me.

I settle my back against his front, thankful for this man, the love I have found.

"Gonna print one of those and put it on the wall, right next to the one from the gardens." His silky voice sends shivers through my body.

He slicks his hands down my arms, taking my glass from me. He drains it in one gulp and sets the glass on the floor beside the bottle. He skims his lips from my shoulder, up my neck, finally nipping at my ear.

"Turn around," he rasps.

I grip the sides of the tub, steadying myself as I shift to face him. Aidan pulls me toward him until I'm straddling his thighs, the bubbles cleared between us. Droplets of water cling to his chest, trembling but not quite ready to slide down to the water. I reach out, tracing a design across each of the bulges and valleys of his muscles, playing an aimless game of connect the dots with the shiny little drips.

"This is where we live now. Just you and me." My whisper muffled in the humid air surrounding us, my fingers dancing down his torso.

Aidan's hands are heavy on my hips, his fingers pressing into the flesh.

"Just us." I watch his tongue dart out and wet his lower lip. Those are the only words he utters, but his heated gaze and the hitch of his breath as I wrap my hand around his hardening dick speak volumes.

I stroke him slowly, almost lazily, languishing in the realization that we are well and truly alone. No roommates, no one. Just us.

Aidan slides his hand between us, his thumb circling my clit mimicking the same lazy pace I've set.

The sun has set and the room is dark, lit only by the candlelight flickering in the mirror over the sink. The only sound, our panting breaths and the gentle splash of the water.

Shadows dance across Aidan's heavy lids as I shift, leaning forward, and lining myself up with the head of his cock. His thumb stills as I slide down oh-so-slowly.

It's completely and utterly silent in the bathroom until Aidan's groan fills the air between us. I hold still relishing the way he feels, the fullness. Our connection.

Rolling his head back to the edge of the tub, Aidan squeezes his eyes shut and blows a breath out through his pursed lips. He's trembling.

I brace my hands on his shoulders, rocking slowly and whisper his name. He pulls me to him, our lips brushing softly. Everything about this is unhurried and perfect.

We rock against each other, movements small but the sensations layer and build until the most intense orgasm hits me, Aidan right there with me.

THIRTY-TWO

I reach to turn off my alarm, just for a minute and then snuggle back into Aidan's warm body. We have been running nonstop since we moved in and hardly see each other.

My clinical hours at the hospital are not overnight this time, but start early, so our mornings are rarely full of leisurely wakeups. More like jumping out of bed, scrambling into scrubs, and running out the door. Hospital. Shower. Bistro. Sleep.

At least, that's what the first week was like. I hated only seeing Aidan when we tumbled into bed at night and ghosting a kiss across his lips as I ran out each morning, not wanting to wake him.

I set my alarm for earlier this week, so I can do this. Take five minutes to soak in his strength and calm before my crazy day starts. I place a kiss over his heart and start to ease out of bed, when Aidan's arm snakes out and pulls me back in.

"Not yet." His voice gravelly still. He closed McBride's

last night, only sliding in next to me a couple hours ago. He kisses my forehead and rubs circles on my back.

"I have to go. Go back to sleep, I'll see you tonight." He holds tight and rolls us over, settling himself between my thighs.

He squints at the time on my phone. "You have two, make that one more minute 'til your alarm." Pressing his hips into me, he peppers kisses along my neck. "More than that, really since your coffee will be made for you while you get ready. Think we have time for a proper *good morning?*"

I groan, knowing we don't have time for a *proper* anything, not even a quick something.

"Tonight, are you working?" He feels so good, his body pressed into mine, hands tickling up my sides. I want to stay in bed all morning wrapped up in him. But...*mwamp— mwamp—mwamp—* Aidan's alarm goes off and when he leans over to turn it off, I crawl out of bed and hear a mumbled curse as I grab my clothes and head for the shower.

After a lightning fast shower, I twist my still-wet hair into a bun, and slide into a seat at the counter. Aidan fixes my coffee and a peanut butter and jelly sandwich. "We need to talk about your sister's wedding. It's in a few weeks, yeah? Have you given any thought to what you want to do?"

I have, and it strikes me that I haven't shared those with him. I bite my lip, feeling bad for not talking this out with Aidan before now.

"I need to go. It's the right thing to do, no matter how much I'd rather spend the day anywhere other than there."

"What's the time, again? I'll make sure I'm covered at the pub." Aidan pops a bite of my sandwich in his mouth and makes a face. "How do you eat that shite?"

"You don't have to do that. I'll just make my appearance and leave." I hike my bag higher on my shoulder and grab my PB & J from him taking a big bite.

Aidan plants his hands on his hips, eyebrows pinched together.

"You think I would let you go through that alone? No, tell me again when it is and I'll make sure I'm free. Not letting you deal with that without me."

My heart flutters at his concern for me. "It's two weeks from Saturday." Popping up on my toes, I give him a kiss and murmur, "I love you," before I head out into the world.

I HAVE BEEN BLISSFULLY AVOIDING my mother's calls for the past couple of weeks. Our relationship is nothing short of toxic and I just don't want to play anymore.

Of course, just as Gracyn and I settle ourselves at McBride's, my phone rings. It's my mother, again. Aidan places our pints in front of us and stares at my mom's name on the screen.

"Just answer it. You're gonna have to talk to her at some point. The sooner you do, the sooner we can go look for a good dress. One we like." Gracyn nods her head at Aidan like they are teaming up on me. "Right?"

His lips pinch together and his eyes sparkle as he agrees with Gracyn.

I close my eyes and swipe at the screen. "Hello?" Passive aggressive, just for this moment, I will my voice to sound like I have no idea who is calling me. It's all I'll allow myself.

"Lisbeth. Have you been avoiding my calls?"

I roll my eyes and shift to climb out of my barstool.

Gracyn grabs my leg as Aidan grabs my hand, both of them holding me in place.

"We need to discuss your part in the wedding. Have you lost enough weight to fit in the dress we picked?" Two sets of eyebrows hit their respective hairlines with record speed and I just shake my head.

"Wow. Um, hmm." Gracyn is looking for a pen to scribble-yell her thoughts on my mother, and Aidan, bless him, sets a glass in front of me along with a bottle of bourbon. I smile at both of these amazing people I have supporting me.

"While I'm sure the dress you and Maryse picked is lovely, I'm going to find my own. Is there a color you'd like me to stick with or a specific detail? Length? Sleeve?"

My mother's displeasure is unmistakable, mostly because she launches into me on how ungrateful and selfish I am. Pot, may I introduce kettle?

I let her rant while I pour myself a little bourbon and before I can even pick up the glass, Gracyn dumps in enough to put me on my ass. Aidan drops in an ice cube and nods for me to take a drink.

I'm so caught up in enjoying these two hovering over me, I miss it when my mom's tirade comes to a close. "...Lisbeth are you even listening to me?"

"No. I stopped a bit ago. So, Bliss Bridal is where you got the dress? I'll consult with them for the color."

"I have your dress here at my house, you'll just have to make it work. You can pay me for it when you pick it up—" At *her house?* As if I didn't grow up there. But it has never been home to me. Never.

"Yeah, no. Sorry, I'll—" Is she for real? "I'll see you Saturday." I'm so over this mess.

"The rehearsal is on—" Can't do it.

I disconnect the call, throw back the bourbon and turn to my sister of choice. "*Shit*. Wanna go shopping?"

TURNS OUT, being a little bit buzzed is a great way to shop with Gracyn. Loaded down with dresses in the most boring shade of pink you could even imagine, I pull Gracyn into the dressing room with me. Much as I love my privacy, I need her in here with me.

"What the fuck is that?" She picks a dress from the hook and looks at it like it has personally offended her. "Nope. Not that one." She rifles through my *maybes* and pulls four more dresses out, chucking them in the corner. "Those are *nos* too."

Perfectly satisfied with herself, Gracyn rolls her hand at the remaining dresses in a "get a move on" gesture.

Miraculously, I find two dresses that look good enough. And while I don't love the color, I'm stuck with it. Thank God for small favors—it at least complements my hair and skin tone.

I plop down on the chair opposite the fainting couch where Gracyn is laid out and put my feet up on the end.

"What do you think? Which one?" She offers me a Twizzler from the package she pulled from her purse. I grab two, because they're Twizzlers.

"Any one of those look fine on you. Just pick one."

I check the price tags and they are all way more than I want to spend. I shrug, not really excited about any of these options.

Gracyn chucks me the bag of candy and stands. "Hang on a minute."

Six of the strawberry-flavored twists later, she comes back and trades the candy for a dress. Heaving a sigh, I push myself up and look at what she brought me.

It's pretty. Like really pretty. Off the shoulder, rouched bodice, and a fitted skirt that ends just below my knee. It's similar in style to the dress I wore when Aidan asked me to move in—the first time.

It fits perfectly and looks drop-dead gorgeous.

"Where's the price tag?" I can't find it no matter which way I twist.

"At the register. It fell off when I grabbed it out of the rack. I think it was like eighty bucks?" She's doing her shifty thing again. "So, that's the one. Let's get out of here and get something to eat."

"G, don't lie to me."

Hands on her hips, attitude in full swing, Gracyn turns and pins me with a look.

"Fine. Francie and the bar boys gave me a wad of cash to make sure you got something beautiful that would knock your mom and Maryse on their asses." She puts her hand up cutting off my protest. "We all know you're all about doing everything yourself, but just take it this time. Really. Strut into that wedding looking like a rock star with your beautiful man and let them know—rub it in their fucking faces—that you got your Prince Charming."

THIRTY-THREE

.

Lis

To celebrate finding something fantastic to wear to the wedding, and mostly because we are out of Twizzlers at this point, Gracyn and I head to the bistro. We grab a couple of seats at the bar, and order a shit-ton of food. Sangria, fried calamari, goat cheese and tomato bruschetta, eggplant au gratin—and tiramisu. The dress is forgiving, so thankfully this splurge won't even matter.

"So, thank you, G—for today. I hate shopping unless you make me."

"Lis, you hate shopping regardless. God, you hate doing anything that's just for you. Seriously, be selfish once in a while. It's okay, you know."

"Yeah, I feel like I've gotten better at it—maybe? How are you doing?"

I scoop some eggplant onto some garlic toast, garlic and spices bursting in the air. "You miss me or are you liking living alone?"

"Mmm, I'm alright. I miss you always, you know that. It'd be nice to find another roommate though. I hate that you're still paying rent and don't even live there."

Gracyn grabs a fork and divides the plate of calamari in half, leaving a huge gap between the piles.

"Yeah. I hate that I'm not paying for anything with Aidan right now. He keeps telling me not to worry about it, but it's killing me, being dependent." I reach past her for the lemon and squeeze it on my half of the calamari.

I lean back in my seat and look out the front windows, watching people go by. There are couples walking hand in hand, families getting ice cream from next door. There is love out there and my friend needs to find some.

"So, what about Gavin? Heard from him?"

The eye roll she gives me is epic—Olympic quality.

"And how would I hear from him, hmm? No contact. That's—you know what? Forget it. He was fun, a fling. Just leave it alone already, please? Please?"

"Someday I'm going to get you drunk enough to spill. Are you dating at all right now?"

She grumps a *no* into her wine glass and grabs a lemon-less ring of squid, popping it into her mouth.

I shake my head and go back to staring out the windows, and watch as a girl crossing the street stops right in the middle. A car screeches to a halt, the driver yelling at her. She doesn't seem to notice, focused intently on something in front of the gelato place next door.

"Holy shit, what is she doing?"

Gracyn's head pops up just as the chick waves off the driver and dashes the rest of the way across.

"Weird. Hey, I'll be right back, I need to check when I'm

working again." And she bolts for the back room with her phone clutched tightly to her chest. She's so making my head spin. I swirl the deep red wine around my glass, lost in thought.

"Hey, can I get a margarita, heavy on the tequila? Rocks and salt, please."

The girl from the street drops her clutch on the bar and slides into the seat next to me. Her phone vibrates inside the clutch, stops and starts in again. She pulls it out, swiping the screen angrily.

"There's nothing you can say that will make this right, so stop. I don't—" The last thing I want to do is listen to her phone call, but she's right there. And pissed. "—no, you do you. It's fine, I'll figure something out and get my shit out." She disconnects and tosses her phone on the bar.

She drains half her drink in one gulp and drops her glass back down on the bar. Gracyn wiggles back into her seat on the other side of me and looks back and forth from me to the girl with her eyebrows up in her hairline.

"Sorry, y'all didn't need to hear my mess." She slams down the rest of her drink and rattles the ice at the bartender. "Just keep 'em coming, sugar."

As she downs the second margarita, tension seeps out of her and sanity finds its way back in. And we all realize that Gracyn and I are just sitting there, watching this poor girl's shit show unfold.

She looks from me to Gracyn to me once again, empty glass and back up to me again.

"Wow. Um, sorry. Really." She reaches out her hand. "I'm Kate, and honestly, I'm not a psycho, I just... Holy shit, my day has gone to hell in a hurry."

Her Southern twang from earlier is working its way out of her voice, like she's willing it to go away. She slides her glass toward the edge of the bar and taps the rim as the bartender looks over.

"You gonna be alright? That's a lot of tequila," Gracyn asks.

"I don't know that there's enough tequila in the world to take care of this day. Month, really. *Shit*." She shakes her head and smiles. Then the giggles start, and by the time she's worked up to a full-on laugh, the last thing I expect are the tears.

Not laughing tears, but the real ones.

"Kate, are you okay?" I hand her a wad of cocktail napkins and slide her water glass closer. "What happened?"

"Oh, my Lawrt." She dabs at her mascara, not smudging it in the least. It's a skill that I absolutely do not possess.

She looks out the window and sighs. "I'm a walking soap opera. I was early, meeting my boyfriend here for dinner. I'm never early, y'all. Never. And I guess he was banking on that, because"—she swallows hard and stares at the ceiling until she gets herself together again—"because I found him making out with his boyfriend at the gelato place next door."

My hand flies to my mouth, trying desperately to hold in the shock. Just as the words whiz through my brain, I hear Gracyn bark out, "Well shit, Lis, you don't have the worst breakup story anymore."

The silence is deafening for all of ten seconds before Kate's laugh fills the bistro bar and her perfectly preserved mascara runs down her face.

Gracyn dumps the rest of her sangria down her throat and I can't hold it back anymore. The laughter bubbles out between my fingers, still firmly clamped over my mouth. We're for sure making a scene.

"I'm so sorry," I squeak out, "so sorry. It's not funny, but—"

"Oh, it's funny," Kate spits out. "It just fucking sucks. I need to find a new place, too, now." Sighing, she wipes at her eyes and mumbles, "*Fuck.*"

"Sorry, again." Nudging Gracyn with my elbow, I ask—silently—and she agrees—less silently.

"I'm looking for a new roommate. I'm Gracyn and this is Lis. She just left me for the love of her life."

"Are you serious? Because that would be amazing." Kate leans over me to Gracyn. "I teach kindergarten, well, I start next month, but I can prepay rent until then. I don't want you thinking I'm gonna mooch or flake or anything. When—how soon can I move in? God, I don't ever want to see that asshole again. Can you believe I moved up here to be with him? Shoulda known a fine dressing, pretty Southern boy wanting to move closer to the fashion district was too good to be true."

She's killing me, all quick wit and Southern drawl. Kate pulls out her phone and shows us a picture. Pretty is most definitely the word for him. His hair is not just styled, but coiffed. His smile is all veneers and the boy is sporting seersucker shorts and original Penguin polo that so needs to be a size larger. I think I saw in Urban Dictionary that it's referred to as a *smedium.*

"Isn't Aidan covering part of fashion week?"

Nodding through my last gulp of sangria, Kate shifts her gaze to me. "Is that your man?"

I show her the picture I took of him at the beach. Shirtless, scruffy, and rugged. Holding his hair out of his eyes and a hint of his crooked tooth where he's biting his lip.

I love this picture the way he loves the one of me from the reflecting pool. "Yeah, he's a photographer...very straight, I swear."

"Mmm—you hope."

Gracyn is shocked silent before busting out laughing, covering up my giggled *If you only knew*.

THIRTY-FOUR

Aidan

She's not answered one phone call. Not returned a single text. No one's heard from her or seems to know where she is. She's disappeared.

I'm not sure how I became the one in charge of finding her, but I am. Lorna's been my best friend for years. I didn't think twice about being there for her and Michael after his diagnosis. Didn't flinch at helping her through the end. But I'm three thousand miles away. In another country. I can't just drop everything and go 'round her flat looking for her.

I'm not sure what else I can do.

For Lisbeth, though, there's no question. She's been working her hours at the hospital during the day. Shadowing the nursing staff, and loving every minute of it. But she's still putting in as many hours at the bistro as she can each week.

As hardworking as she is, she's just as stubborn. I've told her the rent is paid. The bills taken care of. I've got us covered with this flat. I want to help alleviate some of her stress, take the load off and give her the opportunity to finish her school and training without having to worry about paying day-to-day bills.

I laugh to myself as I fix her coffee in the huge travel mug she likes. She takes hers to the hospital with her in the wee hours of the morning, so I bought a second one. One for me to treat and spoil her with.

Gracyn pulls up to the curb, just as I lock the door behind me.

"Thank you, for doing this." I settle into my seat, and pinch the travel mug between my knees pulling the safety belt across me.

"No problem. I love that you're taking care of my girl." The drive to the hospital is slow with traffic at this hour. "We should get done at the same time. You don't need to sit at the bar all night."

Sliding my sunglasses down, I take a sip of coffee and shake my head.

"Erm, no. She's my girl." I wink at Gracyn forgetting that she can't see past my aviators. "And since she insists on working so much, I'll at least spend the evening in her presence."

"Good answer. Why—forget it. Stupid question."

"Why, what?" The red light gives her a moment to look at me.

"I was going to ask why she's killing herself working—what? Seventy hours a week between the bistro and the hospital when she could just accept some help? But we both know that she's not wired that way." She brushes away her question.

The car behind us honks and Gracyn turns her attention

back to the road. She pulls into the car park and drops me by Lis' car.

"Thank you, Aidan. Thank you for seeing how amazing Lis is. Thank you for loving her the way she deserves." Her voice is quiet and her knuckles pale as she grips the steering wheel tightly.

I wait for her to face me, but Gracyn doesn't break her stare out the windshield.

"I wouldn't have it any other way. Thank you for taking care of her until I found her. She's lucky to have you for her friend."

I lean against the trunk of Lis' car to wait for her, and as I watch Gracyn drive away, I swear I see her swiping at a tear.

The look of confusion on Lisbeth's face turns to sparkling eyes and smiling face when she sees me leaning against her car.

"What are you doing here?" She hikes her bag higher on her shoulder as she steps into my arms.

"I'm here to take care of you." Much as it pains me, I keep our kiss chaste, polite for her professional workplace. "You're changed already for the bistro?" I take Lis' bag and keys, and hand her the coffee.

"Yeah. I had to wash off the hospital germs before I go serve food and drinks. God, can you imagine?"

I settle her in the passenger seat and the relief washes over her as she takes her first tentative sip of coffee.

"You're incredible, Aidan. I needed this so bad."

I smile at the little humming sound she makes while she enjoys the moment to relax, to let the caffeine work its way into her system. To allow herself to be taken care of. She's getting better at it, but I want to do so much more for her.

"How was it today?"

"Good. It was really good. I learn so much every time I'm there." She sinks into the seat, head back, eyes closed. She needs this. Her alarm goes off before five o'clock every morning and she's been running for the past eight hours.

As she relaxes into a quick nap, I reach over to stop the travel mug from sliding out of her hands. I tuck it between my thighs and reach back to take her hand in mine.

I need to check my schedule, between McBride's and my expanding photography commitments, to make sure I can do this for her as much as possible. Make sure she has what she needs.

She blinks away the fog as I park and open her door. I offer Lis my hand, and she climbs out stretching the rest of the nap away.

"Do you need me to help you set up for the night?" I run my hand down her ponytail, giving it a little tug at the end.

"No, I'll be fine." She grabs at her coffee and leans in to brush a kiss across my lips. "Thank you, so much. I'll have G drop me off when we're done. But will you bring my bag in for me when you get home?" Home. It is home with her things strewn about.

"I will, but I'll be back to fetch you home." I stop her protest with a quick kiss to the lips that deepens into the promise of more. When I know she's good and breathless, unable to protest, I pull back. "Let me take care of you, Lis." My lips brushing hers with each word.

It's hard won, but her whispered "okay" is the only thing I want to hear. With a final kiss, I send her on her way and head home.

I throw her scrubs into the washer, well aware that she

likes to wash them separately to keep the hospital cooties away from our other things.

While I wait, I run around the flat straightening things and tidying up. I set a fresh towel on the edge of the tub, place her favorite candle on the windowsill. I straighten the bed and grab her robe to hang by the tub so she can wrap herself in it before she falls exhausted into bed.

As soon as the dryer makes its awful buzz, I pull out her warm scrubs and hang them so they are ready for her in the morning.

Done with the domestic shit, I grab my rucksack and head back to have dinner with Lis, needing to carve out whatever time I can to spend with her.

THIRTY-FIVE

Lis

I catch Aidan watching me in the mirror as I swipe on a final coat of mascara. He's laughing at my mascara face, the one everyone makes—brows up, but lids half closed, mouth open, tongue out.

"Would you stop? Making me laugh is not gonna move this process along." I screw the tube of black goop closed and chuck it in my makeup drawer.

I am doing my very best at dragging my feet. This wedding is the last thing I want to do on this gorgeous Saturday. I just don't want to go.

And like he can read the thoughts running through my brain, Aidan pulls my dress from the closet. "We can leave as soon as you've had enough. Before that, really. I'll entertain you, make you laugh."

He sucks a breath in, the sound hissing between his teeth, as I drop my robe and reach for my dress hanging from his finger. Aidan's eyes take in my strapless bra in pale pink with matching lacy boy shorts, lingering lazily until he finally meets my eyes. His are dark and heavy-lidded, almost black with desire.

"I don't see any reason for us to linger at the party after." He steps closer as I slide my dress over my hips. With his hands on my hips, Aidan turns my back to him and slowly slides the zipper closed. He places a kiss at the back of my neck, my hair pushed to the side. My skin tingles where his lips rest and I have to concentrate really hard on why we need to leave—soon.

Pulling myself together, I step away from him and into my shoes.

"We need to go. No more distractions."

I try to pull off sassy and all I hear is breathy and desperate.

WITH MY HAND firmly tucked in the crook of his arm, Aidan and I walk up the steps to the church. Not the church we attended on Christmas and Easter growing up. No, it's the big showy church in town, the one that will look better in the pictures.

"Doing alright?" Aidan asks with an extra squeeze of my hand.

I blow out a shaky breath and slowly nod.

"Sure?" I'm not sure. The closer we get to the back of the church where the ushers wait to seat us, the more nervous I get. I don't want to claim being here for either side. It's childish, but honestly, who can blame me.

"Didn't think you'd actually be here." His voice is far too loud and draws way too much attention. The muscles beneath my hand tense, as Aidan recognizes Tyler, Rob's best friend. "You here to make sure she doesn't spill any drinks later?" he laughs and slaps Aidan's shoulder like they're friends. "I'll, uh take her from here." He winks, jutting his arm out to escort me down the aisle and the loud and obnoxious becomes absolutely uncomfortable.

Outwardly, Aidan is the image of calm and serene, but I can feel his tension as he rolls his shoulders and shifts his body between us.

"You won't, actually." Tyler takes a step back and stares at us, not quite sure what to do. "I'll escort Lisbeth, if you'll just show us where we're to sit."

"Fff—wherever, man. Enjoy the show, Lis." Tyler puffs out his chest and tries to brush past Aidan to the couple behind us. What I'm sure he intended to be an intimidation, has Tyler looking like a fool as he bounces off of Aidan's shoulder, stumbling.

This stupid exchange, the posturing, has garnered far too much attention. Whispers are rippling through the church and like the wake of a pebble dropped in a still pond, bodies stretch and turn. People are staring at me, comments hush through the church.

"What do you want, love? Shall we strut to the front of the church or take a seat back here, and not worry about it?" Aidan's warm soft voice calms my racing heart.

I smile up at him, knowing there is no one I'd rather do this with.

"Let's sit back here. It'll be easier to make a quick getaway if we need."

Aidan

The look Lisbeth's mum tosses at her as she's escorted down the aisle is nothing less than judgmental. I don't understand the dynamics. They seem to thrive on judgment and condescension, going out of their way to make this strong, lovely woman doubt herself at every turn. I want to protect her—rescue her from them.

We definitely made a mistake in sitting at the back of the church. While it made perfect sense to not parade down the aisle, we do have to endure the stares and whispers of everyone as they file out after the ceremony. As guests file out, I feel Lisbeth getting tense, her discomfort floating around us like a cloud. I run my hand down her back, landing on her hip and pull her close to me.

"Do all of these people know it's you he was dating a few months ago?" I get a stiff nod, and she reaches back for my free hand.

My phone buzzes a text notification. It's the third one since the ceremony ended, but it'll have to wait. When it's finally our turn, we leave the sanctuary and make our way outside, breathing a sigh of relief when we are safely tucked into the car.

"That was awful. I'm not going to make it through the reception." Lis drops her head back to the seat and stares at the ceiling of the car. "Why did I bother getting a dress to match the wedding party? It makes no sense. This is ridiculous, I shouldn't have come."

I hate the doubt and self-deprecation. Shifting in my seat, I turn her face to mine, making sure I've got her attention. "You're here because it's the right thing to do, you know that. If I'm honest, your family is like nothing I've ever seen before. They are absolutely toxic." She rolls her eyes and huffs out a small snort. "I don't know how you're related to them, seriously. I can't for the life of me figure out why that arsehole picked her over you," I rush to smooth what was not meant as a hurtful comment, "but I thank God, every day, that he did. I may thank Rob personally at the party, buy him a drink. I definitely have the better of the sisters."

"Thank you." The smile, the peace spreading across her face makes me feel good. Like I've gotten through to her. "You're very sweet, but you know you don't have to say those things, right?" I start to protest in earnest when she winks. "And if you play your cards right, I'll even go home with you tonight. Let's just get this done. Make our appearance, have a couple drinks and leave."

The reception is even more of an event. It's not just a couple drinks type of party. There's a formal dinner with table assignments and dining partners.

I grab a couple whiskeys from the open bar handing Lis a glass as her mother sidles over to us.

"I didn't realize you were bringing someone with you. We'll have to make space at one of the tables for your friend." The dismissive flip of her wrist should have bothered me. But the fact that she has no interest, no respect for her daughter is what has my ire up.

"Aidan, this is my mother, Anna Rittenhouse. Mom, this is—"

I extend my hand, all my manners on full display. "Aidan Kearney, ma'am. It's a pleasure to meet you."

She reluctantly places her hand in mine. Her handshake is as cold as her assessment of me.

"You're not from here." The woman is brilliant.

"No, I'm not. But I've found the best reason to stay." I pull my hand back and place it possessively around Lis' waist.

Anna looks from my hand to Lis, from Lis to me and back again.

"Well. I'll figure out the seating." And away she goes snapping at the poor wait staff lugging a tray laden with champagne glasses. *"We've had an unexpected guest show up. You'll have to add a place to table—"*

"So, that's my mom." Lis takes a tiny sip of her whiskey and shakes her head. "And you've already met Maryse and Rob, so now is your chance to run. Take off before it's too late." Her small laugh and nervous smile trying to cover her discomfort.

"Love, it's already too late. I'm not going anywhere." The kiss is just barely on the right side of appropriate, flushing her cheeks a beautiful rosy pink.

My hand at her back, I guide Lis to our table when the announcement is made to please enter the dining room. As I pull her chair out for her, my phone buzzes a text—and immediately starts the phone call buzz. I pull it from my pocket and see it's Francie.

I decline the call and see a stack of text messages from him, the last demands *CALL ME NOW*.

"Lisbeth, I have to take this. I'll be right back, love." I set my glass in front of her and swipe to call Francie as I make my way out to the lobby.

"Christ, ye need to get your arse here, now. Did ye know? Did ye think to tell me she was comin'? How does Lis feel about this?"

It's rapid fire, question after question.

"Francie, what are you talkin' 'bout? Slow down."

"Aidan, Lorna is here. In the pub. Said she's here to bring ye home. Ye want to tell me what this is about?" I can practically hear his blood vessels popping through the phone.

"I don't know. I've been trying to reach her for weeks and have heard nothing. When did she get there? And what the fuck—she wants to bring me home?" My mind is racing. What is she doing here? Why now? Should she even be traveling?

"She's been here an hour or so. I tried to feed her, but the girl's exhausted. Looks like she's been up for days. Aidan —"

Pinching the bridge of my nose, I huff out, "Tell her I'll be there in a minute. Let me—let me tell Lis I have to go." I end the call and see Lis' sister smirking at me over her glass of champagne.

Fuck.

THIRTY-SIX

Aidan

The look on Lis' face nearly killed me. The disappointment. The resignation. And ultimately the acceptance that I was leaving her to the wolves. I could see them circling with their teeth bared, ready to descend on her.

I hope with all my racing heart that Maryse didn't hear as much of my phone call as I think she did. I can only imagine how she would spin things if she had half a mind to.

I cringe thinking of the way she smirked at me like she had the world's juiciest secret.

This day could fuck right off.

I'M RELIEVED that she's okay. She looks fantastic, actually. She's sitting at the small table at the back of the pub, feet on the chair across from her, smiling down at her phone.

"Hey, how are ye?" Lorna's head pops up at the sound of my voice and a huge smile breaks across her face.

"Aidan—God, it's good to see you." She struggles a little as she stands, rolling her eyes at my offered hand. "I've got it, come here and give us a hug. I've missed you."

I wrap her up in my arms, relief washing through me.

"What are you doing here? Should you be traveling like this?" I pull back and look at her round belly.

"Yeah, I'm fine for a few more weeks." She smiles softly as she rubs her hand across her bump. "I missed you, Aidan, a lot. I needed to see you before—before this has me all tied up. How are you doing?" She sits back down, reaching for the other chair to prop her feet up again.

"I'm good, really good. Can I—let me get us a couple drinks, are you hungry?" She shakes her head and I pop into the kitchen to grab myself a sandwich and crisps.

The hors d'oeuvres from the cocktail hour are long gone and I'm starving. I throw a couple extra pickles on my plate, not because it's a pregnant cliché, but I've known Lorna forever and pickles are her thing.

I set the plate down and grab a water for her and a pint for myself.

"Did ye put extra pickles on here for me? You're a prince, man. God love ye." She's tearing into my plate without abandon.

"Jesus, d'ya want your own?" Lorna smiles at me and around the bite of turkey sandwich—my turkey sandwich. I push the plate in front of her and head back to the kitchen to make another for myself.

Francie pokes his head out of the tiny office off the kitchen. Pinning me with a glare, eyebrow cocked, he silently questions me. "Francie, she's just here for a visit before the baby comes. That's all."

"Not the way it sounded earlier when she showed up." He folds his arms, resting them on his paunch trying to make himself look the part of the stern father.

"Lisbeth?"

I cringe, knowing I deserve his judgment for this. "She's at the wedding reception, her sister's. I'm sure she'll be here soon."

"I don't like it, Aidan."

I feel like an arse for leaving her there, but what other choice did I have?

My thoughts run in a muddled mess as I turn back to rejoin Lorna.

Holding my plate out of her reach, I drop a few more pickles to hers.

"You're lovely, ye know that? Mmm, so good." She mumbles, brushing the crumbs off her hands. "Sorry, didn't realize I was so hungry until I saw yours. So, you're good? Better? Ready to come home?" Lorna bobs her head from side to side while taking me in. "You're dressed awfully posh, were ye out, then?"

"I am good, much better, and I was out. At a wedding, actually."

"You're working again then? That's fantastic. You're far too good at what you do to waste time tending bar and mucking about."

"I am, but—" My words forgotten when Lorna grabs my hand and places it on her belly, pressing it flat.

"Was that? That's the baby moving?"

"It is. He's really strong." She says gently.

He. It's a boy.

"I'd like to name him Michael Aidan. After the two men who mean the most to me."

"Lorna, that's—I-I'd be honored."

It's not fair that my brother is missing all this. He wanted to be a father more than anything. It kills me knowing the last thing he did before finding out his death sentence, was create this life. He should be here. He should have his hand on his wife's belly, feeling his boy kicking and rolling and moving. These moments should be Michael's.

Lorna slides both hands over the top of mine, holding me in place. She talks quietly, telling me everything will be okay. Soothing me, like I'm the widow facing this alone. I cover my face with my free hand, letting the tears come.

Not the wracking sobs from right after his death, but silent sad tears mourning Michael's loss of this gift. Tears for this child having to grow up not knowing his father and the man he was. Not truly knowing how desperately he was wanted.

The slamming of the pub door against the quiet of the room, pulls me out of my moment. I wipe my tears and take some deep breaths, pushing down the pain in my heart.

"I'm sorry. I thought I was over it, but—God, he's really gone. And this sweet child will never know him." I brush at the tears that continue to fall.

"I know. Believe me, I understand. I've done nothing but cry and ask *why* for months." Lorna slides my pint across the table. I take a healthy draught and steel myself.

Of course, she has. She's been alone through all of this. Dealing with the pain and the guilt and the loss of her husband. Knowing she's going to have to be both mum and dad to this child.

"There is a way." I lift my head and meet her eyes, hesitancy clouding them.

"There's a way for what?"

"For his father to be in his life. For him to know Michael in a sense." Lorna's voice wavers with uncertainty.

I shake my head, not understanding what she's trying to say.

"Come home, Aidan. Come home with me and...we're a good team. We can do this. Together." Her plea, the only thing sounding in the pub.

"What?" Not sure that I heard her right, I search her face, fear written all over it.

"You were close to Michael. You were there with me through everything." She can't mean it. "Aidan, you're the only one who truly understands. He would want you to be a part of his son's life. You're so much like him it would be like his father was here. Please."

Nonononono. "Lorna, I can't take Michael's place. I—"

"Sorry. No, you're right. I shouldn't have asked. Shouldn't have even implied."

She's a flurry of nervous hands and false laughter, not meeting my eye. "I should have gone on a beach holiday instead. This was a mistake. I'll—I'll just call a cab and go. I'm sorry."

"Lorna, stop. You can't just turn around and go. You've got to be exhausted." She's staring at her bag, sniffling quietly. "Come on. Let's get you settled and we'll talk in the morning, after you've slept."

She nods and wipes at her cheeks.

"Where are you booked in?"

Still not meeting my eye, she replies barely audibly, "I didn't book anything. I-I thought I could stay with you."

I run my hand down the scruff on my jaw and nod once, pulling my phone from my pocket. I need to call Lis and let her know we have a guest tonight. Shit, I need to call my mum and let her know that Lorna's alright. That she's here, I'm not sure that she's alright. Swiping at my screen I see a text from Lis.

L: At Gracyn's. Staying here tonight.

A: Sounds good. Need to talk in the morning.

I grab Lorna's bag and guide her out the door, feeling eyes on me the whole way. Holding the door, I catch Francie leaning in the doorway of the kitchen, the corners of his mouth turned down. I know he's worried, but it's Finn who makes me pause. Hands braced on the bar, his eyes are narrowed and full of disgust. And they're aimed right at me.

He throws the towel to the bar and brushes past Francie, muttering *feckin' bastard*. I'm all but certain I hear the sound of his fist hitting the wall as the door shuts behind me.

Lorna falls asleep on the short drive to my flat, exhausted, I'm sure from the travel and emotions resurfacing. Wanting to wake her gently, I smooth her blond hair back from her forehead. "Lorna, we're here. Come on, let's get you to bed."

I take her bag straight back to the bedroom pointing out the bathroom and kitchen on the way. With Lis spending the night at Gracyn's, it makes sense for Lorna to have the bed. I grab a pair of shorts and a t-shirt from the dresser before turning to face her.

"I'll take the couch. My girlfriend is spending the night at her friend's flat, so just make yourself comfortable. I'll, erm

—I'll let her know you're here and we'll all chat in the morning."

"Girlfriend? You're living with her? Is it—is it serious?"

She wraps her arms around herself, again keeping her gaze from meeting mine.

"It is. Go to sleep, we'll talk tomorrow." I drop a kiss on her forehead and wish her a good night. My heart breaks for Lorna as I head down the hall.

I loosen my tie and grab some blankets and a pillow from the hall closet, throwing them to the couch.

Relieved to see nothing new from Lis, I call my mum, peeling off my suit while I fill her in on Lorna.

Lis

I can't stay at this reception any longer. I have smiled and nodded politely through all the comments about everyone assuming it would be me and Rob getting married. I have answered all the tacky questions about when Rob and Maryse "started" dating. I stuff down my desire to tell every single one of them what a lying cheating bastard he is and how much they deserve the misery of each other.

But I don't.

I sip my drink, far slower than I want to. It's the same one I started the night with. Aidan was supposed to be by my side for this. He was supposed to be my buffer from all of these shitty meddling people. When he told me he had to leave, that Francie called with an emergency, I tried to be understanding. I tried to have a brave face.

I tried.

I set the watered-down whiskey on the table with a sigh

and reach for my bag to order an Uber and meet Aidan at McBride's.

Somehow, I've been able to avoid Rob's parents. Do they know he cheated on me? Do they care? I don't know. I've managed to avoid Maryse and Rob, too.

Until now.

Like she's on a mission, Maryse bustles through her audience cutting off my escape. "You weren't going to leave without saying goodbye, were you?" Hand on her hip, champagne glass in the other, she literally blocks me from leaving.

I paste a smile on my face. "Of course not, Maryse. Congratulations to you both and thank you for inviting me to celebrate with you. Your wedding was just lovely." My words are as fake as our relationship and it shows.

I try to step around her, but she's not done with me.

"Where'd your date go? Couldn't keep hold of him either?" she sneers.

"What? For the love of God, Maryse, leave it alone. You won, okay? You have Rob, and really, Aidan wanted to thank you both for that in person, but he had to leave unexpectedly. There was an emergency and he had to rush off."

I have never understood why she hates me so much, but this is the end.

"Mhmmm—his *emergency*. I heard him on the phone earlier, have fun dealing with that...again."

Why? What is wrong with these people?

The Uber driver tries to make conversation, but I have nothing more for him than an occasional *uh-huh*, and a *thank you* when I hop out at the pub. Thinking my night can't get any worse, I step through the door and my heart—my heart stops.

I close my eyes, trying desperately to convince myself that I'm not seeing this. When I open them again, my heart cracks, the pain slashing through my chest almost convinces me I've died from this.

I drag my gaze to the bar and see Finn seething at Aidan. The sound of a pregnant woman soothing Aidan as he rests his hand on her belly, his shoulders shaking. Telling him they'll be okay.

That's what truly breaks me.

Hopeless and destroyed, once again, in less than a year, I turn and walk away from the man I love. But it's worse this time. So much worse.

Tears stream down my face as the door slams behind me.

What am I going to do? Where am I going to go? I can't go home. Home. God, I can't do this.

On autopilot, I head up the street to my old apartment praying that Gracyn is home. My mind is blank but spinning a hundred miles an hour. My car, he has my car. Kate. Gracyn has a new roommate. I shake my head, running up the stairs. I don't know what I'm going to do if they're not here. I knock on the door and wait. It's Saturday night, they're probably out.

I knock again, *pleasepleaseplease* falling off my tongue.

"Gracyn—please." I call into the crack of the door.

"Lis, honey, what happened? Come here." The sound of her voice, here at the door of this apartment—Gracyn ushers me in and when my back hits the wall, I slide down to a heap on the floor. Down into the misery of another broken heart. Down into the familiar place of despair and confusion.

I let the sobs wash over me and cling to Gracyn. Just

barely registering when she hisses, "I'm gonna fucking kill him."

I CRY.

I sob.

I fall apart tucked into Gracyn's side. And once again, a wad of tissues is thrust into my hand as my best friend soothes my hair out of my face and rubs my back.

"Hey, come on, Lis. Tell me what happened. Where's Aidan?"

All I can manage through the hiccupping sobs is to shake my head. I can't say the words. I can't. I want so much for this not to be real.

"Oh shit." Kate huffs out as she walks out of my bedroom —her bedroom. *What am I going to do?* "Do we know yet if this is a chocolate cry or are we going straight for the tequila?"

"I sure as hell need some tequila, maybe a dull steak knife to castrate the bastard," Gracyn grits out. "I warned him—I told him I'd cut it off if he broke her heart. Jesus."

It should bother me that Gracyn and Kate are talking about me like I'm not here. But their murmured threats and plans to take care of me, protect me, calm my sobs to a steady stream of tears.

"C-can I stay here tonight? I can't go home, G." Kate's face is filled with sympathy as she pushes up off the floor and heads down the hall. "Sorry. I don't—I can find somewhere else."

"Why would you do that?"

Glasses clink in the kitchen before Kate comes back

around the corner. Dropping a t-shirt and leggings on the back of the couch as she passes, with her hands filled with tequila, my bottle of bourbon, and a couple shot glasses.

"Go get changed, Lis, we're gonna need the whole story."

After changing into Kate's clothes and scrubbing my face, I shuffle back into the living room and drop down in the corner of the couch. Gracyn hands me a box of tissues and a tumbler of bourbon while Kate finishes sending a text—from my phone.

"What—did he send a message?" I hate the hope bleeding through my question, my voice still thick with tears.

"You let him know that you're spending the night here." Kate glances down as my phone pings. "And he says he wants to talk in the morning. You ready to spill?"

She powers my phone down and sets it in the kitchen.

"This whole day can eat a dick." I gulp down half my bourbon and revel in the warmth as it slides down my throat. "I was leaving the reception to catch up with Aidan, and Maryse had some shit comment about him running off and that she heard all about his emergency and—"

"Wait, he left you at the reception? What the hell?" Gracyn plops herself on the other end of the couch.

"Yeah, he had a bunch of texts and missed calls. Francie was blowing up his phone. Said there was an emergency and he needed Aidan at McBride's immediately. So, he left and, the things people will say—unreal."

As bad as the wedding was at the time, relaying the horrors of it are far better than thinking about what comes next. I know the wait is killing Gracyn, but she gathers all her patience and fills my tumbler while I tell them about Tyler at the church, the comments at the reception. I even laugh at some of the shit people thought it was okay to ask me.

"But why did he leave you, Lis? What was the big issue at McBride's?" Gracyn pushes me, knowing I'll avoid this as long as I can.

It's not cold in the room at all, but I pull the blanket off the back of the couch, wrapping it around me. When I have that settled, I reach for a throw pillow still feeling far too exposed. Hugging it to my chest, I blow out a big breath readying myself for opening the scabs and scars on my heart.

"I walked into McBride's and he was bent over a pregnant woman with his hand on her belly, crying."

I almost can't get the words out. Tears stream down my face again, the little details I couldn't process at the time are all I can focus on now. The way they held hands, the soft way she looked at him. The sweet lilt of her voice as she talked about this baby—their baby.

"She's Irish, I heard her talking, shushing him while he cried over her. Telling him..." I have to pause. I grab tissues from the table and wipe my tears.

I'm so sick of crying.

"Telling him what, sweetie?" Kate folds her long legs into the chair across from me.

"...that they can get through this together. That everything will be okay, now. They were both folded into each other, crying and holding on to the baby between them. This is worse—so much worse."

The pain where my heart used to beat is excruciating. It's off the pain scale. The pile of tissues on my lap is growing with each passing minute.

"Maybe...maybe it's not what it looked like?" Kate offers

hopefully. "How pregnant do you think? Could it, I don't know..."

"It doesn't matter. Tonight, we drink and eat ice cream. Tomorrow, we'll deal with this shit." Gracyn nods, her plans made, everything in its tidy little box.

I just can't with this whole thing. I reach for the bottle, filling my tumbler again.

I FELL ASLEEP CURLED into the couch with Gracyn tucked into the opposite end. My face is swollen from crying, my head hurts from bourbon and I drag myself into the bathroom to see just how bad the damage is.

One quick glance in the mirror and I get the shower going. With my forehead on the cold granite counter top, I dig deep, building the wall back up around my heart. With repetition, comes strength. There are so many sayings for moments like these. Lemons and lemonade. Bootstraps. Not getting more than you can handle. I run through them like a mantra as I shower and grab some clothes from Gracyn's room.

I braid my hair, and tiptoe to the kitchen, grabbing my phone. There are no new messages when I power it back on. Just the one Kate sent last night and Aidan's response.

I order an Uber and jot Kate and Gracyn a note. Gracyn would go with me in a heartbeat, but I need to do this alone. I grab a coffee from the bakery across the street and send Aidan a text that I'm on my way.

THIRTY-SEVEN

Lis

I haven't heard from Aidan, but the door is unlocked like he's waiting for me. I shouldn't feel nervous walking into our apartment, but my palms are sweating and the hairs are standing up on the back of my neck.

"Aidan?"

He doesn't answer, but I hear water filling the tub. Could I have totally misread what I saw? Maybe it's not what I thought. I drop my purse on the counter next to where he left my keys and head down the hall.

The sheets are rumpled on my bed, my candles are lit in the bathroom. And the woman he was with last night walks out of my bedroom with my robe wrapped around her perfectly round pregnant belly.

Nonononono.

"Back already, love? Did you forget your wallet?" Her singsong voice slices through me and I can't help the gasp that escapes me. Startled, her hand flies to her chest and, "Jaysus wept, ye scared me."

I have no words. My mouth opens and closes, but nothing. I stand there like an idiot staring at her, my heart trying to decide whether to race—or just stop.

"You're Lis, then." She looks me up and down, appraising me. Her tone is not as sweet as when she thought I was Aidan. Her eyes narrow. "He's not here. He ran out to grab a few things, for the next couple days, just until we go to the city this week."

"Who—wh-what do you mean?" There they are, those words I've been waiting for. And they are absolute gibberish.

"Aidan and I are going to the city. He's a job there this week and then we're on to Dublin. Did he not tell you?" Her hand rubs lazy circles on her belly drawing my attention to the baby growing in there.

She knows his schedule. She's in my house.

Cocking her brow, she jeers, "He didn't tell you about this then, either? To be fair, it happened just before he left. Aidan didn't even know about the baby for a few months. He needed to get away and I love him enough to have given him that. But you have to understand, we always planned to raise our kids together. Always. And that didn't change with Michael's death."

Her hands are splayed across her, smoothing my robe. Showing off the innocent child that will kill me.

There is no way in hell that I can come between them. I can't do it. Aidan was obviously hers first. They have a past.

And that past is growing into Aidan's future.

Nodding my head, listening to her words, it becomes

clear to me. I love him too much for there to be any other choice.

"I-I need to grab some of my things. I—"

"Of course. I'll just pop in to take my bath, stay out of your way." She smiles victoriously.

I won't keep him away from this baby.

The quiet click of the bathroom door launches me into action. I grab my suitcase and fill it with clothes, throwing shoes on top of my scrubs, clearing out as much as I can jam in there. Shoving my makeup into my computer bag.

With a quick look around the room, my eyes land on the picture on Aidan's nightstand. It's from the beach. He's squinting at me, the bright sunlight glinting off the water. We're laughing, his arms thrown around me. Arms I thought would keep me safe, give me comfort.

Arms that will soon be holding and loving a new baby.

Willing my tears away, I twist off the beautiful ring he gave me and set it in front of the picture frame. My bags behind me, I rush through the apartment stopping only to grab my purse and keys.

I stumble on the stairs, laden down with my heavy bags, barely catching myself before I fall. I need to go. I need to be gone before Aidan comes back.

I shove everything into my car and drive straight back to Gracyn's curling up on her couch and losing what's left of my heart.

Aidan

My love-hate relationship with the pub is strong this morning. Finn insisted on ripping my arse, face to face, and I missed Lis' text while he was stressing just how badly I'd fucked up with her.

"Fuckin' watched 'er 'eart break when she walked in the door."

His fist takes me by surprise, snapping my head back.

"Told ye I'd kick yer arse, if ye fuckin' dicked 'er 'round."

As his fist struck my jaw for the second time, it pounded home the fact that what she walked in on may have looked very different from what it was. I thought I would be introducing my best friend and the love of my life, but now I need to do a little crisis management instead.

Busting through the door of the flat, I call out for Lisbeth.

"She's come and gone already. I was in the bath, but it sounded like she packed a bag and left," Lorna answers around her cup of tea.

I push past her, striding into the bedroom. The bed is perfectly made, everything looks in order, but her case and computer are gone. Her drawers and closet empty. I pull out my phone and click on her contact. Six rings. Six hundred beats of my heart, and no answer. I try again. And again. I try until my calls are automatically rejected.

I send text after text. I'm on the tenth message when I see they're not being delivered.

"What happened? What did she say?"

This is so much worse than I ever imagined. I turn, facing Lorna, pleading for her to help me make sense of this. My skin is too tight, and my jaw aches from Finn's right hook.

Lorna gasps as she feathers her fingers over my swelling cheekbone. "Oh my God, Aidan what happened? Were you attacked?"

I push her hand away, shaking my head.

"Lorna, what happened?"

Tears cloud her eyes. "I'm sorry, Aidan. She said she made a mistake. That you were just a distraction." She puts her hand on my arm trying to ease the bomb she just dropped on me. "She said if you love her at all, you'll respect her need for time and a little distance. She suggested you go home, visit your parents while she sorts herself." Tentatively, she wraps her arms around my waist, hugging me.

Resting a hand on her shoulder, I close my eyes trying to figure out what to do.

How often have I told Lis that I don't want to be a distraction? That I won't come between her and school. Maybe I pushed her too hard. Wanted her too fast.

She pulled back after our first dinner out, it took her weeks to come back 'round and talk to me. The time we spent in the garden and then the darkroom. That's when things really changed. I should have held back, not taken advantage of the heat of that. Fucking hell, I couldn't even help her study for her class, without having to push things further.

And then pushing her to move in—make this commitment.

I look at the wall above our bed. The picture I took of her in the garden, sunlight filtering all around her. The one of her soaking in the tub, bubbles spilling over the edges. Moments of love captured and frozen in time.

"Can you give me a minute? I need to talk to—" My voice thick with emotion, I realize the only person I want to talk to, is the one who needs space. The one who needs time away from me. I untangle myself from Lorna and wait as she closes the door softly behind her.

I sag down on the edge of the bed, elbows on my knees. I shouldn't have left her last night. She needed me and I left. Finn was fucking right. I failed her when she fucking needed me the most.

I call Gracyn, desperate to know where Lisbeth is, but the call goes nowhere. She must have blocked my number.

The only thing I can do is give her what she's asked for. All I've wanted was to help her, to make things easier for her. To give her the love and support she needed to reach her goal —and I fucked it all up.

I drop my head into my hands making peace with what I know I have to do. The light streaming in through the window glints off the photo Lis took of us at the beach.

I pick up the frame and knock something to the floor. When my fingers meet cold metal, the lump in my throat becomes too hard to swallow around. I clutch her ring over my heart. My arse hits the floor when I slide down off the mattress, my back propped against the side of the bed. I don't know how long I sit there, the symbol of all I hoped for clutched to the spot Lis always rested her hand. I held it right fucking there yesterday.

Scrubbing the tears from my face, I stand and slide the ring on the little finger of my left hand. Without thinking I reach for Lis' school bag knowing she keeps a pad of paper in there. My hand drops to my side and with a shuddering breath it hits me again that she's gone.

I shuffle out to the kitchen and pull my credit card from my wallet, letting it fall to the counter. I slide it to Lorna. "I have to run out, need to let Francie know I'm leaving. Can"— Jesus, I can't believe I'm doing this—"can you book me a flight home? End of this week, if you can get us on the same flight. I'll be done with the shoot late Thursday, so—I don't know, as soon as possible."

My eyes never leave the counter as the images of eating breakfast—making dinner—with Lis flash through my memory.

FRANCIE OPENS his door after three raps of my knuckles and zeroes right in on the bruise blossoming on my cheek.

"Looks like Finn talked to you already. Come in and tell me your troubles, then."

Francie's little house backs up to the pub and looks like an eighty-year-old grandmother lives here. He straightens a lacy circle on the back of a chair before offering me a seat on the dainty floral couch.

It's my first time here and I can't help looking for the twenty-three cats he's probably collecting.

I perch on the edge of the uncomfortable couch, hating what I came here to say. There's no reason to put it off any longer. I twirl my key ring around the key to McBride's.

"I'm leaving."

He leans back into the uptight chair he's sitting in, his forehead wrinkled in surprise. "That's not what I expected. Have ye told Lis?"

"It was her idea, Francie. Said I was a distraction. To go home and see my family while she sorts herself."

I feel him staring at me, but I can't face him. I can't look him in the eye.

"I leave in the morning for a photo shoot in New York City and then we'll fly out Friday. Don't know when I'll be back."

I pull the key to the pub off the ring and place it on the glass-topped coffee table.

"We?"

"I'm booked on the same flight as Lorna." My voice catches and I have to swallow back the tears that burn behind my lids. "It just makes sense to travel home with her."

"Not a thing about this makes sense and ye know it." He fixes me with the same look he gave me last night.

"Leaving Lisbeth is the last thing I want to do," I grind out, pain shooting through my bruised face as I work my jaw back and forth.

"Then why are you doin' it? Stay. Tell 'er how important she is. That you'll do what she needs, stay out of 'er way, if that's what she wants. But do it from here."

He's spent so much time in the past six months threatening me—pushing me away from her. The change of heart throws me off.

"Why? She doesn't want me here. Why are you so invested in this now? You've been warning me off at almost every turn."

"Because I love that girl like she's my own. And I've not seen her this happy, this settled in all the time I've known her. Let me talk to her, find out her reasoning before you go."

He's right. Nothing makes sense anymore.

I pull the envelope from my back pocket, her ring safely tucked inside. "I'm going. I'll visit my family, then...I don't know, then I'll come back if she wants me. Will you give her this, though? Please?"

He makes me wait a lifetime, before he reaches out to take the envelope.

A tight-lipped nod.

A heartfelt hug.

A silent farewell.

And I go back to the flat I shared with Lis for far too little time. Avoiding Lorna, I go straight to the bedroom and pack my bag, only what I need for work and a visit to my parents. The rest of my stuff I box up and move to the storage room off the kitchen.

THIRTY-EIGHT

Lis

Five days. He's been gone five days and I'm pretty sure I'm dying.

He's not even really gone, though. Or maybe he is. I don't know.

I knew he would be in the city all week, I was prepared for that part. I was prepared to spend all weekend just being with him, neither one of us scheduled to work.

I never imagined that I would lose him.

Stupid.

So instead of hanging out all weekend with Aidan, I wake up on Gracyn's couch again. Not that I really slept. I can't.

"Hey, what are you doing awake so early?" Gracyn shuffles out and drops down in the corner of the couch.

"Not really sleeping all that great." I push up so I'm sitting in the opposite corner, blankets all wrapped around me. "What did I miss? I just don't understand, G."

She doesn't have the answer any more than I do.

There is no answer.

"You should come out with us tonight, Lis. Just for one drink—" She starts pushing as soon as I start shaking my head.

"I don't think so. I...I have things I have to take care of today. I need," Lord, this hurts, "I need to find a place to live."

I twist the blanket around my fingers, avoiding looking at her.

"Nuh uh. This is your apartment too. You can stay here as long as you need."

"I can't. It's not fair to you and it sure isn't fair to Kate. She moved in here to get away from relationship shit, she doesn't need mine."

I'm feeling so sorry for myself, I can't even pretend to hide it.

"Fine. Look for a place, but you can't commit to anything today. Promise me. And come out for a drink with us. You can't sit here all weekend, you have to get out."

I open my laptop and start looking for a place to live while Gracyn makes coffee. There's nothing. Nothing I can afford alone.

"Mornin'." Kate stumbles out in a hungover haze and heads straight for the kitchen.

I know it's fruitless, but I do a search for roommates wanted and come up empty there as well. Kate and Gracyn bring steaming cups of coffee and the rest of last night's pizza, dropping the box on a stack of magazines on the table.

Kate dives into the pizza, not saying another word until

she's downed two slices. "So, you're going out with us tonight?"

Jesus, it's not even ten o'clock in the morning and the hungover kindergarten teacher is making drinking plans for the night.

I tilt my head side to side, not ready to commit. "Maybe? I guess?"

Kate nods like it's a done deal—set in stone—while I'm still trying to think of ways to get out of going.

"I'm gonna run some errands this morning, I-I'll be back later."

I climb off the couch, starting back toward Gracyn's room. She cleared some space in her closet for me but this needs to end. I can't stay on the couch for much longer.

"Want me to come with you?" Gracyn is right behind me. Ready to catch me, like she knows I'm gonna fall.

"No, I just..." I don't know what I need. Well, I do, but he's gone. "I just need some alone time. I need to figure this out, G."

I grab some clothes and shower as fast as I can. I miss my bathroom. I miss my tub. I miss Aidan.

I get in my car and drive aimlessly. People are out, living their lives and I'm—I'm what? Sleeping on my best friend's couch, because someone else is living in my old room.

Just like someone else is loving my old boyfriend.

I stop at the farmer's market on my way through town and grab a couple peaches and a scone. Cold pizza didn't do it for me earlier.

Without thinking, I drive north toward the river and head to the mansion. I sit on the massive stone deck, leaning against a marble column. Usually this place gives me such peace, a sense of calm. Today, my heart hurts and being here, looking out over the water does nothing for me.

I wander down to the gardens. *The gardens.* If I can't get him out of my mind, I might as well surround myself with him. Make myself sick on the memories of us. Maybe then, I can purge them. I sit on steps where Aidan stood taking the picture of me that hangs on our bedroom wall.

My mind won't stop racing through our time together. Looking for the signs I obviously missed. The signs that there was someone else and once again, I am temporary and easily replaced.

"LISBETH, YOU HAVE A MINUTE?" Francie calls to me from the bakery across the street. I'd stayed in the garden far longer than I had planned and of course, got nowhere on finding a place to live. "Come, let me buy you a cuppa and a treat, yeah?"

With a quick check for traffic, I cross the street and run straight into Francie's arms. He holds me tight and pats my back, shushing me until my grip around him relaxes a bit. He guides me inside and to the counter.

"Hey, Roxie, can I have a large iced coffee with almond milk?" I place my order and move to the side.

"A cuppa black for me and two of those chocolate tortes for us. Thanks, love."

I hit the trifecta—groan, eye roll and smile at sweet Francie. "The chocolate. How'd you know I need that?"

"Figure we need it for our chat. How're ya?"

He steps back giving me the lead to find a table. We

settle in by the window and Roxie places our yummies in front of us and skips away. I want to feel that carefree again.

"I'm alright." I shrug a shoulder and pick at the smattering of raspberries centered on the torte.

"Yeah? You're not a very good liar. Never have been." Francie eyes me over his steaming mug and chuckles. "Haven't seen much of ye this week."

I fight the tears and push a big sigh out through my nose, lips rolled in between my teeth. I shrug again.

"I didn't really feel like peopling this week."

"Stop playin' wit' your food and eat it already. Where've you been? Stayin' wit' Gracyn? Doesn't she have a new roommate now?"

I nod, taking a bite of the dense chocolate cake. Trying hard not to think of all the times Aidan and I shared this dessert—the heat in his eyes as I slid the decadent confection off my fork.

"Mhmmm. I looked online for a new place, but I can't afford anything on my own, and the whole strange roommate thing freaks me out. I-I miss—"

"I know. Still don't understand what happened," he says.

I have nothing to say. I don't really know what happened either, so I stare out the window and avoid looking at my friend. When enough time has passed, that he knows I'm not going to make eye contact, Francie pulls an envelope from his shirt pocket and places it on the table in front of me.

"He came by Sunday. Asked me to make sure ye got this. I held off hoping he'd come to his senses, but..."

I tear my eyes away from the pot of flowers I've been staring at and look at the envelope. My name is scrawled across the front of it. Aidan's ridiculously beautiful writing over the top of an odd bulge.

"I don't want it. I don't need his excuses."

I push it away, the bulge taking shape.

Nonono.

Tears form and hang on my lashes. "I can't, Francie."

"Lissy, I don't know much about anythin' other than nothin', but I can recognize when things have gone tits up. You're both thinkin' the worst and maybe...maybe you're both wrong." He slides a napkin across the table to me. "Do you want me to leave ye while ye read it?"

I dab at my tears and shake my head. "Stay." I hold the envelope, feeling the weight of it, knowing that it's going to rip the scab off the barely stemmed flow of my fragile heart.

I unfold his note, placing the ring on table next to my plate. The words blur as my hands tremble and shake.

Lisbeth,

This ring is yours, always. How you wear it is up to you. I want it all, but I'm afraid I've driven you away and that was never my intent.

I'm away to Dublin to see my family and give you the space you need. The last thing I ever wanted was to become a distraction. You and your needs were always first and foremost in my mind.

Our flat is paid up through the end of your school term. Stay there. I want to know that you've a safe place to stay. I'll stay at the loft when I get back.

"Too many people know the price of everything

and the value of nothing." I value every moment we've spent together, and every memory we've made.

I love you always,
Aidan

OSCAR WILDE—HE quoted Oscar Wilde. My heart tap dances beneath my ribs.

"I don't know where you both got lost, but I've not seen that man as devastated since he showed up in my pub after his brother died, Lis. Sure, it didn't help that Finn got his fists to him first, but Aidan was ruined."

I twirl the ring around on the table, lift it and test it out on my pointer finger, spinning it around. "What do you mean? Finn hit him?"

Something feels off—wrong—somehow.

"Called him to the pub Sunday morning and laid him low. Told him how things might've looked to ye, not knowing Lorna." Francie stacks his empty plates and pushes them to the edge of the table.

"What?"

THIRTY-NINE

Aidan

"These were the only seats available when you booked us?"

I fold myself into the postage stamp-sized space. In the center of the plane. In the middle bank of seats. In the center of the row. And all I have running through my head is the song "Stuck in the Middle with You," Bublé's version, not the old one. We're so tucked in here, changing seats with Lorna won't win me any extra leg room.

"There were the two seats in first class." She smirks at me.

This last-minute fare set me back a ridiculous amount of money, no way was a first-class upgrade even an option. I push myself back into my seat as far as I can, hating everything about this trip.

I check my phone for the millionth time this week, the millionth time today. Not that I really expect Lisbeth to call or text, not if I've been labeled a distraction. I have seven hours of absolutely no distractions to think about what happened. To think about Lis.

The past week had been so busy with shoots, editing the final product and getting things squared away for the week or so that I'll be gone. I don't intend for it to be any longer than that. I've started building my life—the life I want is here in the States.

I scrub my hands over my face, and check my phone one last time before turning it off for the flight. I try again to relax and get comfortable, but it's just not going to happen. The flight attendants run through their bit and I really only pay attention when they get to the part about the booze available.

"You excited to go home?" Lorna tries to chat with me, but I'm tired. I'm cranky.

"Yeah. Sure." I close my eyes, hoping she'll stop. I just don't want to talk.

"Your mum will be so happy to have you back." She's not getting it.

I tune her out for a bit as the plane taxis and takes off, counting the minutes for the pub in the sky to open and let me drown my sorrows.

It's pretty obvious I've been ignoring Lorna when my eyes pop open at the formal offer of a beverage. I order whiskey for me and the three pregnant women in my row, not that I plan on sharing with them.

How does that even happen? How is it that I'm squished into this tiny space with three women growing tiny humans? Maybe that's why it feels so damn crowded in here.

"Thanks," I mumble as the four little bottles of liquor are distributed through the row, along with the drinks the ladies actually wanted. I'm not fooling anyone and we all know it.

The stewardess, Marta, must feel for me, or something. The little bottles appear on my tray table as soon as Marta moves on to the next row.

As the third one empties down my throat, Lorna starts again, trying to draw me out of my fit.

"It's been almost six months, Aidan. It's time you're home. Your family needs you. The life you have in Dublin is still there for you."

"My life is in New York," I huff out, disgusted with this whole thing. "What—what exactly did she say to you, Lorna? It's killing me. I feel like I finally found what you and Michael had. I love her, fought so hard to get her to trust me, to give me a chance."

I roll my head on the seat back to face her. I line the empty bottles up in a nice neat row across the top edge of my tray. "What did I do wrong? How did I screw this up?"

We've been friends for so long. So. Long. Surely Lorna can help me understand where I went wrong. Her cool hand picks up mine, stilling it from the nervous fiddling with the bottles. She holds it possessively on her belly, my nephew moving and stretching. The pressure calming both of us, lulling both the baby and me into a state of security.

Lorna's melodic voice is quiet, soothing. She practically coos at me.

"She said she made a mistake. That she was wrong about your relationship. Said you're not right for each other, and she was going to go home, spend time with her family as well, and focus on herself. That she needed time for her."

Lies. Nothing but lies and they roll off her tongue effortlessly.

I pull my hand back and glare at her while keeping my voice even and low. "You're full of shite."

Lorna and the woman on the other side of me both gasp.

"Wh-what? I—no—that's what she said." Lorna's face is turning red and her left eye is twitching. It's her tell.

This girl and I lied our way out of all kinds of mischief growing up, I've seen that eye twitch more than I care to think of right now.

"Her family's not in her life. Certainly, they're not her 'safe' place. Not where she'd go to sort herself." I turn toward her as much as I can in this tiny seat. "What really happened? Tell me the fucking truth, Lorna. The truth."

HER DECEPTION IS TOO MUCH. The way she played Lis, the lies she wove, there's no excuse for those. Having to sit next to her for the remainder of that flight while she cried and I seethed was uncomfortable for everyone around us.

All of that is enough to send me off the deep end. As soon as the plane lands, I pull the airline website up on my phone and try as I might, I can't make a reservation on a flight back. I close down my phone and tuck it away as I approach the customs area. The anger vibrating inside me is barely contained as I stride through to the next available agent.

"Papers."

I shove them across the counter.

"Can you help me? I tried to make a return reservation as soon as I deplaned and the system won't let me. Do you know what that's about?"

I need to get back to the States as soon as possible. I need to explain to Lis what happened—that Lorna lied.

To both of us.

"Sir, there seems to be an issue with your last visa. How long were you out of the country?" *Fuck.*

"Since March? But I started the process of renewing it—changing the designation before I left the States. I need to get back."

He flips my passport closed, hands it back to me and waves me through.

"You'll want to go to the state department and start working on that to get things sorted. Should be able to travel back in a couple months. Next."

"What? No, I can't wait. I have to go back soon—now."

He yells, "Next" again, and I'm absolutely fucked.

Lorna sniffles as she takes her papers from the agent next to mine and moves slowly toward baggage claim to collect her case.

"Did you hear that? Did you, Lorna?" I'm doing everything not to draw attention, but I'm livid. "I'm stuck here, for months. Months until I can get back to Lis and try to fix this shit."

I'm tired. My face is red and I am shaking all over and no matter how much control I want to have, my voice is rising. I'm not surprised to see a TSA agent striding toward us.

"Is there a problem here? Ma'am, do you need us to escort this man away? Is he threatening you?" He's got a hand on his baton and one on his walkie, ready to call for backup.

"No, I'm fine. Thank you." Thank Christ.

"About fucking time you start telling the truth." I

grumble it low. The last thing I need is to be detained in the airport.

"I'm sorry, Aidan. I'm so sorry."

I'm done with her. Done. But I'm not a complete asshole. I grab both of our cases from the conveyor and head for the exit.

It's pissing rain and my phone pings as I move off to the side of the door.

It's my dad.

Traffic is snarled and he's going to be a bit.

It's the middle of the night in Beekman Hills, but I don't care. I send the first of what will be a million texts to Lisbeth, hoping she'll listen—that she'll forgive this mess.

FORTY

My phone has been pinging with incoming texts since two o'clock in the morning. I only hung with Gracyn and Kate until about midnight. We'd had dinner and gone to a club dancing, but when they decided to go to McBride's, I just couldn't.

Not yet.

Instead I grabbed my bag from their apartment and drove home.

Home.

All of Aidan's stuff was in the storage room behind the pantry. His closet empty, his drawers cleared, toiletries gone. I had a new understanding of how he must have felt when he saw the empty spaces I had left last week.

Only a week has passed. How was that possible? It feels like a lifetime.

I twist my ring in my pocket. I still can't put it back on,

but also can't bear to not have it near. I'm not sure I'll ever be able to.

Searching for signs that *that woman* left some mark while she was here, I dragged my bag back to our—my room.

I hate her.

There was no way I was willing to take any chances that she'd had the decency to change the sheets before she left, so after taking care of that, I crawled into bed. I flipped and rolled until I finally got comfortable only to hear the pinging of my text notification. I had turned it off, but now—now it's time.

THERE ARE MORE than twenty messages. Mostly from Aidan, telling me he loves me, needs to talk to me. They are full of excuses, claiming I don't understand. *No shit.*

The last one though, is long. Desperate, almost. His tone is different, prompting me to really read it, not just scroll through it like I did with the others.

A: Please call me as soon as you get this. I'm stuck. I can't get back to you. This is the biggest cockup ever and I need to talk to you, I need to see you and I fucking can't. Please, Lis. Please call me.

I lay there thinking. Do I want to talk to him? Do I want to give him a chance to feed me lines and bullshit excuses?

I feel so overwhelmed between the letter yesterday and all of these messages. I don't know what I want.

That's not true. I know what I want, I just don't know that I can have it, that it's still in my reach.

The messages and calls continue, making my phone buzz and ping until I just turn it off again.

I let days pass—weeks. I'm getting ready to start my last semester of college. I can't piss away all my hard work because of a bump in my road. Because I made a mistake. I gave too much of myself, too soon and it ended poorly.

He's all I think about. It's taken until tonight to even step foot back in McBride's, and it was awful. I was nervous walking in there, but it was so much worse than I'd imagined.

The unfamiliar face behind the bar caused my steps to falter. The accent, the lilt of his voice wasn't right when the new bartender asked for my order.

It surprised me, shocked me, that this is what affected me so severely. This was Aidan's place. This was where we started, and in a way, it's where we came undone.

I felt his loss like a heavy blanket, weighing me down. Suffocating me. I couldn't stay, everything about being there felt wrong. I turned and left without a word, shaking the tears away.

Safe in my bed, I read each of his messages. I've read them so many times, I have them memorized yet they give me nothing, no direction. No idea of how to put this behind me and move on. Gripping the case so hard it creaks, I swipe the screen waking the display and see another text from Aidan.

Please.

My thumb hovers over the button, and something in me cracks. I need closure.

The message was sent hours ago. Probably as he was lying in bed. I talk myself in and out of calling him a thousand times before I do it.

"Lisbeth." He answers right away, like his sole purpose since he left was waiting for my call.

It's three o'clock in the morning in Dublin.

"Hey." Now that I've done it, broken down and finally called him, all my thoughts fly from my head, leaving me with nothing.

Silence drags, weighing the air between us. There is so much he needs to explain to me, so much I need to say and suddenly, it doesn't feel right, doing this over the phone. We're too far apart, too disconnected.

"I need to see you." I hardly breathe as I force each syllable past my lips.

"I can't come back, I—there's an issue with my visa. I—"

The words tumble from my mouth. "I'll book a flight. I have a few days right before classes start. I need to know what happened, what I did, where I went wrong. This is my last semester and I can't afford to flake on this now. You owe me this."

I don't know where that strength came from, but the lead blanket that has been sitting on my chest for the past couple of weeks seems to have shifted.

"I'll pay—please—anything." His voice washes over me wrapping me in his sadness.

I'm glad. Glad he's upset, glad that I'm not alone in this.

"No. I've got it. You've paid the rent on our apartment, I can do this. I-I'll send you my arrival information in the morning, but I have to finish up some things here before I leave."

"Of course, yeah." Relief with a touch of desperation, bleeds through the miles.

"I love you, Lisbeth."

"Okay. Um...I'll text you in the morning. Bye." I disconnect quickly, harshly, but that's all I can handle right now.

I pull my computer off the nightstand and book a flight to Dublin.

WHY AM I DOING THIS? The customs area is jam packed with tired cranky people wanting to get their luggage and breathe fresh air for the first time in hours.

I pull my phone out to let Aidan know I've landed. The guy behind me in line taps my shoulder and point to the sign that mobile phone use is strictly prohibited in this area. With a tight smile and a nod of thanks, I put it back in my bag catching the glare of a customs agent.

The line creeps forward so slowly. The thoughts I've barely suppressed since I boarded the plane bombard me. Tired and nervous, I shuffle my feet, one step forward, wait, wait, wait.

Am I going to have to see her? Being civil to that woman is not something I think I can do.

It takes almost an hour to make it through this mess and to baggage claim. The conveyor is empty, bags lined up along the wall—all of them except mine.

My bag sits on the floor next to the man I'm here to see. Hands shoved deep in the pockets of his jeans, he shifts on his feet and smiles tightly.

"Hi." I wipe my sweaty hands on my pants.

"Hey. Did ye have a good flight?"

His gaze bounces from my face to the ceiling, the wall behind me, finally landing on mine.

Pressing my lips together, I nod and lean in to grab my bag.

Aidan stoops, grabbing it before I can get to it, settling it on his shoulder.

All I want is to step into him, his arms wrapped around me—enveloped in him. Instead, I follow silently out to a small blue SUV.

We stand staring at each other over the top of the car, neither of us saying a word.

Things have changed. Every single time we've gone out together, Aidan has always—always—opened my door for me. Until now. I blink back the tears threatening to fall; I shouldn't have come.

"Think you're up to drivin' after your flight?" His voice is soft and a little hesitant. Maybe I'm not the only one feeling off balance right now.

"What? No, I..."

Of course. I'm on the wrong side of the car. My lip between my teeth, I walk around to where Aidan has the door open for me and climb in. I watch him stride around the car, appreciating the way he moves, missing everything about him.

"I brought you a coffee." He nods at the cup holder as the aroma makes its way through my foggy brain. "You probably want to nap, but it really is best to just try and get on the local time." Hotels and long-term parking fly by as I sip. It's perfect—of course it is.

"Thank you. This is great." I don't know what to say, the awkwardness is creeping in. I should have planned this better, I'm here for three days and I didn't think to get a hotel room. Never considered how this would go beyond getting on a plane and seeing Aidan. Talking to him.

I lean my head against the window as we wind through the city, eventually pulling onto a tree-lined street more than an hour after leaving the terminal. "I'm sorry, I didn't know you lived so far from the airport. I could've taken a cab or something."

With my bag in his hand, Aidan guides me through a bright red front door and whispers, "I just wanted to have a quiet moment with you before the pandemonium."

I almost miss his words as he tucks my bag inside the door and a toddler comes tearing around the corner, hands in the air squealing. Aidan scoops him up and tosses him in the air, blowing raspberries into his tummy.

"JAYSUS WEPT, was yer flight delayed getting in? What took ye so long? Come in, love, come in. Och, Aidan, don't wind 'im up like that. We've got 'im all day."

Aidan's mom swoops in and wraps me in a warm strong hug. "I'm so glad to meet you, love. Come in and have a seat. Can I get ye something to eat? Did Aidan show ye through the city in the morning traffic, then?"

She's a flurry of efficiency, taking my jacket, setting my purse on the table by the door.

I try to keep up with her, I do. But I miss half of what she says, unable to focus.

"Um, I-I'm fine, thank you. Mrs. Kearney."

Swaying slightly, I reach for the closest solid surface to steady myself, and find my hand on Aidan's arm.

She smiles as she takes me in. Is it significant that I reach for Aidan when I'm unsteady?

"Love, it's Ann. Come on, then." She's lovely, of course she is.

"D'ye need a moment? To freshen up after your flight?" My breath catches in my chest at Aidan knowing I need to catch my breath.

I turn to him and nod, grateful for him.

"I'll show you up. Henry, go with Granny for a treat, yeah?"

He sets the sweet boy down and grabs my bag, leading me upstairs to a bright sunny bedroom at the back of the house. The pale creamy walls are covered with pictures of Aidan and his siblings. And as much as I want to fall into the soft ivory bedding, I step closer to one of the more recent photos, studying the faces.

"Are you a twin?" I glance over my shoulder knowing that Aidan is still with me.

He's leaning against the doorjamb, arms folded across his chest, looking past me to the framed photograph.

"That's Michael. He was fifteen months older than me."

It hits me then; how little Aidan has talked about his brother with me.

"I'm so sorry." I take a step toward him and stop. I want to go to him, put my hand over his heart. Comfort him.

His gaze settles on mine and he sucks in a deep breath, almost like he's bracing himself. "I want to do this now—talk —get things sorted, but." He glances at his watch and scrubs a hand down his face. "But all hell is about to break loose and we need time."

I scrunch my brows together, not really getting what he's saying, when the front door flies open and the sound of love and laughter float through the house.

"They're all dyin' to meet you, insisted on it, so we'll not have a quiet moment for quite a while." Meeting his family is not what I came here for. This is not how I imagined this would go. Not at all.

"Take some time. The bathroom's just across the hall. I'm so sorry for the chaos, I'm sure it's the last thing you want to do after traveling and...everything." Aidan backs out of the room shaking his head, his smile forced. "Just come down when you're ready, yeah?"

I flop down on the bed, disappointed, annoyed as shit. I feel dizzy, light-headed. Closing my eyes, I breathe deep, trying to calm my racing heart and push down this bitter pill.

Did he plan this? Is this to throw me off balance? Why am I here? Why the fuck am I spending the day with his family? I'm here to say goodbye—to let him go.

I allow myself ten minutes to wallow and curse and mentally stomp my feet before dragging myself to the bathroom. I wash my hands and brush my teeth, trying desperately to center myself for what is, no doubt, going to be the longest day ever.

I swipe on some lip gloss, hoping it's enough armor for what I'm about to face.

FORTY-ONE

Aidan

Chaos is the only way to describe it. My niece and nephews are running around the house. My mum and sisters are waiting to pounce the minute Lisbeth comes down the stairs. And I just want to have her alone. I hate every minute that we have to put off talking. Clearing this mess up.

Good or bad, our day has been taken over by my family. Just as Lis comes down the stairs, Henry rounds the corner at full two-year-old speed. I catch him as he slips, falling on his arse. This is the best age, when they fall and can't quite decide whether they should cry or not. Eyes wide, he looks to me for a hint at what he should do.

Lis claps her hands and smiles huge. "Good job, Henry—look at you!"

It's exaggerated and so over the top, but does the trick and the little monster giggles and reaches for her.

I'm jealous, and horribly in love, as he wraps his chubby little arms around her neck. I want this. Christ, how I want to have this with her. Babies, and little monsters and all the love in the world.

"Thank you," I murmur.

"Of course. He's darling, two-ish?"

"He is. My oldest brother, Sean's, son. They'll be by later." I take a deep breath and blow it out between pursed lips. "Actually, they'll all be by for dinner. I'm sorry. I tried to get them to hold off a day, but—"

"Everyone? What does that mean?" I've not seen her face this hard, tense, not ever. She narrows her eyes at me, her voice cold. "*She* won't be here, will she?" Lis is practically vibrating, she's so tense.

"No. Of course not, they wouldn't do that to you—I wouldn't do that."

The air is thick with tension. I'm ready to grab her hand and pull her out the door. Take her out of here so we can sort this.

My mum's voice rises above the clamoring in the kitchen. "Aidan, bring Lisbeth in here and let us have her a bit. You'll have plenty of time tomorrow." Any hope I had of talking to Lis today dissipates immediately.

I shake my head, afraid to meet Lis' gaze. Her frustration is written all over her face.

Lis slips into the kitchen pasting a polite smile on and sits at the table. Mum and Bridget start asking about her trip and school and how we met while my youngest sister, Kathleen, splashes a little whiskey in each of their coffee mugs.

"Uncle Aidan, will ye take us to the baker for a treat? Mum and Granny said ye would while they talk to yer pretty friend." Eagan's big blue eyes are joined by his big sister's and Henry scrambles down out of Lis' lap.

"Me, too. Wanna go too."

I throw Bridget a look and am met with a bright evil smile and a five-pound note.

"Here's a list for me as well, love. Pick this up while you're out." Mum hands me a scrap of paper and waves me off.

I end up trotting the kids down the lane and back. The baker, the grocer—Mum's planning is impeccable. She's kept me out with the kids until they're all starving and it's Henry's much needed naptime.

"Erin, take this for me." I hand the baker's satchel to my niece and scoop a whining Henry into my arms where his thumb goes straight to his mouth and his blond curls tickle my neck as he nestles in. It takes about four steps for his breathing to even out and he relaxes into me, his bum resting in the crook of my arm and his little legs tucked up between us.

"You gonna marry her? Can we call her Aunt Lis?" Erin lisps over Lisbeth's name, not quite used to the gap in her smile. Ever since she lost her first tooth, Eagan's been working on his.

It's not that I haven't given this question a ton of thought over the past few weeks—longer, if I'm being honest.

"Erm...well..." We've been talking about school, and the zoo, and her friends and dance class. She's hardly spent any time with Lis. "I'd like to, but I'm not sure she feels the same."

"Why?" And here we go, Eagan's favorite game.

Sighing, I try to figure out how to put the quickest end to his questions. "I might've hurt her feelings, made her mad at me." As soon as the words leave my mouth, I realize my answer is far too open ended for a five-year-old boy.

"Why?"

I stop outside the house and wait for Erin and Eagan to look at me.

"Because I'm but a simple man, and while my love is big and strong and my intentions are good," their attention is fleeting and both kids are looking up toward the door, "I made a mistake and now I need to beg forgiveness."

Erin scowls at me. "You should buy her flowers and chocolates. That's what Da does when he messes up." And with that bit of advice, she skips up the steps and into the house.

Eagan, however, is very serious in his response. "You should share something very special with her. That's what I did in school when I hurt Josi's feelings." This must be his little friend that Bridget was telling me about. "I shared my most favorite crayons with her, the ones I don't let anyone use because they're my favoritest. Girls have to feel special sometimes, Uncle Aidan." He nods like he imparted the world's greatest secrets on me. And maybe he has.

The rest of the day is filled with my family occupying Lis in every way. We eat and talk and the kids fawn over her, wanting every bit of attention they can get.

Lisbeth is polite and engaging. I'm sure no one can see how hard she's working to keep it together. I see it. I don't miss a thing. Each time she looks at me, I feel her stress, her frustration straight through to my soul.

And at dinner it starts all over again. The introductions as my brother Declan and Bridget's husband, Cian, follow my dad in from work, chatting Lis up. Sean and Aileene waltz in a half hour later beaming with happy news of another baby on the way.

Dinner winds down and Mum shoos us out to the lounge while she and Kathleen clean up, and Lis grows quiet. She's settled in at the corner of the couch with Henry on her lap and his sturdy book in her hand.

I take in the way she cradles my nephew to her, not just reading him the little book, but asking him about the animals on the pages. Both have heavy eyes, and I watch as they slip into sleep, his head on her chest and her check nestled against his curls. And my heart squeezes. I hope it's not too late.

"Aidan, why don't you get Lisbeth settled, you've a big day tomorrow." Mum rests her hand on my shoulder, drawing my attention. "She's lovely, I'm glad we had today with her." She pins me with her mum look. "Be honest, but don't let her go. She's one worth fighting for."

"She is." I squeeze my mum's hand and stand. "What was this about today? We could have had this sorted by now, if you'd have just let us be."

I need to know why she bombarded Lis like this.

"I want her to know your family, the good in us. If Lorna's the only one she's met, after the mess she's made, Lis would have no problem telling you to piss off." She wraps her arm around my waist and nods toward the faces staring at me from around the room. "The way you've talked about her since you got home, it's obvious you love her and that she has your heart. I love Lorna, but she had no right to do what she did and I won't let her be the reason you lose the woman you love."

Sighing, I scoop Henry up and deposit him still asleep into Sean's arms. "Thank you, Mum. I hope it works."

I shake Lisbeth gently, waking her. "Lis, let's get you to bed."

Her eyes go wide and dance nervously around the room. Much as I would love to take her to bed, we're in my parents' home and we have a lot to sort before we're ready for that. I smile and shake my head slightly, ruefully.

She says her *goodnights* and heads up the stairs.

"I'll be back down as soon as I've got her settled."

Sean stands, adjusting his son's sleepy body. "I think we're away, then. See you tomorrow." Aileene gathers up Henry's things and they file out. But not before she has her say. "I like her, Aidan. Make things right."

IT'S late morning when I finally give in, I can't stay away any longer. I lie on the bed, watching her. Every cell in my body drawn to her. Wanting to take her pursed lips, kiss her senseless.

I slide a lock of hair off her cheek and through my fingers causing her to stir awake.

"Morning," she mumbles.

"Not for much longer." I tuck the hair behind her ear, caressing her cheek. "Are you up for a drive, or d'ya want to stay in? Everyone's gone for the day."

I don't want to do anything to pop this bubble of time where there's no stress, no fuckups and nothing but sleep-rumpled Lis.

"Yeah. Let's go out. Just give me thirty minutes to clean up?" She doesn't make any move to get up.

"Lis, I'm sorry. I didn't know she was coming to visit. I —" She rolls away from me, throwing her arm over her face.

"Stop. Just forget it, this was a stupid idea." Her words are muffled, but she sounds defeated. Like she's giving up.

Christ, I don't want to lose her.

"She's my sister-in-law. Was my best friend growing up. But none of that excuses me leaving you when you needed me. I should never have walked out of that wedding without you. I broke my promise, and you have every right to be mad, but..."

Her arm flies off her face, and she sits up clutching the duvet to her chest.

"You don't get it, do you? I'm not mad, Aidan. I'm hurt. You discarded me, threw me away like everyone else has. You made me trust you—fall in love with you. I gave you my whole heart and you went running without a word."

I sit up facing her. "Lisbeth, I—"

"No. I came here for me. So I could have my say." She blinks away the tears glistening in her eyes. "You didn't say a word to me about what that emergency was. Did you think that I wouldn't understand? That I'd hold you back from a friend? All of this could have been avoided, if you'd just talked to me.

"Instead, you left me clueless. Guessing at what I was seeing in McBride's with you bent over her, crying. Why? Why would I have thought it was anything other than what it looked like? You hadn't even told me Lorna was pregnant. Have you asked yourself why? Why you didn't share that really important tidbit with me?

"Because it's just about all I've thought about. All that's

been going through my head. That and why I'm not enough. Never enough." Tears gather, threatening to spill.

"Lisbeth. My God, I love you. I was thinking of all the things I need to do to create our life together. Lorna and Michael's baby never crossed my mind aside from a few phone calls with my mum. I was so focused on us—you and me. Getting work to support us. Sorting my visa. Finding a way to make me irresistible to you—so that you'd have no other option but to choose me."

I want to touch her, need the connection with her. Wiping the tears from her cheeks, I push on. "I wasn't hiding anything from you. Not intentionally. It just wasn't relevant. I'm so sorry. I fucked this up with us. I made you feel less than the most important thing in the world to me." I run my hands down her arms, taking her hands in mine, rubbing circles on her wrist. "You are my world. I failed miserably, but please, please give me a chance."

She tugs at her hands, trying to pull them away from me. I hold on for dear life, not wanting to let her go.

"Sh-she said you were going to raise the baby together. She—"

"Yeah. I found out what she said to you halfway across the ocean, stuck in a seat next to her for another three hours. I was livid, tried to get right back on the next flight out. She had no right to try and play us like that. The shite she told me you said—"

I shake my head, shoving the anger back down. It won't do us any good now.

"Lis, I don't know why she thought she needed to do that, be manipulative. That's not how she was growing up, that's not anything I would have ever expected from her. I think...I think the grief, the loss of Michael—maybe the raging hormones?—made her act irrationally. I don't want to make excuses for her, but it's just not who she is.

"This whole thing is a mess and you're absolutely right. If I'd told you, if I'd stayed with you..." I lift her chin so she's looking at me, so she can see my sincerity. "You're my world. Lisbeth. My bloody world, and I will do anything to prove that to you. Please tell me it's not too late. Please tell me we've a chance—that I've a chance to share your life with you."

Her gaze bounces back and forth between my eyes for far longer than I'm comfortable with. My heart forces the blood through my veins.

That's it.

I close my eyes and nod slowly, sure that this is the worst day of my life. Far worse than burying my brother, my best friend. He was taken from me by an awful disease, one that has no cure. I've lost Lis through no fault but my own.

"It's not." My head whips up, searching her face. "It's not too late. I-I want to try, I want to be with you, Aidan. I love you." She leans in, brushing her lips across mine.

FORTY-TWO

Lis

The minute my lips touch Aidan's I feel the spark, the shock of electricity as it courses through my body. I'm finally able to breathe for the first time in almost a month. My world spins in the right direction and my heart fills with hope and possibility. It hits me, just how lost I've been without him. My heart only stuttering, not truly beating, until now.

Before Aidan, love was conditional, sometimes even cruel. I let Lorna's words get to me, affect me, because that's what I've known for most of my life. Much as I thought I'd given my whole heart to Aidan, I realize that I've still been holding back, shielding myself. Only giving him pieces of me. This is it, though, it's time to bare my soul and give him all of my heart— cracks, scars, flaws—all of it.

He releases my hands, grasping either side of my face and pulls me to him deepening the kiss. Not wanting any space between us, I crawl forward onto his lap, my knees firmly planted on either side of his thighs. I need to be close, need to feel our connection again. Show him how much he means to me.

Aidan groans deep in his throat as I settle myself, grinding against him. My skin tingles as he runs his hands over me, touching me everywhere. Pulling me closer until there's nothing between us but thin layers of cotton. His touch, warm and comforting, singes my skin through my thin sleep shorts and t-shirt. His warm palms press my ass closer, closer, closer as I push his shirt up his torso, revealing the bumps and valleys of his muscles.

My need for him making me forget all rational thought. I pull back just long enough to get his shirt over his head and out of my way, crashing my lips back to his as soon as it's clear. His muscles shift and flex across his back as his hands glide up my thighs and dig into the flesh of my hips—pushing me, pulling me.

I work my hand between us and fumble desperately with the button of his jeans. Frantic to feel him, to be with Aidan, I struggle with the closure and groan in frustration.

"Lis—" he breathes across my lips. "Jesus, I can't believe I'm saying this. Lisbeth, stop." Aidan grabs my hands and stills them, clasping them tightly.

I pull my head back panting and search his eyes, not understanding. "What? Why...?" Surely, I didn't misread him.

He leans back, putting even more space between us.

"The last thing I want is to take you in a rush, fuck you like a secret in my parents' house." He looks to the clock on the nightstand and then over his shoulder to the open bedroom door. "I'm not sure when they'll be back, but I sure as hell don't want that to be on my mind while I show you how much I've missed you. I want you to myself, Lis. Completely to myself."

I look past him, out the door, biting my lip.

"Yes. But—" My brain is fuzzy with lust and I blink several times trying to make sense of what to do next. My body physically aches for him. My heart thunders in my chest, pushing the blood through me in the familiar rhythm I've come to associate with Aidan. His grip on my hands loosens. I feel his thumb graze the skin on the underside of my wrist like he's measuring the beats.

Aidan brings my knuckles up to his lips and stops, staring at my fingers. "Where's your ring? Did Francie not give you the letter?"

"It—it's in my bag. I brought it to give back to you. I couldn't...I just couldn't wear it," I whisper, not wanting to give the words life, to admit that I was coming here to say goodbye.

With one arm wrapped around, holding me tightly to him, Aidan leans to the side grabbing my purse from the nightstand. "Where? I need it." His words rumble through my chest, making me catch my breath.

I pull out my wallet, unzip the inner pocket. Fully prepared to return this ring, I never expected to wear it again. The thought that I will, brings tears to my eyes. I place the ring in his waiting palm, giving him my right hand. He kisses my knuckles again and places it over his heart, before reaching for my left hand. "Lisbeth, this is more, so much more than just dating. I won't lose you again."

He flips the ring so the point is out, toward my fingertips and slides it on sealing it with a kiss over the ring and one to my lips. "This is just a place holder until I'm home with you. But I won't—let—you—go."

Each word is punctuated with a brush of his lips across mine.

I feel like time has stopped. And once again, the thought flies through my head, that this is not why I came here—but it's so, *so* much better.

"You good with that? Or we can go to the jeweler right now and get you a proper engagement ring."

"No. No, this is perfect. I don't need anything else, just you." The beat of my heart syncs with the thump of his beneath my palm. I bow my head and press a kiss to his chest, tasting the salt of the single tear that escapes my lashes. The veil of my hair covering my emotions.

Aidan lifts my face to his with a lone finger under my chin. I want to hide, but I know I need to let him in. Let him see me.

With a shuddering breath, I look up into his eyes. This single moment is so much more intimate than any we've shared. The recognition of what this is, what is passing between us, spreads across Aidan's face, changing his look of confusion to one of tenderness and love.

His gaze slides down, landing on my lips. His kiss filled with the love and emotion his features hold. Breaking the kiss, he rests his forehead on mine, sighing. "Let's get dressed and go. I'll show you a bit of Dublin before we can check in." His words give me all the pause I need to collect myself.

. . .

TWENTY MINUTES LATER, I meet him by the front door catching the tail end of his phone call. "...right, so that's the soonest? You've nothing earlier? Right, yeah, that'll be fine. Thank you." Aidan slings his bag over his shoulder and grabs mine from me.

"You ready?"

"Where are we going?" My stomach growls as we walk out, locking the door behind us. I slap my hands to my stomach and feel my cheeks flame red as he turns, a smile stretching across his beautiful face.

"Erm—we're going to get you something to eat and then I'm going to share one of my favorite things with you." I cock an eyebrow at him trying to suppress a giggle-snort.

Aidan chucks our bags in the back of the car and straightens up. Hands low on his hips, shaking his head as he laughs. His eyes sparkling with mischief and desire.

"Yeah, I intend to share *that* with you later. But Eagan gave me his views on love yesterday and how to win over the girl. I want to test his theory."

"Really? Advice from your five-year-old nephew? You're that desperate?" Chuckling, I climb into the correct side of the car this time.

"If I were truly smart, I'd have taken Henry's lead and wrapped myself around you last night." He pulls my hand to his lap and drives us into Dublin. We park near the Woolen Mills at Ha'penny Bridge and go in to the café there.

WE SETTLE in to our lunches and watching the people pass outside the huge plate glass windows.

"Is this what you're sharing with me? Your favorite thing in Dublin?" I sip at the best pint of Guinness I've ever tasted. "For the love of God, this is amazing. It tastes so—so different."

"Yeah, it's fresh here. Better, right?" He smirks at me; our easy conversation is back. God, I missed this. I missed him. I think a part of me knew all along that I was coming back to clear things—that I couldn't live without him. "And, no. This is just lunch to keep you from scaring off my next surprise." He pops a bunch of fries in his mouth being particularly obtuse.

"You're not going to tell me. Is it that awful?" I'm teasing, baiting him when suddenly my blood runs cold. He wouldn't, would he? I press my shaking hands flat to the tabletop, and stare at him.

She's his best friend. And she sure as shit should be scared of me, but I'm not doing this today. No way in hell. I take a bracing breath and bite back the anger and disappointment that threatens to bubble up and overflow.

"Lisbeth, what? What's wrong?" Aidan's fork clatters to his plate as he reaches for me.

A hot flush climbs up my neck, setting my cheeks on fire. "I can't see that woman, Aidan. I won't do it. Not yet."

His roaring laughter snaps my attention.

"What the fuck is so funny about this?" I'm seething.

"Lis, no. Give me some credit, I'm not that daft."

I'm not so sure.

"I want to take you to Howth, a fishing village up north— to feed the seals. Sammy's a local celebrity, loves getting a fish head thrown to him, waving at all the pretty girls. He's quite a flirt." He gazes at me over his pint glass, and I'm not sure if he's being flippant.

His eyes go dark then, intensely serious—dangerous.

"Then I'm going to take you to spend the night in a castle and remind you—repeatedly—how much I love you."

Oh.

FORTY-THREE

Aidan

Over and over and over again.

I show her how much I've missed her. How much I love her.

I drink in every single moment I can with Lis, savoring the time we have. I don't want to spend even a minute sleeping.

Her laughter as she fed the seals was musical. Hearing my name on her lips as she comes undone, is something I will never get enough of.

The pale light of early morning filters through the castle window, highlighting Lis' kiss-swollen lips, and her messy hair.

I don't want to let her leave.

I check my watch and think of how little time there is until we have to leave for the airport.

I have her. But I have to let her go.

I still have to say goodbye.

"Hey, you let me fall asleep." Lisbeth's voice is raspy from sleep. I feel her graze my neck as she runs her finger down to rest over my heart. "I didn't want to miss out on any time—I didn't want to waste this, any of it." Her warm palm rests on my skin and her fingers toy absently with my nipple.

"What's...what's the plan? How are we going to do this, until you get back?" And there it is. Her need to know and my complete and utter lack of answers. It could be weeks, yet. It could be months.

Sifting my fingers through her hair, watching the light play with the silken strands, I press a kiss to her forehead. "We'll do whatever we need to to see each other. I'm going to bust my arse to get everything taken care of here as quickly as possible, but..." I move her on to my chest, needing to have her closer, hating the words that hang between us, "...but it could still be some time. Are you going to be okay?"

I search her face, cradled between my palms needing reassurance that this will work. That we'll be okay.

"I will be. I'm going to dive into my classes, get lost in studying for the nursing boards. I'll be busy, but I will miss you every single moment." Lis leans forward brushing her lips across mine in a slow sensuous kiss. One full of all the emotions that neither of us seem to be able to put into words.

I roll us gently so I'm braced above her, breaking the kiss only enough to whisper against her lips, "I love you, Lisbeth. Don't want to imagine being without you."

I want her, but more than that, I want her to know it's with my heart—not just my cock.

She shifts beneath me, pulling me closer.

"I came here to say goodbye. To be done with us, to move on." Lisbeth slides her hand down my torso, fitting it between our bodies. She wraps her long slender fingers around my cock and strokes me gently. "I never imagined that we would be here. Together but still saying goodbye."

I kiss a trail down her neck, across her collarbone, tasting her, breathing her in. Memorizing every detail until we are together again. There's nothing between us, not a fucking thing. No history, no past, no misunderstandings.

"Not goodbye. This isn't goodbye, Lisbeth. This is forever."

She gasps as I slide into her, twining her legs around me. With my heart beating against her hand, I hold the other one above her head, my thumb rubbing circles on her wrist. Each of us feeling the pulse of this love that neither of us expected to find.

I rock slowly, not wanting an inch of space between us. Wanting to draw this out as long as possible. Wanting to stay here forever in this perfect bubble and never let her go. I suppress every primal urge to mark her as mine for all the world to see.

Instead, I love her, worship her body, and thank God she's given me another chance.

Lis' gasps mix with mine as we move against each other— with each other. Climbing. Building. I want to touch her everywhere all at the same time, desperate to show her how much I love her, how she owns every piece of my heart.

Slowly, we reach the top of the wave, our orgasms thrumming reverently through us. The world falling away leaving only the two of us, nothing else.

WE'VE DELAYED IT—WE'VE actively avoided it.

And now we're late to the airport.

"Ohmygod ohmygod... I'm not gonna miss my flight, am I?" Lis is frantic, bouncing and shifting in her seat. "Aidan, I cannot miss this flight. My classes start tomorrow."

Her eyes are wide and pleading, all the serenity from the hours of losing ourselves in one another, gone.

I whip the car into a spot blessedly open in the front row of the car park. Lisbeth jumps out and meets me at the boot of the car.

I grab her bag and her hand and we run like mad for the terminal.

"You won't miss it. Boarding isn't 'til half ten. You'll"—I glance at my watch and grind my teeth—"you should be okay."

Hands clasped, we weave and dodge through the crowds of slow-moving people—people who actually showed up on time. People who are on holiday. People who don't have to put half of their heart on a plane across the ocean not knowing if it will be two weeks or two months until they can be together again.

We're both panting, breathing heavy as we skid to a stop at the airline desk.

"I-I need to check in for a flight to New York?" Lis is digging through her purse for her passport spilling bits and things onto the desk and floor. "Um—sorry, I know it's here. Aidan? Where did I put my—oh God, here it is. Sorry."

"Well. You are cutting it close, then. Checking any baggage with us today?" The attendant is obviously put out by our tardiness.

"No. I just have a carry-on."

"Gate 414. Security is to your left. You'll want to hurry."

This is the part I've been dreading. The line through security is short, almost nonexistent.

I want to beg her to stay. And I absolutely can't. Instead, I walk with her as far as I can, clinging to her hand, spinning my ring around her finger.

When I've gone as far as I can, I turn her so that she's facing me, mere inches between us.

I'm stalling.

Time is running out, and all the things I couldn't find the words for earlier, are fighting their way to the surface. I open my mouth and close it again. There's too much to say and not nearly enough time.

"You'll call, yeah, when you land?" I pull the lapels of her jacket together, not wanting to let her go. "When you get back to the flat?"

I'm fighting to be strong for her, fighting to keep my tears at bay.

"I will. I promise." She settles her hands on my forearms, a tear rolling down her cheek. "You'll come back to me soon?" Her eyes overflowing with emotion.

I swallow hard and nod, echoing her words. "I will. I promise." I kiss her thoroughly, tasting the salt of her tears, only letting go when I absolutely have to. With whispered *I love yous*, our fingers slowly sliding apart, I watch Lisbeth— my entire world—walk through security and away from me. I watch her as long as I can, until she disappears in the sea of people. Only then, when she's no longer visible, do I let go and let the tears stream freely.

Lis

Once I'm through security, I do my best to get lost in the throngs of bodies moving toward the departure gates.

I need to catch my breath.

I need to talk myself into getting on this plane.

I need to see his face one last time.

Twisting to look over my shoulder, I see him. I see the moment he thinks I'm gone, consumed by the crowds.

My tears matching his, flow down my cheeks.

Leaving Aidan like this is the hardest thing I can imagine. The only thing making it bearable, is knowing that our love is strong enough to endure whatever gets thrown our way.

EPILOGUE

Gracyn

Lis stumbled through the door late this morning, arms full of pies and wine for Thanksgiving. She practically dropped everything trying to get her boots off. I had to hide in the kitchen, slugging back the rest of my mimosa afraid of what would come flying out of my mouth.

She bitched at me for not helping her. Laughed at me for trying to pull off Thanksgiving dinner. To be fair, I don't know what I was thinking. I figured fried chicken was close enough to turkey and we'd make it work, but Kate vetoed that and went on a cooking spree. Food was never the point of today anyway.

Lis wanders back into the kitchen as Kate takes the turkey out of the oven. "Smells amazing in here. Kate, what can I do to help?" Neither of us did much cooking when we lived together, but Kate is ah-freaking-mazing.

"Nothing, really. Gracyn just needs to set the table and

we should be ready pretty soon. Wait, can you open the champagne I have in the fridge?"

Lis goes to the fridge digging around for the bottle I hid behind every available condiment jar.

I check the big clock over the bookshelf and grab plates and silverware, hurrying out to the table we set up behind the couch.

The cork makes a deep satisfying pop and Lis brings the bottle out setting it on one end of the table. "Are we—is there someone else coming?" she asks as she scans the table set for four. "Oh shit, is Kate still on that dating site? Do we finally get to meet one of them?"

Kate slides out of the kitchen, leaning a shoulder on the wall, not wanting to miss anything.

"We do have someone joining us, but it's—"

And right on time, almost like we planned every little detail, the door swings open.

It takes all of four strides for Aidan to cross the room, weave his fingers into her hair and kiss Lis silly.

Aidan asked me to help him surprise Lis when he got his visa mess fixed. He wanted this to be a special moment. One that will become so much more.

And by the shock on her face it looks like we did it. This is worth all the planning and lying and scheming I've done over the past three weeks.

Their love is palpable, seeing them finally together after so long. Lis touching his face, his arms, his chest like she can't believe he's really here.

Aidan beaming at her, his fingers threaded through her hair, pulling her in for a kiss that promises so much more.

I drag Kate into the kitchen, feeling bad, like we're intruding, giving them a little privacy.

No one deserves this kind of love more than Lis. She's been through enough and seeing her happy makes my heart swell and my eyes leak.

Someday, I want what they have—the kind of love they share.

I brush at my tears, stowing my emotions quickly, trying to keep my thoughts from running straight to Gavin. This moment is all about Lis.

I love it.

Love her being in love.

Love the ring I know he has in his pocket.

Love that she's going to say *yes*.

Thank you for spending time in Beekman Hills with Aidan and Lis. I would love to know what you think of these two! If you can, please drop a quick review on your favorite retailer for me!

To stay up on releases and happenings, make sure you're signed up for my newsletter at www.kcenderswrites.com

...now, jump into **Twist** for more of Finn and Addie, or **Tombstones** to meet Kate and Jack.

If it's Gracyn's story you're looking for, grab **In Tune** (formerly Tunes).

ACKNOWLEDGMENTS

Thank you from the bottom of my heart to each and every one of you that have touched my life along the way. You all mean the world to me.

Kate. This would have never happened without you.

Lynsey. Your inspiration and input are what started this mess. Credit or Blame...it's up to you.

Marisol, Kate S., Shawn, Chad B., and Chelsea. Your support, encouragement, and feedback have made this book what it is. Thank you.

The ladies in McBride's on Main, A Novel Bunch KC, and all the real-life bartenders at Cinder Block Brewery, thank you for the words of encouragement, your enthusiasm and the pints poured and endured while I wrote at the bar. Someday I'll try to figure out the bottles of bourbon and the barrels of beer that went into the writing of this!

When everything started to crumble and the world demanded I quit this crazy adventure, thank you for seeing me through to the finish.

TWIST

BEEKMAN HILLS

Twist
BEEKMAN HILLS

To my 'fiends'
I wouldn't be doing this without you.
Thank you.

ONE

"ARE YOU AN ANGEL FROM HEAVEN?"
"NO. SATAN LET ME OUT IN COSTUME TODAY."

Adelaide

People suck. I mean, not all people, but having to meet with them and listen to their "creative ideas" on what they want on their websites is the least favorite part of my job.

God, and having to meet with them out in public? Where there are people? I am not Ariel. I do not want to be where the people are. It takes everything I have in me not to roll my eyes. I need to be professional and land this job.

I creep down Main Street, cursing the plows for not doing any kind of a decent job of clearing the snow from the roads. Maybe my anger is misplaced because Mother Nature should have checked with me before dumping a foot of snow overnight. The four and a half years I've spent here in New York for college have done nothing to put me at ease while driving in the snow. It snowed in Kansas City, but nothing like it does here.

The snow grabs at my tires, pushing my car toward the one other car on the road, coming from the opposite direction.

Shit, shit, shit, shit.

The car swerves across the road, cutting in front of me just as my tires catch, and I barely get things under control. I seethe every curse I can think of at the snow, the plows, the universe, and the asshole who almost hit me and made me miss my turn. And, now, I'm going to be late.

Twenty minutes later, after turning around, getting stuck in stupid one-way streets, and finally getting back to Main, I gingerly pull into the parking lot of McBride's. This is my first time actually going to the Irish pub in the almost four and a half years I've been in New York. With the millions of stories I'd heard throughout college about the pub and the whorish Irish guys working here, I'd have been fine with not coming at all.

With my messenger bag slung across my body, I shove my hands into my pockets and hurry to the door. I should know better; I really should. Just as I start to stomp the snow off my boots, my bag shifts and pulls me off-balance. Arms wheeling through the air, hands reaching for anything to stop the madness, I lose it. Bust ass and end up flat on my back in the snow bank to the left of the door.

Late.

Cold.

Ass covered in snow.

I'm so not getting this job. The wind whips my magenta-and-pale-pink hair up into a twirl of gourmet cotton-candy mess. I haul myself up and dust the snow off my black leggings, cringing when a chunk of snow finds its way into my boot. I don't have time for this. I should be home, cozy in my apartment, with some coffee and a blankie.

Small favors, but my glasses stayed on, and my computer is okay. Carefully, I get myself together, inhaling deeply and slapping what I hope is more smile than grimace on my face, and step into the pub.

The door slams shut behind me on a gust of wind, and all heads turn to face me. I clear my throat and approach the tall, dark-haired guy, pretty sure he's the photographer whose website I'm supposed to be building. "Mr. Kearney?"

"I am. Please, call me Aidan. Are you Miss Huntington?"

He reaches out to shake my hand, so I grit my teeth and firmly clasp his. Yeah, I don't like touching strangers either. They can have all kinds of germs. Like, how do you know if a person just picked their nose right before shaking your hand? His hand feels smooth and clean, so I hope for the best. Maybe I can discreetly grab my hand sanitizer as I unpack my computer.

"Adelaide," I tell him, following suit. "Great, so what are you looking for with your website?"

I really want to just get this started and done, so I can go home and hang out with Eric. He's the best roommate I could have ever asked for after living in the dorms for the first couple of years of school.

Aidan pauses and rests his hand on the back of the chair across from me. "Erm, I don't know really. I thought, with you being the expert, I'd let you guide me."

More small favors. Maybe this won't suck.

"Can I get you something to drink? A pint maybe?"

I stare at him for a second, not quite sure what to say. Is it professional to drink while working? Not that it matters. I don't really drink.

"I'll just have some coffee, I think. Thanks."

"You're sure?" His voice is deep, the accent a little more pronounced than when we spoke on the phone.

I nod and watch as he makes his way to the bar.

He grabs a tall glass of dark beer for himself and a steaming mug of coffee for me. "Do you take anything with it? Some sugar? Creamer?"

"Fuck's sake, I'm sure she doesn't need any sugar. She looks sweet and lovely to me." The bartender comes out of the back room with a basket of French fries, a cheesy smile stretched across his face. "She radiates sunshine and sweetness."

Dear God and sweet baby Jesus, help me have the strength not to roll my eyes. Please, please—

Obviously, those little prayers just did nothing for me. Aidan and the older guy sitting at the bar each bark out a loud laugh. And there goes my attempt to be professional.

"Just creamer, thanks," I tell Aidan.

Scowling, I turn back to my computer and pull my hair up into a messy bun, securing it with a couple of pens. The feet screech against the floor as I shift my chair in. I pull my feet up and wiggle around until I'm sitting crisscrossed on the hard wooden seat. I tuck a third pen between my lips and start typing, pulling up the site template. It would be great if he just gave me creative license, but we'll see. People say that shit all the time and then change every last detail on their sites.

"And look at how she folds herself up so neatly on that chair. She's sweet and bendy, like Twizzlers."

Out of the corner of my eye, I see this guy leaning forward over the bar, dousing his fries in vinegar, a wide grin practically splitting his face.

Is he serious?

Aidan's jaw twitches as he stares past me. There are only the four of us in here, but the silence is deafening.

"Finn," he grits out before mumbling, "Christ," under his breath. "Adelaide, I'm sorry. He thinks he's pretty slick, but—"

"Please don't hold this against me," I manage to say quietly before turning in my seat to look at this guy, Finn. "Twizzlers can leave some nasty whip marks, given the right velocity. Maybe you should watch yourself." Facing forward again, I push my glasses back up my nose and ask Aidan, "Are we ready to do this?"

Eyes wide, Aidan is working really hard to contain himself, but the older gentleman sitting at the bar barks out a deep belly laugh. Cheeks red above his full beard, he says something to the bartender in not English—maybe Irish? And the dude frowns and goes back to washing glasses or something.

"Sorry. Francie—he's the owner—just told Finn he's not going to be able to charm his way into your good graces. He thinks...well, I told you already." Aidan waves his hand and drinks down about a third of his beer. "What have we got then?" He scoots over and peers at my screen.

We work for a bit, and I think I'm getting a pretty good idea of what he wants for his site. It's all good until the air shifts, and I square my shoulders, the skin prickling along the back of my neck.

"Thought you might like a little warming up." Leaning heavily on the back of my chair, Finn refills my coffee cup. But he lingers, crowding me.

Don't react. He's just looking for a reaction.

And, when I think it's safe, I release the breath I'm holding.

He lets loose with another comment. "Personally, I think you're smoking hot. You've got me burning up."

He seriously thinks he's good at this.

I pull a strained breath in through my nose, hard enough to wiggle my septum ring I neatly tucked up—again, trying for that professional vibe. "You're burning up?"

"I am," he purrs. "Think you can help me?"

I twist my lips, assessing him. He's tall and lean. Just starting to put on some muscle. He looks like he's close to my age with an artfully tousled mop of dark-red curls. He's cute, but for the love of God...

"I'm not a doctor, but generally, antibiotics are a good idea to nip that shit in the bud. Some of those"—I dismissively flap my hand toward his pants—"diseases can be cleared up pretty quickly, from what I've heard."

TWO

"What's your sign?"
"Stop."

Finn

Francie might be right. This girl is quick on the comebacks. And seriously witty. I like that.

"Should I sit and keep you company? Be your inspiration?" It looks like she's working on something for Aidan. I pull out the chair next to her, thinking I'll slide in close and keep working on her.

She looks at me over the top of her glasses and deadpans, "Or you could not."

"What's your name, love?"

"Don't you have work to tend to, Finn?" Aidan pipes up, giving me his annoyed big-brother look.

"Sure, yeah. They're knocking down the doors today. Clamoring for drinks with the storm going. Pretty shite move of you, making this lovely lady risk her safety out in this weather." I throw a wink her way. Girls cannot resist the Finn wink. Not in the least.

"Right, well, Francie just took the rubbish out to the bin, so you'd best look busy when he gets back, or he'll be on your arse."

I shoot Aidan a fuck-off look and take in the shades of deep, dark pink fading out to a delicate, light cotton-candy hue in her hair, which is all wound together on the top of her head. She looks like she's trying to hide behind her big sweater and wild hair, but there's no denying how cute she is. Fucking adorable really.

"Let me know if I can get you anything. I'm at your service..." I draw the last word out, hoping that she'll fill in her name for me.

Instead, she gives me a side-eye and goes back to her laptop. Fingers flying across the keys, her tongue resting against her top teeth. Not biting it, but kind of.

I need to up my game. Pour on the charm—the lucky charms—and see if I can get a taste of her. "Can I get you—"

The slamming of the back door cuts me off, mid pickup.

"Christ, Finn. Go move your car, and park it straight. Have you lost all your spatial awareness?" Francie bellows as he bursts through the door from the kitchen. "You'll be lucky to make it through the winter without your car getting hit again."

I roll my eyes and slide behind the bar to grab my keys. Aidan barks his obnoxious laugh and looks from the pink-haired pixie to me and back again, not even trying to hold his laughter back at all now.

"What?" I pause, pulling my jacket on. "What're you

laughing at?" I scowl at Aidan sitting smugly with the girl I want to be chatting up.

"I just said it was kind of disappointing that someone so suave couldn't seem to get it in the right place on the first try," she replies. This girl keeps an absolutely solid dead stare while Aidan is laughing so hard, I think he might fall out of his chair. Actually, I hope the arse does.

"You don't need to worry about me sliding into tight spots. I can maneuver just fine."

Francie scoffs and shakes his head at me, pointing to the back door.

"I avoided a collision just today as I turned into the car park." Having made my point that I am in fact a stellar driver, I hustle out to straighten my car at the back of the building.

It takes me three tries to park my little Kia perfectly straight and even within the lines. I should probably get my eyes checked and see if I need a new prescription for my glasses. Maybe I'll get contact lenses this time. Though I've always heard that girls like a nerdy-looking guy, and I try hard to be everything the ladies could possibly want.

I wonder how long she's going to be here, working with Aidan. Maybe I should clean the snow off her car. Maybe she'll tell me her name if I do. It's not like there's anyone inside, waiting on me to serve them. It's just been the four of us since we opened, and I don't see the evening filling up too much.

When her car is cleaned off, I knock the snow from my boots at the back door and shake the flakes from my jacket before returning to the bar. My glasses are completely fogged up from the sudden change in temperature. I slide them off to clean them and I'm caught off guard by the finger in my chest.

"You're the asshole who swerved out front? You almost hit me!" She really is quite little, her head just clearing my shoulder.

"What are you on about?" I slide my glasses back on, so I can focus on her adorably annoyed expression.

"That car you almost hit this morning? That was me, asshole."

Her royal-blue fingernail jabs repeatedly into the center of my chest. And it hurts.

I grab her hand and bring her knuckles up to my lips, kissing them. "See then, we were destined to meet today," I croon at her. I totally have this thing in the bag. There's no way she can resist me.

My attention is drawn to the front door where Aidan is coming back in from outside. I don't see it coming, not at all. But, when she yanks her hand from mine and shoves her shoulder into my sternum, it knocks the wind from me.

She's a hell of a lot stronger than I gave her credit for.

"Your car's all cleared off. Is there anything I can carry for you, Adelaide?"

The arse just took credit for my work. I cleared the snow off her car, me.

"Thanks, but no." She shrugs on her coat and wraps a blue-and-teal scarf around her neck. And then she pulls bright-green mittens out of her pockets.

She is a riot of color that I can't seem to take my eyes off of. She's captivating.

And she's walking out of the pub.

I have to do something. I need more time with her. I need

for her to realize she wants me, needs me, can't live without me. I don't like losing.

"Maybe I'll run into you again sometime," I toss out to her. I lean back against the bar, feet spread and thumbs hooked in the pockets of my jeans. That leaves my fingers dangling, framing my goods. This move always works, gets the focus where I want it. The ladies can't resist me when I point out what I've got to offer.

When she turns in the doorway, framed by the snow falling outside, I give her the smile and wink. Hope lights up her features. I wiggle my fingers a little to draw her attention to what I'm sure she's thinking of.

And, with her eyes never leaving my face, her lip twitches as she says, "All flirt and no follow-through."

My smile fades as she turns and walks out of the pub. I almost don't hear Aidan laughing at me through the sting of her words, my mind locking in on her brush-off.

THE PUB never does fill up. Probably has more to do with the fact that it's a Tuesday night in January than the bit of snow we've gotten. Unfortunately, that means I'm bored. Nothing to do but wipe down bottles, bullshit with the handful of regulars who never miss stopping in, and think about what comes next.

I should probably go back to university and try again for a degree. I pull up the college website on my phone and look at the offerings. Teaching, nursing, business, computers. I have a fair bit of money in the bank. That happens when you share rent and work all the time.

I love my job; I do. I get to sleep late, drink at work, and have constant access to lovely, willing women. But I can't *just* tend bar for the rest of my life. I don't know what Francie's plans are for McBride's, but he's not getting any younger. Maybe a business degree will give me some options. Maybe I can help Francie, show him I'm responsible and that I can take on more responsibilities here at the pub.

"Finn, my man, how's the single life treating you?"

Andy's a regular, and he has been giving me shite for as long as I can remember. I slide his usual down the bar to him before continuing to wipe down the liquor bottles.

"Yeah, I'm good." I spin a bottle of whiskey round in my palm before dropping it back down in the well and picking up the rum to run my bar rag over it.

"Tell me about your latest. I have to live vicariously through you."

He quickly drains his pint, and I take it straight from him to refill. Andy needs a beer on the house every now and again. His youngest has been poorly, and things are tough at home for him.

"Erm, no one new today, man. Not since Marlee last weekend." I throw him a smirk as the words tumble out of my mouth.

Marlee was really damn appreciative of the time we spent in her bed, her kitchen, and after that thing in the shower.

Christ, that shower.

I follow through. I had all kinds of follow-through with Marlee, and her neighbors can vouch for it.

"Andy, can I ask you a question?" I lean my hands against the bar for a moment, arms spread wide.

He wipes the beer off his upper lip and nods. "Sure."

"I follow through with things, yeah? I-I don't leave you hanging and wanting for more?" I pull at the label of the vodka bottle resting in front of me in the well.

"Uh, you give me beer when I need it. Is that what you're looking for? Validation in your job, Finn?" Andy chuckles as he takes another draught of his beer.

Everyone treats me like a joke, and I'm not sure what that's all about. I work hard. I'm here on time for almost all of my shifts, certainly more often than not. Chat with the patrons and entertain the ladies. I'm good at what I do. Better at some things than others, and I sure as shite haven't had any complaints in a long time.

THREE

Adelaide

Aidan's website is about finished. I have a handful of questions that I have to ask him, but they're things we need to go through in person. Face-to-face, and I'm avoiding that at all costs. He has been really easy to work with, making changes and adjustments, but I just don't want to have to leave my cozy apartment.

It's been snowing on and off for the past week since I went to McBride's for our initial meeting.

Eric is snuggling with me hard today, burrowed into the blanket draped across my big, comfy chair. He sighs and starts snoring lightly as I run my fingers down his back. This should be reason enough to never leave my apartment. There is so much contentment right here. It would be inconsiderate to disturb his peace.

Just as I'm about to close my eyes and take a little nap, my phone pings with an email notification from an older client wanting to tweak things yet again on her site. It's like the thousandth time she's decided to change everything. Everything. This is one of those reasons I don't like having to deal with people.

Maybe I did actually fall asleep for a bit because, when I open my email, I have four unread messages. Three from the continuing education program I work with and one from Aidan.

I fire off a response to my pain-in-the-ass client and let her know what to expect for additional fees. Thank God I put a PITA clause in her contract, outlining incremental charges for all changes after the third round.

Aidan is checking in to see if there is anything further I need from him. His girlfriend is ridiculously lucky. He is such a nice guy—kind, thoughtful, always concerned that he's being a pain in the ass.

Hardly.

The last set of emails gets progressively more urgent. The instructor who was lined up to teach a course on basic computer use bailed at the last minute. And they know I can't say no to them. Their computer programs are heavily attended by the cutest little old ladies. They help me when I'm missing my grandma, and I can't seem to resist them.

The new class starts this afternoon, so I slide out from under Eric and drag myself to the bathroom to shower and do my thing. I take a few extra moments to twist my hair into a funky braid before swiping on a coat of mascara and a little tinted lip balm. Though they frown at my septum piercing, the older ladies seem to like my colorful hair, and with Valentine's Day approaching, they'll probably make a big fuss over my festive pinks.

I shuffle through the posted syllabus for the continuing ed class and update the slides I have from the last time I filled in for this course. After checking my pantry and finding it woefully lacking, I pack up my computer and press a kiss just behind Eric's ear.

I need to stop on the way to the community center and pick up some cookies from the bakery. My ladies will be bringing me homemade cookies for the remainder of these classes, but since they don't know yet that it's me teaching, I need to make sure to bring some goodies.

The parking spot right out in front of the bakery and coffee shop opens up just as I approach. I park carefully, being mindful of the never-ending snow as I turn in. The selections inside are nothing short of mouthwatering, but knowing my ladies as I do, I stick with the giant, chewy chocolate chip cookies and the biggest, darkest roast coffee they have. My nap wasn't nearly long enough to knock the cobwebs from me.

Glancing at my phone, I check the time and hurry back out to my car. As I settle the box of cookies on the front seat and straighten up to grab my coffee off the roof of the car, I see a little silver hatchback careen past me down Main Street. There's no mistaking the fact that I know that car. It almost hit me, running me off the road the last time I was over this way.

Peering down the road, I see the car turn into the parking lot of McBride's, the wheels skidding wildly, the back of the car swerving until the driver regains control. A tall form unfolds itself from the driver's seat, and there's no doubt in my mind that it's him—Finn.

Is he out to get me for real?

By the time I get to the community center, my coffee is half-gone, and I have just enough time to make copies of my handouts before the ladies start showing up. Several of them have taken this course before. With me or one of the other instructors. I think they use it more for a social hour, but between this and the knitting classes they teach, they have a place to be. A place to hang out with each other and spend time with their friends. Lord, even in my head, it feels like I'm commenting on wayward youth as opposed to members of the grandparents and great-grands clubs.

Loaded down with coffee, cookies, handouts, and my computer bag, I stumble into the computer lab and almost drop it all before I catch myself. Thankfully, the only thing I manage not to save is the stack of handouts. They slide out of my arms, seemingly in slow motion, and scatter across the floor.

"Well, shit," comes the sweet voice behind me. Louise looks at the mess before waddling over to me to wrap me in a warm, rose-scented hug. "I'm so glad we have you this go around, Adelaide. That other guy they have teaching sometimes doesn't let us have cookie and coffee time." She looks genuinely put out by that inconvenience.

Squatting down, I gather the papers into a neat pile, placing the slightly wrinkled ones on the bottom. "I stopped by Sweet Treats and brought the first round. Sorry. If I'd known I had this session before today, I'd have baked them myself." I look up and smile as the others start filing through the door. "Afternoon, ladies."

"Adelaide, honey, why do you bother with all that paper? You know we're not going to take them, sweetie." Connie sets her big floral bag on the floor next to *her* computer and makes grabby hands at me until I stand and let her hug me.

I'm so not a hugger. Nope. I don't like people, and I don't like being touched, let alone hugged. But this is different. And not a one of these surrogate grandmas is going to take *no* for an answer.

I unpack my laptop and connect it to the projector in case there's actually someone new signed up for this session who plans on learning the basics of using a computer. The roster I have shows my usual suspects, but there could be a last-minute attendee.

"Are you going to pass those treats around, or are you going to make an old lady walk for her cookie?" Virginia asks from the desk right next to the door. She's perfectly capable of walking the twenty feet, but she likes to play the poor-me card every now and then.

Connie turns and calls her out, "Virginia, how's that tai chi class you teach twice a week going?"

"Fine."

"Then, get your wrinkly ass up, and get your own damn cookie. You make people bend and breathe, but you think you can't walk for a cookie?" Connie dishes shit like no one else. No one, except Virginia because that woman is the master shit-slinger.

My heart is happy with this crazy crew. I make my way around the room, offering up cookies before we get started to avoid any catfights. It's blatantly obvious that I was not listed as the instructor for this session. My usually early attendees are dribbling in the door right up until the published start time. I guarantee, they will be early from here on out.

"Should we start this thing?" I ask while approaching the front of the room.

"Lord, yes," Ellie responds. "I thought we were getting stuck with that stuffy Richard this time around. Did you switch with him, dear?" She's looking at me over the top of her glasses as she turns on her monitor.

The rest of this crew though is snickering, a few mumbling about how stuffy Dick is.

I tilt my head from side to side and consider how to respond. I believe in honesty above all else, but I hate drama and sure as shit can't acknowledge their twelve-year-old sense of humor. And there is nothing a bunch of little old ladies love more than drama.

"I think you might have scared poor *Richard* off."

Eight sets of magnified eyes pop up to stare right at me. Some are surprised, a few are a tad bit confused, but most of them show nothing but barely contained mirth.

Master manipulators, the lot of them.

FOUR

Finn

I'm late. But it's not like this is a real class anyway. Once I made the decision to go back to university, I went out and bought myself a new laptop. The spot-faced salesman promised me the graphics were worth the extra money, and since I'll be using it mostly for social media, mostly Tumblr, until I can get into classes this summer, it seemed like a fantastic rationalization.

Now, I just need to get the instructor of this little community class to go through the setup on this thing, and I'll be good to go. I had to beg Aidan to fill in for me this afternoon, but once my laptop is all set up, I'll drop out and have no need for anyone to cover my Tuesday and Thursday shifts. Instead of having to squint at my tiny phone screen,

I'll have a crystal-clear, high-def, fifteen-inch screen for my Tumblr time.

I check the room number against the confirmation email I got when registering. The instructor is listed as Richard Johnson, but the voice I hear going over the course outline does not belong to a man. I planned on a guy getting the importance of Tumblr in full HDMI, but I can work with this. Maybe I can even get some extra credit out of the experience.

"I know we have a system, but we need to accomplish something this time. Turn your computers on, and..." The sweet voice does not match the vision at the front of the room.

It's the girl from the pub, Aidan's computer girl. Instead of being twirled up on top of her head, her hair is twisted into a pink rainbow plait hanging over her shoulder.

This is fantastic. Fan-fucking-tastic.

The last row of seats to the left of the door is empty, so I saunter over, drop my ruck on the desk, and shed my jacket. My zipper is the only sound in the room. I open my ruck and pull my new toy from the bag. The outlet is inconveniently located on the floor under the desk. Down on my knees, I plug in the cord and take a moment to make the necessary adjustments in my jeans.

Had Richard shown up to teach this, there would be no adjustment. But this girl? This girl has me off my game once again. In fact, she's got me so in my head, I don't notice the red Converse that have settled next to my desk.

"What are you doing here?"

Startled, I hit my head on the underside of the desk and pray there's no chewing gum stuck in my hair. I crawl out from my hiding space and look up at this girl. "I thought I'd brush up on my skills." It's not lost on me that I am literally on my knees in front of her, and I want to beg for a date, a taste, her name.

She rolls her eyes like it's an Olympic event and turns to take her place at the front of the room. I slide into my chair and finish setting up my command center. Laptop, phone, "water" bottle. I push my ruck down to the end of the table and lift the lid of my computer before cracking open my beverage.

"Are you ready?"

I look around the room and notice that I am the only guy here. And that all the ladies, other than the pink-haired love of my hour, are over the age of seventy and could give my gran a run for her money. But they're not giving me that hostile vibe. They look like they're thinking. Scheming. Up to no good for certain.

"Ready and willing, love." I swear, I see one of the ladies dabbing at her cleavage with a napkin. They all have napkins, some with half-eaten chocolate chip cookies from the bakery on them. "Erm, did I miss the portion of class where treats were handed out?"

I feel like I'm back in McBride's with the way she's rolling her eyes, and the over-seventy crowd is laughing at me.

"If I give you a treat, will you sit nicely and stay quiet?"

"Adelaide," the cleavage-dabber chides, "that's no way to speak to the nice young man."

Right, I knew I'd heard Aidan call her by name in the pub. "Addie, I'll do whatever you want, if you ask nicely and give me a little something for the effort."

The collective gasp momentarily wipes the smile from my face. But I didn't say anything too bad, did I? Plus, at least half of them have to be hard of hearing, right?

"Adelaide. It's Adelaide," she says with some bite in her tone, her teeth grinding against each other. "And you obviously aren't getting any treats." She stops herself just shy of stomping her foot and flicking me on the nose.

What does she think I am, a naughty dog?

"A word, dear. Stick with her full name, and you'll do fine." The lady across the aisle reaches over and pats my arm. "What's your name, cutie?"

"Finn O'Meara, ma'am." I shake her hand and use the manners my mum hammered into me. "It's a pleasure to meet you."

"Call me Virginia. You're not a native either then? Our Adelaide is a transplant from the Midwest," she says while offering me a cookie from her stash.

"No, ma'am. From Dublin, but I've been here for a few years." I reach out to take the cookie from my new best friend but pull back when I hear an outrageously loud throat clearing from the front of the class.

"I thought not," Addie scolds.

I grin innocently over the top of my bottle. "I'd be happy to share, if that would make amends."

The nip of whiskey I have in my bottle warms me as it slides down my throat. Not that I'm doing hard drinking, just a bit to make the class more tolerable. I offer the bottle to Addie because, if I'm honest, the only lips in the room I'm interested in sharing space with are hers. Especially her plump lower lip. The one that she's abusing with her teeth. The one with just the tiniest smear of chocolate that she somehow misses with every nibble and bite. The one I've dreamed of having wrapped around my cock every night for the past week.

I throw her the Finn wink, hoping to distract her as I adjust my growing problem—again.

All I'm met with though is a mumbled, "Antibiotics," and a flip of her braid as she walks away.

FIVE

"Are those space pants? Because your ass is out of this world!"
"No, these are baseball pants because my ass is out of your league."

Adelaide

Finn's very presence is annoying the shit out of me. Why is he here? This is my place, my zone. These are some of the only people I actually like, and this is one of the few places I enjoy hanging out, outside of my cozy apartment. For the love of God, he's tainting it.

I do everything in my power to push him and his crazy, infuriating existence out of my mind. I'm here for my ladies. To fill my cup and get my grandma time in.

We go over the basics, just like I do at the start of every session. Turning on the computer, signing in, connecting to the internet. This is pretty much as far as we'll get today because the cookies are gone, and Esther is out of coffee. We all have our limits.

"Okay. So, we'll pick up here on Thursday. Does anyone need a handout?" I take the stacked papers and chuck them in the recycling bin.

"Erm, that's it? We're done for the day?" His feet are on the corner of the desk, and his crap is spread across all three workstations at the very back of the room.

"Do you really need to be here? Surely, you know how to check your email and Google shit." I shove his feet off the desktop and twist my lips to try to suppress my grin when he falls forward to catch himself.

"Adelaide, be nice to the young gentleman. He's a long way from his family, too," Virginia appeals for her new friend. Hers, not mine. "Maybe you'd like to be friends. Get a drink or a bite to eat after class."

Is she serious? Making playdates for me? Setting me up on a date with her grandson was one thing. This is entirely different. And not okay.

"We met last week and didn't hit it off, so...I'll pass."

"Surely, we can't be done. I've still not made it all the way through the setup, and—"

"What?"

"The laptop is new, and I thought...well, I thought you could help me get things set up, so I'll be ready to take classes in the next college session." He has the nerve to look around the room, silently pleading his case.

"You're ridiculous, you know that?" I just can't with him. "Go. You're perfectly capable of setting up and using your laptop. Why the hell did you get this one anyway?" I turn the machine, so I can see what the specs are and laugh. "Jesus

Christ, you already have a shortcut on your desktop to—" I snap my head up, staring into his eyes, and clamp my lips tightly together.

Oh my God.

"Adelaide, are you okay? Your face looks like a tomato."

Lord have mercy, nothing gets by Connie, and she is closing in on me and the screen full of Tumblr GIFs.

I slam the top down and push the now-offending computer away from me. "This is not what we do here." I glance around the room before narrowing my eyes at him again. "If you plan on coming back on Thursday, you will be following the syllabus in an appropriate manner. Do you understand?" I used my stern voice. My I-mean-business voice. My do-not-even-fuck-with-me voice. And I expect him to be intimidated, embarrassed, something.

Instead, Finn stands up, so we're chest-to-chest—more like chest-to-stomach in my case—and he leans in to pick up his laptop.

"Oh, I plan on coming back, love. For every single class. I'll also be planning on that drink and the bite as well." He nods toward his new best friend and the class traitor. Taking a step back, he addresses the group as he slides all his miscellaneous crap into his bag, "Ladies, it's been a pleasure. As for you, Addie, I'll see you soon."

"It's Adelaide."

He slings his backpack over his shoulder and walks backward out of the room, waving as he goes.

* * *

"HE'S A CUTIE, ISN'T HE?"

"And did you hear him with that accent?"

"And manners. With his, *Yes, ma'am*, it might just make an old lady swoon a little."

Not one of them is bothered by the shade I'm throwing their way. I pack up my computer and straighten the chairs, making my way to the door. My jaw is tight, and my head is down. I don't want to engage. I feel like they all turned on me a little.

A warm hand settles on my arm, startling me out of my thoughts. "Adelaide, you should give him a chance," Louise says softly.

I can't help but roll my eyes again at the idea of going out with Finn.

"Louise, he's just..." Sighing, I try to think of what I want to tell her. That he's a cheesy flirt? That the rumors I've heard are that he's a man-whore and more likely to have a flavor of the day as opposed to being the gentleman he's led them all to believe he is? And why do I care? I have Eric; he's all I need.

Louise wraps her arms around me and pulls me in tight. Maybe it's time for me to move back home. I miss my family, especially my grandma.

Squeezing her back and stuffing down my tears, I bark out an ugly laugh when she pats my back and says, "If nothing else, honey, get laid. You'll feel better."

SIX

*"Your pants would look great on my bedroom
floor."*
*"You can buy the same pair at Target for twenty
dollars."*

Finn

I should have probably gone back to my flat after that
exchange with the fiery little thing, but I'm too keyed up.
Instead, I stop in at McBride's for a pint and some food.

"You're done then? I'm away, home to Lis." Aidan claps a
heavy hand down on my shoulder and plants a bar rag in the
middle of my chest.

"Fuck's sake, you said you'd work for me tonight. I'm just
in for a—"

"Sorry, Finn. Lis is home. She got done early and
needs me."

"Christ, I can't catch a break anywhere today." I stow my
ruck under the bar and grab a glass for my pint, mumbling,

"Just wanted to get my setup done, check out some GIFs, and take care of myself."

"What are you on about?" Aidan asks. "I thought you had your class today, yeah?"

I set the glass down to let the thick black beer settle and lean my ass against the bar. "I did. Didn't go to plan though."

Aidan huffs a laugh at me. "Turn out the instructor was a man?"

I hang my head and roll my shoulders. The last thing I want to do is let on that I'm hung up on—*haunted by*—his web designer. Aidan's such a protective arse; he'd probably never have her meet him here again if he knew. *What if they're done meeting up? What if his work with her is finished?*

"Finn, you all right? Need to talk something out?" He steps back up to the bar, concern written across his face.

"I'm fine," I mutter. "Just gonna drop some chips in the fryer before you leave, yeah? Give me a minute."

In the kitchen, I take a few moments to cool off in the walk-in freezer and try to collect myself. I should have just gone straight home. Addie has me off-balance and aching for her at the same time.

When I can't avoid it any longer, I grab a fresh bag of chips and drop a healthy—or rather, an unhealthy—portion into the fryer. I busy myself, cleaning the already-spotless kitchen while I wait for my food to cook. Aidan will be fine for a few extra minutes. And Lis won't be that upset with me for keeping him.

"You about done back here?" Aidan pops his head through the door, eyebrows raised, pupils dancing. "Lis is waiting for me in—"

"Christ, man, don't rub it in. I'll be out in a second." I need to find someone to take my mind off matters. Or take them into my own hands.

"Let's go then. I don't want to keep her waiting." He smacks the doorjamb twice in quick succession and fixes me with a glare. The glare of a man about to go home to a beautiful woman. His beautiful woman.

Shaking my head, I drain and plate my chips with a liberal application of salt. I grab the vinegar and go back out front to the bar.

WHEN I SHOW up to the community center on Thursday afternoon, I'm prepared. I have water in my water bottle instead of whiskey and my own little snack pack of cookies, and I'm not entirely late. I've even hidden the shortcuts to Tumblr and Pornhub in a folder on my desktop titled *Homework*. Perfectly respectable.

My new friend, Virginia, nods and smiles to me as I take my seat across the aisle. Like a ripple effect, each row of ladies turns, smiles, and nods, murmuring their hellos until sweet Addie raises her head and fixes me with her gaze.

"You're back." Not a question, it's more of an annoyed observation.

"I am," I reply, smiling. "And I've brought my own snack." I hold up my store-bought treat, feeling like I've got this thing handled.

Addie does the eye-roll thing again, and I have to admit, I'm a bit concerned for her. She seems to have a problem controlling that particular response. Like, I'm afraid she's going to strain herself.

Virginia though stands, grabs the bag of cookies out of my hand, and throws them in the rubbish bin. "We don't allow that shit in here, Finn. We have standards," she scolds.

My protest is on the tip of my tongue when she hands me a still-warm, gooey cookie from the plastic container on the desk in front of her.

Addie grumbles something about me not knowing standards if they smacked me upside the head, which isn't true at all. If I didn't have standards, I'd have gotten into more trouble in Dublin with my Humanities professor.

"Thank you, ma'am." I make an exaggerated show of manners that everyone seems to appreciate. Everyone, except Addie.

She turns back to her computer and prattles on about files and organizing them into folders.

I get a bit lost inside my head, listening to the gentle melody of her voice. She's lulling me into a trance with her soft, almost accentless tone. Well, she has no accent compared to most of the girls I chat up in the pub. They all seem to have that harsh edge that screams New York, whereas Addie is all rounded vowels and steady cadence.

Christ, she's stunning when she's focused on what she's doing. I'm so entranced, watching her, listening to her, that when I take a bite of the cookie Virginia so kindly bestowed upon me, I embarrass myself a little. The chocolate and sugary flavors explode in my mouth, causing my eyes to close and a groan to escape from low in my throat.

The room goes absolutely silent, and when I open my

eyes, everyone's head is turned, and the cleavage-dabber is dabbing and fanning.

I drop my feet down from where I rested them on the desktop and swallow quickly. "This is spectacular." I hold up the remainder of the cookie and smile.

While the prevalent response is a murmured, "Oh, dear," the louder response, the one that makes its way to my waiting ears, is more of a, "You have got to be fucking kidding me."

"Are you done?" she asks more loudly, glaring at me across the room.

"I'd never finish before you," rolls off my tongue before I can think better of it. So, I wink at her. I wink hard and play it off like it's no big deal because, really, it's true. Despite what she threw at me in the pub, I flirt *and* follow through.

And the ladies? They're not nearly as hard of hearing as I hoped, as they are stifling their laughter while Addie's face turns the color of her hair.

SEVEN

Adelaide

I can't believe Finn just said that. I can't fucking believe it. I bite at my lip while my face flames red, and I try to compose myself. *Does he mean to say shit like that all the time? Does he not know how to tone it down?*

Putting forth my best effort to ignore the fool, I carry on with the rest of the material, sneaking an occasional glance Finn's way to make sure he's not doing anything inappropriate, like cruising Tumblr. Sadly, the only way I can even think of to check on that is to find his hands and maybe look for any exuberant adjustments.

Each time I glance up though, he's smirking at me, hands in his lap, stroking his pen, but still. And, of course, he winks.

Every. Dingle. Time. *Single.* I meant, every *single* time. Damn it. I just roll my eyes, unchecked, not giving a shit anymore if he notices.

I hang back as the room empties, hoping to avoid any more awkwardness. Finn holds the door and acts all valiant and chivalrous to the ladies. *My* ladies. I had them first, and now, I feel like I'm losing them to him. We haven't even been out on one date, and we're already having a custody battle. Wait, there will be *no* dates with the cheese-slinging Tumblr monkey. Nope.

Finally alone, I check my email and see that my Susie-change-a-lot client has yet another overhaul she wants me to do. My bank account gets fatter with every one of her whims, but she's starting to drive me insane.

Aidan responded to my meeting request, and thankfully, he's agreed to meet at the coffee shop. I pack my stuff up and notice that no one really said good-bye to me. Shoulders slumped, I grab my bag and head out the door, flipping off the lights as I go.

Finn is opening and closing car doors for Virginia and Louise. Maybe he is chivalrous. Maybe he misses his grandma, too. I don't know. But my heart breaks a little when I see Louise wrap him in a hug before she settles in her car.

With a deep breath, I tuck my head down against the wind and power-walk to my car. It's time for a change.

"THANK you so much for being flexible." Aidan assesses me as I settle at a table in the back corner of McBride's. "I have to cover for one of the bartenders for a bit and couldn't get away to the coffee shop. We shouldn't be bothered much over here." He's searching, trying to figure out what's different with me.

"It's green," I say, thinking that's all he needs, but he's still squinting his eyes and furrowing his brows. "My hair. It was time for a new color, so..." I just shrug. *Do I really want to share with him that I was feeling a little jealous, so I needed my hair to match? Probably not.* It sounds crazy enough when I think about it too hard, but I guess, if he pushes it, St. Patrick's Day would do for an excuse.

"Huh. It suits you, but so did the pink. I like it." He smiles as he brings me a fresh mug of coffee and a small pitcher of cream. "The website is fantastic, by the way." Aidan pulls a chair around next to me and places his glass of whiskey down on a coaster.

"Great. So, I just wanted to check with you on a couple of details before we launch it and optimize the search engines." I slide my finger across the touchpad, waking the screen, just as the door flies open.

Virginia, Louise, and Connie come tumbling in—with Finn.

They pass through the room to a table out of sight and settle into what looks like a conversation that's been going on for a while. I would like not to be sad, not to feel left out, but I do. They didn't even notice me. I wrap a lock of my mood-matching hair around my finger and try to ignore the cackles of laughter and blatant flirting across the room.

He's flirting with them. Like real flirting, gentle touches, eyes sparkling, genuine smiles. Not the cheesy shit he gives me.

"You all right, Adelaide?" Aidan's brows are pinched, concern written across his features.

"Um, yeah." I shake my head, clearing the errant thoughts away. "Let's get through this and get your new site launched."

Aidan looks back at the table full of whispers and laughter, pausing before turning back to me. "He's a good man. A little lost maybe but a good man."

My breath catches, and my spine stiffens. "Okay. What... what does that have to do with anything?" I ask. The edge in my voice is a little sharper than it needs to be.

"Not a thing. Just doing a good deed for the lad." He smirks at me before nodding at someone over my shoulder.

I assume it's the cheesy leprechaun, but I don't need to know.

"Well, charity is good for your Karma, I guess." The desire to finish this up and escape to home washes over me. I would love to call in sick to class tomorrow, but I know that'd just end up biting me in the ass. Hell, I'm the substitute. Who knows whom they'd call to fill in for me?

We make a few minor adjustments on his site and take care of finances, and then I'm done. Quickly and quietly, I wrap my scarf around my neck and grab my bag. I forego my jacket to escape just a little bit sooner.

"Okay, so thanks. Let me know if we need to tweak anything, make changes, whatever."

Aidan nods his thanks, and I bolt. I'm out.

Eric is surely waiting on me. At least he'll be excited to see me.

EIGHT

Finn

I wasn't really sure what to think when the lovely ladies from class asked me to lunch on Monday, but I had the time free and figured I could pump them for some information on Addie. I never expected to see her in the pub with Aidan. I might have volunteered to work for Jimmy if I had known they were going to be meeting up here.

"I think you'd make a lovely couple." Virginia leans close, like she's sharing a secret.

"I don't think she's interested," I huff out. "She has a tendency to—"

"To cut you to the quick. I know," Louise cuts me off with a knowing nod. "Have you considered maybe a different approach?" She peers at me over the top of her reading glasses.

This conversation seems to have taken quite the turn.

Hell, I didn't even know I was looking for Addie to be interested. I thought I was just fixated on her since she seemed impervious to my obvious charms. I mean, I've tried all of my best moves. She just seems to dislike me more and more.

"Maybe bring a coffee to class for her tomorrow. And, of course, you'll want to work on your cookies." Connie grabs a pad of paper from her bag and starts writing a list or something.

"What do you mean, *my cookies?* Is that a euphemism for something?" I like getting a rise out of the girls, though I do need to know more about the cookie situation.

Connie passes me the top sheet of paper from her pad. "Here, just follow this exactly and bring them tomorrow with that coffee. Dark roast with—"

"A bit of cream, yeah." I look over Connie's recipe for chocolate-chocolate chunk cookies as I think about what I need to grab from the market on my way home.

The closing of the front door draws my attention away from my mental shopping list. Addie is gone, Aidan's getting the bar ready for the night, and all the girls are staring at me. I push my glasses back up my nose and run my hand through my hair as I look at each of them in turn.

"What?"

"Nothing, dear." Virginia pats my arm again and smiles at Louise and Connie. They're quite obviously plotting something.

They file out the door shortly after, talking about where to go for dinner. That adds to my confusion since it's only three o'clock in the afternoon.

"Who eats dinner this early?" I ask the empty table.

Aidan, of course, can't leave well enough alone. "Erm, your demographic is aging, yeah?"

I slouch back in my chair and throw him a glare over my shoulder. I wish I could just ask him for advice. Talk to him and be taken seriously for a change.

"Are you pouting then? Did they turn you down for lack of experience?"

Shoving back my chair, I stand and shrug into my jacket.

With my recipe safely in my pocket, I stalk toward the door before a gruff, "Oy," stops me in my tracks.

"What? Not done? Need to pile on more shite?" I'm a bit touchy, yeah, but I have reason to be. I take a lot of crap from Aidan and Francie.

"Not piling more on, just...she's lovely. Maybe you should tone it down and ask her out." Aidan sets a Guinness on the bar for himself and an extra, though there's no one else here just now.

I check the time on my phone and sigh. There's just enough time for a pint before the doctor's office closes. The market is right by my flat, so I should be able to get it all done tonight.

Shrugging my jacket back off, I settle at the bar. The cold pint gives me something to focus on for a bit while I compile my thoughts.

"You're concentrating on that awfully hard. What're you thinking?" Aidan settles against the counter behind the bar and takes a pull from his own pint.

There's no way I'm going to tell him how his jab bothers me or why. Sure, I miss my brothers and would love for

Aidan to fill that role, but there are some things I'm just not into sharing.

"When did you know with Lis? How did you know that she was worth taking out?"

"Worth taking out? If you're interested at all, take the chance. It might turn out to be nothing, not right for either of you. But it might turn into the best decision you've ever made. What's holding you back? I've not seen you leave with anyone in over a week."

My head snaps up to meet his inquisitive look. "I..." He's right. I think back to the last time I entertained one of my lovely friends. *Was it Marlee?* "I don't know why you're paying such close attention to my love life. Things on the rocks with you and Lissy again?"

Aidan levels me with a harsh glare, choosing to ignore my last statement. I set him to rights several months ago, and he's not above giving it back to me.

Christ, why have I been leaving the pub alone? It's not that I'm hurting for willing participants. My phone is full of numbers, and the pub is usually full of options.

"Finn, maybe it's time to stop fucking about. Get serious about something for a change."

"You marrying me off? I haven't even taken her out, for fuck's sake. What if we're not, erm...compatible?" *He's got to be kidding me.* "Just because you moved right in with Lis doesn't mean I'm on a similar schedule." Fucking lunacy is what this is. I push back from the bar and drain my Guinness. I've heard enough of his wisdom, and I grab my crap from the barstool next to me.

"Finn—"

"Nah, I'm done. I've things to do. Places to be."

The door slams behind me just after I throw him the finger over my shoulder. Aidan can fuck right off.

NINE

Adelaide

"Did the instructor from the last class leave their coffee?"

There's an odd vibe in the room today. The ladies are looking far too innocent for real life.

"I don't believe so, dear."

Something is up for sure; Connie never calls me *dear*. And no one has opened the cookies.

"The coffee's for you. Just the way you take it," Finn casually throws out. He's here—not just on time, but early. And he's not wearing his glasses.

"Do you need to sit up here? Closer to the front, so you can see?" *Maybe he forgot them. Maybe they're just another one of his cheesy props.*

He looks so different without the frames. I mean, he's

good-looking regardless. I'm sure that helps his man-whore ways, but I can't seem to stop looking at him.

"I can see just fine, thanks. I went with contact lenses. Do you like the change?" He winks.

There is so much winking with him.

I'm getting a little lost in Finn's eyes. When he unfolds himself from his chair and stalks toward me, I force myself to look away. Aidan's words, his comments about Finn, run through my mind as he approaches. I pull my lower lip between my teeth when he stops in front of me and leans in close. I level him with my best side-eye. No way, no how is he going to make a move here. Not in front of the ladies.

Instead, he pops the lid off the cookie container, deftly flipping and catching it. The most amazing smell wafts out, enveloping me in chocolaty goodness. "I'll just pass these round the class before we get started then," he murmurs. And, like a gentleman, he takes the stack of napkins and makes his way through the room, stopping and chatting with each of the girls. Polite. Kind. Considerate.

This is not what I expected to see from him. I catch Virginia giving him a quick wink when she pats his hand. Seeing this side of him has me off-balance. It's so far from what I've come to expect. And, this time, when he saunters toward me, I'm biting at my lip for an entirely different reason.

"I think you'll find this a far better thing to chew on than that lovely lip. Though I'd be happy to help with that if you need." He holds a cookie out to me.

"It's huge." I look up at him, not registering what I said until the cocky smile spreads across his face. Shaking my head, I prepare myself for the inevitable.

"It is—" Whatever he was going to say gets cut off by a loud throat clearing from over on Louise's side of the room. Finn snaps his mouth shut, nods, and goes back to his seat.

Flabbergasted. I'm completely flabbergasted.

I have no idea what's going on today. Turning back to my computer, I take a bite of Finn's cookie and moan.

A-fucking-mazing.

The buzz that started in the room goes completely silent. I chance a look over my shoulder and find all the ladies smirking. And Finn is staring at me, wide-eyed, shifting in his seat.

"I...'s really good," I mumble around the warm, gooey treat. "Sorry. Let's, um...should we..." I never get flustered like this. "Fuck." This can't get any worse. I need to get a grip.

I DON'T KNOW how we make it to the end of our class time, but I'm pretty damn sure it's the least productive class I've ever led.

"So, we'll just pick up here next time."

And, with that, the awkward filing out of the room commences. The air has been charged for the entire hour and a half that we've been here. I pack up my stuff, eyeing the rest of my cookie. There's no way I could risk taking another bite with an audience.

Finn, however, hasn't moved from his seat.

"Did you make these?" I wave toward my half-eaten treat. His response is nothing more than a slow nod. "They're delicious."

"Thank you," he rasps, still not moving from his seat.

"Here." I shove the container holding the remaining cookies toward him.

He shakes his head, pulling his computer off the desk and settling it on his lap. "No, you take 'em." His accent is thicker, more pronounced than usual.

"Okay. Are you, um...are you ready to go?"

"Erm, I am." He nods, sliding his stuff into his bag, waiting for me to pass before coming to his feet. "Can I help you with your coat?" He takes it from my hand and holds it for me, guiding it up my arms and settling it on my shoulders.

"Thank you." I have to clear my throat to make the words come out. I gather the rest of my things from my desk and pop a stray crumb in my mouth. A moan bubbles up unbidden, and I try to stifle it by pressing my hand to my lips. "Sorry," I mumble, cheeks flaming.

Finn follows me out of the room, turning off the lights and closing the door behind us. He walks me to my car and gets the door for me—just like he did for the ladies.

"I guess I'll see you...later?" I don't know why that comes out as a question. I mean, I assume I'll just see him back here in a couple of days.

"Sure." He nods at me, tight-lipped, and closes my door.

Finn steps back, and as I pull out of the lot, he's still standing in that same spot. Bag slung over his shoulder, jacket clutched at his waist, shivering in the winter cold.

TEN

"Your place or mine?"
"Both. You go to your place, and I'll go to mine."

Finn

I hope to God she didn't notice my struggle, my discomfort. But Jesus, Mary, and Joseph, when she moaned around that cookie, my cock was paying attention and didn't seem to want to let the issue go. Instead, I sat there, imagining the sounds she'd make with my lips around her clit.

Christ, I wasn't sure I had it in me to behave like a gentleman and not slip back into the tried-and-true methods that have yet to fail me. Until now. She seems impervious to my usual charms.

Today was different though. She didn't just dismiss me like usual. Maybe Virginia is right about tempering my approach.

Addie's eyes didn't hold the same disdain that they had in

the past. It was like she appreciated my manners. But, fuck me, when she made the *huge* comment, it took everything I had and a quick reminder from my cheer squad to bite my tongue.

Much as I would love to get a handle on my *situation*, I've traded a lot of shifts with Jimmy, and I need to go to the pub and work. And shake myself out of this slump I've been in.

Maybe Virginia was mistaken about Addie's interest, though. Aidan is off his tits in love and thinks everyone should fall in line with that. I probably just need to find a lovely someone to help ease my suffering, to take my mind off relationships.

NONE of them strike my fancy. Not a single one.

Not a second glance.

Not a twitch.

Nothing.

The only thing that interests me and might possibly occupy my thoughts is another whiskey. I've already drunk more than my share tonight. But, as I pour another measure into my glass, the door opens, and finally, there's a reason to smile.

"Hey. I, um..." She approaches the corner of the bar and nervously looks around. "I brought your container back." She sets the plastic box on the counter. Nods and turns toward the door.

"Stay for a bit, Addie. Can I get you a drink?"

Any progress I thought I was making with her disintegrates as her spine stiffens, and her shoulders rise until they're practically lost in the green tresses twisted up at the base of her neck.

"It's Adelaide." I can practically hear her molars grinding, but I follow her to the door, like a lamb being led to slaughter.

"What's wrong with ye, Addie?" Before I realize I've done it, my finger is wrapped up in a soft green tendril that's escaped from the rest. "I like this color. It suits you."

Her sneakers squeak against the cement floor as she spins. She pulls her head back, releasing her hair from my grasp. "It's just Adelaide. Nonnegotiable."

Her head is tilted back, so she can meet my eyes. And glare at me evidently. My eyes dance across her features, taking in her deep-brown eyes and the silver hoop pierced from one nostril to the other. She's so unique, so different from other girls.

"What? Did you hear me? Nonnegotiable."

"I heard you, Addie." I open the door of McBride's, taking my business outside. Stepping into her, I lean down; she's ridiculously short. "And everything's negotiable," I whisper across her mouth, letting the door swing closed behind us.

Since she doesn't pull back, I press a kiss to those delicious lips.

Christ, they're more perfect than I imagined. And, when I sweep my tongue against the seam, she opens for me.

The last thing I want is for her to come to her senses too soon and pull away, so I slide my hands round the sides of her neck. I tilt her head a bit, just enough for me to nip at that plump lower lip that has been haunting my dreams for the past week or so.

Her hands grasp my forearms, and for a moment, I fully expect her to push me off. But she clings to me instead. So, I deepen the kiss, diving in for more. Tasting her. Teasing her. Taking my breath away—and, hopefully, hers as well. There's a current, sparks, crackling beneath the surface of my skin, and I want nothing more than to take her home. I want to peel back her layers and lay her bare. My mind swirls around the things I want to do to her. For her. With her.

So, when she pulls back a little, breaking the kiss, I try to blink my lustful thoughts down.

"I..." Her fingers ghost across her kiss-swollen lips, quivering slightly. "I have to go."

"You could wait until I'm done and go with me." I pull her hand and press her fingertips to my lips. *Fuck's sake, what if she says yes?*

Her pupils are blown wide, but she shakes her head. "I can't. I have to go home. There's some—I just...I have to go." She takes a wobbly step backward before fumbling in her pocket for her keys. "I'm sorry. I..."

Having her flustered is such a change. I like this.

"Good night, Addie. Sweet dreams." I shove my hands into the pockets of my jeans, watching to make sure she gets in her car safe. Without even thinking, I throw her the Finn wink.

She'll be back.

AS I'M CLEANING up for the night, Marlee floats through the door and settles herself at the bar.

"Hey, Finny," she purrs, leaning over the bar and flashing me her tits. "You almost done here?"

I can practically feel her gaze raking up and down my body. And, for the first time ever, it doesn't have any effect.

I just don't care.

"Marlee." I toss her a smile but have no real desire to engage her more than that.

What's happened? Our time together was spectacular, fucking mind-blowing. A couple of weeks ago, I'd have been looking for a repeat performance—or several. I mean, our evening was great. I was phenomenal, and Marlee certainly had nothing to complain about—repeatedly.

"So, do you already have plans tonight?" Her arms are crossed on the bar top, and with the way she's leaning over, her tits being pushed up as high as they can go, there's no awkward eye contact.

"Erm, no." I could so easily take her home and lose myself in physical pleasure. Making her scream and leaving her with just enough energy to give me a quick blow job before making her come until she passes out. I could, but—

"Your place? Or mine?" She licks her lips while she talks to my dick, her eyes not venturing higher than my belt.

Why? Why does this feel cheap? Why does that bother me now when it never has before? Maybe I'm broken. It's been weeks since I've indulged with someone. In fact, I'm almost positive that Marlee's the last girl I've spent time with like that.

I casually fist a bar rag in both hands in front of me, shielding my poor, uninterested cock from her inspection.

"I think I'm going to pass, yeah..." *Think, Finn.* I search through the files in my brain for a solid excuse. "I've a headache, just going home to sleep."

Marlee stares at me like I've lost my mind before she shrugs and turns, walking out the door.

Maybe I *have* lost my mind.

ELEVEN

Adelaide

The entire drive home is lost to me. I was there, awake and aware but not. Completely on autopilot. I've never needed a friend to help me sort something out like this before. My friends here have proven to be more than biased toward the Irish Casanova, and since it's after eight at night, they're most likely in bed already anyway.

That whole antisocial thing I have going on is totally biting me in the ass. I could talk to Eric about it, but I need more. Another girl's perspective.

Climbing the stairs to my apartment, I text my friend Brielle, hoping she's not out with her fiancé, Brad. She's one of the few girls I hung out with in high school. We were pretty tight even though she's a couple of years older than me.

Instead of pinging with a notification, my phone buzzes, and Bri's smiling face lights up the screen.

"Hey, am I interrupting anything? You didn't need to actually call me."

"Oh my gosh, Adelaide, no. How are you?"

Hearing her voice makes me kind of miss my friend in Kansas City. I was so eager to get away, spread my wings, and start fresh that I never thought twice about the things I would be without, true friendships being one of them.

"I'm okay. I didn't pull you away from Brad, did I?"

"No." She snorts. "We need time and a bottle of wine for that story, but that's over. No more Brad. What's going on? You sound...I don't know...thinky." There's nothing like a librarian making up words.

"I am *thinky*, I guess." I don't touch on the Brad issue, because I'm thrilled that asshole is out of the picture.

"Is it a guy? A one-night stand who wants more? Is Eric still the only man in your life?" She giggles at the notion of Eric.

I unlock my door, grab his leash from the end table, and go straight for his crate. His little sausage-shaped body wiggles excitedly.

"He's more than enough testosterone for me. Usually." I settle him in my arm and head back down the stairs to let him do his thing.

"So, it is about a guy. Spill it."

I sigh heavily, thinking maybe I should have just slept on the whole thing and then ignored it with every fiber of my being.

"I don't need a guy. Relationships are a pain in the ass. As a general rule, I don't like people enough to want to spend large amounts of time with any of them. I'm just not wired that way. I don't *people*."

"But?"

"But this guy has me all confused and rattled. I don't know, Bri. It makes no sense."

"What doesn't make sense, Adelaide?"

"He tends bar, and I thought he was nothing but bad pickup lines and one-night stands. Thinks his shit doesn't stink, and he's God's gift to women. I can't stand that shit." I scoop Eric up since he's done with his business and his short, little legs aren't conducive to two flights of stairs.

"Keep going. There's more you're not telling me."

"He's in my class—one that I'm teaching at the community center. And he's so sweet with my ladies. And he kissed me tonight. And, Bri, I thought I was going to die—like, my skin was all tight and tingly."

"Adelaide, sweetie, did your toes curl?"

"They did. They so did. And he stole my breath. Brielle, I don't know what to do," I whine, pushing through my door.

Eric scampers off to find his squeaky toy.

"Go out with him, Addie," she says softly. "Give him a chance. And, if nothing else, get laid. You'll feel better."

Letting the Addie thing slide because it's Bri, I snort-laugh at her advice. "That's exactly what Louise said."

"Well, listen to your elders. We've got experience on you. Let me know how things go, okay? And, if all else fails, rub the nub."

"Okay, thanks. Maybe I'll come home soon. Catch up with you and the Brad sitch?"

"You know it. Night, babe." She hangs up before I can respond.

I throw myself back in my chair, hugging my knees to my chest. Not once since leaving Kansas City have I had a problem with a guy. Finding a release. Getting off and walking away.

It's not like I'm warm and fuzzy. I don't really like feeling —feelings. It's just sex, endorphins. And it's been a long fucking time. Since Eric came on the scene, the dachshund has been the only wiener in my apartment. Not even the guy who delivers my General Tso's chicken has stepped foot inside, and we see each other on the regular.

Pushing up out of the chair, I pad through my apartment to the fridge and grab a carton of leftover Chinese and a pair of chopsticks. The flavors bursting in my mouth elicit a small moan that makes me think back to class earlier.

To Finn.

To that kiss.

When he let go of his goofy, cheesy persona at McBride's and kissed me, more than my toes were affected. I felt that kiss race down my spine, expand through my skin, and set every part of me on fire.

It might have even sparked something in my soul. Thus, me off-balance. Feeling prickly and uncomfortable.

I can practically feel his warm hands grasping and tilting my face, moving me where he wanted me. With our height difference, he could so easily overpower me, but it was nothing like that. He didn't try to take over in that moment; he just took control.

My God, if he's anything like that in bed...

Maybe I should listen to Brielle and Louise. Maybe they

have a point. If nothing else, it could be some pretty amazing sex. And, really, I won't have to see him anymore after this class is done in a couple of weeks. This could work.

I finish eating and drop my bowl into the dishwasher. With all the thoughts of Finn's lips and the hint of getting laid, I'm definitely feeling twitchy. There's really only one thing to do, one thing that will afford me some relief.

Eric nips at my heels as I traipse down the hall to my bathroom. I fill the tub, testing the water temperature, adding cherry-and-vanilla-scented bath oil. Fragrance hangs in the heavy, humid air as I light a candle and slip out of my clothes. I hit the light switch and push Eric out, closing the door behind him. The last thing I need is a wiener ruining my moment.

With Eric safely out of my way, I sink low into the tub, steaming water caressing my curves. I slide my hand down my stomach and slip it between my thighs. Brielle's suggestion bounces around in my brain as my fingers tease and hint at the release my body needs.

As my climax builds, all I can think is, *What's Finn doing right now?*

TWELVE

Finn

The door slams behind me, interrupting the halfhearted moans coming from Jimmy's side of our flat. I stalk straight to the kitchen and grab a bottle of whiskey. Marlee's offer and my refusal sobered me far beyond where I want to end the night. I drain a fair bit of the bottle before resting it on the counter next to me.

"What's up your arse, Finn?" Jimmy walks out of his room in nothing but his boxers, slung low on his hips. He reeks of cheap perfume and sex.

"Nothin'." I rub at my eyes, not quite used to the contact lenses. I take another long pull from the bottle and wipe my mouth with the back of my hand. "Did I interrupt your big moment then?"

The whiskey is just taking the edge off whatever shite is running through my head.

"I got what I needed." He shrugs, reaching for the bottle.

I pull away, guarding it for myself. "You're a fucking selfish bastard, man."

"And you couldn't find a warm body to bring home, so you can fuck right off."

"Had the offer. Just wasn't the one I wanted," I boast, pushing off the counter and heading down the short hall toward my room. Green tresses swirl through my mind.

"You giving up the game?" Jimmy shouts after me.

"Just getting choosy," I toss back.

I strip down and warm the shower. The whiskey bottle gripped tightly in one hand, I step beneath the stream and tilt my head under the water. Surely, I can get some relief. My free hand slicks up and down the length of my cock, jerking, as thoughts of Addie fill my head. The way she tasted. The way she gripped my arms—not quite pulling me in, but not really pushing me away.

Christ, I've gotten my release any number of ways, but when I think of Addie, the feeling is entirely different. With my eyes squeezed shut, cock aching in my fist, my thoughts go straight to her. I wonder what she's doing at this God-given moment. The inkling that maybe, just maybe, she could be thinking of me has me stroking faster, harder.

I steady myself on the wall of the shower, whiskey bottle clinking against the tiles. And the face I see when I come is Addie's, the look of pure lust when I took her lips earlier.

CHRIST, *can I not wake up just once in the morning with my cock not aching for a change?*

I close my eyes, hoping to fall back to sleep, but the ear-splitting wails of, "Jimmy, oh, Jimmy," are far too loud and not at all genuine, but they do the trick for me, killing any fantasy I might have fallen back into.

The man needs to pay attention to his girls' tells. Or have some fucking pride and find a girl who's a step further away from desperate.

I grab my earbuds and crank some music at a high enough volume to mask what I'd rather not experience. At least I take my time. Pay attention and leave whoever the lucky lady is satisfied but wishing for more.

WHEN I PUSH through the door of McBride's, only five minutes late for my shift, the last person I expect to see sitting at the bar is Francie. He's not been around much for the past few weeks, but with St. Patrick's Day quickly approaching, it makes sense that I'd be seeing a lot more of him.

"You're late again, Finn." Francie peers at me over the top of his coffee mug. "What's your excuse's name this time?"

"Erm, Jimmy? That bastard is loud as fuck when he—"

"I don't need to know that." Francie holds his hand up, palm out, stopping my words. Hell, no one should be subjected to it. "What's goin' on wit' ye? I've heard that you've been keeping company with some *older* ladies again, not acting quite yourself."

"Been talking to Aidan then?"

I can take their shite and them riding my arse about things. I grew up with two older brothers who showed no mercy for taunting me until the day I left Dublin, but there are times I just wish the McBride's men would leave well enough alone.

"I have. Don't want you repeating history," he puts out there without any pretense. "He also mentioned a lovely little thing who is doing some work for him. I like her."

At that, I snap my head up to meet his inquisitive stare. "What did he say about her?"

"Finn, maybe it's time you settle yourself and take a break from the quick and easy."

My eyebrows disappear into my hairline at that.

He stands from the stool and pauses a moment, swaying a bit on his feet. "You're off this year for St. Paddy's. Why don't you ask her out? Take her someplace nice, treat her like a lady. And keep things respectful for a first date for a change." Francie nods at this sage advice and turns for his office.

THIRTEEN

"Do you have a map? Because I keep getting lost in your eyes."
"No, but you're right on track with getting lost."

Adelaide

I put off starting class, waiting to see if Finn will show. It's fifteen minutes after the hour, and he's not here. While I would've totally expected that the first week of class, I'm concerned now. He's been so punctual, early. And so involved with the ladies.

"Has anyone heard from Finn? Should we wait for him?" I flit my gaze from face to face and back to the door, searching for his now-familiar wide smile.

"He texted me that he's not feeling well, so he won't be here today," Virginia volunteers.

"You text?" The question falls out of my mouth, unbidden and completely without thought.

"Of course I do, Adelaide. I also tweet and snap." The

look she gives me over the top of her glasses is nothing short of condescending.

"Is he okay? Does he need anything?" As soon as the questions tumble from my lips, I see the gears turning, and Virginia types furiously on her iPhone.

"He says not to worry; he'll manage. He'll maybe try to go to the market after a while if his fever's down." She reads from her screen. "I think it would be a nice gesture if one of us stopped by to check and see if he had everything he needed." She looks around the room, meeting everyone's eyes, before she blinks up at me. "Unfortunately, I've got to bounce after this, so..."

Virginia's declaration is followed up by a chorus of, "Oh, I wish I could," and, "I'm just not able to today."

"I would go, but I don't know where"—*ping*—"he lives." I glance down at my phone and see a text from Virginia with an address. When I look at her, her face is a mask of innocence.

"Might be nice if you brought him some soup or something from the market, dear."

I should have paid closer attention.

AFTER FINISHING up at the community center, I swing through the market and pick up some homemade chicken noodle soup, crackers, and some ginger ale. And Twizzlers because, even when I'm feeling icky, it's nice to have a treat.

THE STREET that Virginia sent me to is full of cars with no parking spots in sight. As I turn the corner, I see a small lot behind the building and a spot open next to Finn's little silver Kia. Once I'm parked next to him, I grab the bags from the grocery store and climb the stairs.

I knock gingerly at the door. If he's feeling badly and sleeping, I don't want to be the ass who wakes him up. I shift my weight, popping one hip out and then the other as I wait. *Should I knock harder? Ring the bell?*

As I lift my hand to rap on the door one more time, it swings open, revealing some guy I've never seen before in my life.

"Oh. Sorry, I must have the wrong address." I back away, looking at the number on the mailbox and comparing it to the one Virginia sent.

"Not at all." The distinctly Irish accent washes over me. "You're looking for Finn then?" the dark-haired man says as he steps out of the apartment. "His is the room to the right, through the kitchen and down the hall a bit." He lopes down the stairs and disappears around the corner.

Tentatively, I step through the doorway and look around. It's every bit the bachelor pad. Worn dark-blue sofa, ridiculously large screen TV mounted on the wall with a gaming system sprawled on a makeshift shelf under it.

"Hello? Finn?"

It feels weird, walking through the space. Surely, the guy who let me in would have texted Finn to let him know I was here. Well, that someone was here.

I pop into the kitchen and set the bags on the table in the corner. Busying myself, I empty the bags and consider digging through the cabinets for a bowl.

"Are you stalking me, sweet Addie?"

I almost drop the container of soup at the sound of Finn's raspy voice. When I turn, I'm faced with a lean, flushed chest and low-slung gray sweatpants, a roll of toilet paper trailing from his hand.

Damn it. What is it with stupid gray sweatpants?

"No. Virginia said you were sick, and I got *volun-told* to bring you soup and sick supplies." I narrow my eyes and point at him as he takes a step closer to me. "Keep your germs to yourself. I do not have time for sick shenanigans."

Finn's eyes are glassy, and his nose is red, like he's been wiping it with sandpaper. "Right. So, no kissing today." The words barely make it out before he sneezes three times back to back to back. "Fuck." He rips off a length of toilet paper and grimaces as he blows his nose.

I roll my eyes and replace the roll of TP with a box of super-soft, antiviral tissues. Then, I reach for the Lysol wipes I bought. Lord have mercy, germs are the devil. Snapping on the gloves I made sure to bring, I go on a mini-cleaning frenzy, wiping surfaces around the kitchen, throwing away trash, and straightening little bits of everything. I've gone completely into mom mode.

"I brought some chicken noodle soup. Which cabinet do you keep your bowls in?" I pull one down from where he's pointing and watch as a violent shiver rolls over him. "Finn, are you..."

He looks like he's burning up, goose bumps all over him, bright red painting his cheeks.

"Have you taken any medicine?"

"I haven't. 'M f-f-fine," he chatters, arms wrapped around his torso.

He's not. I shuffle him out to the couch and get him settled.

"Hang on, let me get you some Advil."

He's half-lying down when I come back with a glass of water, some pills, and the bowl of soup.

"Here, sit up for a minute." I hand him the water and pills, watching his grimace as he swallows. Replacing his water with the soup, I look around the room. "Do you have a blanket? Want me to get you a shirt or—"

"In my room, there's a quilt on my bed," he says as he starts in on the soup.

I don't know what I was expecting from his room, but the tidy, well thought-out space is not it. The soft cream-colored sheets, rumpled from sleep, are not the nasty dark ones that single guys usually go for. Like, since they're dark, they can get away with not washing them very often. His closet is open but organized. His shoes are lined up, clothes hung up neatly. It's just not what I imagined.

I pick up the handmade quilt pieced together in a mix of blues and grays. When I hug it to me, the fresh smell of fabric softener wafts up, and I inhale deeply.

"Did you find it?" Finn looks at me over the back of the couch. "Christ, yes." He reaches back toward me, making grabby hands. "Are you sniffing my woobie?"

Eyes wide, I push it away from me and huff, "No. Did you finish your soup?"

I round the end of the couch, shaking out the quilt. Finn takes hold of it and pulls hard, sending me toppling to the cushion next to him.

"I did. Thank you." He stifles a yawn and settles into the

corner of the couch. Broad shoulders, pale and lightly dusted with a smattering of freckles, slide out of sight as he wraps his blanket loosely around them. "You didn't bring me a pillow, too?"

"Would you like me to get you a pillow?" I ask, trying to force patience into my voice.

"I would." He tries to do his usual douchey smile, but cuddled with a blankie, his nose bright red and hair a tousled mess, he just looks freaking adorable.

"Fine," I sigh and grab a pillow from his bed. His very large, comfy-looking bed. I roll my eyes. The bed where he's taken countless women, if the rumors are correct. "Here." I chuck the pillow to him when he turns, and I start tidying up his tissues and bowl.

"Will you stay for a bit?" Finn calls as I scrub my hands under scalding water to kill any germs that might have gotten to me.

I dry my hands and bring him a fresh glass of water. He's completely snuggled in. Completely.

I shift from one foot to the other after setting his glass on the coffee table in front of him. "I don't know. I don't do germs well." Reaching up to center my septum ring, I panic for a beat, wondering if I washed my hands thoroughly enough.

"Please? Just till I fall asleep?" His eyes are drooping, so surely, it won't be long.

I slide onto the far end of the couch and suppress a shudder when he tucks his feet under my thigh. *What do I do?* I don't like feet any more than I like germs. Feet are disgusting unless they belong to an itty-bitty brand-new baby.

Oh my God. This is why I don't like people. They have germs. And feet.

Finn sleepily mumbles, "Thank you," as his eyes close and his breathing evens out.

I count to thirty, and then unclenching my fist, I tentatively reach out, touching his calf. The muscles are relaxed under my hand, so I push myself off the couch, trying not to disturb him. Finn rubs his feet together, the warmth of my ass no longer warming them. I pull at his quilt to cover him up better, but when I lift it, he shifts in his sleep, tucking one hand up under his pillow. And the other? The other is firmly in place, cupping his dick.

Of course.

FOURTEEN

"I KNOW HOW TO PLEASE A WOMAN."
"THEN, PLEASE...LEAVE ME ALONE."

Finn

I wake from what had to have been a dream. There's no way Addie would've been in my flat, tending to me while I was sick. But I'm wrapped in the quilt my mum made me while on the couch with a glass of water in front of me instead of whiskey. My quilt holds a subtle scent of something. Something soft and warm. Something I can't quite place, but it's familiar at the same time.

The distinct smell of disinfectant hangs in the air, and as I stumble into the kitchen, I take in the polished surfaces, the perfectly straight canisters, and a small stash of pain relievers and cold remedies. The fridge holds half a container of chicken soup and a full bottle of ginger ale. Things I know we did not have in the flat when I fell ill because I looked. I was fucking desperate for them. And the tissues are soft, soothing ones. Not the prickly roll of toilet paper I was using.

My smile stretches across my face as I read the note tucked under the meds. It's loopy girlie handwriting with the time marked for when I'm due my next dose. Christ, I slept like a baby. I shake out a few Advil and throw them back with ginger ale straight from the bottle. It wasn't a dream.

I shuffle to my bedroom, wrapped in my blanket, pillow tucked under my arm, and check my phone. No messages. No new contacts added. I dial the pub, and after no one answers, I text Jimmy.

Me: Did you buy food?

Jimmy: No.

Me: Did someone stop by? One of your...women?

Jimmy: Just the girl. Green hair, pierced nose, nice rack.

Me: You saw her rack?

Jimmy: She has great tits.

Me: I haven't seen them. How did you?

Jimmy: Relax. Used my imagination. She was being swallowed by a huge sweater thing. Nice legs though.

Me: Fuck right off. Did she leave a number?

Jimmy: No.

Me: Is Aidan there? Ask him for her number.

The bouncing dots taunt me while I straighten my bed and adjust the angle of the TV. I tilt the blinds so there's no glare on the screen, debating what to do next.

Jimmy: Sorry. He says no.

Why are they all against me? Because, now, I don't have her number, and all I can think of are her tits. Or the possibility of them since she always seems to be hiding under big, bulky jumpers.

Since Francie won't let me back to work yet, I watch movies, read, and think long and hard about what to do for myself—the next step in finding my place in the world. My purpose.

The application for university isn't difficult, but I hold my breath when I hit the request for my records from Dublin to be sent. That could ruin my chances. Francie and Aidan think I'm young and stupid now. I roll my eyes at the thought and can't help but think of Addie. Christ, she can roll her eyes gloriously. She thinks it's all tough and off-putting when she does it, but it just makes me wonder what she looks like when she loses herself in a moment of rapture.

Fuck, I've taken a lot of showers since she was here in my flat, and my cock has never been cleaner. I was sick, sure, but not sick enough to ignore the thought of her going into my room, into my space. If only I'd had her here and not been feverish. The mental image of her splayed out on my bed, green tresses spread out across my cream sheets, a hint of her perfume lingering. Her eyes rolling entirely from my efforts.

The frustration of not being able to break through her shell feeds the tedium of having nothing to do for the next few days. Add that to all of the anxiety from submitting my uni application and I can't seem to stop fidgeting. I glance at my phone for the fiftieth time today, just as a text pings in.

Virginia: How are you feeling, honey? Better?

Me: Better. Bored though.

Virginia: Did you have a visitor?

Me: I did. I have no way to thank her. Can you help me?

Why did I not think of this before? Of course Virginia has Addie's phone number. Maybe I really am young and stupid, but at least, now, I know what I'm doing in some respects.

My phone pings again with a phone number from Virginia. One not from this area code. I send a quick winky face and enter the new number under Addie's name in my Contacts.

Jimmy busts through the door, balancing a six-pack of beer and a large pizza box. "Fucking lazy bastard. When ye coming back to work?" He empties the contents of his arms onto the coffee table and glares at me on the sofa.

The smell of Italian sausage and mushrooms wafts through the room as I lift the lid of the box snagging a piece. "I'm bored as fuck. Would love to get back to it," I mumble around the huge bite of pizza.

Jimmy pops the top off a couple of bottles of beer and hands me one. "Right. So, you'll take a few of my shifts this week to make up for all your hours I worked?"

I owe him for certain, but I know what he's getting at. And the answer is no.

"I'm not taking St. Patrick's Day. No."

"I've had to train the new kid all by myself," he whines. Legit whines, like a child. "Finn, you fucking owe me."

"Not that. I've not had a break on St. Paddy's in four years." I reach for another slice of pizza. "And my flute is feeling neglected," I deadpan.

Jimmy snorts beer out his nose.

I pop the pizza crust between my teeth and type out a quick text to the number Virginia sent me. My thumb hovers over the Send button, not quite ready to commit. I could call. Francie would tell me I should call instead of text. He'd tell me it was the proper way to say thank you.

But, if I call, she can opt not to answer and then just

delete my voice mail. I'd never know if she listened or not. A text though? I can see that it's delivered and when it's read. With a text, I feel like I'll have a better grasp on her level of ignoring me. *What are the chances she didn't turn off those notifications?*

FIFTEEN

"If these walls could talk…"
"You'd probably masturbate less."

Adelaide

Unknown: Thank you for coming by and taking care of me.

Me: Who is this?

Unknown: How many sick people have you been tending to?

Me: Finn? How did you get my number?

Unknown: It is. I wanted to thank you, and I didn't want to wait for days to pass.

Me: You're welcome.

I slide my glasses to the top of my head and rub at my eyes. This is about the last thing I expected. I've been working nonstop for…glancing at the three-foot round clock hanging high on my wall…six hours. I lost track of time again, and now, I'm stiff. Hefting my computer and lap desk to the table next to the chair, I slowly start to unfold myself.

A low grumble of discontent sounds from under the blanket by my feet, and Eric wiggles his little body out, blinking at me. It's a standoff. If I hold perfectly still, he'll go back to sleep, but if I move an inch, there's no way I'll be able to put off his walk for even a minute. His eyes are just drifting closed when my phone vibrates with a handful of text messages back to back.

The sensation, while not at all unpleasant, startles the shit out of me since I dropped it in my lap after responding to Finn. It might have slid to strategically rest right against my lady bits. Eric takes my subtle shift as confirmation of his deepest desires, and he bolts for the door, sliding to a stop before he dances in an awkward circle.

Sighing, I push myself up, grab my jacket and bright-yellow scarf, and shove my feet into my boots. "Buddy, it's cold out. This is going to be a quickie," I tell Eric as I scoop him up to expedite the whole process.

Eric, of course, is oblivious to the cold and hops and skips down the sidewalk, looking for the ideal spot to poop. Honest to God, what makes the spot three blocks away from my warm apartment so much more desirable than the snow bank right outside the door? Dogs are stupid. Or maybe the male species in general are the stupid ones.

I'm frozen solid by the time we walk back through the door. Eric does his helicopter dance in front of his bowl for his post-poop feeding. So gross. I scoop out some kibble for him and go straight for my coffeemaker, fixing myself a fresh pot. The aroma fills the air around me as I fix myself a cup.

With my hands wrapped around the warm mug, I realize I have a big decision to make. *More work? Or lose myself in a book for an hour or two?* There's not really a question to it. I grab my Kindle, and after a few minutes, just when things are starting to heat up, the cushion under my ass shakes.

Shoving my hand down into the side of the chair, I dig around for a bit before scoring. There are a ton of text messages, almost as many emails, and a missed call. I don't talk to this many people in a given day, but there is someone new who has my number now.

"Eric, should I even look?"

Eric truly acts like he doesn't give a shit.

Swiping at the screen, I see that Brielle sent me a ton of pictures of her and Not Brad. The guy is seriously hot and looks super familiar, but I can't quite place why. The emails are from clients, and I decide to answer those later. The missed call is my dad. That's a no.

Nothing further from Finn. Another surprise. I figured he'd be all up in my business now that he had my number. He's not used to hearing no, and I have given him nothing but. I stare at my phone for a minute. Look around my apartment and take stock of my life. I'm twenty-five, I live alone, I work from home, and my best friend lives a thousand miles away and is sending me pictures of her and a hot guy who is definitely not her fiancé. My only consistent interaction is with a foot-long wiener named Eric. And, now, I'm bothered that one of the man-whore bartenders has my number and is *not* blowing up my phone. I don't know what to do with this, but it doesn't look good for my social life.

I drop my Kindle and send a quick text to Bri, asking who the guy is, but the bouncy dots never bounce. Nothing. I pull a strand of hair from my braid and wrap it around my finger while I wait. The colors blend and shift as the strands wind and layer from deep, dark green to a much paler hue. I glance at my phone and still no bounce.

I'm lonely.

Really freaking lonely. It's never bothered me before. I like to be alone—like, really like it. No people. No germs. No feet. No attitude.

But it's lonely.

I check again, and there are still no bouncy dots. It's fine. My book will keep me company. I don't need anything else. I mean, I moved here to get away, so I'm away. I turn off notifications and drop my phone in my lap, diving back into my steamy story. But the silence is interrupted by a voice. Eric cocks his head from side to side, staring at my lap. At where my phone rests.

"Bri, is that you?" I call, fumbling with the button, so I can just put it on speaker. "Hang on, you're stuck between my thighs."

The laughter is deep, deeper than Brielle's voice. Maybe she's with that guy in her pictures. Lord, that would be mortifying. But, when I check my phone display, it's not my friend's number I see.

"I can't think of a better place to get stuck." The accent is raspy and a touch nasally, but it's his.

My fingers slide through my loose strands, and I groan. "Hey, Finn. I, uh...that wasn't meant for you."

"I'm not your Bri, but I wouldn't mind getting messages like that." He coughs out the last word and pulls the phone away from his mouth until he's back under control. "Sorry, that got away from me. Probably the excitement."

"You're not better yet? Do you need anything?" I guess I just assumed he was over this cold.

"Mostly better, no more fever, but—" He grunts a little, and it sounds like he's walking. "Sorry, I wanted some privacy. Since I've got you, erm...I, ehm..." He laughs quietly and blows out a barely audible, "Wow."

"You don't have me; let's just get that straight." Realizing how prickly that came out, I try to soften things. "But what do you need?"

"That didn't make it any easier to ask." Finn huffs out a laugh. "I would like to show you a good time."

"Show me a good time?" I snark. "You really think you're up for that?" *Does he even hear himself?* I gave him a chance. I tried to be nice. "Why don't you just—"

"That's not what I meant. I want to take you out," he rushes out. "Will you..." I hear a muted thud, like he banged his head against the wall or door or something. "Would you allow me to take you out on Friday evening?"

I'm stunned silent.

Whatever smart-ass direction I was about to tell him to go fuck off scatters from my brain when I hear a quiet, "Please."

"Okay."

"You will?"

I don't know what possessed me to say yes. Well, I do. It has everything to do with that whole lonely thing going on with me.

"Yeah. But I should go. I, um...I have to...I'll see you later."

"Bye, Addie."

"Adelaide. It's—"

And he's gone.

"Adelaide."

SIXTEEN

Finn

I don't know what to do.

I'm absolutely mental over this, where to take her, and Francie is not making things any easier. He keeps riding my arse about being a gentleman and not trying to get in her knickers on the first date. I've been trying to do that since I met her, and I don't know how to flip that on its head now.

Giving in to Jimmy's constant whining and begging for me to take his shift is starting to look like a good enough idea. I could tell her that I had to make up work from when I was sick, but that wouldn't be right. I don't think I can lie, nor do I really want to.

"Where are you taking your girl?" Francie asks.

"I don't know." I polish the very clean bar top.

"You have a date?" Aidan pulls the bottle of Jameson from under the taps and pours himself a substantial one.

"I do, but I..." I look around the pub. All the preparations for St. Patrick's Day are done. "Maybe I should cancel and help Jimmy and you." It makes sense really.

"*Pfft*, we've the new kid all trained up. Are ye nervous, Finn?" Francie, bless his heart, looks like he's worried for me.

I do feel a little off. Maybe I'm still sick.

"Who're you taking out that has you tied in knots?" Aidan looks from Francie to me and back again.

Jimmy picks this God-given moment to walk through the door. "Your Adelaide. Gonna loosen her up, yeah?"

"Christ, you're not." Aidan's eyes are wide, and his mouth is hanging open as he tries to make sense of what's happening. "Don't you fuck that up. She's a nice girl. You're not allowed to drive her away."

AND, because she wouldn't give me her address, we're meeting at McBride's.

On St. Patrick's Day.

With people packed in here and no room to fucking breathe.

Francie's at the door, checking IDs. Jimmy, Aidan, and the new kid, Kieran, are behind the bar, and I'm just standing here with my hands in my pockets, looking like a prat. The shattering of glass pulls my attention from the door, and Kieran's standing like a deer in headlights. He sputters an apology at Aidan, but when he leans down to pick up the bits of the bottle he dropped, Jimmy trips, sending the kid to his hands and knees. When Kieran sits back on his heels, there's a huge shard of glass sticking through his palm.

"Finn, can you..." Aidan nods toward the crowd of people filling the pub as he wraps Kieran's hand with a clean bar rag. He and Lis shuffle the kid out the door—taking him to the hospital, I'm sure.

I jump in and start pulling pitchers of beer and taking money, falling into the familiar rhythm of the past four years. Money. Beer. Whiskey. Flirt. As soon as I'm able, I reserve a spot at the bar for Addie, hoping she'll understand. *Hoping.*

I look up from another pitcher of green beer to see cascading emerald curls tumbling around the shoulders of an oversize cardigan. At least it's a million different shades of green. I set a mug of coffee in front of her, grabbing a carton of cream from the fridge.

"I'm so sorry," I start.

"It's okay. The guy at the door told me there was an emergency. Should we just forget this?"

I splash a bit of cream in her mug and tuck the carton away. "No." I'm leaning in, so I don't have to shout at her. "You look far too lovely and festive to waste this opportunity." I push the mug closer to her. "Do you mind waiting a bit? Maybe Aidan will come back." I get pulled back into the flurry of empty pitchers and waving dollar bills before she can answer.

It's an absolute madhouse, just as it is every year, and far too much time passes before I can take a breath and make my way back to Addie.

"Is this normal?" she shouts.

I grab her mug, refilling it as I knock a tap closed with my elbow.

"Pretty much. It's Francie's favorite day of the year." I nod toward the door and see the line is not going to let up anytime soon. "Usually, we have three of us back here, one at the door, and Francie keeping supplies stocked. We were a bit shorthanded to start and then..." I just shrug because more empty pitchers are being waved at me.

A few hours pass with Jimmy and me scrambling to keep up, and each spare moment is spent making sure Addie won't give up on me.

"Finn, baby, give me a beer and a shot!" a familiar voice yells.

I look up, and Marlee has her tits spilling out of a tiny green shirt. I do the best I can to make eye contact as I slide her a shot of whiskey and hand her a plastic cup of beer. Taking her money, I see a handful of guys behind her staring. Of course, she's wearing the shortest plaid skirt I think I've ever seen. And I've seen some short skirts over the years. The guys' jaws drop as she leans across the bar, grabbing my shirt to pull me in for a kiss.

Thankfully, Aidan and Lis breeze through the kitchen door just then, and I turn my head to greet them. And Marlee's lips land square on my cheek.

"I missed. Give me another chance, Finny."

Christ, she's off her tits already. I probably shouldn't have even served her.

I back away and nod at Aidan, wiping at the goopy, glossy mess on my cheek. "You back then? He's all right?" I look around for Kieran and only see Lis and her friend Gracyn.

"A bunch of stitches and some painkillers, so he'll not be back tonight. What was that?" Aidan nods at Marlee dancing her way over to the side of the bar. Right next to Addie.

"She's not taking no for an answer. I need to get out of here with Addie." I wipe my hands on a bar rag and hand it off to Aidan.

"Who?" He reaches out for an empty pitcher and falls into the repetitive motions of the night.

I glance to the right and smile as wide as I can—until I catch Marlee looking from me to Addie and back again.

I stalk over to them, smile firmly in place. "I'm done then. Let's get out of here, yeah?"

Unfortunately, Marlee is more than a little impaired.

"Sure, lemme jus' finish my beer," she slurs.

And the look Addie gives her is priceless—and more than a little intimidating.

"Heeeyyy, you don't have your glasses on. You look shexy like that."

Adelaide slides out of her barstool and makes her way through the crowd to the front door.

"I'll jus' sit right here." Marlee slides into the newly vacated seat, making herself at home.

"I'm out, Aidan. Maybe she just needs an Uber." I nod toward Marlee as I grab my jacket from where I stowed it under the bar and push my way through to catch up with Addie. "You're not leaving, are you? Can I still take you for a bite?"

"Absolutely. I just hit my limit with people. Had to leave before Skankzilla got too close," she deadpans at me. "She always like that?"

"No. She's a hot mess tonight." I laugh as I guide Addie to my car.

She pauses when I open the door for her. "I've seen how you drive. Maybe we should take my car."

The way she bites her lip when she's being snarky does things to me. Things that make my jeans uncomfortable.

I manage to keep the car door between us to hide my growing erection. "I promise, you're in good hands. We'll be perfectly safe."

She climbs in, and I close the door, thankful to have the barrier while I make the necessary adjustments.

Unfortunately, with her seated, Addie's face is exactly level with my hand as I shift my cock.

SEVENTEEN

"Haven't I seen you somewhere before?"
"Yes, that's why I stopped going."

Adelaide

There is no denying that he's got something impressive there.

Finn clears his throat as he closes his car door and starts the car.

"Forget that was a window?" He pastes on his smirk and shifts his hips, opening his mouth for what I'm sure will be bullshit, but I cut him off, "Just be real for a change; no need to get cocky."

We both freeze. Neither one of us is willing to move a muscle until it can't be contained, and we bust out laughing.

"Cocky." When Finn repeats it, the snort-laughs start.

"Oh my God. Sorry, that was too funny." I swipe a finger behind my glasses, dabbing at the tears. "What's the plan? What are we doing?" I shift in my seat to face him as he whips his car out of the space at the back of the lot.

"I had a plan, though it's all kind of gone to shite now with getting stuck at the pub for so long. Are you hungry? We could go get something to eat."

I've thought some horrible things about Finn and his driving. Who could blame me after he almost hit me and the way I've seen him zipping around town. But watching the way he handles the little hatchback, the confidence he has here, it not only matches how he moved in the chaos behind the bar, but it's also somehow better.

"I could eat." And I lose a little hold on my decorum as I watch him palm the stick shift, the way he grips it and strokes it like he's stroking himself.

He shifts in his seat and glances at me. I quickly look back up, hoping I didn't get caught staring, but—

"Whatcha looking at?" He quirks an eyebrow as he pulls into an impossibly tight parking spot at a restaurant.

"Nothing," I huff out.

He parked so that I have more space on my side of the car, so watching him slide his lean body out of his barely cracked door takes all of my attention. Hips flexing, ass tight, legs driving him up and out.

My hand clutches the door handle, knuckles going white as I grip it tightly. By the time Finn's around the car, opening my door, I have my breath under control, though my libido seems to be marching right along without a care in the world.

"You all right?" He puts his hand out to help me from the low seat.

Much as I need the help, I insist that I don't—because I'm not sure I can handle the contact—and almost wipe out as my feet hit a slippery spot on the ground. Finn catches me with a large hand firmly planted high on my waist, high enough that his thumb is almost grazing my boob. And the smug smile tells me he *knows* he's close.

"You sure you're okay?" he asks.

He's getting to me in more ways than he knows.

After the rocky start, we have a surprisingly normal dinner. My burger is perfectly pink and juicy, dripping in cheese, mushrooms sliding off the bun. My double-fried fries melt the mayo as I dip them.

"So, you came here for college and couldn't bear the thought of leaving?" Finn asks before licking some ranch off his thumb.

I'm wound so tight, everything he does makes me shift in my seat, seeking relief.

"Kind of. The program was great, and my scholarship was amazing, but I stayed"—I don't know how to say this without sounding like a petulant brat; maybe I am—"to win a passive-aggressive battle with my dad. He's a super-conservative lawyer, and he doesn't appreciate my style." I shrug, laughing a bit. "He'd rather I have golden highlights and clutch my pearls instead of my ever-changing hair and my pierced nose." I watch Finn for his reaction. We've hardly had a conversation, let alone a serious one touching on my less than conventional looks. "What about you? Came for the women? Using the accent to its fullest potential?"

"Eh, no." He smiles, embarrassed. Maybe rueful. "I had an incident in Dublin and felt the need for a new start." He shoves a huge bite of his bacon cheeseburger in his mouth, darting his tongue along the seam of his lips.

I mentally shake the lust away, trying to focus on our conversation. *Conversation, good, Adelaide. Fucking him with your eyes, bad.*

"There's more to that story, Finn. You're going to have to tell me." That wasn't flirty at all, and the wink didn't really count. I might have potentially had dust in my eye. Or something.

"Ehm, well..." His blush comes hard and fast, but an answer doesn't.

Finn concentrates intensely on his fries, popping three into his mouth. Again with the licking of his fingers.

Why am I so focused on his mouth?

"I had an incident with my Humanities professor that ended poorly. My *married* Humanities professor." His smile is tight as he spins his pint glass back and forth on the table. "She kept her position, and I was asked to quietly leave university. My mum and dad told me to figure it out, so I did. I bought a plane ticket and came to visit my uncle in New York, and he hooked me up with a job." He shrugs and finally dances his eyes up to meet mine. And he's biting his damn lip.

"Wow, so...a married woman?" I stare at him, not quite sure what else to say.

"It was four years ago. I've learned a lot since then," he says earnestly.

There's an awkward pause, and then, with my eyes bugging out, I bust out laughing, my mind completely falling into the gutter. "I'm sure you have," I jeer.

"That is *not* what I meant." Finn laughs with me. "Christ, not what I meant at all."

We finish dinner and move on to discussions of Finn's seven siblings and the multitude of ways I've embarrassed my dad. Then, my work and his renewed thoughts of taking college classes.

Finn pays our bill and drives us back to my car at McBride's. He slides his car in next to mine. When he cuts the engine, his playlist continues softly with an amazing mix of indie and alternative rock.

"Thank you for sticking round and having dinner with me." He bites his lip and winks.

The wink has an entirely different effect than it used to. Or maybe I'm just really horny, but whatever. All I can think of is the way his lips feel and how sweet he's been.

Finn leans closer, tongue flicking across his bottom lip, drawing my gaze there. Again.

What starts out as a chaste, wholly appropriate good-night kiss is not nearly enough. The memory of our first kiss and all the lip-biting and finger-licking. The stick-shift-stroking, the cock-adjusting. I need more.

Unbuckling my seat belt, I plant my hand on the dashboard and push closer, deepening the kiss. But it's still not enough. I reach down between his legs and release the bar, sliding his seat all the way back.

Finn's eyes snap wide open, and a surprised smile stretches across his face. "Thanks for the ride."

I climb over the center console and settle on his thighs, straddling him. "Don't ruin this, Finn," I say against his lips, running my hands up his chest, grasping the zipper to open his jacket.

He pulls me closer, hands on my hips, grinding me on his very impressive cock.

Very impressive.

My elbow hits the steering wheel controls for the radio, raising the volume of the music, and the beat of the drum and thump of the bass fill the car. Finn pulls me against his chest, hands sliding up to push my cardigan down my arms. He leaves it wrapped around my wrists, trapping my hands behind me. There's no hiding my boobs like this, and the way he's staring is hungry and raw. He skims his hands up my waist, pausing high on my rib cage.

The anticipation is killing me. It's like he knows exactly where to touch me, how hard or light, to caress or squeeze. I lean in, ravenously kissing him, grinding down on him, fighting to free my hands. There's not nearly enough room in the front seat of this car, and in my struggle, I hit the steering wheel, blaring the horn.

"Christ, Addie. You're driving me mad." He pulls me tight against his cock, the pressure bringing me dangerously close to orgasm.

The windows are fogged, the air in the car heavy with lust. I'm so close. So fucking close.

"Finn, 're you in there?" a very drunk female voice calls from outside the passenger side of his car.

We both freeze, panting and frustrated but trying to be completely still.

"D' you leave your car running, Finny?" The shadow of a palm is faintly outlined against the window by a streetlamp. "Finn?" Her singsonging his name is cut off by someone calling, "Marlee?"

Fingers trail away, a door slams, and the other car takes off, crunching gravel beneath the tires. It feels like we've been holding our breaths forever until it finally spills out in stuttered laughter.

"I guess I should go." I'm just as stuck, trying to get back into my sweater, as I was getting out of it.

Finn grasps the sides, sliding it up my arms, his knuckles

resting against the swell of my boobs. "Maybe," he says gravelly. "Can I see you again though? I liked this—tonight."

"I'd like that."

He pulls me in for a sweet kiss before opening his door. He crawls out after me and makes his adjustments as we round the back of his car.

"Good night, Addie." Finn tucks me into my car with a final kiss.

I let it go, not correcting him this time.

EIGHTEEN

*"Sex with three people is a threesome. With two
people, it's a twosome."*
"Then, I know why they say you're handsome."

Finn

I sit in the parking lot of the pub for at least another half
hour. The windows need to defog, and so does my brain. Or
maybe I just need to get the blood flowing back in that
direction.

I tilt my head back against the seat and close my eyes,
willing my erection away. It's not an easy task when each
time I think of Addie, I imagine the feel of her luscious tits in
the palms of my hands. Jesus, I had no idea she had that body
hiding beneath her loose T-shirts and oversize jumpers.
Tight little arse, strong thighs, and that rack.

The drive home takes far too long, and the trek from my
parking spot to the door feels like it takes even longer. I want
nothing more than to sink into the memory of what Addie

and I started in my car, but unfortunately, there's a ridiculously drunk girl passed out in the corner of my sofa.

Marlee's low-cut shirt is askew, and her skirt is doing very little to cover her arse. This is not the arse I was thinking about during the drive home.

I shake her, getting no response. Nothing.

Swearing, I drop my keys on the counter on the way to my room. I grab my quilt and a pillow. As soon as she feels the blanket on her, Marlee slides down on the couch, mumbling about steamed-up windows and breaking in. I grab a bottle of water and a bucket, setting it in front of her, just in case. This is not how I saw my night going.

After a quick text to Jimmy, explaining that there's an inebriated girl on the couch, I lock my bedroom door. I strip to my boxer briefs—the ones with the cartoon horseshoes all over them. I wore them for luck, and they worked perfectly—until Addie and I were interrupted.

My phone pings as I climb into bed.

Jimmy: Right. Couldn't make it to your room?

Me: Not Addie.

Jimmy: Fuck's sake?

Me: Marlee Ubered here. Picked the lock maybe and passed out.

I get a thumbs-up and nothing further. Jimmy's still got hours till closing and probably pitchers three bodies deep that need filling. If I were a better man, I'd have gone into the pub to help out instead of coming home straightaway, but I've been working there the longest out of all of us boys. I've earned my night off. And, with Addie on my mind, I'd have been useless anyway.

Christ, I'd probably scare the drunks with the ridiculous

tent in my trousers. I'm concerned that the horseshoes on my briefs will forever be stretched out, never quite snapping back into shape. And there's no way I'll ever be able to sleep until I take matters in my own hands. So, I cue up my playlist from earlier—The UnBroken or maybe it was Of the Room— and reach deep for my much-needed release.

I WAKE in the morning to the sound of retching in the bathroom I just cleaned yesterday—you know, just in case. I should go help Marlee, bring her a glass of water, a spare toothbrush—something. But I don't. I lie in bed, waiting for the sounds of bad decisions to quiet, when it hits me. She fucking broke into my flat. Who does that?

Suddenly, I'm motivated to get dressed and talk to her, get to the meat of the matter. Find out what the fuck she was thinking. I pull on my jeans from last night and take a deep breath before stepping out into the flat.

"Marlee, you all right?" I ask, passing the bathroom, on my way to the kitchen. I grab a fresh bottle of water and take it back down the hall. "Marlee?"

The door swings open, and the wreck of a girl walks straight out, popping the bottle from my hand and wiping at her mouth. "Have you seen my phone?" She looks around the living room, shoving her hand down the side of the sofa and beneath the cushions. She plops down on her knees, her barely covered arse arched high in the air as she rests her head on the floor. "There it is." She stretches her arm flat under the sofa and retrieves her phone. Her dead phone. from the sneer and the hateful look she gives it.

"Can you give me a ride?" she asks. There's far too much suggestion in that simple question as her eyes rake down my bare chest, settling on the open button of my jeans. I really wish I had taken the time to throw a shirt on as well.

Fuck no.

"Erm, let me check my messages real quick." Hightailing it to my room, I grab my phone and shoot a text to Aidan, letting him know I'll take opening the pub today.

"Sorry, looks like I've got to fill in for Kieran, the new kid," I call out. Turning toward the door, I jump at the sight of Marlee propped against my doorjamb with her tiny T-shirt in her hand. "Ehm, here." I toss her my phone. "Call an Uber and go."

She catches the phone with a huff and scowls as she pulls up the app, tapping away at the screen.

"Just leave it on the kitchen counter, and lock the door behind you," I shout.

I'll have to ask her another time about how she got in here. Gathering my clean clothes, I head into the bathroom, making sure to lock the door behind me. It's a completely pointless act; if she broke into my flat, the lock on the bathroom door won't stop her.

I hold my breath and take the world's fastest shower, certainly the quickest I've ever done the morning after a first date. But, when I'm dried and dressed with contacts in, I'm thrilled to see my phone on the counter, the flat empty, and the front door locked.

PEOPLE SLOWLY TRICKLE in the day after.

St. Patrick's Day is Francie's favorite day, and while the tips are amazing that night, the day after is significantly less impressive.

Aidan texted me a very appreciative, *Thanks*, from both him and Lis.

Normally, my mind would head straight for the gutter, but he mentioned something the other day about a gallery showing or a photo shoot he had planned for this weekend. Between his talent and Addie's new website, his photography seems to be taking off.

I busy myself for the first couple of hours, stocking the beer cases, wiping down the bottles of liquor, and putting the tables to rights.

Francie ambles in mid-afternoon, box of doughnuts in hand, and settles himself at the bar with a cup of coffee. "I thought Aidan was taking the kid's morning shift," he grumbles, rubbing at his tired eyes.

"He's got some artsy shite to take care of, so I stepped in." I open the box from the bakery down the street and pluck out the chocolate-glazed doughnut, popping a big chunk into my mouth.

The look of surprise on his face makes me feel good and terrible at the same time. If a simple kindness shocks Francie, then it might be time for me to make some changes.

"How was your evening with the girl?" He blows at the steam from his coffee.

"Lovely. She was absolutely lovely." The door opens, and my words get lost in my smile. It takes over my whole face; biting it back is fruitless.

"Well, and there she is," Francie announces, killing any

doubt she might have had that we were talking about her. "Are you going to introduce me then, Finn?" he says, laughter dancing in his eyes. He can be such a prat when he wants to be.

"Addie, this is Francie." I gesture between them, adding, "And, Francie, this is Addie."

"Adelaide actually," she states.

I'm not thick. I catch it every single time she corrects me, but she's so bloody cute when she does it. Plus, I think she's starting to like it.

"Finn, get the lady a pint. Sit down, love, and tell me how your evening was."

Instead, I set a mug of coffee the way she likes it in front of her with a wink and smirk firmly in place.

"It was fine, good really."

My eyes are trained on her mouth as she takes a sip of coffee and then licks a drop off the rim of the mug.

Jesus, Mary, and Joseph, she's killing me.

I take a sip from my pint of Guinness as Francie asks, "And he was a gentleman? Kept his hands to himself, yeah?" The timing is unfortunate as I choke on a bit of foam, beer dribbling down my chin.

I'm stuck coughing, so I can't even respond.

Addie, thank God, has more grace in the moment. She assures him that I was perfectly well behaved. I grab the box of doughnuts and offer one to her before grabbing another for myself. Taking a bite, I hope the doughnuts are a distraction, and they get off this topic.

She chooses the other chocolate-glazed and moans around a sizeable bite. I must be staring. I'm honestly not quite sure that I'm breathing because I heard the start of that noise last night for an entirely different reason.

"Right. I'll just, erm...I have paperwork to do in the office," Francie states as he slides out of his seat, chuckling. "It was a pleasure, Adelaide." He nods and turns to face me, pinning me with all the fatherly warning he can cram into one look. "Finn."

That look speaks volumes. He knows something. Nothing specific, but I'm thinking he has a good idea that I was less than honorable.

I wait until I'm sure he's gone back before speaking. "Sorry about that. Francie can be a tad protective at times. He has a tendency to collect wayward youth and parent us."

I take another generous sip from my pint, and her lips quirk up on one side.

"Careful. You don't want to blow your load again."

How she can deliver lines with a straight face like that is fascinating. I, on the other hand, struggle to swallow my beer yet again.

Wiping the palm of my hand down my face, I collect myself and answer with, "Maybe I do." I hit her with the wink that's almost automatic.

Addie looks away, dunking the doughnut in her coffee and giving me another moan.

"No, definitely, I do."

Her lips are wrapped around a delicate finger, licking the sticky glaze clean.

Surely, I'm developing brain damage, considering how often my blood seems to flow rapidly away from there. Closing my eyes, I count to ten and silently recite a Hail

Mary before clearing my throat. "So, what brings you in today? I can't say this is normal, just stopping by."

"Hmm..." She pops her finger out of her mouth and tilts her head back and forth. "I wanted to see what your weekend looked like. See if you wanted to, um...watch a movie...or hang out?"

"Addie, are you asking if I want to Netflix and chill?"

NINETEEN

"If there's a sock on my doorknob, don't come in. It means I'm having sex."
"Yeah, probably with the other one."

Adelaide

Finn ends up working all weekend, covering for the new guy. There's no way he can work with the twenty or so stitches in his hand and all the bandages.

Really, it's okay. I have my crazy client's website to completely redo. Again. So, I spend my weekend working on that, cleaning my apartment, and stroking my wiener. And reading.

But, when Finn has a lull at the bar, we text. All the texts. I've never really done this. It's a little like peopling but not. Flirting with a filter—I can handle that.

Late Monday afternoon, my phone pings and vibrates while I'm hooking Eric up to his leash. My doxie is not big by any means, but he is a mighty little dick when properly motivated. He pulls and tugs his way down the sidewalk until he sniffs every tree, rock, and blade of grass, looking for the one that is magically just right.

I scramble to keep hold of the leash while checking my new message and trying not to drop my phone. Surprisingly, it's a lot to handle.

Finn: Are you still in your meeting?

Me: Nope.

The dots bounce for just a second, and then his number pops up with an incoming call. It's so weird to actually talk on the phone, and my skin feels itchy and tight as I hit the green button, answering, "Hey."

"Hi. How's your day? You met with a new client?"

"Yeah, someone Aidan referred. Um, it sounds like they want to work with me, so that's good." None of my calm and snark works on the phone. I feel put on the spot and stumble over my words.

"Excellent. Done enough of a deal to celebrate it?"

"Yeah. I thought—aren't you working tonight?"

"I plan on getting off and buying you breakfast," Finn responds. I can practically hear him wink with his comment.

"When and where should I meet you for food?" This is getting easier. I bite my lip and check to see if Eric is done yet.

"I might need a nap after, so eleven o'clock? And where depends on what you're up for."

"Who has good sausage?"

Finn's groan turns to a chuckle, and he mentions a diner not far from the community center.

"M'kay. I'll see you tomorrow," I say and end the call.

Kneeling down, I scoop Eric's tiny poop into a bright-green bag and chuck it in the nearest trash can. "Let's go, man."

BREAKFAST LASTS until well after noon with countless cups of coffee, a shared order of sausage, and ridiculous amounts of flirting. I really didn't even know I had it in me to flirt. Usually, I stick with prickly bitch. It works for me.

"Here." I pull some cash out to cover the bill.

"As if I'd let you pay for my sausage," Finn scoffs, shoving the money back at me. "You can have it for free."

I still roll my eyes at his cheesy comments but not quite as strenuously. I think there's more to him than he lets on, and it's kind of cute.

"Thank you." I slide out of the booth, and he places a hand at my back, guiding me out into the cloudy spring day. There's still a chill in the air, and a shiver runs through me.

"Are you cold?" Finn starts peeling his jacket off, but I wrap my black cardigan around me and smile.

"No, I'm good." I stop him. "I might just go to the coffee shop and work until it's time for class. It's warm there, and..." I shrug to heft my bag higher on my shoulder.

"They have tiramisu and coffee?" Finn adds, scooping said bag from my shoulder to his. He walks me to my SUV and settles me in the driver's seat. "I'll meet you there after I run by my flat. I just need to grab my laptop—unless you're going to share your Tumblr with me?" Winking, he leans across me, setting my bag on the passenger seat. Crowding me, pressing me into my seat.

"Yeah, no. I, uh, have to do actual work." His clean,

citrusy scent surrounds me, invades my senses, as he slowly pulls his torso across me and smiles.

"Sorry, did I squish you? That was unintentional." He lingers a moment before closing the door with another wink.

Did he always wink this much? Is it his contact lenses bugging him? I kind of miss the nerdy glasses sometimes.

LOST IN CONVERSATION, we walk into class together after spending the rest of the afternoon in comfortable silence, working at the coffee shop. Or at least, as silent as Finn could manage. The timing and our newfound amiability do not escape the ladies. Maybe it's the fact that Finn's hand is on my back as we walk through the door.

"Well, finally," Louise says as she pops open the top of her cookie container.

Setting my laptop and coffee on the desk, I scoff, "You know we don't have a designated snack time for this class, right?" When I look up, eight sets of owl eyes greet me.

"Oh, Adelaide. Not what we were referring to, dear." Virginia gives a side nod of her head toward Finn and waggles her eyebrows.

"You just make the cutest couple," Connie declares, followed by a chorus of, "Adorable," and, "Sweet," and other sentiments I usually bristle at. All the descriptors that my dad wanted me to embody back home. He wouldn't know what to do if he heard this crazy crew referring to me that way now. Like this.

My shoulders relax as I shake my head. "We went on one

date. We're not a couple," I huff out, trying to blow them off a little.

My gaze is drawn to the back row where Finn is leaning his chair back on two legs with his hands clasped behind his head.

He smiles his cocky smile, replying, "Yet."

All of those owly eyes look back and forth between me and Finn.

"Shit. And, now, we're back to just a bunch of available old women in here, eating cookies. I signed up for a computer class, thinking I might meet a nice young man," one of our first-timers states.

"Really, Delores?" Connie asks. "All the nice young men know how to check their email already. You want to find nice young men, you have to go to the gym. Hell, even the hardware stores only have young moms doing DIY projects or grumpy old men trying to get away from nagging wives for an hour or so."

"It's true," Louise chimes in, plucking another cookie out of the box. "And is it even worth it at this stage? I'd rather just take care of *things* myself."

Oh sweet baby Jesus, no.

"Maybe we should talk about scanning and printing documents?" I'd really like to avoid where I think this conversation is headed.

"*Maybe* what we should do is have one of those Love Nest parties," Connie suggests, looking around the room. "You know, like a Tupperware party but with vibrators?"

TWENTY

Adelaide

My apartment is by no means large. It works for Eric and me, and really, I don't have anyone else over. It's my space. Just for me. In fact, I don't think I've had anyone in since Eric was a puppy, and I had Chen set my takeout in the kitchen while I cleaned up an accident. That was months ago.

This is supposed to be casual, just our Netflix and chill, but after cleaning and straightening my living room three times, I decide I need a distraction. I dig through the pantry and find what I need.

The noodles are done, the four cheeses blended and melted into an amazingly smooth sauce. The bacon is crisp and crumbled. I assemble everything, unable to resist tasting as I go. With another heaping handful of cheese and the rest of the bacon on top, I slide the funky blue-and-green casse-role dish into the oven.

Focused on getting things cleaned up before Finn arrives, I'm elbow-deep in suds. And he knocks. I grab a towel to dry my hands and hurry to the door, quietly opening it.

"Hey, come in. Quick." I tug on Finn's hand.

"Don't want the neighbors to get jealous?" he asks while leaning back into the hall, looking left and right.

"Oh my God, just get in here, and keep your voice down." The door finally closed, I pause with my finger on my lips and listen. Releasing my breath, I turn to Finn and smile.

"What was that about?"

And there it is. The thud of a body rolling off the bed, evidently taking my book and tablet with it.

"Is there someone else here? I thought you lived alone?" Finn looks totally disappointed.

"Yeah, brace yourself. That's Eric."

At that, Finn takes a step back and shoves his hands deep in his jeans pockets, disappointment turning abruptly to anger. His molars are grinding, his jaw twitching, cheeks flushing red.

"We've lived together for almost a year now." I can't contain my smile at Finn's scowl.

"Right." He nods and takes another step toward the door. He stops when I crouch down as the long reddish-brown body bolts down the hallway, skidding his back end out as he tries to navigate the corner.

I lift the doxie up and snuggle him into my side. "This is Eric."

Finn's jaw stops spasming, but his cheeks redden even more.

"Eric's a dog," he says, smile spreading slowly across his face.

"He is, and sometimes, he's a real dick, too. He tends to bolt out the door, and he thinks he needs to go as soon as he wakes up, so I was hoping to sneak you in, so he'd stay asleep for a while longer." I sigh, reaching for the leash. "Consistency is key with this guy, so I'll just—"

"I'll take him. It smells like you're cooking?" He inhales deeply and grins. "Let me tend to your wiener while you finish up." Scooping Eric out of my arms, Finn drops his voice, chuckling, "I'll slowly stroke him till we're out in public."

"CHRIST, THIS IS FUCKING AMAZING." Finn groans around a bite of mac and cheese. "Orgasmic."

It's good, I won't lie, but watching Finn enjoy it is so much better. "Do you want more?" I ask.

His tongue darts out, licking at the corner of his mouth. Swear to God, it does things to me.

Naughty things.

"I'd best hold back, so I don't explode."

My spoon clatters into the bowl at his words. Intentional or not, the double meaning zings through my core.

"Here, let me get that for you." Finn takes our dishes to the kitchen, giving me a moment to calm my shit down. Not an easy task because the way those jeans hug his ass should be illegal.

"Do you have something queued up for the evening's

entertainment?" he asks, coming back from the kitchen with fresh glasses of water for us.

"Guest's choice," I respond. "Sorry, I should have gotten some beer or something for you." I nod at the water glasses.

"This is fine. I can't claim that you got me drunk and took advantage of me." Finn grabs the remote and plops down in the middle of the couch, crowding me. Scrolling through the options, he finds a movie and starts it.

As he leans back into the sofa, he thrusts his hips up, sliding lower into the cushions before relaxing with a sigh. Shoulders melting, hand resting in his lap, legs falling open. He's completely comfortable while I'm wound so tight, I'm practically vibrating.

"The film is better than whatever it is you're looking at." He bites his lip, sliding his gaze to meet mine.

Suddenly warm, my cheeks flame, and I pull at my cardigan, settling it low around my arms. The air on my exposed shoulders does nothing to cool the fire burning through me as Finn traces my collarbone with his eyes.

"Maybe." I try, really try, to turn my attention to the show, but I have to fight the constant urge to look at him.

His hand slides over my thigh, coming to rest with his fingers tantalizingly close to my core. He stops progress and squeezes, digging his fingers into my muscles. I close my eyes, tensing even more.

"Then again..." he says, lips brushing softly against the side of my neck.

His tongue darts out, tasting my skin. Licking a trail down to my shoulder.

I tilt my head, granting him even better access. He sucks and licks and bites until he's pushed the strap of my tank top down to where my sweater sits, gathered at my elbow. His lips nudge at the lace of my bra. It's one of the few I have that can tame my boobs, and it happens to be the sexiest one I own. Turquoise, lacy, and makes the girls look fucking fantastic.

"I love this color. The pale of your skin peeking through the lace." Finn cups my breast, pushing it up, his thumb brushing over my hardened nipple. "The green tips of your braid splayed across it."

He closes his lips around my breast, sucking on my nipple through the lace. I arch my back, a soft moan tumbling from my lips.

Finn lavishes attention on one boob while tugging my tank top lower, revealing the other. "Christ, I'd never have guessed that you were hiding the most perfect tits." He licks deep into my cleavage—because, let's face it, there's *a lot* of depth there. "Fucking hell, Addie, you're gorgeous." He plants a kiss between the swells and meets my gaze. "And I mean more than just your magnificent tits."

Wrapping his fingers in the bulk of my sweater, he drags the material down, down, down, bunching it at my waist, my tank top going with it. I pull my arms free and run my fingers through his hair, grasping it in my fists. Pulling him into me.

"Oh my God, Finn."

His lips dance down the soft planes of my stomach, his arms wrapped around my hips, hands splayed across my back. We've shifted. Finn's body is covering mine. His chest resting between my thighs vibrates with a deep chuckle exactly where I need to feel him. My crazy-sensitive girl parts just fucking got a zing in the right direction.

Licking across the band of my leggings, Finn looks up at

me, eyes hooded and full of lust. He grips the sides of my pants, fisting them in his warm hands. Waiting for my nod, my permission.

A breathy, "Yes," spills free, and Finn tugs, revealing the lacy boy shorts that match my bra.

Did I plan this? No. But I fucking hoped.

My tank top, leggings—all of it is stripped off and tossed to the floor. I lie on the couch with Finn sitting back on his knees between my legs. Fully clothed.

"You're a riot of color and beauty, Addie." He bites at his lip and palms the front of his jeans.

"You have far too many clothes on," I whisper.

"As do you," Finn replies as his finger dances down the lace of my panties, pausing and circling between my legs.

I slowly shake my head, pushing up onto my elbows. "Nope. Your turn." I clamp my thighs together to halt his hand but end up trapping it instead, between my thighs, driving myself more than a little insane.

With his free hand—the one not circling and kneading me—Finn reaches behind him and pulls his shirt off over his head.

Sliding his hand from between my thighs, Finn tosses the shirt aside and lowers himself, pressing his lips to my clit, rubbing and licking through the lace. He pushes my thigh toward my chest, his thumb hooked around the side of my knee.

And his other hand? That one is working overtime, his jeans gaping open now, his hand gripping and sliding along his cock from root to tip and back again. I can barely see, but I know. I know what he's doing, getting us both where we need to be. Aroused and riled. Panting, thrusting, hearts racing.

"Finn. God, Finn—*uhngmagawd*—" I gasp as he pushes two fingers into me. Curling, stroking. His thumb circling my bundle of nerves. Never have I ever...*never*...

His name tumbles from my lips over and over, louder and louder. Until...until...

Fuuuuck...

"Addie..." Finn grunts, jerks, and stills just as my world explodes in lights and tremors and the most blissful release.

Ever.

TWENTY-ONE

"I could make you very happy."
"Why? Are you leaving?"

Finn

Never have I ever...

The way Addie came undone. The way she looked, wrapped up in that fucking turquoise lace. I never even got her completely naked. But I have never in my life seen sexier lingerie than Addie's. Doesn't even compare to the strappy scrap of black lace that books and movies seem so fond of.

And, as hard as we both came, that evening at her flat was...different for me. It changed something. Shifted it.

Made me think.

Consider.

She made me want the thing I hadn't allowed myself to even acknowledge since leaving Dublin. Jesus, fine. I'd considered it a million times but only in theory. Just the idea of it, not the reality. Not seeing it through. But, with Addie, things haven't followed my usual path in any way.

I have more time and energy invested in this thing—whatever it is—with her than with any other girl before, including my fucking Humanities professor.

Addie is a bundle of badass and pushback, but I can't imagine anyone I'd rather wrestle with.

And her dog, her little sausage. Eric and I bonded like men. Sure, I'd offered to walk him, but the little prick didn't seem to want to acquiesce and find a suitable place to piss. I had to encourage him, show him the way. We shared a moment behind the Chinese restaurant around the corner from her flat and marked the brick wall together.

Christ, and the way she moaned my name.

"HEY, LOVE." I look up as she walks through the doors of the pub. "You're early. Kieran's not quite in."

His hand is finally healed enough for him to work again.

"Hey. How are you?" She's not shy with her affections, just shy around people in general.

I lean across the bar and push her boundaries a bit. "Give us a kiss, yeah?" I'm practically on my stomach, lying across the bar. But I get contact. Brushing my lips across hers, deepening it, savoring it.

"Remember when we had to kiss Finn for beer?"

"Yeah...it was only a year ago."

Lis and Gracyn are set up at the end of the bar, smiling at the interchange between Addie and me.

"You must be Adelaide. I'm Lis, Aidan's girlfriend"—

sweet Lisbeth raises her whiskey glass toward Addie—"and this is my friend Gracyn."

"Hi. Yeah, I work for Aidan. With him really. Um, nice to meet you." Addie shifts her gaze from the girls to me, narrowing her eyes. "Do you kiss everyone? Like, all the time?"

Lis and Gracyn snort out a laugh, big grins and brows high. I don't mind them laughing at my shit near as much when Aidan and Francie do it.

Addie leans back, away from the bar, and snarks, "Damn, and I thought I was special."

"Oh, you are," Lis offers with Gracyn nodding in agreement.

"You've changed Finn—tamed the feral bartender."

I shake my head and finish stocking the beer cooler, leaving them to their conversation for a moment.

I guess I have changed. Sharing cookie recipes with the sassy seniors. Looking past all the enticing, willing women in the pub. I've kissed my share, pleasured more than a few. But the only one I think about now is Addie.

And she might have "tamed" me, but I've had some positive effect on her, too. Like tonight. We're going to see a band play live. If fucking Kieran ever shows up. He's late to every one of his shifts. Every single one. *Does he not consider his coworkers?*

Loaded down with a couple of cases of beer, I head back out front.

"Kansas City? There's a huge music festival there in the summer, right?" Gracyn's eyes are wide as she leans across Lis toward Addie.

"Yeah. The lineup is pretty amazing every year, but I

think this year will be unreal. Did you know Lightning Strikes is from there? And so is Of the Room; I think they might be headlining."

Gracyn sits back in her seat, gnawing at her lip. She had a fling over her spring break last year with some guy in a band. I don't know details, it had a lasting effect on her, and not in a good way.

Kieran finally strolls through the door, tapping at his phone.

"Nice of you to grace us with your presence."

He nods his head, blond curls bouncing, not looking up from the screen, and mumbles, "Right," as he passes through to the kitchen.

"It's safe to leave him?" I look to Lis. "Does he even have a clue as to what he's doing?"

"That's part of why we're hanging out here. Francie asked us to 'check up on him,'" she whispers with air quotes in full effect.

"Jimmy trained him up, so..." I shrug. "When did *I* become the responsible one round here? Ladies, you're all right if we go then?"

Lis waves us off while Gracyn stares off into space, still lost in her thoughts.

"Adelaide, it was really nice to meet you finally." Lis smiles warmly.

"You, too." Addie waves as we push through the door.

"THAT WAS AMAZING. I kind of like your taste in music," Addie says as we leave the venue.

The show was fantastic. The lyrics raw, the bass and drums heavy, like I prefer. And the swaying hips of the gorgeous green-haired girl nearly killed me. More than once, I had to recite the rosary in Gaelic to keep from embarrassing myself.

"It was." I run a hand down the ocean that's her hair, my fingers lost in the waves. "Do you need to get home to Eric straightaway?" I open the car door for her, praying for her answer to be no.

Spinning so that she's facing me, wedged in the space between my body and the door, Addie runs her hands down my chest, curling her fingers around my belt. "Nope. He should be good for a while. Solid sleep when he's been properly exhausted."

Her breath is warm, and her lips are soft as I get the response I wanted, followed by a kiss to the hollow of my throat. She's gone far too quickly as she tucks herself into the car and winks at me.

I run around the back of the car, promising my cock the wait is done if all goes well. And, as short as the drive is back to my flat, it's considerably too long. The engine revs, and I jerk the stick shift from one gear to the next, abusing the transmission in a way I normally wouldn't.

Practically skidding into my parking space, I lean over, roughly kissing Addie before jumping from the car.

She meets me round the back and pushes me against the boot, pressing her little body into mine. "I really liked that band. They were...sexy, sultry." Her hands roam while mine pull her closer still.

I shove off the car, guiding her up the stairs to my door. "Keys are in my pocket," I mumble against the shell of her ear. Now that I've got her, I don't want to stop touching her for even a moment.

Her hands go to my jacket, finding them empty before sliding round to my arse and squeezing.

"Only one other place they could be." I think I'm being cheeky, but when she reaches in and slides her hand against the line of my cock, I suck a breath in through my teeth. *"Déan deifir.* They're right there." I resist the urge to grind my cock against her, knowing that's not going to get the keys in her hand any faster.

"What?" she gasps.

"Hurry up, love. We need to get this inside."

"Yeah, we do."

Keys finally in hand, I fumble with the lock, desperate to get inside.

We tumble through the door, grasping, kissing, nipping at one another. Lips and hands everywhere. Pushing and pulling at the layers of clothing separating us.

The timing couldn't be better. My mind was made up earlier that this would be it.

Addie's delicate, little hand cups my cock, squeezing slightly, and waves of lust and pleasure roll through me.

I spin us and pin her to the door when a voice breaks through the haze, a bucket of ice water to our sizzling passion. "Are you finally back, Finny?"

Addie's eyes go wide when she looks past me, but even that doesn't prepare me in any way for what I find. Marlee is on my fucking sofa, wearing nothing but knee socks, wrapped in my blue-and-gray quilt.

"Christ, Marlee. Not now."

Driving me back with a shove of her shoulder, Addie

steps away from me. "Why is the drunk chick from McBride's naked on your couch, Finn?" Her glare is deadly.

"I let myself in, right, baby?" Marlee doesn't make any move to cover up, her tits on full display. Instead, she hoods her eyes, trailing a finger across her collarbone. "Just like St. Paddy's Day."

I cringe with everything I have.

"Oh, fuck no. Nope. No." Addie seethes, her green waves crashing with a vengeance around her shoulders.

I look between the women squaring off in my flat. This looks really bad. "Marlee, you need to leave."

"But you let me stay last time, Finny."

Sweet Mother of God, what is wrong with her?

"Yeah, I'll go. Leave you to have your fun with Bitchy McCuntface here." Addie shoves past and pulls the door so hard, it slams against the plasterboard, the handle denting it.

"Addie, wait."

She moves far faster than I would have ever guessed and is nearly to the cross street, tapping at her phone.

"Let me—"

"Nope. I don't have time for this shit, for your games. Go do your thing, Finn." She swipes at her cheek.

"That's not what this is." I reach for her arm as she slows to look for traffic.

She turns, her brows stretched high, and snorts out a laugh. Shaking off my hand, Addie spits out, "Obviously, I'm stupid, and you have your nights confused."

"Addie, I can explain," I plead.

A car pulls up to the curb across the street, and Addie rushes toward it.

"It's Adelaide." She slams the door of what I hope is an Uber, and she's gone.

Pissed off, I storm back to my flat and slam the door behind me. I hope to shit that Marlee is dressed and gone, but it turns out, I'm only half-right. Maybe more like twenty-five percent.

Pulling her long white-blonde hair out of the collar of her shirt, Marlee turns to me, smiling. "So, she's upset?" The simpering idiot pouts at me like she thinks she's being coy.

I drop my hands to my hips and start counting to ten.

Somewhere around seven, she laughs out. "But, damn, the green-haired chick is good with her bitch names." Marlee saunters across the room, stopping only when she's thoroughly invading my space. "I don't like to share, Finn. And I don't feel like I've been getting enough attention in this relationship." Her fingers curl into the waistband of my jeans, pulling me flush against her. Surgically-enhanced tits act as a barrier between us.

"Marlee"—I step back and remove her hand from where it sits far too close to my cock—"we hooked up, but that's it. One night. Not a relationship."

"But you ruined me. Finn," she purrs, sliding a hand up my chest, the other one gripping my completely uninterested knob, "I can't live without this in my life anymore. In my mouth, my p—"

"Stop. You'll live and find a sufficient replacement for your mouth." I put some serious distance between us, bending down to scoop up her tiny shorts.

But Marlee's forward, and her hands go straight for my arse. The contact propels me forward out of her reach once again.

Needing to keep some distance, I toss her the rest of her clothes. "Get dressed, and go, Marlee. No means no, and I'm not interested."

"But"—she pouts, stepping into her shorts—"you're the best I've ever had."

"You never actually had me, love. Now, tell me, how the fuck do you keep getting into my flat?"

"I borrowed my daddy's keys. He's your landlord." Marlee throws me a devious little smirk.

Fucking hell.

"Christ, are ye fuckin' kiddin' me?" My accent grows thicker with my anger.

"Not even a little. And you'll probably lose your security deposit." She runs her fingers over the dent from the door handle. "Unless you want to work out a trade."

"No." *Fuck no. No fucking way in hell.*

"What about your roommate?"

"Go." *What was I thinking when I took that one home? Oh, that's right. I wanted affection and looked for it anywhere I could get it, even with a scary skank like Marlee.*

"So, I'll just ask him directly." Her high, nasally giggle follows her out the door and down the stairs.

I need to warn Jimmy and start looking for a new place to live. But, first, I need to figure out a way to talk to Addie.

TWENTY-TWO

"What's it like, being the most beautiful girl in the pub?"

"What's it like, being the biggest liar in the world?"

Adelaide

Furious.

I don't talk to the Uber guy. There's no reason to bite his head off. I just seethe and cry angry fucking tears.

Irate.

Fucking incensed.

The words tumble through my mind as I search for the best one to describe this feeling. Sanskrit has ninety-six different words for love. The Eskimos have fifty. And I'm just sifting through all the words I can find for angry. There are some good ones, but none are quite strong enough.

Livid.

This whole thing can fuck right off.

I should have known, paid attention to the fact that he was nothing but a cheese-slinging Tumblr monkey. All about the lines. Picking up chicks. His conquests, scoring what he could, when he could and bragging all about it. Lowlife piece of shit.

The truly devastating part is that I did know. I'd heard all about the bar boys at McBride's when I was in college. I'd seen his flirting in class and in the pub and been on the receiving end of his cheese. And I still let myself be convinced that I was different.

Turns out, it doesn't matter how I set myself apart from whatever cookie-cutter mold there is, I'm just another chick. Apparently, there's nothing special here.

I don't know what to do with this feeling. I mean, I do.

Tears are still streaming down my face as I step out of the car and make my way up to my apartment. Fuming, raging, indignant tears.

I grab Eric from his crate and his leash from the table, and I head right back down the stairs. Consistency with this dog. Hooking the leash to his collar, I pause, letting a small laugh bubble its way past the tears. Every wiener should be properly restrained. The more I think about it, the more I giggle and snort. Thank God I have the sense of humor of a twelve-year-old boy.

I try to steer him to his usual patch of grass, but he tugs and pulls until he's found the perfect spot on the wall of the Chinese place. I probably have to find a new place to order my General Tso's since my dog is now peeing here.

And there it is. I have no control over the wieners in my world. None.

The rest of my night is filled with brownie batter. No need to waste time cooking that shit. It does the job just fine with a bowl and a spoon.

Eric burrows under the blankets and snuggles with me, doing everything he can to make me feel better, and after scrolling through my Pinterest board, I decide it's time for a change.

MY PHONE PINGS and vibrates during the next couple of days. Most of the calls and messages are from *Cúl Tóna*. I Googled how to say dickhead in Gaelic. Those go unanswered, and I don't bother even looking through the peephole when anyone knocks on the door. I'm not hiding. I just don't want to mess around with the Dick Who Shall Not Be Named.

I stepped out of my comfort zone and peopled, putting myself out there, and obviously, it didn't have great results. Not quite ready to deal with any of that, I throw myself into my real job.

Referrals have been flying in since I did Aidan's website, so many that I can easily lose myself in the quiet orderliness of designing and coding. All I need to do is get Eric's sleep cycle adjusted a little so that I don't have to leave my apartment as much during normal people times.

Eric, of course, is resistant to change. Most change since, all of a sudden, he can't seem to pass the damn Chinese restaurant without having to pee on the wall. When there are treats involved, he's even quiet when the inevitable knocking starts on my door. Although the little dick does go cry at the door when he hears Finn's voice through it. There is nothing worse than a weepy wiener.

We'll get through this.

I work nonstop through the weekend and email the director at the community center, Anne, letting her know that I'm out for the rest of the classes. There are only a handful left, and to be honest, Virginia can cover them. She's taken that class so many times, she knows the material inside and out.

Anne isn't having it though.

"Adelaide, you're one of the best instructors we have. You're gifted with the ability to break down the concepts for the...more mature attendees," she quips.

I couldn't blow off her phone call.

"Maybe age is the problem," I mumble.

"Problem with what?"

"Nothing. Just thinking about a different problem."

"The young man currently enrolled in the class? Is he the one you're concerned with?" she asks softly.

"What? No—it's—he's—"

"Virginia called to let me know he won't be back. Was he inappropriate, honey? I've seen him around, usually helping the ladies into their cars, holding doors. Always using lovely manners, but then I'm sure age could be a factor there."

"He quit?"

"Mmhmm. Virginia didn't give a reason, just to let you know. She said you'd most likely be calling to back out of the rest of the session. So, since he's not an issue, we'll see you tomorrow." Anne's singsong voice fades well before she ends the call.

AND, true to that message, Finn's seat is empty. But they all are. There is not a soul here today. My ladies are never late. I glance around the room—from the door to the clock and back again.

Finally, at five after, Louise walks in and hands me a cup of coffee before sitting down.

"Thanks, Lou." I take a sip. "Where're the others?"

Before she can answer, Esther comes in with a box of cookies. A small one just for me, and they look suspiciously like the ones Finn made. She hands them to me and hugs me.

Ellie walks through the door with a beautiful scarf tie-dyed with pinks, teals, and blues. She wraps it around my neck and plants a grandma kiss on my cheek. I'm stunned absolutely silent.

Connie's next with a to-go container from the diner. I crack open the lid even though I know what's in there. The smell of sausage wafts out, and I snort-giggle, thinking of how his cheesy comments started being kind of cute.

The gifts keep coming. A fresh box of the super-soft tissues I brought him when he was sick. That one I open right away to dab at the weird emotions leaking out of my eyes.

"What is all this?" I sniff. Katherine just smiles and pats my arm.

No one responds. Instead, Sue walks in with a stuffed dog toy—Flounder from my favorite animated movie. She squeaks it twice before handing it to me and taking her seat.

Delores, the new student, walks through the door with a dog leash coiled in her hand. There are goofy sharks sporting oversize fins embroidered all down the length of it. Fins for Finn? I huff out a laugh, pursing my lips. I really want to just be pissed off, but he's making it really hard.

The ladies have dribbled in the door, bearing gifts, over the past half hour. Looking up, I'm met with seven sweet smiles. The only one missing is Virginia.

"He set you all up to do this?" I ask through some errant sniffles.

Not a peep. Normally, these women don't shush long enough for me to get through what I'm supposed to on a given day, but today, they have nothing to say.

Nothing.

Virginia slides up to the door and props her hip against it. "I like the new color." She nods at me, eyeing my blue-and-silver ombre waves.

"Thanks."

Virginia extends her arm, an envelope in her hand. "This is the last of it, honey. I'll take over class and keep the girls in line." She follows this up with a wink. A Finn wink.

I side-eye her pretty hard as I fumble to open the card without spilling my coffee. Surprised by the beautiful handwriting, I take in the words before looking up at Virginia. "Did you write this for him because—"

"Nope. My handwriting sucks, and you know it." She leans in and wraps me in a big hug, whispering, "Hear him out. That boy has it bad for you."

Connie hands me my computer case and a big floral bag full of all my presents.

Loaded down, I bite at my lip and reread his words as I stalk outside.

Adelaide,
> *Please come outside.*
> *—Finn*

"Why are you blocking my car, Finnegan?"

His car is angled behind mine, preventing my escape.

"It's just Finn. And I need to make sure you listen to me."

It's warm for the end of March. The sun is shining, and Finn has his sleeves rolled up past his elbows. He's leaning back, ass against the hood of his car, ankles crossed. Thumbs in his pockets, fingers dangling.

"What do I need to listen to, *Finnegan*? Stealing my best friends and having them do your dirty work isn't going to fix having BMCF naked on your couch." I pop my brows as high and judgy as I can manage, taking an exaggerated sip of my coffee.

"BMCF?"

"*Bitchy McCuntface.* Or has she been replaced with a new one since then?"

"No." He snorts out a laugh. "Well, yes, actually. And it's just Finn."

"We're done. Move your car, please, and let me leave, *Finnegan*."

He pushes off his car and walks toward me. Relieving me of my bags, he plucks my coffee from my hand and takes a sip before setting it on the roof of my SUV. "I won't. Not yet, not until you listen to me, Adelaide.

"Your BMCF, or Marlee, has been replaced. She was

replaced a couple of months ago, about the time I tried to use a continuing ed class to get my new laptop set up. I met someone with a quick wit and a smart mouth, someone who's far more interesting." He takes a step closer to me, reaching out to slide a lock of hair through his fingers. "And it's just Finn. That's it, not short for anything."

"Fine, whatever. That doesn't change the fact that you were playing me. Having her spend the night after we went out? That's fucking shitty, *Finnegan*. And she has a key to your apartment?" I am full-on pissed, finger poking his chest, punctuating each word. "I was just the challenge. The chick who didn't buy your line of bullshit and give it up at the first flash of your cute fucking wink."

"You think my wink is cute?" He steps closer again, and his smile splits his face.

"Jesus, that's all you took from that?" Pushing against his chest, I try to give myself some space. Lord knows, I have to remind myself not to get lost in his eyes as it is.

"That was just my favorite part. But, no, I'm not toying with you. I did go home with her—once. Well before I met you. And, as for having access to my flat, her father is my landlord. She stole the key and let herself in. She was passed out drunk on St. Patrick's Day when I got home from our date. Christ, I had to sit in the fucking car park of McBride's for a half hour to let my windows clear and get some blood flow back to my brain. I was too exhausted to try to take her home, so I covered her up—on the sofa—and locked my bedroom door.

"And the other night? I don't know what that was. I've told her it can't happen again. Told her I'm not interested. At all." He takes the final step into my space, my back against the side of the car. "And, if you'd like, I'll call my mum. Right now, so we can settle the name thing." He slides his phone out of his pocket, taps at the screen, and holds it between us.

"What are you doing?"

The screen lights up with a video of a woman who can only be Finn's mother. They have the same dark-red curls, same cheekbones. The same mischievous grin.

"Mum, I need you to settle something for me."

"Of course, hon. Is that Addie with you? Hello, dear."

I try to blink away the fact that his mom knows who I am, but it's useless.

As I say, "Hello," Finn talks over me and says, "It's Adelaide, Mum. Anyway, what's my name? My full name."

He winks at me. That fucking wink kills me.

"Finn Francis Michael O'Meara. Have you hit your head and can't remember?" She winks the same damn wink.

"So, Finn's not short for anything?" His left eyebrow is creeping higher up on his forehead as he waits for her answer.

"Of course not," Mrs. O'Meara scoffs. "What else can I help you with?"

"That's it, Mum. Thank you. I'll talk to you again at our regular time on Sunday, yeah?"

They blow kisses at each other and end the chat with a quick, "I love you."

"So, Adelaide, I am just Finn. And I never encouraged Marlee's behavior, and I hope to never encounter her again outside of McBride's. I'd be fine with never seeing her there again either. And I'd really like for us to pick up where we were so rudely interrupted." He tilts my face to meet his gaze.

He stares at my mouth as I chew at my bottom lip. I briefly look away before he draws my attention back to him, swiping his thumb over my poor, abused flesh.

I quickly rise up onto my toes, delivering a sweet kiss. "It's Addie."

TWENTY-THREE

*"I DON'T WANT TO MAKE WAVES, BUT YOU COULD
DEFINITELY FLOAT MY BOAT."*
"I AM FEELING A BIT WET."

Finn

I follow Addie back to her flat, sliding my car into a spot right next to hers. Jumping out, I grab her bags—all of them—from her car and sling them over my shoulder. I will proudly sport the big floral tote that Connie brought to get all the small gifts home in.

"You know, Eric is going to need attention before..." She trails off, and God love her, I hope she means...what I hope she means.

"I'll tend to your wiener while you put your prezzies away." I steal a kiss and snatch his new leash out of the bag.

"Oh, and I don't know what's up with him, but he's been liking the Chinese place lately. He pees on the wall about halfway down the alley."

The dog and I share a look; he's a bit sheepish, but I'm nothing short of proud.

I scoop him up and run him down the stairs, outside and straight to the alley he seems to favor now. Of course, the little prick wants to take his time. Sniffing around, rooting under trash, generally drawing out the conclusion of his business.

"Be a good lad and go. Just get there, man."

But no...he's in and out of boxes, not even quick-like. He slowly drags his long snout along the top of each box as he slides back out, sometimes only to rush right back in and do it all over again, snuffling and panting as he goes.

Finally, when I'm about out of my mind, I swear, I hear him sigh. Having found what he was looking for, whatever that might be, he trots over to the wall and takes a long-drawn-out piss.

With his business done, I wrap my hands around Eric's girth, holding him tight and stroking him from tip to tail the whole way back to Addie's flat. When we burst through the door, he practically vibrates in my hands, and I release him with a bit of a grunt, relieved.

"Adelaide?" I almost can't breathe with my need to touch her. "Where are you?"

"Hey, right here," she replies from the doorway to her bedroom. "You okay? You're breathing kind of hard."

Her hair tumbles over her right shoulder, curling around her lush, gorgeous breast. The silvery blue is a stark contrast to her deep-purple T-shirt. A riot of color.

Closing the distance, I thread my fingers through her hair, thumbs tilting her head just so, and kiss the ever-loving fuck out of her. Not as sweet as I should be, not as reverent as

I want to be. But heated, flaming passion spreads through every fiber of my being.

I pin her against the wall, unable to get close enough, needing to feel her against me. Addie slides her hands under my shirt, her palms cool against my blazing skin. I need more. Releasing her face, I kiss a trail down the side of her face until my nose is buried in the crook of her neck. I inhale her sweet, heady scent—a mixture of cherries and vanilla. She smells like dessert, good enough to eat.

I nip at the flesh where her neck gracefully meets her shoulder, soothing it with a kiss, and wrap my hands around the backs of her thighs. "Hold on," I rasp.

She gasps when I lift, clutching at my neck to steady herself, not that she needs to. I don't think I'll be letting her go anytime soon. I stalk through her room, not really looking where I'm going.

When my leg hits the side of the mattress, I plant a knee and set Addie in the middle of her soft bed. Not willing to let her go for even a moment, I cover her body with my own, forearms planted on either side of her. She's tiny, and now that I've got her here, I don't want to squish her. But, dear God, do I ever fucking want her.

Piece by piece, I peel off her layers. Her bright-yellow jumper, the black leggings she's got a preference for. Sitting back on my heels, Addie's thighs resting on my knees, I take a moment, allowing my gaze to wander over her pale, creamy skin and amazing fucking curves. I've certainly seen her in less, but with her splayed out on her bed—eyes bright and blue hair slashing color across the crisp white bedding—I want more than anything to see this through.

"I think," Addie draws out while hooking her feet under

my arse, "you should get rid of some clothes, too." She curls up to sit and whips her T-shirt off, chucking it to the floor. She undoes the top few buttons of my shirt, trailing a delicate finger along my chest as she does.

I should move, rip my shirt off, but all I can do is stare. I'm not even sure I can breathe. Because, as Addie patiently undoes each button, I'm mesmerized by the vision in front of me. She's wrapped in creamy satin, a little navy bow nestled between her gorgeous tits. I'm definitely not breathing. In fact, I might pass out.

"Finn? *Finn?*"

I pull in a big lungful of air and try to focus.

"I thought I'd lost you for a minute."

"You did. You completely did."

Her hands are working at my belt, flipping open the button of my jeans, sliding the zip down. It's not until her delicate hands slide around my waist, pushing at the denim, that I snap out of my haze.

I twine my fingers through her hair, grasping a fistful, and pull her head back, exposing her neck to me. The swell of her breasts spills over the top of her bra. Kissing and nipping down that lovely valley, I push one strap down and then the next. As gorgeous as this is, I want it gone, out of my way. Addie reaches behind to release the hooks, freeing what have to be the world's most magnificent tits.

"*Fucking perfect,*" I murmur against them. Stretching my fingers wide to try to contain them, not wanting to allow an inch of her skin to go unworshipped, I kiss and nibble from one to the other. Sucking and biting at her nipples. Drawing each one into my mouth and letting go with a pop.

Kicking out of my jeans and trainers, I push her back

down into the pillows scattered across the top of her bed. "I want to taste every inch of you," I say, trailing my tongue down, down her flat stomach, teeth grazing and nipping at each of her hip bones.

The vanilla lotion on her skin tastes as good as it smells. She's fucking delicious.

I slide my hands beneath her hips, grab her navy-blue knickers, and pull at them until Addie lifts her hips.

She plants her feet on my hips, her toes nudging at my cock through my boxer briefs. "Finn?"

I close my eyes, taking a deep, controlling breath. "Addie?"

"Is that—"

"All for you, love."

"The four-leaf clovers on your undies?"

"Mmhmm. I wore them for luck." It takes all my concentration to keep my eyes from rolling to the back of my head. "You're going to want to stop doing that, love." I grab her ankles and push her feet to the side, sliding my palm up the length of her leg.

I wedge my shoulders between her thighs and lick her, slow and lazy. Circling the tight, little bundle of nerves, sucking gently.

Today, this, with Addie will be an exercise in control. Patience. My feelings for this girl are so fucking overwhelming in every way. She has pushed me away, challenged my bullshit, and made me grovel and beg in a way I never have before. I've never been this invested. Not even back in Dublin when I thought I was surely in love. It never felt like this.

I slide one finger through her wetness and dip inside,

pumping deliberately. Her moans, her gasps, the breathy sounds she makes drive me. I add a second finger and curl them, stroking and massaging that spot, the one that makes her gasp and shudder and sigh.

"Finn...oh dear God..." She tugs at my hair, not quite deciding whether to pull me closer or push me away. Her legs tremble and shake as she comes apart with my tongue on her clit and my name on her lips.

I leisurely kiss my way across her hips, up her stomach. Lavishing attention on her gorgeous tits, lifting them, feeling the heft of them resting in my palms. I bite her nipple, lightly tugging at her flesh. Addie reaches for me, drawing my lips to hers, tasting herself on me.

"You good?"

"So good. Do you have..." She lifts her hips, sliding her slickness against me. "Do you have a condom?"

Fuck, is this really happening?

"I—" *I can say no.* "I'm—"*I might be falling for you.*"I've —" I don't know how I'm capable of even the smallest thought.

"Top drawer on the left," she breathes against my neck.

I have one. I'm prepared, but the drawer is closer. I stretch across her body as she slides her hands into the waistband of my briefs, pushing them down my hips. I hand the foil packet to her and push back, freeing my cock and shoving the briefs away.

Addie rips the wrapper open, pulling the condom out.

Jesus, Mary, and Joseph.

The sight of her biting her lip, wanting me has me ready to explode.

I squeeze my cock and breathe deep, trying to find all the control I possibly can.

It's not a matter of wanting to. *Fuck's sake, I want this with her.*

My jaw muscles twitch as she reaches out, rolling the condom down my length. Nothing has ever felt as good as her fist on my cock. Nothing.

She squeezes lightly, and any thoughts I had of waiting, wondering are gone. All of them, gone.

Unable to keep my lips from her, I lean in, kissing her breathless. Or maybe I'm the breathless one. Addie shifts beneath me, sliding against me, nudging me closer...closer. She tilts her hips the last little fraction of an angle, and I'm right there.

Not moving.

Addie pulls back, searching my face, her gaze bouncing between my eyes. The connection is stronger than I could have ever imagined.

"You okay?"

"I am. Are you?" If nothing else, I have to make sure there's no doubt. None.

"God, yes."

She slides a foot up the back of my thigh, wrapping her legs around me. I inch forward, and a breathy moan escapes Addie as I slide the tip of my cock in. I thought her fist on my cock would send me to an early grave; I was mistaken.

In fact, nothing has ever felt as good as this.

"Addie, God help me...You're sure this is okay?"

"Yes, God, yes. Give it to me, Finn."

Her foot pushes against my arse until I'm there. Fully

seated, bottomed out. Balls deep. Fucking surrounded by her in the most amazing way.

Every moment of intimacy before now were just lies wrapped up in a pretty little bow because sliding into Addie is the best feeling in the entire world.

Nothing has ever felt as good as this.

"Oh my God, Finn..."

I don't dare move a muscle. I don't fucking dare.

Gritting my teeth, I try desperately to run through the months of the year in Gaelic. Anything to keep control of myself.

"Holy Christ, woman. Fuck." *I think I might pass out.*

"You're not allowed to pass out, Finn. Let me...let me... please...*ohmagawd*..."

I thought I'd kept the passing out comment to myself, but I guess it slipped out. "Are you...are you okay? Sweet Jesus, please tell me I can move, Addie. I don't think I can hold still."

Before the words are out of my mouth, her hips start rocking, and I'm back to Gaelic. This time, I'm counting...

"*A haon, a dó*..."

Thrusting with each new number.

"Yes, Finn...more..."

Christ, her sounds are distracting in the best possible way.

"*A trí, a ceathair, fuisce, cíche*..."

Addie is meeting me thrust for thrust, and I'm fairly certain I've died and gone to heaven.

"*Ungmagawd*, Finn...Finn..."

Ah, fuck, God, she's amazing.

"*A cúig, a sé, glas, gorm*..." I reach between us and circle her clit, thrusting, counting, and saying random words in Gaelic. My spine tingles, and I know I don't have much time left.

"*Finn...*"

"*Tá tú álainn...*"

"*Please...*"

"*Ghlacann tú mo anáil ar shiúl...*"

Throwing her head back, Addie comes undone—again. Squeezing me, pulsing around my cock. When she opens her eyes, staring deep into my soul, I let go. My release ripping through me, like nothing I've ever experienced in my life.

Because until this moment, I haven't.

TWENTY-FOUR

Adelaide

I run my nails down the center of his back, humming softly. "Finn, are you okay?" I laugh. "You didn't really pass out there, did you? Or die? Because that would really suck."

I can feel his chest expand and contract with each breath, but when he shakes with silent laughter, I don't fucking know what to think. Maybe it's relief or something.

"Addie, *is tú mo neamh*," he mumbles into the crook of my neck.

"What does that mean? You said a lot of things in there I didn't understand. It was almost like you were speaking in tongues." I smooth back his hair as he pushes up and smiles down at me.

"It was Gaelic. I said a lot of different things. I should, erm...get rid of this now, yeah?" Finn looks down to where we're still joined.

"The condom? Absolutely."

He grips the base and pulls out, both of us gasping a quiet, "Fuck," at the loss.

"Flush it then or..." He looks absolutely lost, like he's never done this before.

Surely, that's not right. Can't be.

"Knot it and trash?"

When he's back in bed, pulling the covers up over us, I settle half on top of him, chest-to-chest. "Can I ask you a question?"

He has a sweet, goofy smile plastered on his face, like he's all kinds of pleased with himself.

"You can, and then I'll tell you what I said in Gaelic." His gaze dances from my face to my boobs squished against his hard chest.

"Was that..." *How do I ask if this was his first time without offending him?* I feel like I should have known something like that beforehand. Plus, it's Finn, and he's known as one of the man-whores of McBride's, not that I really want to think about that. I'm no virgin, but...*holy shit*.

"My first time?"

I just stare at him, waiting.

"Was it terrible? Christ, I'm sorry, Addie." His whole body tenses, and he avoids meeting my eye. His jaw muscles twitch.

I place a palm on his cheek, drawing his attention to me. "Not terrible at all," I tell him. "Truly, you blew my fucking mind, Finn. But..."

Finn snaps his eyes to me. "After what happened in Dublin, I just..." He licks his lips and looks deadly serious, shrugging. "I wasn't ready to actually go through with it. But it didn't completely suck?"

Oh, my heart. "We have a lot of things to discuss, but *that* did not suck at all. Not in the least." I place my hand on his belly and bite the lovely pectoral muscle that's right there, asking for it. "Now, tell me what happened in Dublin. Why did you have to leave school and the...Humanities?"

He nods, confirming that little nugget of knowledge.

"Why did she get to stay, and you had to leave?"

Finn flops his arm across his face, avoiding me as much as he can. "I mentioned she was, ehm, married, yeah?"

I nod slowly, and he peeks out from under his arm, quickly darting his gaze away.

"Her husband was the dean of the school. He walked in on us during her tutor hours. She was splayed out on her desk. I was there, about to slide in and..."

Holy shit. I'm not quite sure that needs to be voiced.

"And she got preferential treatment while you were asked to go." *Who would ever guess this tender, vulnerable soul was hiding under all the cheesy lines and bravado?* "I'm so sorry, Finn." I paint his chest with kisses over his heart. His beautiful heart.

"There are eight of us kids. My two older brothers were already through uni or almost done. But the younger ones didn't need to suffer for my mistake. I was young and dumb, flattered by her attention, and thought I was untouchable." He shrugs and lets his arm fall to the pillow. "The whole thing freaked me out. The dean said it was a good thing we'd not actually done the deed yet. Said he'd have called the constable. Just seemed a better idea to not take that step until I found someone worth the risk."

My heart melts when he reaches up and tucks a lock of hair behind my ear. "So the girls you've taken home, you didn't...?"

"I didn't. That's not so say that I don't have other skills." He gives me a cocky smile before turning serious again. "I'm not proud of what happened in Dublin or the aftermath. Thank you for not judging me." His knuckles trail lightly down my shoulder and across the swell of my boobs smashed against his chest.

"We all have shit to deal with, and how we deal with it is up to the individual. It would be crazy for me to judge," I scoff, sliding my hand down his abdomen, making him squirm as I trace the V of his muscles.

"Like this?" Finn runs a finger down the bridge of my nose, tapping my silver septum ring. "And this?" he asks, grabbing a fistful of my hair, tugging my head to the side. He kisses me, licking at the seam of my lips before wrapping his free arm around me and pulling me closer.

"Some people wear their hearts on their sleeves. I change my hair with my mood, and nothing pisses my dad off more." The light, easy kisses I trail up his neck flames and smolders into a passionate thing that runs away from us.

"Tell me what you said earlier." I lazily stroke his cock, running a finger around just below the crown.

He groans and gently thrusts his hips. Scooting down his body, I slide my leg across his hips and straddle his thighs.

Not needing any encouragement, Finn reaches into my drawer and grabs another condom, tearing open the packet. He hands me the condom and tosses me a Finn wink. "It was sexy as fuck, watching you sheath my cock. Do it again?"

I take the condom, arching a brow at him, waiting.

"Fine. I was counting in Gaelic, trying to distract myself so that I wouldn't blow too quickly."

With the lightest touch possible, I slowly roll the condom down his length. Finn watches me with hooded eyes.

"Then, I got distracted and went with whiskey, your tits, and the different colors you've had your hair." He runs his hands up my hips until he's cupping my boobs, pinching and rolling my nipples in the same lazy way I stroke him.

I lift my hips, positioning him at my entrance. "What else did you say?" I ask on a gasp as I lower myself until I'm completely and deliciously full.

Finn thrusts slow and deep, our bodies rocking, hands caressing and touching. He pulls me down, so we're chest-to-chest, the new angle robbing me of my ability to breathe.

"I said, 'You are lovely.'" He slowly drags his cock out until we're just barely connected. "That you take my breath away." He murmurs against the shell of my ear as he thrusts back in, "And that you are my heaven."

"More..." Dear God, his words squeeze at my heart.

He wraps me in a mixture of Gaelic and English as he brings me to a shattering release.

TWENTY-FIVE

*"Can you imagine if someone wrote you a list of
reasons they loved you?"*
*"No. It would probably be the shortest list in the
world."*
"You're right. All it would say is, Everything."

Finn

I pull on the soft gray T-shirt I had done up for today. It's not
a holiday, nothing special to the rest of the world. Just to me.

"Finn, you're working tonight, right?"

I quickly slide into a button-up as Addie exits the bathroom in a cloud of vanilla-scented steam. The blue of her
hair is so much darker when it's wet and twisted into the
complicated braid that I can't quite figure out, no matter how
many times I unravel it.

I pull the sides of my shirt together, buttoning over the
letters first. "I am. Will you keep me company for a bit?"

Addie slides her hands round my waist and pushes up

onto her toes to kiss me. This is dangerous because there is nothing I want more than to deepen this kiss and take her back to bed, losing myself in her.

Addie breaks our kiss and nods. "Yeah, I have to get some work done though. What time are you going in?" She sifts through the few bits of clothing she keeps at my flat.

I've not moved yet, but I did talk with my landlord about his daughter breaking in. He installed a keypad lock for us instead, and I've not seen Bitchy McCuntface around the pub in ages.

"Erm...I have some things to get done before my shift, and Kieran needs to leave early again. I should probably go soon."

"Again?" She spins, hands on her hips. "What the hell does he do? He's never at work on time. Never works a whole shift. Why does Francie keep him?"

"The accent, love. He's got it, and he can pour a pint. I'll get him sorted."

Addie rolls her eyes and plops down on my bed, shoving her foot into a red Converse. "That's stupid. If he can't show up and do the whole job completely, then he needs to be replaced. There should be ramifications for not..." She's lost in her head and mumbling about McBride's.

She's so fucking cute; I can hardly stand it. With all the stealth I can manage, I tackle her to the bed, caging her in and kissing her until her hands are pulling at my belt, and we're both panting.

"I have to go, Addie. But I promise you, we'll pick this up later, yeah?" I drop a last kiss to her thoroughly swollen lips and climb off the bed, tucking my erection away the best that I can. Then, I head to McBride's as she goes back to her flat.

Adelaide

Finn is up to something. He thinks he can hide shit from me and have all the surprises, but I have a few of my own.

I didn't lie to him when I said I had work to do today. I have several new clients and have been busier than ever. Nope, I didn't lie. I just didn't tell him the whole truth.

Aidan has been outrageously generous in handing out my name, recommending my work, and the inquiries have been shocking, to say the least. Through his photo shoots with several bands and ever-expanding client list, I've been hired to overhaul the website and promo materials for one of the big music festivals in Kansas City.

Timing has been weird, and the organizers had some issues with some of the bands and their branding, but in a show of good faith, they gave me a pair of tickets and are flying me and a guest out next week. We don't just get to attend the show; we have full access to the venue, the musicians, and an amazing setup in my hometown.

It took all of a minute for me to decide who my plus-one would be. Finn's mild obsession with music and specifically Of the Room made it a no-brainer. That, and he's weaseled his way into my cold, dead heart.

Things are all cleared with his boss for me to steal Finn away for a few days.

Back at my apartment, I set Eric down, and he scampers off to find the Flounder toy Finn gave him. I make my way to my bedroom to finish getting ready, drying my hair and styling it in soft, beachy waves. It reminds me of ocean waves, and I love it, but it might be time for another change.

Maybe purple? Maybe the soft pastel rainbow that Finn sent me for my Pinterest board?

I swipe on mascara and some lip stain and swap out my total nerd glasses for cute nerd glasses.

Grabbing my laptop, I settle on the couch to print off the flight vouchers and festival info, making mental notes of a few major things I want to completely change on the website and a few other cool touristy things that are must-dos in Kansas City.

After a couple of hours of work, it's time. I take Eric out to do his thing, pop him into his crate, and change into the shirt Virginia scored for me. I text her on the way to my car to make sure everything is all set for Finn's surprise at McBride's.

Francie

I settle into my usual seat at the corner of the bar, waiting for the show. Neither Finn nor Adelaide has any idea of the other's surprise. Maybe an inkling that there is one, but by no means what it is.

It settles my heart to see the boy find his way, and Adelaide is good for him. He needs someone to challenge him, keep him in line, and keep his head from getting too big. He's grown up a lot in the time he's been at McBride's. Training up the new lad, Kieran, has been a challenge—one that Jimmy wasn't quite up to and didn't manage nearly as well as I'd hoped. But Finn's got him sorted. I have all the faith in the world that Finn will be able to sort Jimmy out as well, if need be.

Applying to the university for his business classes was

the final little step the boy needed to get himself lined up for the future. He needed to put the events from Dublin behind him. Know that he's capable of taking the courses he'll need to run a business. To secure his future. Because, as much as I love all my boys here—Aidan, Jimmy, Finn, and now, Kieran—there is only one completely suited to take over when the time comes.

Finn has a love for McBride's in a way the others don't quite possess. He loves the patrons, loves the lifestyle. It's the perfect fit for him to carry on, looking out for the boys here now, for the Irish lads along the way who need a place to land for a bit, and for himself to grow into who he's meant to be.

He'll do well.

Finn hustles through the pub, getting the last little details set. Making sure that his ladies have what they need. They are all wearing their matching shirts, newly altered to add an additional line of text, and drinking whiskey like only classy women can. Neat.

I lean in as he comes back to the bar. "Make sure the grannies have a round on me, yeah?"

He gives me a sly look and asks, "Want me to put that on your tab, old man?" He sets a fresh pint of Guinness in front of me and winks.

I check the clock above the bar. "It's about time."

Finn looks over his shoulder, and with a quick nod, he pulls his button-up shirt over his head, leaving him in just the T-shirt he's so proud of.

An outrageous smile stretches across my face as Adelaide makes her way through the door. The air stills as she searches the dark interior, looking a little unsure until her eyes adjust and her gaze lands on Finn. The dramatic gobshite plants his hands on the bar top and hops over it to get to her, unwilling to wait the seconds it would take to walk the twenty or so feet.

"So, you're on board with the ladies." He nods to the round table in the center of the room after taking in Adelaide's #TeamFinn shirt.

Adelaide shrugs and runs a finger across his own shirt emblazoned with #TeamAddie in pinks, greens, and blues. "I like this." She looks up at him, her smile matching his. "So, this is it? This relationship is officially defined?"

"It is," he answers with just as much cheek.

He pulls the tickets he bought for them to go to a concert in Kansas City from his pocket. The same tickets that she has in a packet for him.

These two are meant for each other as much as Aidan and Lis are. Gracyn will find her man when she stops trying to hide from the truth of who she is.

All in all, these people are my family. My boys and their ladies, my girls and their men.

Sometimes, you hold tight to the secrets that need to be kept.

For love. For life. For the best.

Thank you for spending time in Beekman Hills with Finn and Addie. I would love to know what you think of these two! If you can, please drop a quick review on your favorite retailer for me!

To stay up on releases and happenings, make sure you're signed up for my <u>newsletter</u> at <u>www.kcenderswrites.com</u>

...now, jump into **Tombstones** to meet Jack and Kate, or
Troubles for more Aidan and Lis.
If it's Gracyn's story you're looking for, grab **In Tune**
(formerly Tunes).

ACKNOWLEDGMENTS

Twist was never supposed to be a thing. I had no intention of writing Finn's story; he was strictly a side character. Sweet and goofy, loyal and protective, but just out for a good time. This wasn't supposed to happen. But sometimes life takes a left turn and you need something light and fun to take your mind off the serious life changes going on in your world. This little project provided me with a break, the laughter and goofiness I needed more than anything. For that, I will forever be grateful to my friend, Finn.

I just hope I didn't ruin things at McBride's! Once a flirt, always a flirt, so, ladies, don't stop teasing him—

Christy Wallingford, without you, this would have never happened! You deserve the biggest thank you there is for this. You held my hand, patted my head, brainstormed, laughed, and snorted with me for countless hours through this crazy little side project and brought Finn to life.

Marisol Scott and Kate Spitzer, thank you for reading, laughing, and adding to the ridiculousness of Finn. The idea started with a comment in McBride's and grew and grew until it couldn't be contained. Thank you for all of your amazing support.

Boy #1 and the infamous Sparky, thank you for having those cheesy pickup lines at the ready. Boy #1 and I were chatting at our taproom—Cinder Block Brewery, in North

Kansas City—and I mentioned needing more pickup lines. He whipped out his phone, texted his friend Sparky and the response was so fast, my head spun! Thank you, love. I hope they work better for you than they did for Finn! ...maybe Sparky needs a book...

Boy #2, your time is coming. Ideas are being discussed.

Thank you to the ladies of McBride's who can't seem to wait to get their hands on Finn, your support and enthusiasm has been AMAZING!

And to my Tribe, my author friends, the bloggers, and readers who always go above and beyond in encouragement, support, and promotion, THANK YOU! You all make me life so full.

TOMBSTONES

BEEKMAN HILLS

Tombstones

BEEKMAN HILLS

To family.
By blood or by other means, you are my reason.

ONE

Kate

HOW MANY FROGS DOES *a person have to kiss before she
finds her—*

Who am I kidding? I'm not even looking for a prince at
this point, just someone who's a little less toad than what I've
found on Tinder, Bumble, and all the other dating sites.

I sit across the café table from tonight's frog, sipping my
wine, and I look, really look, at this guy. He's taller than me,
just barely. Works out, probably too much because that really
is a thing. Dude is stacked with gym muscle, finely honed
and aesthetically pleasing in the bodybuilder-Instagram-
profile sort of way. He's dressed nice, he doesn't smell bad,
and he hasn't picked his nose or anything, but may the good
Lord help me, I might just die of boredom right here in this
chair. I don't have even the slightest clue what he's droning
on about. I tried, really tried, to follow the conversation, but
when my mind starts wandering and the first thing that pops
into my head is whether or not I cleaned the turtle cage in

my classroom, I feel like that's a sign from up above to cut my losses and move on.

What might I have to do to make this dude stop talking and pay the bill, so I can just go home? Let's be real; there's a part of me that's wondering if he's going to cough up the cash for the bill or if I'll be the one paying. That nonsense has happened to me far too many times in the past year.

"Excuse me. I'm just going to run to the girls' room real quick," I say, sliding my chair back from the table.

All I get in return is a quick nod, more of a chin lift if I'm being honest, and the frog date goes back to his phone. If he's smart, he'll be trolling Tinder while I'm gone to set up a sure thing for later because the only thing I'm sure of is that this is a one-and-done. That the role of tonight's good-night kiss will be played by the shaking of hands and moving the fuck on.

The tiny restroom is full of other Friday night dates, and while I wait my turn, I create each of their fictional backstories to entertain myself. The chick at the sink grabs my attention, and with her huge purse/overnight bag splayed open, she's either getting paid to be on her date or hoping she reaps some similar payoff. Or maybe she's a Boy Scout wannabe, perpetually prepared for any emergency. She could probably save a small Third World country with what she's packing in that bag.

A stall opens up, and I do my business as quickly as I can. Not that I'm in any hurry to get back out to the Frog Prince, but I feel for the very pregnant mama-to-be who's wedged herself into the cramped room. If there weren't three angry-looking girls between me and her, I'd have let her skip to the front of the line. But New York girls are way different from what one might find in Hattiesburg, Mississippi. Maybe I should go back home. Lord knows that state could do with some more teachers.

I love my students here in New York though. The past couple of years, I've gotten to know so many families, and I want the chance to teach the younger siblings of my kiddos. Or at least watch them come on through kindergarten.

I thoroughly wash my hands. Twice, just to kill some extra time because, let's be honest, I really don't want to go back out there. I contemplate waiting until the pregnant lady comes out, so I can congratulate her, ask about the baby, pretend for just a moment that I'm next. But that would be creepy and weird. I might have a touch of baby fever but not enough to have a restraining order slapped on me for randomly stalking pregnant baby mamas in public restrooms.

With a fresh coat of red on my lips and a cursory fluff of the blonde beach waves I labored over for this stupid date, I go back to the dining room, only to find the Frog Prince exchanging phones with the chick from the restroom, the one with the huge bag and desperation spilling off of her.

"Took care of the check while you were gone. You ready to get out of here?" he asks, throwing his napkin on the table. He hikes his pants high on his hips, almost past his navel, and moves toward the front of the restaurant. "You, uh ... you need me to call you a cab or ..."

"I'm good, thanks." I pluck a valet ticket from my bag and hand it off the moment I'm out the door. I pull a couple of dollars from my wallet and press it into the valet's hand, letting him know I'm in a hurry. Actually, I'm desperate to get out of here. Turning to the frog, I paste a polite smile on my face the way my mama taught me. "Thank you for dinner. It was lovely meeting you." I leave the statement dangling in the air between us, hoping, praying that this night will end here. Now. Done.

"Okay, so I'm going to bolt, Kasey. It was great, really. I, uh ..." He shifts his weight, gunning for his escape. "So, you want me to call you or ..."

I don't bother to correct him on my name; there's no need. "Not necessary. You take care now," I say, reining in the bless your heart that is begging for release.

Thankfully, the valet pulls up and holds open my car door. I slide behind the wheel and let out a sigh of relief, one much like I imagine a deer lets go of when a bullet whizzes past, missing him by a mile. And then the gun jams. And the hunter falls out of the tree. That kind of relief.

Something has got to give. I can't keep dating these assholes. There has got to be some real men left out there for a girl. I don't need a prince or a knight in shining armor. Just a regular person, one with manners. And, if he happens to fill out a pair of jeans just right, that'd be fine, too.

Streetlights blink through the car's interior as I drive toward my apartment. I have no desire to go home. None. My roommate, Gracyn, is gone, down in the city for her first client visit since starting with her dad's accounting firm. Our apartment is far too quiet when she's not there.

Quiet and lonely. And I just can't, not yet. I take a left at the next intersection, and three blocks down, I turn into the parking lot of McBride's Public House. Park. Purse. Phone. Patrón? Maybe that should be the drink of my night.

Pushing through the door, I sidle up to the bar and claim the one empty seat at the corner. "Finn, we're drowning my sorrows," I say, dropping into the barstool. "I'm gonna need a shot of the good stuff with a chaser of his friends."

"Grand. You're ready for the whiskey then?" The redheaded bartender's brogue carries over the din of conversation filling the air. He snaps a coaster down in front of me and grabs a couple of shot glasses. Lining them up in a pretty little row, like soldiers marching off to war, Finn O'Meara places both hands on the bar and dares me to make a change. Dares me with a wink and a smile, knowing full well that it's not going to happen.

"Sweet boy, no. I need Señor Patrón, my friend. He's the only one for me, the only man who hasn't let me down yet."

Finn nods, reaching high on the shelf behind the bar, past the rows of Irish whiskey and brandy. Past the high-end vodka and gin. Sitting pretty in the middle of the back row, closest to the lights, is the squat bottle with the lime-green ribbon lovingly wrapped around its neck. That's the one for me. In fact, I'm pretty sure that I'm the only one who drinks it.

"So, you had another date then?" Finn asks as he pours the fiery liquid into the glasses. He pauses, waiting to see just how bad my date tonight was.

I nod at the third shot glass, giving him the go-ahead. "I did, and it was at least three tequilas bad." A hint of honey tickles my senses as I lift the glass, savoring that moment in time where it's all sweet promises and anticipation. Tipping back the first glass erases all illusions of grandeur. Reality sets in as the peppery blast burns its way down the back of my throat. Cleansing me.

By the time shot number three slides past my lips, the demons of my most recent dating disaster have just about been exorcised.

TWO

Jack

JUST THIRTY DAYS STATESIDE, and then we'll be back in the sandbox for another six months. Not enough time to do all the things I want to do at home. Not enough time to see all the people I need to see, but I've got to plant my feet on American soil again. That simple act will somehow ground me enough to make it through my final tour in the desert. Not having to shake sand out of fucking everything for that time alone is worth the price of the plane ticket.

Steak. First thing I want to do is get a big-ass steak, medium rare. Wash it down with an ice-cold IPA and maybe, if the mood strikes, a fresh bright green Caesar salad. Croutons, sharp Parmesan, and creamy, tangy dressing. Forget a reprieve from the sand. Food is worth the damn plane ticket.

"I'll drop you at your house and take off for a bit. Give you and the fam some time together. Get reacquainted," I tell my best friend, Dallas "Tripp" Triplett. My brother in arms.

I steer the rental car onto the parkway and head north toward Beekman Hills.

"Like hell you will," he drawls, adjusting the satellite radio to an alternative rock station. "Chloe'll kill me if I let you leave. And don't even with Jake, man. That boy'll tear you up if he has to wait any longer to see you."

I'm not worried about Chloe. I know she loves me, but she's not about to harm a hair on her husband's head once she gets her hands on him again. But their son, Jake? Totally different story.

That kid has a serious case of hero worship that doesn't make a lick of sense. His dad is just as badass as me, if not more so. But, for some crazy-ass reason, Jake looks up to me; he is completely obsessed with me.

"You want me to take Jake out for a burger or something? Give you and Chloe time to—"

"Nah, man," Tripp cuts me off. "Come in. Have a beer and get settled. You know she's made a ton of food for us, and it'd break her heart if you bolted. Really."

I check my blind spot and press the gas pedal down, passing a string of slow-moving vehicles. They're probably doing the speed limit, but I don't have time for that shit. I have a lot to pack into a short stint—a lot that I need privacy for—and I'm not wasting a precious second puttering along on a perfectly good highway. Hell, my team moves faster than this over shitty sandy roads while searching for IEDs.

"Fine. I'll come in, have dinner, and say hello, but I'm not staying with you. You need time with your family, man, and I need time alone. All by my lonesome." I glance over at Tripp, dead serious and not willing to give an inch. "I don't even want to consider the possibility of hearing your sorry ass snoring for the next month, so don't fight me on it. Not negotiable."

"Fine," he says, the matter done.

TRIPP SNAPS AWAKE as I bump the car into his driveway, gravel crunching loudly under the tires.

"Damn. Fell asleep," he grunts, as if I hadn't noticed.

The windows of the car have been rattling for the past half hour. It never ceases to amaze me how he can lock that shit down when we're in the field, but the minute he knows everything is squared away, he lets loose. I haven't slept like that in longer than I can remember—probably the eight damn years since my plebe year at West Point when I went home for Christmas break. That was the sleep of the dead. No stolen naps, no bracing for the upper classes, no pinging or squaring corners. Just quiet, blissful sleep when my pop wasn't dragging my ass out to run fence line.

The front door flies open as the car rolls to a stop spilling Jake out into the yard, followed by Tripp's hunting dog, Bronson. Tripp throws open the door and scoops his boy up into his arms as the white-and-black-dappled hound dog bounces around him, demanding his own slice of attention.

"You're home, Dad. You're really home," Jake screeches.

He's so overcome; the poor kid is on the verge of tears. And the dog? Bronson is beside himself, hopping around and squealing almost as much as Jake.

After a tight hug, during which my friend somehow completes the transformation from Special Forces sergeant to dad and husband, Tripp says, "And guess who I brought with me."

Jake leans back from his dad and narrows his big brown eyes at the car, searching. Darkness of the fall evening keeps me mostly hidden in shadow, and before long, Jake is squirming to get out of his father's grasp.

Just as his little feet hit solid ground, I open the driver's door and step out of the car, beaming at the kid.

"Uncle Jack."

The volume he's capable of producing is unreal, but I know from experience that I've got to be on the ball now or else my balls are getting nailed. And not in a good way.

Jake launches himself at me, running full throttle, no brakes in sight. I pivot just a hair and brace for impact. Sure, I could pick him up before he gets to me, but this run-and-hug thing has become part of our shtick. It's just that Jake has grown, and a man, home on leave, has to protect his goods from the wrong kind of overzealous greetings. Specifically, the exuberant greetings of children of unfortunate height. Yeah, I've been head-butted in the junk before, and that shit is for sure something I don't ever want to experience again.

"Hey, little dude," I say, letting him hug me for all he's worth.

This kid holds my heart in his sweaty little hands, and I couldn't begin to tell you the *why*s or *how*s of it. It just is.

The vise grip around my body loosens enough for me to crouch down to eye-level with my namesake. Well, my sort-of namesake. As much of an honor as it was for them to want to name their kid after me, the Wyatt Jacksons from my father on back were nothing but overbearing assholes. Hell, I don't like sharing a name with the old bastards, so Tripp and Chloe flipped what my parents gave me, hopefully breaking the cycle of asshole, and Jacob Wyatt Triplett has been my man ever since.

"Tell me something good, Jake," I prompt.

His eyes go wide with all the seriousness a five-year-old can muster. "You're home. And my dad is home. And you can be my lunch buddy at school every day." His excitement starts to build again, and the motor on his mouth is about to kick into high gear. "And you can meet my friends. I tell them about you all the time. And my teacher, Miss Beard, she's the best and you can see my seat and my cubby and ... and ..."

"Jake, baby, let's let Uncle Jack and Daddy in the house, you think?" Chloe calls from the front steps, Tripp's arms wrapped casually around her.

They do the whole separation-reunion thing with style and grace. Never making those around them feel as though they're in the way or that they are desperate for a private reunion. They just fall back into absolute normalcy.

"Hey, Chloe," I greet, straightening up and ruffling Jake's sandy hair. "You look gorgeous, as always." I climb the steps and pull her into a hug. "When are you gonna get smart and leave this bas—sorry—bad boy for a real man?"

"You couldn't handle me, Jack"—she swats my chest—"and I wouldn't know what to do without Tripp. Now, grab your kit bags and come in, so I can feed you."

The look Tripp gives me screams, *You tell her*, as he hustles down to the car and pops the trunk, grabbing both of our bags. And then he kicks the lid onto my coffin. "Where do you want me to put this, Jack? In the house or in your truck?"

"The house," Chloe says as I call, "Truck."

Chloe props her hands on her hips and hits me with the mom look, her bright blue eyes narrowing.

"Truck," I say again with more determination. "Chloe, you know I love you—all of you—but you need family time, and I need some solitude."

"But, Jack—"

"I appreciate the offer—you know I do—but a man has needs."

She shakes her head, laughing softly as Tripp joins us again.

"And I need some relief from this man's ridiculous snoring. This is the official transfer of custody. I don't want him back for a month."

Chloe ushers us all into the house, the scent of home cooking in the air. "Jack, you know you're family, and you're welcome in our home. You can't stay in a hotel for the entire month. What are you going to do there, all alone?"

"Actually, I can, and you don't wanna know, darlin'." I chuckle. "Now, tell me what smells so good before I die a starving man."

Jake runs ahead, into the kitchen, and pulls out his chair, plopping down onto the seat. "Mom made roast and potatoes and gravy. And chocolate cake and ice cream, if you eat all your dinner. Uncle Jack, you get to sit by me, so Mommy and Daddy can hold hands while they eat." His little face wrinkles up in disgust at the idea.

Tripp pulls a couple of beers from the fridge, handing me one and drinking deep from the other. We tuck into the meal that Chloe made, warming us from the inside out, filling our stomachs, and welcoming us home. Conversation is light and decidedly normal during dinner with Jake telling us all about going to school, his friends, and the best teacher in the world, and Chloe sharing her thoughts on a group of moms she refers to as Teacup Terrorists, trying to run playdates with an iron fist.

The evening drifts easily, and with full bellies, we all get a little sleepy. Well, Jake and I do. He's on my lap, head tucked into my chest, eyes getting heavy.

"Chloe, you want me to put him to bed?" I offer.

"Not tired." Jake yawns. "School ... lunch with me ..." he mumbles bits and pieces as he finally gives in, and his body goes limp with sleep.

"I'll tuck him in if you have lunch with him tomorrow," Tripp says softly, rounding the table to take his son from my arms.

Jake doesn't move a muscle in the transfer, and again, I marvel at how Tripp slides seamlessly out of operator mode and right into dad mode.

I push back my chair and gather the dessert plates, helping Chloe load up the dishwasher. "Thank you. This was perfect."

"Not perfect enough to stay with us though?" she challenges.

"Jesus, Chloe." I huff out a laugh. "Give me a break. I've had him nonstop for the past six months. You all need to reconnect, and I need to do the bachelor thing." I close the dishwasher and drain the last of my beer. "But tell me about lunch. How do I do this shit? I have no clue."

Chloe gives me all the details on where to go, when to be there, and what to bring. She stops just shy of telling me to make good choices and use my manners or I might get sent to the principal's office as Tripp stalks silently into the room.

With his son tucked away for the night, the air between him and his wife changes, charged with electricity, and without a doubt, it is time for me to leave. Tripp tosses me my truck keys and promises to take care of returning the rental car in the morning, practically shoving me out the door.

This is why I need to give them some space. They need to complete the fall into normalcy. My friends are incredibly welcoming, inviting me into their home and their lives, but I refuse to be *that* guy. They need alone time, and I find what I'm after—a clean hotel, a bottle of Don Julio 1942 tequila, and room service.

And, though I'm sure as shit not looking for Mrs. Right, I can at least venture out and maybe enjoy the company of Miss Right Now.

THREE

Kate

I SHOULDN'T HAVE FAVORITES in class. Not supposed to give one kiddo more chances than any other to get his poop in a group. Normally, I'm pretty fair, but Jake Triplett has burrowed his little self into my heart in a way that I couldn't fight, and now, the little shit is acting six different kinds of crazy. Bouncing around the room, talking a mile a minute, generally disrupting the entire class. And it doesn't matter how much patience I have with these littles; I can't lose control of twenty five-year-olds and expect to walk out of here alive today. Mob mentality applies.

"Jake, please take your seat. It will make my heart sad if I have to ask you to move your pin, friend," I sternly tell him. Well, as sternly as I can because, no matter what I tell myself, this little guy is my damn favorite.

"But, Miss Beard, my uncle Jack is a soldier and he's a hero like my dad and he's here," Jake shares as loudly as he dares, completely ignoring the warning tone in my voice. "He was at my house last night and had dinner with me and my mom and my dad, and he told me about the big desert and did you know they don't get play time? He doesn't get to play in the sand at all even though he's there all the time with my dad. And-and-and they don't even like going to the beach anymore; isn't that weird? And—"

I can't. I just can't.

"Jake." I lower my voice and raise my brows, cutting him off before he has a chance to really kick it into high gear. "I'm sorry, but you need to move your pin and take your seat."

The shock that registers across his sweet little-boy features about breaks my heart. It's like a personal affront that I asked him to move his little Jake-looking clothespin off the green dot and onto the yellow one. Any other kid, and I'd have probably already had him on orange and well on his way to the dreaded red dot, followed by a note home to his parents. But I adore this kid, and he is normally so damn sweet and minds so well.

"But, Miss Beard—"

"Jake, move your pin, please, and have a seat," I repeat.

My heart fissures as his little face falls, tears gathering in the corner of his big brown eyes as he does the walk of shame to the pin board.

"Yes, ma'am. I'm sorry." He sniffs. With all the solemnity that this very dire situation deserves, Jake moves his pin to yellow.

Head bent and shoulders slumped, he walks back to his seat and gets to work. I feel like I've sent him off to his doom. With his tongue out and curled around his upper lip, pencil clutched in his chubby little hand, brows pulled tight in concentration, he traces his letters, practicing the skill, though he's probably one of my most advanced students.

Before long, Jake's wiggling in his seat, checking the clock over the door, sneaking surreptitious glances at me. I shake my head and jot a quick note to myself to check in with his mama and make sure there's nothing else going on in his little world that has him so out of sorts.

AFTER HANDING MY CLASS off to the lunchroom monitor, I hightail it to the teachers' lounge and grab my lunch from the fridge. Thank God my roommate, Gracyn, went food shopping this week. She's an amazing friend but a real shitty cook; she could barely tell you what the inside of a grocery store looks like. She did good this time though.

I pull the big roast beef on rye out of my paisley-printed lunch bag and peel back the wrapping. Crisp lettuce and tangy onion give each bite a perfect crunch, and the flavors positively burst in my mouth. Slathered with cheesy Parmesan mayo and bright red tomato, this sandwich is nothing short of heaven. I wash down each bite with a hit of water, focused on getting the food in my belly as fast as I can.

"The hell, Kate? Where's the fire?" my fellow kindergarten teacher Annie asks. She plops down at the table next to me and empties her own bag of goodies.

Teaching the youth of America to properly form their letters is hard work; we tend to take our food quite seriously.

Speaking around another mouthful, I answer, "Something's up with Jake, and I don't want him to get in trouble in the lunchroom. He's a frickin' spaz today, and Martha'll send him to the office if I'm not there."

Martha is the elementary school equivalent of a SWAT team. She runs a tight ship, and nobody messes with that.

Chew, swallow, gulp of water, and another huge bite. My sandwich is almost done, and I pray that I have a mint in my bag for later because this onion is seriously strong.

"You've got it bad for that little boy, don't you? What happened to not having a favorite this year?" Annie teases.

Shrugging, I shove the last bite in my mouth and chew furiously before responding, "What can I do? His daddy's gone a lot, and he just needs a little extra patience right now. I'll talk to his mama, but he just ... I don't know."

"Doesn't hurt that he's cute as a button either."

"Who? Jake or his daddy? Have you met Mr. Triplett?" I ask, chucking my trash in the can.

"I haven't, but I bet the apple didn't fall far from that tree. And who knows, maybe that uncle Jake's always talking about is single," Annie tosses over her shoulder as I leave the oasis and fast-walk down the hall to my kiddos.

It's not unusual for me to pop in and check on my class, but I startle Martha, laying a hand on her back as she's gunning for my class table.

"Little Mr. Triplett needs a write-up to the office, Miss Beard. In fact, I was just about to take him down there and get things back in order here," she huffs at me.

"Yeah, Jake's had a rough morning, but let's give him a hot minute and just see if he can pull himself out of whatever this is. What's he been doing?" I ask, glancing over my shoulder toward the table reserved for my kids.

Hot damn.

That is most definitely not one of my kindergartners.

Making a show of fanning myself, I tease, "Miss Martha,

you sure you don't just want to go over there and flirt with that fine specimen of man sitting next to Jake?" *Because, holy fuck, is he ever?*

Martha pauses and looks at the tall man folded awkwardly into the bench-and-table combo that perfectly fits our smallest students. "Miss Beard," she says exasperatedly, "I'm old enough to be his mother." She flutters her hand at her throat, clutching at the neck of the candy-cane-printed turtleneck that complements her black sweater vest, which has presents and bows appliquéd festively down the front.

"Doesn't mean you can't look." I hit her with a wink and lean in conspiratorially. "You calling dibs on him? Or can I go see what's got Jake all riled up?"

"Dear Lord, you're just terrible," she mutters. "But, since you're here, I'll let you deal with your class issues. I see a potential situation that needs to be handled with that long-term substitute's class." And, with that, Martha scurries off, leaving me to my musings.

The man sitting smack-dab in the middle of the bench is obviously a source of great interest to my kids. Jake alternates between sitting so close to the man that a piece of tissue paper would feel squished and standing, holding court with his tall, muscly friend. Probably his dad. He did mention that his father was home earlier. He's got all the telltale patience of a father visiting his excited kiddo at school. Helping each child open whatever container or snack bag they hand him. Chatting with each of them in turn.

Chloe Triplett is a very lucky woman if that man is warming her bed at night—when he's in town anyway. His broad shoulders test the tensile strength of the fabric of his plaid shirt, molding almost poetically around a muscular back, tapering in that perfect V to a well-formed ass.

God, forgive me for lusting after my student's father, please and thank you, I pray silently.

Closely cropped dark brown hair fades into maybe two-day scruff that peppers a strong jawline. Plump lips hitch up when the question of the moment is interrupted by Amelia telling him he's got pretty eyes.

His shoulders shake ever so slightly as he rumbles out a, "Thank you, and so do you."

Be still my heart.

I take a deep breath as I approach the table, pushing aside any and all of those lustful thoughts that might still be floating around me like fireflies on a hot summer night. "Jake, can you have a seat, please?" I rest a hand on his shoulder, giving him a little clue about which direction he needs to make his body go.

"Hey, sorry. Hope I'm not causing any trouble." The man turns and thrusts his hand in my direction, trying to stand.

Bless his heart for trying to have manners, but that table has a hold on him, and I'm not quite sure it's ever going to let him go. I wouldn't.

"Not at all. Actually, I'm thrilled to meet you, Mr. Triplett. Jake has been talking about you nonstop. Thank you for your service." I smile and nod my head before slipping my hand into his, and no matter how wrong it is, my heart does an extra little dance when our hands connect. *All the good ones are taken.*

"That's not my dad," Jake says, screwing up his face at me like I'm an idiot. "That's my uncle Jack, Miss Beard. Uncle Jack, didn't I tell you she was pretty? I did, right?"

Electricity jumps along my spine as a smile spreads across this man's beautifully tanned face. Blue eyes flecked with green and gold stay trained on my muddy browns, not breaking eye contact, even as his smile wrinkles and creases the skin at the corners of his eyes.

"You did, my man. You absolutely did. I'm at a disadvantage here, Miss Beard. I seem to be trapped and can't stand to properly introduce myself." He's still got my hand firmly clasped in his, deep golden-brown skin wrapped solidly around my winter-paled hand. "Wyatt Jackson. Uncle Jack to this guy." He nods toward Jake. "It is an absolute pleasure to meet you, ma'am."

If I were a less jaded woman, I'd swoon. But I'm not, and this slick soldier is too smooth, too good-looking, and probably just like all the other assholes out there. I need to shake this off and get myself together. Somehow, it was safer to lust after Jake's very happily married dad. His apparently single and possibly interested uncle is dangerously enticing.

I smile politely and pull my hand from his warm grip, his palm rough and callused, his hold strong. "Thank you for visiting with us today, Mr. Jackson. Jake speaks very highly of you," I tell him.

"As he does of you." He winks a golden-greenish blue eye at me "Every time we talk, right, buddy?"

Jake wiggles out of his seat and bounces in front of me. "Can Uncle Jack come to class? Can I show him my seat and my cubby and all of my pictures? Can I, please?"

"Chill, bud. You're bouncing like a bunny," I tell him through a chuckle. "We've got a busy afternoon—"

"Please, Miss Beard. Please? I promise I'll be good the rest of the day. I promise," Jake begs.

Maybe I could resist his folded hands and the puppy-dog eyes on a normal day, but this is special. Jake's been talking about his dad and uncle coming home forever, and as rocky as the morning was, the afternoon won't be any better if I say no to this.

Pick your battles, Kate.

"All right, but you need to pinkie promise me that you're going to calm yourself down." I hold out my right pinkie to Jake, and he carefully wraps his around mine and places his other hand over his heart.

"I promise, and soldiers never break their promises, right?" He looks to his uncle and returns the nod of acknowledgment he gets.

"Without a doubt." That deep, gravelly voice sends sparks down my spine.

FOUR

Jack

JAKE CLUTCHES MY HAND as we walk down the hallway, our free pointer fingers resting tightly against sealed lips. Not a sound aside from the slap of rubber soles against the shiny linoleum—that, and the click of Miss Beard's heels. Those shiny black heels lead up to legs that could only have been created by God himself on his most inspired day in heaven. And that ass. Is that sway normal for a kindergarten teacher? Thank Christ she's not teaching middle school; boys would be throwing 'bows, trying to gain just the tiniest bit of her attention. Hell, I'd fucking throw down just for the chance to hold her hand again.

How many times can I get away with shaking her hand before I solidly enter creep territory?

"Okay, boys and girls, please put your lunch bags away and take a seat on the floor. You may bring your mat or snuggle buddy if you want," the hot teacher says. Her voice is like silk, smooth and calming with just a hint of a Southern accent.

I'm not a linguist, but I learned early on that it pays to pay attention, picking apart accents and speech patterns. The more I can piece together about people when I meet them, the better my life tends to be.

"Uncle Jack doesn't have a mat or snuggle buggle," Jake calls as he darts to his cubby. "But we can share. I'll use my coat, and you can use my dino mat." The kid is dragging half of the coat closet with him.

"Jake, maybe your uncle would like to sit up front and read to us today?" Teach raises her eyebrow at me.

Questioning me? Daring me? I'm not sure, but I am sure as fuck getting lost in the way her eyes sparkle at me.

I stalk to the fluffy pink chair at the front of the classroom, my very best panty-melting smile on my face. Being the teacher's pet right about now sounds like an excellent way to spend a day. Maybe more than a day while I'm in town. I sure as shit don't remember any of my teachers filling out a tight skirt like she does.

"I'd be honored to read today." I throw her a wink and settle myself into the frilly deep-pink chair. It might be petite and delicate, but at least it's adult-sized, not like the minuscule chairs dotting the rest of the room.

Miss Beard approaches me from behind, and I force myself not to react like I'm in the field. Multiple tours in the devil's sandbox have made me a little jumpy about not having my six covered. Dropping a sparkly purple purse and a book into my lap, she explains what we're reading today. She stands to my right and leans into the side of the princess chair I'm planted in, her hip jutting dangerously close to the side of my head. I grip the shiny purse in my hand, the plastic groaning under the pressure as I force myself to keep my hands firmly and safely on my lap. The temptation to reach back and trail a finger up the back of her curvy calf, across the back of her knee, and up that thigh is almost overwhelming. But I'm disciplined; I've had that shit beaten into me, hazed and burned into my very being.

A rhythmic snapping draws my attention from inappropriate thoughts, and with that subtle little noise, the kids all find their spots on the floor in a semicircle around me.

Softly, melodically, Miss Beard praises the group, "Thank you for being such good listeners. Let's take just a moment to say thank you to Jake's special guest for taking time to read with us today."

A chorus of, "Thank you," jumbles into a mix of, "friend," and, "Uncle Jack."

I've seen soldiers who don't follow direct orders half as well as these little kids do with nothing more than a kind voice and some gentle prodding. How much of that can be attributed to the woman who's got them for the majority of their waking hours each day? Hell, after just a handful of minutes with her, I'm ready to fall in line and do whatever she wants.

I steal a glance at the delicate hand propped on her left hip—right where I almost can't miss it. I mean, I *can't* miss it. Relief floods me when I see that her hand is completely unadorned. No rings. None glinting on the hand in the air, reaching to turn on a lamp resting on the edge of her desk. That's a damn good sign for me. Surely, she felt that surge when we shook hands earlier. For fuck's sake, I didn't want to let go.

She saunters across the room, blonde waves bouncing, to turn off the overhead light, casting the room in a soft glow, and with a collective sigh, the kids settle in for story time.

I'm not going to lie. The purple purse story doesn't really hold anyone's interest. Before long, heads are nodding, eyes are closing, and there's complete and utter silence. I close the book and set it on the bookshelf next to me with the purse and silently push myself up out of the chair. There, in the shadows, is a stunning beauty, lit by a desk lamp and the glow of her laptop.

"Is this normal, or did I bore them to death?" I whisper.

"This is a golden miracle, and we don't look a gift horse in the mouth," she says softly, her accent weaving its way around the words. "I love each and every one of them, but peace is peace, and I need it today. Thank you."

She looks around the room, taking stock of the lax, snoozing bodies strewed across the floor. Gracefully standing, she motions for me to follow her, and we slip out into the hall, the door barely cracked behind us.

"Seriously, thank you. Some days are rougher than others, and if I'm being honest, I think they all need the break. Being five is hard work." She smiles, really smiles for the first time since I met her, and it's breathtaking.

"Shit, I'm sorry. Was it me, do you think? Jake's got a tendency to get himself worked up, and he takes the rest of the room along for the ride."

Her hand darts out, landing on my arm, her intent to soothe my worry away. But with her movement comes a waft of perfume, and the effect is the absolute opposite of what is good for either of us in this moment. Soft and buttery like whipped cream, fresh but not overly sweet, her scent is nothing short of heady and intoxicating in the very best way.

"Not at all, and please watch your words," she says, pinning me with a stern teacher look. "I think it has more to do with the phase of the moon or the fact that Christmas break is looming around the corner."

I place my hand on top of hers, holding it in place. "Miss Beard, thank you for all that you do for Jake. People don't usually get how hard it is on those left behind by deployments. You've made a huge impression on him."

Her smile takes on a hint of shyness.

"I'd like to thank you properly. Can I buy you a drink? Take you out to dinner?"

"That's sweet of you, but no." She's still relaxed, not pulling away.

"Just no?" I lean in, testing her commitment to that response.

"Yes. A simple no. Perhaps a *no, thank you* would be more polite." She gives my forearm a little squeeze and pulls her hand away.

"May I ask why?" Without conscious thought, I widen my stance and fold my arms across my chest, slipping into my standard pose when a soldier gives me a bullshit answer that I don't like.

"You may."

Sighing, I drop my chin to my chest before meeting her eye again. "Why did you refuse an offer for a lovely dinner out?"

"Professionalism. Do they have that in the Navy?"

"Army, Special Forces. SEALs just fucking write books. I

actually do work," I respond automatically, busting on my Naval counterparts.

Given the same situation, guys from the other services all do the same thing, but when shit goes down, there is nothing but mad respect.

Her head snaps back, eyes blinking wildly, making her lashes flutter. "Same difference, and I asked you to watch your language," she scoffs, glaring. "I just don't think it's right to see my students' people socially. It would raise questions of impropriety, but thank you anyway."

My lips pull up on just one side in a smirk that has never failed me. I lean in, crowding her space just a little—not enough to scare her off because, let's face it, the last thing I want to do is give her any reason to refuse me. "I'm not related to Jake. He's my best friend's kid, and while I think of them as family, we're not a blood relation."

"And yet, my student calls you Uncle Jack, thus the need to maintain distance. So, *no*, but thank you." She gives my in-charge stance right back, feet planted, arms folded, attitude in full swing.

I like it. Fuck that, I like it a lot that she's a little cocksure and sassy. Color me intrigued.

"True. But I can assure you, I have sufficient security clearance to keep this on the down low if that's what you need ..." I taper off, waiting.

And waiting.

Nothing.

This chick has her shit locked down tight, making me the first to break. "Christ, will you at least tell me your name, or do I have to keep calling you Miss Beard?"

The attitude on this one, seriously fucking hot.

She screws up her mouth so that her plump peach lips are twisted up, the right side of them getting downright abused by her pearly white teeth. "Doesn't matter if y'all are actually related, the answer is still no. And you keep pushin', we're gonna ramp that no right on up to a hell naw, ya hear? And my name is Katelyn Hays Beard. I'll allow Kate, should we happen to run into each other outside of school, but within these walls and with Jake, I expect you to respect my professional relationship with your nephew and his family, referring to me as Miss Beard. There's more to family than just blood."

Yeah. Her Southern roots are showing big-time, and I definitely like ruffling those feathers.

"Right. I hear you. Thank you for your time today, ma'am." I nod and saunter down the kindergarten hallway like I own the fucking place.

FIVE

Kate

THERE IS NOTHING I need more than dinner and a handful
of drinks to help wash away a week from hell with twenty
five-year-olds and a full moon. At least I hope that's what I'm
getting up to tonight.

This is the third, maybe fourth time I've gone out with
this guy, and while he's not the worst I've found on Tinder,
he's sure not winning any awards either. In fact, Dr. Barnes,
as he refers to himself, is kind of an asshole. He's got potential to be a lovable one at times, but still. I mean, for the love
of God, he's a chiropractor; he can't even hook me up with
antibiotics when the sweet little angels in my class lovingly
share their damn germs. It's time for him to up his game, but
I probably need to cut him loose. After dinner because, to be
completely honest, a teacher's salary doesn't go very far, and
I really do need a night out to counterbalance this week.

"Yes, I made a reservation," he says, rapping his knuckles

on the hostess stand. "My time is valuable. You think I have all the time in the world to stand around, waiting for you to find me a table? I'm a doctor, for God's sake."

"I'm so sorry, Dr. Barnes. Perhaps you can have a drink at the bar while we get your table ready for you?" The poor girl is beyond flustered and falling all over herself to make Matt happy.

Yeah, I refuse to refer to him as a doctor. Maybe I would if he wasn't such an asshole. But he is, so there's that.

I lean on the bar and signal the bartender. "Two shots of Patrón and a margarita. Rocks and salt, please," I order quickly, hoping I can get some liquid calm before the not-a-doctor loses his shit.

As the bartender sets the full shot glasses in front of me, a most delicious smell drifts around me. I check over my shoulder for the source of the clean, spicy scent with a hint of citrus and leather, but no one stands out to me. Downing the shots, one after the other, I slide a wad of cash across the bar and scoot to my left, making room for Matt.

He's fine. At the very least, not visually offensive.

"Can you believe how they treat medical professionals here? Honestly, if I ran my practice like this, I wouldn't have any patients," Matt huffs indignantly. "Did you get a drink, KB? That bartender take care of you?" He's talking to me but looking anywhere but at me.

"I did. What do you need?" I turn and smile at the bartender, hoping he comes right over.

Maybe this was a bad idea. Maybe dinner and drinks aren't worth the time I have to spend with this guy.

"Yeah, I'm gonna need an appletini," Matt calls over my

head, doing the douchey bro nod at the sweet man pouring drinks tonight. "And that's on the house since I have to wait for my reservation."

I want to disappear. Usually not offensive just became full asshole.

What self-respecting man drinks appletinis?

None. The answer is not a damn one.

Matt's froufrou girlie drink is placed in front of him with a look that might be classified as heated interest from the bartender.

I catch his eye and give him a quick shake of my head, mouthing, *Don't waste your time.*

Lifting the full glass to his lips, Matt takes a delicate sip and loudly smacks his lips. A move that does not go unnoticed by the bartender despite my warning. Perhaps they're better suited for each other than Matt and I are.

"So I had a new patient today. Fucking hot as shit. Tight body, locked in on clean eating. She was totally a CrossFitter; I could tell. She had these rock-hard thighs and this ass. She's going to need me for a long time coming." He snickers, mumbling, "Come," under his breath like he's saying a naughty word—like the twelve-year-old boy he really is at heart.

Sweet baby Jesus in a manger, this date is going downhill in a hurry. There is not a damn thing I can think of to say. Matt's practically panting over some other chick while he's out with me. When is this shit going to end? I need to find a nice man. One with ethics and morals. One who knows how to treat the woman he's out on a date with. One who refrains from looking for or lusting after his next conquest. Doesn't have to be a forever thing. I just need to know that the apparent unicorn exists.

The front door opens, ushering in a gusty breeze from outside, and that spicy, citrusy scent swirls around me once again. The owner must be somewhere close by. I search the surrounding area, and just as I lock eyes with my favorite student's not-a-real-uncle, Matt's commentary on his better business practices rumbles across the room.

"So, really, I mean, it's only malpractice if they complain, am I right?" Matt's booming, slightly grating voice carries across the sudden lull of conversation in the bar area.

There is no escape. None.

"Dr. Barnes, your table is ready. Would you care to follow me, please?" The hostess smiles politely, indicating the way to the dining room.

Matt rises from the barstool he commandeered for himself, leaving me to stand in three-inch heels. "About time. We've been waiting well over ten minutes."

The more he talks, the more I realize I'm not just not interested; I'm downright embarrassed to be associated with him. Resigned to just get through tonight's dinner and call it quits.

Again.

I can't seem to catch a break with the whole dating thing since I showed up early to meet my ex, Chance, for dinner and found him pressed up—from hips to lips—kissing on the prettiest boy I had ever seen. Needless to say, I moved out the next day, and the rest has been one dating disaster after another. The only good thing that came out of that day was meeting my roommate, Gracyn George, and her best friend,

Lis Rittenhouse. Thank God those girls were all about making friends with a poor, displaced girl from the South.

We're seated at a table by the window, and Matt immediately launches into ordering for both of us. Not a damn thing that I want to eat since the self-proclaimed fitness guru has decided that kale and brussels sprouts are the food of the hour.

I excuse myself as quickly and politely as I can manage, seeking the relative silence of the women's restroom. It strikes me out of nowhere that this is becoming my thing. My date starts going south, and I take off for the sanctity of the restroom—the one place I know the guy won't follow me. I wash my hands, check social media, and waste as much time as I think I can get away with. Maybe our super-healthy, flavorless food will be at the table, waiting, by the time I get back. Doing a quick calculation of how much time I think I can handle spending with Matt Barnes—full-naming him is a fantastic middle ground for me, not too familiar, not at all professional—I push through the restroom door and stop dead in my tracks.

Wyatt Jackson. Standing just like he did outside my classroom earlier today when he was trying his damnedest to look intimidating. Feet shoulder-width apart, arms folded across his broad chest, biceps straining against the confines of his flannel shirt. Waiting. I inhale deeply, readying myself to be just as indignant as I can when the spicy, citrus scent from earlier stops my brain mid-thought. Of course it was him— the source of the scent that calmed me, caught my attention, and yet eluded me in the bar.

"That's the kind of guy you go for?" A smirk pulls at the corner of his mouth.

"What?"

"I got turned down for that asshole who thinks it's perfectly fine to throw a tantrum for a table and talk to his date about the hot woman he met today that he apparently gets to have his hands all over. What does that say about you, Miss Beard?" His smirk grows as he talks.

The hallway seemingly narrows. Or maybe that's just my reaction to being in a confined space with him.

"You teach those kids about respect and honor—yeah, Jake tells me all about class and his favorite teacher every time he's got the opportunity, so I am well aware of what you're instilling in those kids—but you don't have it in yourself to demand the same of the people you date?"

Hot and flustered, I'm not sure what to say. Maybe I should try to push my way through and put some space between us, so I can think. I mean, I just met this man for the first time today, and he's getting all in my business?

"I think you're worth more than you're billing yourself."

He straightens his already-rigid spine, and I can't help but notice the striking form he presents. Confidence rolls off of him, swirling around me, filling the air, but he's not cocky. It's just the unspoken assurance that he's a bigger badass than anyone else in the room.

"Mr. Jackson—"

"If you insist on formalities, it's Captain." His head tilts down ever so slightly as his brows rise up the same amount.

We're just posturing, dancing around each other.

I purse my lips and pull deep at my teacher voice, the voice of calmly rational sternness, but before I can address him further, he relaxes his shoulders and continues, "I'd prefer if we could drop it though. Jack works a whole lot better for me, Kate. And, if I'm completely honest here, I think you should let me take you out. Show you how a gentleman acts on a date. Bet he doesn't open doors or get your chair for you." He nods his head toward the dining room, and a knowing smile spreads across his face.

I'm dumbstruck. He exudes masculinity and control, not sacrificing even an ounce of respect in the course of it though.

"Why? Why do you want to take me out so badly?" I ask hesitantly, not sure that I can handle his response.

"Because you've got the hardest job in the world—hell of a lot harder than mine. You give all you have to those kids, and I think you don't have an inkling of the impact you have on their little lives. Because you exude a confidence that screams sexy and self-assured, but you lower yourself to letting a schmuck like that think he's worthy of your company. It doesn't make sense, and I want to puzzle it apart, figure out why." Uncrossing his arms, he slides his hands into the front pockets of his jeans. And waits.

My brain whirls and swirls. Thoughts bouncing around, not really sticking on any one thing. My breath catches in my lungs as I search for anything intelligent to say. Anything at all.

And all I can seem to come up with is, "Okay."

He nods once, controlled and almost curt, but even that small movement grabs my attention. "Excellent. Give me your number, and I'll call to work out the details—day, time, your address."

I snap out of the trance I somehow slipped into in the haze of his self-assurance. "No," I say, shaking my head.

"No? No what? Not going to allow me to take you out? Or—"

"I'll meet you out, somewhere public." He opens his mouth to protest, but I push on, "I just met you. It would be foolish of me—actually stupid—to give you my address at this point." I wave my hand toward the restaurant's dining room, realizing I've probably been gone way longer than is polite. "He doesn't even have my address yet, and we've gone out several times. Not all my choices are bad ones. You could be a murderer or something."

He huffs out a laugh and says, "Smart girl. I feel a little better, knowing you're not relying on that douche to get you home safely. Not sure he can hold his liquor. Fucking appletini? What is he, trying out for a remake of *Scrubs* or something?"

"Right? Who drinks those?"

The remaining tension drains out of his body, his stance much more relaxed now. I dig through my bag, looking for a pen and a scrap of paper. Normally, I have Post-it Notes, a full set of colored pens, and highlighters of all shades in my purse, but I opted to leave my Mary Poppins bag at home tonight, and there is nothing in my clutch to jot my number on.

"Just text yourself from mine."

This would be a fantastic time to let my sass shine, but I'm coming up short, so I just text my name.

He slightly shakes his head and lets out a determined breath. "I know it's presumptuous, but will you ... will you let me know that you've gotten home safe tonight? After dinner?"

I smile, laughing softly at his request. "That is pretty

presumptuous. I'll be fine, but I'll talk to you soon," I say, slipping past him to return to my very last date with Dr. Barnes.

If this goes nowhere in the long run and Mr. Right remains elusive, Jack has a point. I deserve more in my evenings ... even if the star is strictly Mr. Right Now.

SIX

Jack

NO MATTER HOW MANY times I check, my phone remains idle. Silent. Dark. A useless piece of shit.

It was a toss-up last night as I sat at the bar, finishing my dinner, on whether to be a creep and follow Kate to make sure she got home okay or to sit tight and be a reasonable human being. I went with reasonable and rational, sending a quick text to the number she'd entered, hoping it was really hers and not a bullshit fake. I have nothing to base this shit on —this concern. But it would have taken nothing for her to send me a damn message. Just a quick, *Home. Safe. Here.*

Something.

But, no, I got nothing from her, and that asshole she was with gave me a bad feeling. The voice mail I left this morning has gotten no response either, and that's just pissing me right the fuck off. I offload my bar and step away from the squat rack. The United States Military Academy gym is fairly empty with the cadets in their academic hours, so I take my time. Pop the clips, add another plate to each end, and get my head right. I don't need an injury, just need to work this woman out of my system.

A quick breath progression once the bar is settled across my shoulders, and I get into position. There is no need to waste time with five hundred-plus pounds on my back, so I get straight to it. Squat and up. Squat and up until my last set's done.

Once the bar is stripped and the plates put away, I flip my phone over, and of course, I have a missed call.

"Hey, this is Kate Beard returning your call. I appreciate your offer, but I think I'm going to pass on dinner. Thank you for the offer and enjoy your day." Her message is pert and professional, just like she wanted.

Well, fuck. I pull on a beanie and my jacket, pop my earbuds in, and head out. I hate running. It's mindless and stupid, absolutely fucking pointless, but I take off through town, hoping that the monotony will clear my head and burn off some of the disappointment. It's not like I've never been turned down before—this is not an ego thing—but she's cute. Sassy. Hell, who wouldn't want to spend some time with a fuck-hot teacher? Maybe coffee? I should take her out for coffee first, ease into this. I told her I wanted to show her how a gentleman treated a lady, give her a different experience than the ass she was out with last night, so I need to do exactly that.

I push through my last couple of miles and take a quick shower, thinking hard about how to change her mind *again.* Get her to go out with me. And, at the same time, I'm doing a fantastic job in avoiding looking at why this has become a fucking mission.

With a quick stop to grab a few things, I pull into visitor parking ten minutes early because, if I'm not early, I'm late. And I can't stand being late. The buzzer sounds, and the lock clicks open, granting me respite from the cold wind whipping past Beekman Hills Elementary.

"What can I help you with today?" the secretary asks, a smile plastered across her face.

I pull out my identification and hand it across the counter, checking the name on the nameplate. "Mrs. Simpson, I'm here to see Miss Beard. This is her lunch period, correct?"

She studies my military ID, flipping it from front to back. "It is, Captain Jackson. Is she expecting you?" she asks, one hand on her phone.

"I'm afraid not, ma'am. If that's a problem, I'd be happy to leave this for her," I say, placing the to-go bag on the counter. I'd much rather see Kate, but I'm not about to rock the boat at her place of employment.

"Miss Beard, you have a package in the front office. Can you swing on by after your lunch drop-off?" Mrs. Simpson quips, giving me a sly wink. "No, I'm sure you'll want to tend to this before you eat. Yes, okay. See you in a bit." Ending the call, she turns to me and says, "She'll be right up, if you'd like to take a seat. And thank you for your service."

I thank her and sit by the window, waiting patiently. Hopefully, this won't be an imposition, though Chloe assured me that it's cool to stop by the school. I might have mentioned wanting to drop a cupcake by for Jake during his lunchtime. It's not a lie, not really. There's a mini cupcake in the bag—his favorite flavor—along with the hot soup, sandwiches, and full-sized chocolate cupcake for Kate.

"Hey, Jenny. What's my package? I didn't order anything. Oh—"

I stand, drawing her attention. "I brought you lunch." I nod, taking her in from head to toe. A long-sleeved shirt and curve-loving skirt have never looked so damn good. Hell, she's more gorgeous than I remembered.

"Thank you." Kate's brows push together, and her lips purse into a biteable pout. "Are you ... did you want to join me?"

"I'd love to."

Familiar with the process, I sign in on the clipboard and grab my visitor sticker before opening the door for Kate. She slides past and leads me down the hallway to her classroom.

"What are you doing here?" She glances at me over her shoulder as her ass sways seductively with each step. "I left you a message this morning that—"

"I got it. You said dinner was a no-go, so I thought I'd bring you lunch."

"Jack"—she pauses to open her door—"that's not what I meant. I just think it's best to keep things separate—personal and professional, I mean."

I nod slowly, having fully expected some kind of resistance. "Gotcha. Well, there's a treat for Jake in there, so if it makes you feel better, you can give him the lunch as well, but I have a feeling he's not going to appreciate lobster bisque the way you might. Totally up to you though. I just wanted the opportunity to thank you for what I'm sure can feel like a thankless job at times."

I set the bag on the corner of her desk and take a step back to pivot and go. No one likes getting their marching orders, and that's exactly what this is. A dismissal.

I might not agree with her reasoning, but who the fuck am I? And can I blame her? I understand professionalism. Understand keeping things compartmentalized. That's how I get through each tour in the desert because that sandbox is so fucking brutal.

A deep sigh and a muttered, "Shit," hits my back as I reach for the door handle.

I pause, turning slightly to face her while I wait.

"I just don't get it. Why are you such a pain in my ass?" Flustered and with her guard down, Kate's accent is more pronounced.

Alabama maybe?

She shifts her weight, popping her hip out, arms crossed over her chest. Classic defensive position, but the way it pushes her tits up is pretty fucking distracting, and I have to briefly close my eyes to find my focus.

"Kate, what's the issue? That I'm a pain in the ass or that I'm pushing your limits of professionalism? I'd like to get to know you, for you to get to know me. It doesn't have to be a big thing. I'm just here for a couple of weeks. Surely, we can have a drink. Dinner." Watching her bite at her plump red lip, I want to do a hell of a lot more than just eat with her, but dinner and drinks would be a great place to start. "I don't want to make you uncomfortable though, so I won't push this anymore. You say the word, and I'll go, drop it, and leave you be. Consider lunch today a good-faith, humanitarian gesture and nothing more." I shrug, nodding to the bag still packed full of food on the corner of her desk. And, of course, my stomach picks that God-given moment to rumble obnoxiously. "Sorry, I'll just—"

"Stay. Eat with me and ... I don't know. Let me think

about the rest of it." She pulls containers from the bag. "It looks like you got enough to feed an army."

Her laughter dances through the air, and that shakes something loose in me, drawing me further into the classroom.

Kate

SOMEHOW, JACK BROKE THROUGH my resolve yesterday. Well, he did it with lobster bisque and manners that I didn't think I'd seen used properly since I moved to New York. He's got country manners. And the way he carries himself, completely aware of everything and in control at all times is some kind of sexy. Try as I might, it was damn near impossible to resist him. So, now, we're having dinner.

I run home after school and change into a more date appropriate outfit. *Not a date, just dinner.* And why is this so hard for me? I'm not normally this wishy-washy, but something feels different. Bigger, more intense. I have gone back and forth in my mind a hundred times on dating Jack—having dinner. It's just dinner.

As I apply the finishing touches to my makeup, Gracyn calls out to me from the kitchen. On a whim, I throw my makeup bag into my big tote along with a few other just-in-case essentials and go check out what has Gracyn yelling for me.

The project supplies I ordered are haphazardly stacked by the front door, so I scoop them up and drop the boxes on the kitchen floor, scaring the crap out of Gracyn in the process. I pull all of the craft supplies out and group them by project before repacking them to take to school while we chat. I could ask my kids' parents to send in bits and pieces, but I like knowing what I've got and that it's ready to go for assembly into the cutest Thanksgiving turkeys ever.

"You want some wine?" Gracyn asks, already grabbing a couple of glasses.

"Couldn't hurt," I tell her. "I have a date—hmm, let's not jinx things. I'm having dinner with someone tonight, but I'm sure the wine will help."

"You're rocking the sexy-librarian thing pretty hard. Who is this guy?" She pours us each a glass of Merlot and leans against the counter. "Another Tinder winner?"

"Nope. And I'm sure it won't amount to anything," I say, avoiding. "Let's concentrate on you for a hot minute though. Things rocky with the rock star?"

She tells me all about their back-and-forth, outlining the what-ifs, and damn if she's not trying to talk herself out of falling in love with him.

I tune back in to her saying, "We've spent next to no time together. What if it's just an illusion and we're not at all compatible?"

"What do you mean? Like, sexually?"

Gracyn about snorts her wine out through her nose, sputtering, "The sex is fine, but what if that's all there is? It's not like we can just date like normal people and then walk away when things go south. He's either in LA or on tour, and I'm stuck here. That doesn't bode well for a normal dating relationship."

"When?" I ignore her look of confusion and carry on, "You said 'when things go south,' not *if*. Are you invested or not? Are you willing to take a risk for real, or are you just playing with him?"

And there it is, folks. The dating disaster handing out relationship advice like I have a damn clue. I can dispense the wisdom, but it never seems to work out for me.

I check the time and drain the last of my wine, handing off my empty glass. "I've gotta shake. I'm meeting Mr. Right Now at the restaurant. Don't wait up. If he plays his cards right, he might get dessert," I toss out, going more for shock value than anything.

But it *has* been a long time, and talking with Gracyn about all the amazing sex she's been having with Gavin has me feeling more than a little frustrated. It's been a long dry spell, and I have a fine man taking me out tonight. One who really won't be around long enough to cause any complications. Maybe I will keep the O option open.

I flip my ruby-red velvet coat around my shoulders, waiting for the inevitable.

"Be safe and make good choices," Gracyn calls as I sashay out the door.

"HOW DID YOU END up teaching here? You don't sound like you're originally from the area," Jack asks as the waiter leaves us with our drinks.

I'd have ordered a shot of tequila if I'd known we were

getting right to the nasty stuff. Instead, I take a healthy sip of my paloma and laugh. Nothing like jumping into the getting-to-know-you portion of the evening.

"I moved here from Mississippi with my high school sweetheart. Go ahead and laugh; it's fine." *Lord, if Jack thinks that little tidbit is funny, he's in for a treat.* "We'd dated forever, all through school and college, and when he wanted to move closer to Manhattan and the Fashion District, I followed him," I say coyly because the rest of the story is where the real kicker is.

Jack leans back in his chair and sets his drink down without taking a taste. "Fashion? He a model or something?" he asks, stroking the stubble along his jawline that gets thicker every time I see him.

"He was something." *Maybe he'll leave it at that.*

"What happened? He run off with a supermodel?" Finally, Jack decides to take that sip of his drink, but the timing couldn't be worse.

He sputters the *añejo* tequila, choking on it, when I say, "I don't know if he was a model, but I caught Chance with his tongue down a guy's throat outside the restaurant we were meeting at for dinner." I shrug because, really ... what else can I do? The whole thing was ridiculous. "That's how I ended up with my two best friends. Gracyn, my roommate, and Lis kind of felt sorry for me as I slammed tequila at the bar of the bistro. It turned out, Gracyn needed a new room-mate since Lissy and her boyfriend were moving in together, and it all just worked out."

Jack sets his napkin down after mopping up his spilled drink and asks, "And the guy? Chance? What the fuck happened there?"

"I moved my shit out of the apartment we shared, and his boyfriend moved in the same day, I think. I see him around every now and then, but I think he does his blessed best to avoid me at all costs."

The waiter comes back, dropping off food and filling our water glasses, giving me a little reprieve from the mess that started my long history of dating disasters.

"So, my mama still hears from his mama, and she just can't seem to understand why I would move all the way up here with her boy and then leave him high and dry, making him take a new roommate he hardly knew at all. I think it's safe to say that Chance hasn't come out to his mama and daddy yet. Lord, I'm not looking forward to going home for Christmas and having to deal with that mess." I tip back my glass and take a bracing gulp.

"Wait, you ... your boyfriend, who you dated forever, is gay? And you had no idea?" Jack's eyebrows can't get any further up on his forehead without him pulling a muscle.

"That's correct," I quip.

He pulls his lips between his teeth, biting back a smile. "And your last name is—"

"Yep."

He folds over, practically face-planting in his dinner, loud laughter rolling out of him.

"My last name is Beard, and I had absolutely no idea that I was his beard." I set my fork down and wait until Jack's at least marginally under control. "I've heard all the jokes about it, made quite a few at my own expense, but aside from my epic dating failures since then, I'm glad. Can you imagine if I'd have married him? And let's be honest; that's where we were headed. Lawd, he's probably still waiting for me to break it to his mama, but that ain't gonna happen, no sir." I steal a glance at Jack just as he registers my *no sir.*

His pupils darken as his posture changes. Gone is the casual and easygoing air, morphing into something heated. Something passes between us that is decidedly sexual. His shoulders broaden, his back goes ramrod straight, and God help me, his tongue lazily sweeps out, moistening his lower lip.

"Katelyn"—his voice holds a note of bridled tension that settles low in my belly, warmth tingling through me—"I like the way *sir* sounds, spilling off your lips."

"Wyatt"—I place my napkin on the table. I am all but done with dinner, the heat and lust quickly bubbling up all around us—"I will *not* call you sir."

"Fair enough. You wanna stay for dessert?" Jack asks, pushing away from the table, poised to stand.

I lean down and grab my purse from the floor. "I think I'd rather be dessert," I purr quietly, standing with more grace than I thought I could muster. I stalk toward the door of the restaurant. I'm not sure what's changed, but I'm ready to break all the rules.

Jack just might be the unicorn I've been looking for. Manners and chemistry that sizzles. And, since he's only here for a short time, what could possibly go wrong? It's not like I'm going to fall in love in a few short weeks. Fun, flirting, and maybe a little fucking on the side—it sure as hell won't be forever, but maybe all I need is right now.

THE DOOR to Jack's room snicks shut behind us, his fingers wrapped firmly around the belt of my jacket. He slowly tugs me into the room, full of quiet confidence and control. And, if I'm being honest, I'm more than willing to follow him. He spins me, untying my belt as he does, my jacket falling to the floor behind me.

With the patience of a hunter, Jack pulls the pins from my hair, letting the waves tumble down around my shoulders. He deliberately flicks the buttons of my blouse, exposing my heated skin, inch by burning inch.

"Christ, you're fucking gorgeous, Kate." He trails a fingertip across my collarbone and down between my breasts.

My skin pulls tight, pebbling my nipples. And, with clothes flying in every direction, we tumble into a writhing, glorious, passionate heap. Thrusting and moaning until both of us are beyond sated and there is nothing left but to pass out from exhausted bliss.

NOISES, MUFFLED VOICES, PULL me from sleep, and it takes a beat or two of my heart for me to remember where I am. That, and the hard slab of muscle my hand is resting on. I trace my fingers along the ridges, accentuating V-cut muscles that point to heaven. Fine, they point to Jack's cock, but sweet Jesus, that's close enough to heaven for me. I thanked God more than once, and I swear, I saw angels when he thrust deeper than anyone ever had before.

I wrap my fingers around his cock, gently stroking, feeling the weight of him in my palm. Leaning over, I kiss and lick my way down his body, sliding my hand along his hardening shaft.

"You gonna kiss it or just rile it up?" Jack's voice is gravelly and full of sleep. His question turns to a deep groan as I take him into my mouth, swirling my tongue around his ridge. "*Fuck,*" he hisses as I take him as deep as I dare.

There is nothing good about gagging or puking when giving a blow job. *Nothing.*

"Jesus, Kate, let me ... *ung* ... babe ... oh fuck ..." he groans, reaching for the nightstand, fumbling for his wallet.

I pop his dick from my lips and lick slowly, languorously from his heavy balls to the very tip. And, from there, I just keep going, crawling up his body until I'm straddling him, rubbing up and down his steely length. Never have I had this kind of craving for someone. The way he moved me, played me, owned me was like nothing I have ever experienced.

"Need a condom," he murmurs against my neck, hands firmly grasping my hips.

I agree. We need a gross of them.

"Mmm, out. Used 'em," he tells me while sucking on the dip of my collarbone.

With hands planted firmly on his pecs, I push myself up and off of him. "Two? That's all you had?"

Jack cocks an eyebrow at me, running his hands up and down my thighs.

"It's fine," I say, climbing off him. "I've got backups."

I dig around in my bag and pull out my condom stash. A girl can't be too prepared, no matter how long and bad her dry spell is. I toss one of the packages to him and place the rest on the nightstand. We are so going to need them before this night is done.

"What the hell is this?" Jack asks, holding up the purple foil square, a smirk plastered on his face.

"Protection?"

"You get them from a vending machine or something?

Are these a joke?" He pushes himself up until his back's against the headboard. "We use this shit on the barrel of our weapons in the desert. Keeps the sand out, but, babe, this ain't gonna work here."

"It's a condom. What's not gonna work?" I climb on his lap and take the package from him, tearing it open. When I try to apply the condom, it becomes abundantly clear what Jack's trying to get at. It's obviously not what he had in his wallet.

"I don't know whether to be flattered by your enthusiasm or concerned that you've just not been properly serviced."

He has the damn nerve to laugh. I mean, I knew right away there was more to him than I was used to, but honestly.

"Humble you are not," I say, pulling my bottom lip between my teeth. *This has to work.*

"Can be when it's warranted."

EIGHT

Jack

"KATE, BABY, LET ME just throw on some clothes and go ..."

She's trying to kill me. I'm absolutely going to die right here.

"It's fine. I got it. Hang on." She's motivated, seriously motivated. "There," she huffs out, lifting up on her knees and rubbing my head through her folds.

"Kinda tight, Kate," I groan as she slides down until I'm fully seated, balls deep.

Her pussy is nothing short of heaven. All nonessential thoughts scatter from my brain, and all my focus is drawn to this woman and the things she's doing to me. Watching her tits bounce as she rides me is a recipe for premature disaster, and there is no way in hell we're going through putting another pencil-sized wrapper on my junk. I grab hold of her ass and flip us over because, with as good as she feels, I *need* to be in some kind of control.

Slowing things down, I pump my hips and drop down

onto my elbows, and I swear on all that is good and holy that some of the pressure dissipates. Maybe it's the workup, maybe the change in angle, but the relief is the sweetest. Suddenly, the torture of getting wrapped becomes worth it, and no matter how much thinking about said torture should dial things back for me, this feels *more*. Infinitely better. I snake my arms under Kate's back, pressing her to me, giving a little extra shove at the end of each thrust, making damn certain I'm bottoming out. Every. Single. Time.

"Lawd-'a'-mercy, Jack ..."

My sentiments exactly.

"Kate ..." I'm not gonna last much longer.

"Close. Oh God, so close ..."

And, like I fucking planned it, I feel her muscles clamp down on me, squeezing, massaging, pushing me right the fuck over the edge. Poetry in motion, we both get racked by waves of ecstasy that I sure as shit have never experienced before in my life.

"Why was that so good?" Kate asks, her words breathy and muffled by my shoulder.

I'm probably on the verge of crushing her, but, for fuck's sake, I saw stars, and I'm not sure I can even move yet. Instead of responding, I grunt and reach deep within myself to thrust into her one last time before pulling out and letting the poor girl breathe.

"It was probably the special prophylactic I provided," she mumbles, arm falling over her eyes.

"Kate?" *Jesus, no. You have got to fucking be kidding me.* "You on the pill? Something?"

"No. Why?" she asks, opening her eyes, trailing them down to my dick. "Oh hell."

There's no denying *why* that felt so good. I sit back on my heels, shaking my head because that prophylactic has become problematic.

"Well, you just busted right through that thing, didn't you?" Her gaze bounces from my cock to my eyes and back again. "Obliterated it. I mean, you just fucked right out the other side …"

"Goddamn it. Not funny, Katelyn," I warn. I don't like the edge in my voice, but this is not good. It goes against everything I've fucking planned for myself. "If you weren't dating pencil-dicked douche bags—"

"Hey now. It's not like you're the only one this affects. Are you even clean? That thing"—she waves at my still-hard dick—"could be diseased for all I know."

"Checked regularly and has never jumped without a parachute. And what about you, huh? I'm not sure I like the odds of Appletini Guy being all that hygienically aware."

She slowly blinks at me, like she's either processing what I said or getting ready to slap me. After several more owl-like blinks, Kate scowls and pushes herself up to sitting, almost nailing me in the junk when she folds her legs Indian style— or whatever the fuck they're calling it in kindergarten these days. "A: no. Just no. He sure as hell was not getting with me. In fact, it's been a lifetime, thank you very much. And B: we just did the deed in the wild. Unprotected. No goalie in the net."

"Yeah? What's that look like? What's my risk factor there?" My heart is pounding, panic threatening to pull me over the edge from kind of an asshole to full-on fucking prick.

She looks completely offended but counts in her head,

eyes focusing on the ceiling in concentration. Meanwhile, I try to roll the useless thing off.

"*Your* risks should be okay, cycle-wise, and since you're so damn concerned with me, mine should be the same."

She deserves to be pissed. I might have gone further into prick territory than I thought.

"What are you doing?"

Dying. I'm dying of dick asphyxiation. Strangulation of my schlong. "Trying to get this off. Christ, it's like—"

"A cock ring," she says, snorting. "Is it supposed to be turning that color? Guess I know where the whole eggplant-emoji thing came from because I feel like that's what I'm looking at."

"Jesus fuck, Kate. Can you help me here? Gonna have to cut this shit off." I fall forward, hand on the headboard to brace myself because, really? I think I could pass out right about now. "You got some scissors in that bag?"

She slides off the bed and digs through her tote. "You bet your sweet ass I do," she sasses triumphantly. "Here we go. Turn around for me, darlin'."

I fall to the side and sprawl across the bed, blankets rucked up behind my back. "Hold real still now."

There is no way in hell I could have prepared for what I see coming at my junk. "What the fuck are you doing? You're a goddamn kindergarten teacher. Where are your safety scissors?" I put one hand out to stop her and protectively clutch my really unhappy Mr. Happy with the other.

"What?" she asks, obviously not getting just how sensitive this situation is.

I swear to God, I fight to keep my shit together, staring down at the glinting metal of the biggest pair of granny shears I've seen in ages—since I last visited my granny, to be completely honest.

"No way you're coming at me with those ... those ... weapons of mass destruction." Ain't nobody in the world I trust enough to come at me with that noise. "Hell, you're a hostile with a grudge at this point. No, just hell no."

"Jesus, Jack. What do you want me to do? Call 911? You look a little peaked—"

"Do you have—I don't know—lotion? Coconut oil? Maybe we can grease it up and slide it off?"

Or maybe calling the EMTs really isn't a bad option. I'd never live that shit down if it got back to my team. Holy hell, I can't breathe.

"Here, let's just ..." Her hand glides down my length, coating me in—of course she fucking has coconut oil in that bag. "Hold on. I just need to get a good grip." She snickers as her fingers slide over the ring of death, not gaining any purchase. "Um ... wow. That, uh, might have been—"

"Counterproductive," I finish, running through baseball stats, trying to think of my sweet granny without actually thinking of her while my cock gets impossibly harder. "Stop. Just ... stop stroking me. Oh my fucking God."

I feel bad for about a hot minute when she jumps back from me, hands up. Her lip taking some serious abuse between her teeth. But then the panic really starts setting in. I can't think.

Of course I can't think. There's no blood flow to my thinking brain.

"Shower? Cold water? Um ... oh," Kate exclaims as she jumps up, grabbing the hotel robe from the back of the bathroom door. Tying it around her, she bolts out the door with the ice bucket and a room key.

Bracing myself, I limp into the bathroom, holding on to the walls the whole way. The last thing I need is to actually trip and fall on this thing. I'm not sure if it'd break in half or put an indentation in the concrete floor.

Deep, cleansing breaths.

Need to clear my mind.

It doesn't look good, not that a raging, strangled purple—*it's fucking turning purple*—dick is gonna look good in any light, but in the harsh light of the hotel bathroom, things don't look good at all. Veins are popping out like it's their fucking job. Slowly, carefully, I attempt to pick at the band of latex that is squeezing the lifeblood out of me.

My God, I think I really could die from this.

I should have cut my nails. They look like fucking talons ready to rip my dick to shreds. *What if ... what if my finger-nail pierces one of the veins in my dick? Could I bleed out from that? For the love of fucks, I have got to get this thing off of my dick before I die. Or pass out. Or die.*

Desperate times. I grab hold and squeeze my base with everything I have, and the damn death ring slides. Just a little. Just enough to give me some hope.

The door swings open, and I don't even care that my ass and angry purple peen are on display for anyone who might be passing by.

"I got some ice. Let me just tie a knot in this. Holy, oh my Jesus, did your thing get bigger?" More snorting that erupts into giggles.

Pretty sure this is the least humorous thing I've ever experienced. Now, if I were hearing the tale from one of my soldiers, different story. I'd be laughing my ass off. And *thing?* She needs to pay some damn respect to my poor, suffering schlong. This situation is so bad.

"What are you ... did you get it to move?" Kate asks, reaching her ice-cold hand out, spilling the ice down my front.

Cock. Balls. All of it is fucking freezing and engorged now. Surely, I'll die soon and just be put out of my misery.

I suck air in through my teeth and glare at her. "Don't." I have never needed freedom like I do at this moment in time. Pulling from my untapped reserves of strength, I repeat my process.

Breathe. Grip. Squeeze. Slide.
Breathe. Grip. Squeeze. Slide.
Breathe. Grip. Squeeze. Slide.

And, by some miracle, the thing slides off, and my dick is free. Finally free. Relief floods me as I sink to the floor, the offending ring of latex discarded to the tiles.

"You okay?" Kate asks softly.

All I can do is nod, my hand gently cupping my cock. Christ, it hurts.

"What can I do?" All signs of snarkiness and sass are gone, and she gently rests a hand on my arm. "Want that shower?"

"Yeah, I think I do." I stand slowly, appreciating my newfound freedom.

Kate leans into the shower, getting the water going, adjusting the temperature until it's just right. Biting her lip, she looks over her shoulder at me, eyes soft and caressing. She stands back and gestures to the pounding water, steam filling the small bathroom. I step under the spray, eyes closed while the warm water washes over me, still clutching my junk. It's like I'm afraid to let it go. I almost lost it tonight, and I really am kind of attached, you know?

I startle and pop my lids up when I feel Kate's hand slide down my arm, gently prying my hand from its protective position.

"Let me see, Jack. Move your hand."

I move it, but don't dare to look until I hear her gasp. *Sweet mother of God, can it be that bad?* I squint one eye closed and look down. Down to where Kate is on her knees in front of me, my bruised dick dangerously close to her lips.

"Does it hurt?" she murmurs, pressing her lips to the tip.

"Mmhmm."

"You think you'll be okay?" Her tongue darts out, licking into the slit.

A groan escapes me as I nod my damn head, watching the show play out before me.

"I'm so sorry," she whispers. "Will you forgive me if I kiss it, make it better?"

My hand slaps the tiled wall in front of me as I fall forward, bracing myself. And, by the time her lips hit the bruised ring around my cock, the tip pushing against the back of her throat, any and all transgressions have been forgiven and forgotten.

"Darlin', if your BJ game is that strong, you're gonna have some bruised knees."

And, as good as I thought it felt with her plump lips wrapped around me, when a laugh rumbles out of her, vibrations slamming down my shaft, I'm almost willing to walk through that fire again.

NINE

Kate

DAMN MY SHIT LUCK. Murphy and his law have nothing on me because, when I finally meet a guy, a man, who checks all the boxes, it turns out, he's only here for a hot minute. Or a cold month, but whatever.

Tall? Check.

Body? Check.

Manners? Check.

Decidedly straight? All the damn check marks for that one.

And leaving.

I rush through my thankfully minimal end-of-day tasks—wiping off desks, stacking chairs, and putting my room in order. I check my lesson plans and make sure all the supplies are organized for my substitute because I need a long weekend away. Pretty sure I can count on one hand the number of times I've called in or arranged for a sub since I've been teaching, and all of those have been for real-life, actual illnesses. Let's face it; kindergartners are cesspools of germs and have learned the art of sharing those germs like it's the most valuable lesson going. But today, this weekend? I'm out of here.

Jack's time here is coming to an end—his deployment fast approaching—so when he asked if I wanted to get away for a couple of days, go up to the mountains for a long weekend, I jumped at that chance. Hopped, skipped, and jumped. There might have even been a little twirl in there, but I'll neither confirm nor deny that tidbit.

I packed my bag before work today, so that I have nothing more to do than go home and change my clothes. The fifteen-minute drive seems to take far longer, and after sliding my car into a parking spot, I run up the stairs to find a tall, yummy man leaning against the window outside my apartment. Long denim-clad legs casually crossed at the ankles, Sherpa-lined barn coat, unbuttoned to reveal his charcoal-gray thermal. Dark scruff thickening into a beard. *Dear God in heaven, this man is the stuff of dreams.*

"Hey." I smile, stuffing my key into the lock. "I won't be but a quick minute. I just need to change and grab my bag." I peek over my shoulder and startle when he's right there behind me. "Lord, how do you do that? You scared the shit outta me."

"Long, painful lessons and years of practice. Moving silently is a job requirement, and Jake's dad beat the lessons home," he says, holding the door wide open for me.

I set my tote by the door and unload my lunch bag in the kitchen before scurrying down the hall to my bedroom. "Be right out," I toss over my shoulder and about bounce off the doorframe because something about Jack in my space has me spinning and off-balance in the very best way.

"Need any help?" Jack calls from the living room.

I pull a sweater over my head and twist my hair into a low knot. "Thanks, but pretty sure I can handle it," I answer, grabbing the handle of my roller case. "All set. You ready to go?"

"Yes, ma'am," he says, collapsing the handle and lifting my bag.

With my jacket over my arm, I grab my big tote, and out the door we go.

"You have everything good to go at school?" Jack places his hand low on my back as we make our way out of the building.

"I do. Projects are lined up for tomorrow, directions have been spelled out, and an emergency backup plan is ready to go. Lord, I can't believe it's almost Christmas break."

I pause on the street, not sure which way we're headed. Lights flash a short way down the block, and Jack steers me toward a behemoth truck parallel parked impossibly perfect. Having grown up in the Deep South, I am not unfamiliar with boys and their toys. Big trucks make up for small *personalities*, but I know for a fact that Jack is not lacking— anywhere. He opens the passenger door and hands me up into the creamy black leather seat. He shuts me in, deposits my case in the back seat, and rounds the back of the truck before swinging himself behind the wheel.

The engine rumbles to life, and I can't help the snort that escapes in a most undignified manner. I'd deny that it was even me if I thought I could get away with it.

"What's so funny?" Jack asks while maneuvering the

huge dark gray truck out into the street. He pulls his seat belt across his broad chest, clicking it into place. Shifting, he pulls his phone from the front pocket of his jeans and hands it off to me. "It should be connected, so just pick a playlist or whatever. But tell me what's so funny."

"Not a thing. Just ... could you have found a bigger truck? I know you're not overcompensating or anything." I scroll through his music app, looking for something, anything that's not R & B or metal.

"You giving me a hard time about my ride?" He smirks, raising a brow. Merging smoothly, Jack slides onto the interstate and heads north toward the Catskill Mountains.

Finally settling on a list, I pick some music—a little bit indie, a touch of alternative, perfect road-tripping tunes. "I would never consider busting on your wheels, but really, this is huge." I can't miss the cocky grin that spreads across his face.

"You like how big it is, sweet cheeks?" He hits me with a roguish grin that makes my insides turn hot and fluttery. "Grew up on a ranch in Montana. Big trucks are all I know. Hauling cattle, moving hay—gotta have size and power to get the job done."

I laugh at his ridiculous play on words and ask, "A ranch? Why'd you leave? That sounds like heaven."

"Mmhmm," he hums. "Hard work that never ends. No vacation, and the hours are shit."

"How's the Army any different?"

Jack glances at me before changing lanes and passing a slow-moving line of cars. "The scenery changes in the Army. Haven't you heard? We get to travel the world."

"You refer to it as *the sandbox*," I say, turning toward him.

"I love the beach as much as any good Southern girl, but how can you tell me the scenery in the desert is better than snow-capped mountains in Montana?"

I turn down the music, not wanting to be distracted from our conversation because, right now, there is something else going on with his tone—anger, melancholy. I thought he loved his job, but I'm wondering if I got things wrong.

Jack stares out the windshield, one hand resting casually over the steering wheel while the other scrapes across the light beard covering his cheeks. Silence stretches between us, so thick that I'm not sure if it might be best to change the subject entirely or just let it go. Let him brood and stew over on his side of this ridiculous small-dick mobile.

"I needed to leave. The *scenery* in my town was working hard to tie me down and suffocate me. I had one shot at getting a college education, and the only way for that to happen was for it to be fully funded and be in the name of service to our country. And the farther from home, the better," Jack says, his voice eerily calm and low.

"You were running."

"I was. Not afraid of going back, I'm an entirely different person now. But, at the time, I needed to go."

The finality of his statement leaves no room for doubt that the discussion is done. Obviously, this is a sensitive subject to him, and it's not like this thing with us is going anywhere other than the mountains. This is not a relationship, just a between-deployment hookup for him and a recalibration for me. A reminder that there are good guys out there. Men with manners and honest intent. He's been perfectly candid about what this is and what to expect when his respite ends. He'll go; I'll stay. End of story. The end of our story anyway.

We exit the highway and wind along mountain roads, slowing to pass through small towns. Snow piled high on either side of the road.

"You, uh ..." Jack clears his throat, breaking the silence that has accompanied us for most of the drive. "You want to stop and get a bite to eat before we head to the cabin?"

"I could eat." Turning toward him, I wedge myself into the corner where the seat meets the door. "I'm sorry if I touched on stuff you didn't want to get into, but is this going to be awkward now?"

"Don't want it to be. I should be the one apologizing, not you," Jack says, pulling up to a small Italian restaurant. He puts the truck in park but leaves the engine and heater running. "Look, I love my family, and I love Montana. Ranch life made me who I am, but I wanted more. My mom and dad have never left the state; they hardly even leave the ranch. They had no idea I went through the application process to West Point. I didn't tell them until I was accepted and everything was in place. And then I left." Finally, he turns his head, meeting my gaze. "Let's go in. We can talk more over dinner, okay?" His eyes are pinched at the corners, a cross between pleading and pain.

I purse my lips and nod. "'Kay, or we can just fill our bellies and go snuggle into the cabin and pray for a snow storm."

He relaxes, and the corner of his mouth lifts into a smirk. "I like that. Hang on," he says as he hops out of the truck and comes around to my side. Instead of just holding the door, Jack steps into my space, offering his hands.

"I'm perfectly capable of landing my dismount," I tell him, pivoting and sliding out of the mile-high truck.

"You are, but maybe I wanted my hands on you a little. Get things back on track before we go carb-load for the marathon later."

He crowds my space, running his hands around to my ass, pressing me to him. Teasing, the promise of orgasms hanging in the air. Because this is strictly physical. Here and now. This weekend and maybe one more, and then he'll be gone again. Nothing but a memory that brings a smile to my face and makes my vibrator a woefully inadequate substitute.

"Let's do this thing then." I push my way past him and pat his firm ass as I go.

Jack's chuckle floats behind me as he closes and locks the truck. His hand settles low on my back just as I reach the door, and he steps aside, allowing me to go first.

"Two, please," he tells the hostess, and we're seated right away at a small table in front of the window, looking out over Main Street of the quaint little town.

"Wine, Kate?"

I nod, and he turns to the hostess before she has a chance to scurry off back to her station.

"A bottle of Chianti, please, and calamari while we decide. Thank you."

The table is covered with an old-school red-and-white-checkered cloth, the dim glow of a candle dancing in the minimal space between us. Our knees brush with each shift as we peel off our coats and settle them on the backs of chairs.

"Your *vino*?" a heavily accented voice asks. White apron, black dress, and the swish of nylon stockings, a short woman approaches our table. Her black hair is pulled back into a severe-looking bun low on her head. She splashes bloodred wine into a glass and hands it to Jack, heavily resting the bottle on the table. "Is good, I know this, but you taste, eh?"

"I believe you." Jack nudges the glass toward her with a broad smile stretched across his face, nodding at the bottle. "Are you the owner here?"

"Taste," the force of nature insists. She lets go of the bottle and crosses her arms under her ample bosom. There is no other way to describe the shelf of modestly constrained chest this woman has.

Jack lifts the glass and sips the dry red. "It's good, perfect," he says.

"Of course," she states on an authoritative nod, pouring a full glass for me before filling Jack's glass. "You listen to Angelina; I no tell you wrong. Now"—she briefly assesses us —"Bolognese for you, and for the lady, my lasagna. You too skinny." And, with that, she marches toward the kitchen, barking in Italian.

I close my menu and pick up my glass of wine, taking a healthy sip. "I guess we're done ordering," I say, checking over my shoulder. The last thing I want is for Angelina to bust me making fun of her. "I wonder what we'll get for dessert."

"You think we'll get dessert?"

"If you clean your plate, you might. I'm too skinny, so I think I'm guaranteed to get mine."

"Oh, you're going to get yours; that's for damn sure." Jack's voice drops low, and he gives me a searing look that holds absolutely no mystery but all the promises in the world.

TEN

Jack

JESUS *FUCK*, **I** **DON'T** know what I was thinking on the drive. *Why the hell did I get all personal?* That shit doesn't fly here any more than it does on a mission. Thankfully, Kate rolled with it and defused what was about to become a shit-show, all three rings running.

Angelina brings our calamari and an antipasto, telling us, "*Mangiate!*"

So, we eat and eat and eat as our newly adopted Italian aunt brings us more food than we can realistically manage.

"Oh my God," Kate sighs as she leans back from the table. "I'm so full." She spreads her hands across her flat belly, eyes wide and pleading.

We've hardly even touched our main courses, and I'm not going to lie, I'm kind of afraid of how little we've eaten.

"I'm not gonna make it through this," I say, scooping another bite of pasta onto my fork. It's savory and thick, full of meat and covered in Parmesan cheese. The best I've ever had, including my time stationed in Italy. That was good, fantastic actually, but this tastes like *Zia* Angelina made it just for us. I pop the forkful into my mouth, effectively throwing Kate under the bus, since it would be bad manners to talk with my mouth full, and our plates are getting checked over.

Kate kicks at my shin, fully aware of my cowardice. "Angelina, this is amazing—"

"Of course it is." Nothing like the confidence in her craft this woman has.

"But I can't eat another bite. Can I take the rest with me? And maybe some tiramisu, too?" She smiles sweetly, and while I know it's not for me, that curve and pull of her lip and the pink blush of her cheeks burrow into my soul.

I push my pasta around my plate as I chew, afraid to put my fork down. Evidently, I can't win with this though because I get scolded for playing with my food. But small miracles, I also get my plate taken away with nothing more than a slap on the wrist.

"Jesus, she's scary as fuck," I murmur, leaning forward in my seat. No doubt, her hearing is as sharp as can be.

"Would you shut up? God help you, if I get guilted into putting one more thing into my mouth, I will literally die," Kate hisses, eyes wide. Her foot impacting with my shin again tells me loud and clear that she sees the lewd thoughts running through my head. "That includes your dick, so just don't right now. I swear, I'm going to explode."

"Let's go while we still can," I suggest.

Standing from the table, I get Kate's chair and help her into her coat, putting mine on as we step up to the hostess. I don't even bother looking at the bill, best to just pay it and cut sling load. I hand over my card and sign the slip as a huge to-go bag loaded down with food appears in front of me.

"Thank you, Angelina. Dinner was a memorable experience."

She hands me the bag, which is way too heavy to just be leftovers and dessert, and pulls me down to her squat level by the collar of my jacket. "You a good boy." She pinches my cheek, hard, and soothes it with a sound pat. "You take care of your girl. Make sure she eats enough, eh?" And, when she moves on to Kate, holding her at arm's length for just a moment, her eyes sparkle, and her lip mischievously curls up. "*Diventerai una brava madre,*" she says, soundly kissing Kate on each cheek.

My Italian is not great, but even I can figure out she's saying something about a good mother. I toss a couple of twenties on the signed bill and wrap my arm around Kate, leading her out into the cold evening.

"What did she say to me?" Kate asks as I hand her up into the truck.

"I couldn't tell you," I mumble, tucking the bag of food behind my seat and climbing in. I hit my GPS and wind out of town, toward the cabin I rented for the weekend.

While Kate spreads out on the couch, red-and-turquoise-striped socks kicked up on the coffee table, I fuck around with the fireplace until the cabin's living room is filled with the crackle and pop of the logs and the cozy glow of flames.

"That's quite the manly feat," Kate says as I plop myself down against the far arm of the leather sofa, tucking one foot under her ass for warmth and the other under her knees. Anything to be touching her. She pulls a blanket off the arm of the couch and throws it over her lap and my legs. "Tell me something." She soothingly runs her hand from my ankle to knee and back again.

"About what?" I scoot my ass down and lean my head back on the plush arm.

"Anything. Work. Home. Your greatest fears or what you want more than anything out of life." This is one of those soft moments where her accent hints at itself. Where there's more drawl to her words, melodic and relaxing.

"A lot of shit to cover there. We already touched on home, so work? I enjoy what I do. I feel a huge sense of purpose most of the time. The missions, the people, their faces, and gratification when we clear out the trash and make way for food and supply drops. No one likes a bully. Doesn't matter the color of your skin, religion, or even what grade you're in." I leave out the parts about hunting down the bully, infiltrating their strongholds, and taking them out in whatever way is necessary. Most people tend to like security better when they don't have to know the details of how it's attained and maintained. "What about you? Greatest fear?"

Kate snorts and shakes her head. "Born and raised in Miss'ssippi, but you know all that. I guess ..." She smooths the blanket, tucking it in around my legs. "Damn it. I guess my biggest fear is that I wasted way too much time on Chance, and I'll never ... eh, forget it. It's stupid."

I wiggle my foot, digging into her side with my toes, tickling. "Tell me."

She drops her head back, focusing on the dark wood beams stretched across the ceiling, her lips pursed with her thoughts. "I'm afraid I'll end up the spinster kindergarten teacher. That the only kids I'll ever have are the ones in my class." Her eyes close briefly before she rolls her head to the side to steal a glance at me.

My brows rise, and my mouth falls open in shock. "Are you kidding me? Because of that asshole? You sure as shit didn't turn the man gay, Kate."

"I know that. Deep down and rationally, I really do, but ..." She shrugs and shifts, turning so that her back is against the opposite arm of the couch and her arms are wrapped around her bent knees. All closed off, visibly protecting herself from the world.

And that's the last thing I want. It's one thing for me to lock up and compartmentalize, my job—my life at times—depends on that, but I want her to feel safe here with me. I'll have to examine the *why* of that later.

I reach under the blanket and pull her feet into my lap, wanting contact, needing to hold on, if just for now. "You're so much more than that. So much better than his shit." And it hits me, what Angelina said before we left the restaurant. "You'll have all of it, and you'll make an amazing mama someday."

She will. Jake has been talking her up nonstop since school started. If I didn't know any better, I'd think that boy had been trying to set me and his teacher up. But that's ridiculous; he's five. A tiny dictator, entirely possible. But matchmaker? I doubt it.

"Mmm, maybe." Her jaw cracks with a wide yawn. "Not something to deal with today, but that's my fear. Total FOMO. What about you? Fears? Desires?"

I dig my thumbs into her arch, kneading the tension away. I don't want to tell her that I have the same fear. That I want the family life that Tripp has, but I'm scared shitless that I wouldn't be able to balance it with my job. That I'd fuck it up. And then it wouldn't just be my life I was ruining. That, if I had a family, people depending on me, and, God forbid, a mission went south, that would be the ultimate failure. One I'm not sure I'm willing to risk.

Instead, I slide my hands up her legs, wrapping my palms around the backs of her knees, and tug. Kate squeals as I pull her across the couch until her ass is nestled between my thighs.

"I'm afraid of falling asleep on this couch. And I desire nothing more than to lay you out across that big bed back there and worship every inch of your body."

Tossing the blanket aside, I scoop Kate into my arms, wrapping her legs around my hips, and stalk to the bedroom. And then I make my desires a reality. Peeling off her layers like I'm unwrapping my final Christmas present. The one you want to draw out and make last forever. I kiss, lick, and nip my way up her body, paying special attention to the dip of her hip, the sensitive skin under her tits. The hollow of her clavicle.

Pulling a sigh from Kate, I swallow a grunt and slide between her warm, creamy thighs, slowly fucking her. Drag and pull. Thrusting and grinding until I feel her clench and shudder, and only then do I let myself go.

ELEVEN

Kate

I bared my soul, and now, it's just a matter of time until Jack pushes me away, and this thing ends. Dies an epic death. Our expiration date is looming, getting closer every single minute. But even I know that when a chick starts talking babies, guys typically run for the hills.

Though with the written-in-stone end date, it's been kind of liberating, knowing I can say just about anything because he's leaving regardless.

I slide from between the sheets and sift through the clothing strewed across the floor. The air is frigid, and the fire needs to be stoked. While I stir the embers and add another log from the basket on the hearth, I pray for some kind of coffee miracle in the kitchen.

As the steaming liquid gurgles out of the machine, hands slide around my waist, tugging me back into a hard wall of muscle.

"Morning," Jack mumbles into the rat's nest that is my

hair. His nose brushes the shell of my ear as he pushes my hair to the side. Goose bumps run along every inch of my skin as he kisses down the column of my neck.

"Jack," I gasp as he pushes me into the edge of the counter.

His front is pressed to my back, contact from his lips down to our hips. The feeling that I handed this thing its deathblow by talking futures and babies dissipates in a puff of smoke and burning desire as Jack turns me and scoops me up onto the counter. All thought blows wide open as he pulls me to the edge and slides between my thighs, making me gasp and shudder. Carrying me while I'm still wrapped around him, Jack takes me to the bedroom where we lose ourselves in each other's bodies until we are nothing short of sated.

"You're going to have to feed me again," I say as I sit on the hearth to pull my boots on. "I'm weak."

Freshly showered, Jack appears at the edge of the room, jeans still unbuttoned, feet bare, T-shirt and flannel hanging from his hand. "We have a few leftovers," he teases. "We could just hole up here all day and—"

"Tempting but no. We need to go out in the world and see what there is to see."

He finishes dressing and shoves his feet into combat boots, pulling the laces tight and tucking the bows into the tops. "What?" he asks, straightening to his full height.

"Not a thing. Just surprised that I like watching you get dressed," I tell him, handing over his coat.

Jack huffs out a laugh and asks, "As much as you like watching me undress?"

"I'm usually too distracted to notice that." My smile

pushes my cheeks high, and for the briefest moment, we stand there, staring at each other. Not with heated, lusty desire, but with something softer. Something scary and dangerous and ... more. I clear my throat and grab my purse, murmuring, "Let's go." I duck out the door, needing to escape the fog of unattainable possibilities.

Sun bounces off the chrome grill of his truck, and the lights flash as the locks click open. Driving into town, down out of the mountain, is nothing short of gorgeous. Bright snow-covered trees line the road and guide us into the picturesque town nestled into the valley. I slide my sunglasses on and reach for the cupholder before I remember that it's empty, the cup I brewed in the cabin abandoned to lust. No coffee. None. And, if I don't fix that soon, I'm going to end up with a headache crippling me.

"A café sound good to you?" Jack asks.

"Dear God, yes. I need some caffeine and a big old plate of something bad for me," I groan. My stomach rumbles loudly at that moment, erasing any question on just how hungry I am.

Once again, defying logic and space constraints, Jack parallel parks his monstrosity and swings out to get my door. I like it. He's attentive but respectful. Masculine but not condescending. Long-term but leaving. I shove those thoughts and feelings away because I knew what this was, going into it. There's no use in dwelling on wanting to manipulate and change the outcome that is so solidly set in stone.

Instead, I focus on the late breakfast of eggs Benedict and breakfast potatoes with strong black coffee, trading bites for a taste of Jack's hash and egg skillet.

I grab the bill before Jack has a chance to set his coffee cup down and hand it and some cash to the server, telling her it's all good.

"Kate," he admonishes, reaching for his wallet. "Let me—"

"Nope. Breakfast is on me," I tell him, taken aback by the shocked look that crawls across his face.

"That's new." Jack stands, tucking his wallet away and reaching for my chair. He helps me into my coat, which, while a nice gesture, is usually more awkward than helpful. Reaching for and missing the sleeve, having to adjust and shimmy around until it's settled just right. But not with Jack. He manages to do even that with finesse and precision. "Thank you," he says, voice gravelly yet soft.

I turn to him as we step out onto the sidewalk. "It's breakfast. So not a big deal," I say, brows pulled together.

"Just has never happened to me before, a woman paying for a meal for me."

"Seriously?"

He shrugs, lifting one bulky shoulder. "Yeah, no. I'm not trying to be an ass, but I was raised to believe that the man pays. Opens the doors, all of that." He settles his hand at the base of my back and guides me down the street.

I let that idea simmer. Stir it around in my brain while we walk along the main street, peeking into shop windows.

"What are you doing for Christmas?" Jack asks as I peer into a stationery store, my love for books and journals pausing my feet.

"Going home to see my mama and them." He chuckles, and I realize that my Southern just flashed itself for all the world to see. "Sorry, my accent just does that when I think about going home."

"I like it." He nods to the door, asking, "Want to go in?"

I do, but the last thing I need is another journal, sitting empty on my shelf. Because let's face it; I love the beautiful books and all the potential their empty pages hold, but I don't want to mess them up with my ramblings.

"Nah, I need to find something for my mom and my friends. This would be purely a selfish store."

I'm a few steps toward the next little shop, the windows filled with handmade mugs and bowls, when Jack's palm lands on my back again.

"Do you mind if we go in here?" Mississippi has a serious thing for pottery, and my mother would love the gorgeous pieces and unique glazes.

"Not at all."

Jack gets the door once again, and as he strolls through the shop with me, I ask, "What about you?"

He pauses, brows lowered.

"Christmas. What are your plans?"

He picks up a small cream-and-brown mug, weighing it in his hands, almost like he's checking it for a good fit. "I fly home for a couple of days and then catch a flight overseas. Tripp'll meet me in Chicago, and we'll fly the rest of the way together." It feels like there's more he wants to say, like he's teetering on the edge of something, and instead of falling over, Jack takes an emotional step back. Forcing a smile, he replaces the mug and reaches for his phone. "Hey, I'm going to step out and take this. Are you good for a minute?"

"Of course. Take your time," I say.

He strolls out to the sidewalk and slides his phone to his ear. His broad back strains under the fabric of his coat, and he glances back at me before walking to the park bench a few stores down.

"Is there anything I can help you with?" a salesclerk asks. She straightens the mug Jack just walked away from.

Smiling, I say, "This is beautiful. Is it local?" I pick up a bowl glazed in blues and greens, the edge of it ruffled and a swirl of deep blue curling around the interior. It's just Lis's style.

"It is. In fact, the artist is due to stop in soon and drop a few pieces off." Her lips flatten into a tight line as she darts a quick look around the shop, nerves rolling off of her.

I tuck the bowl under my arm and move on to the next display.

"Oh, let me take that for you." The clerk scoops the bowl out from under my arm and protectively clutches it to her chest as she hurries to the counter.

A set of plates with soup bowls grab my attention, so I carefully add those to my bowl on the counter, almost dropping them as the shadow of a man appears in the doorway to the storage room.

His dark brown eyes skitter around the store, landing on where my hand curls around one of the soup-bowl-plate things. Silently, he approaches and places a crate on the floor behind the counter. "Nora," he says to the woman helping me, "these are ready to go. Anything you're low on?" He scratches at his chin, fingers getting lost in his beard, and scans the store, eyes landing back on my hands.

"No, I think we're good," Nora says quietly.

The interaction is kind of weird.

"There's a round platter in here that would go well with

those soup-plates." He awkwardly nods at me. Shifting his weight, he steps back in the direction he came from.

"Okay." Nora watches as he disappears out the door as quietly as he came in.

"That was ..." I start, but I'm not sure where to take that statement.

"Intense. He's intense, very defensive of his craft." She relaxes visibly and asks, "Do you want to see that platter?" She sifts through the crate, pulling one beautiful piece of art after another out until she sighs. "Here we go," she says, placing a stunning platter in front of me.

Even though I'm sure it's way more than I'd normally spend, I can't walk away without it.

"My mama will absolutely love it. I think that'll be it though." I hand over my card and watch as she carefully wraps up my purchases, placing them in a beautiful red bag. Hell, with the bow she adds to the handle, I can use it as a gift bag for my mama's pieces.

I thank Nora and step out onto the sidewalk. Scanning the area, I find Jack leaning against the side of his truck, legs crossed at the ankle, hands shoved in his pockets and his eyes sparkling as he takes in my approach.

"You find something good?" Jack asks, reaching to relieve me of the bag.

"I did. Got my mama and one of my friends taken care of. I just need to find something for my roommate, and I'll be in good shape." I watch as he carefully sets the bag on the floorboard of the back seat of the truck. "How 'bout you? You get your call taken care of?"

"Yeah. Just confirming flight plans home for next week."

Next week. No matter how I cut it, I've not had enough

time with Jack. I'm not ready for this to be done. I'm not ready to say good-bye. Instead of risking emotion spilling into my voice, I purse my lips and nod. I need to lock my emotions down. There's no use in showing my hand. Making things uncomfortable. It's not Jack's fault I'm falling for him, and it'll just be easier all around if I shove it down and ignore the way my heart beats faster, the way he's burrowed his way into my soul. He's leaving. It all comes back to the fact that he's leaving.

<h1 style="text-align:center">TWELVE</h1>

Jack

EACH TICK OF THE second hand is like a bomb timer counting down. Silent and ominous. Inescapable and unignorable.

The call I took gave me a headache and made me think about how much better Christmas would be with Tripp and his family or maybe in the Mississippi Delta as opposed to going home. Home. Home is so much more than a place on the map. An address. And the last place I want to spend the final days of my leave is with my judgmental family and the lying, cheating manipulator who tried her very best to fuck over my escape from them.

Jessica is ancient history. She just doesn't seem to be willing to acknowledge it yet. We dated through most of high school, and everyone in town had us practically married off at the start of my senior year. Yeah, no. By that point, I was pretty well on my way to the United States Military

Academy and wasn't going to do a damn thing to jeopardize that once-in-a-lifetime opportunity.

And, now, she's harassing me. Badgering me to get together while I'm home. Catch up. Over my dead body.

Of course, at the mention of our time coming to a close, Kate withdraws, turning inward. Shutting down. I close and lock the truck, her packages safely tucked over top of the bag from the stationer's shop. It didn't escape me, the way she stared at the gorgeous red leather-bound journal in the front window. I saw her hand drift toward where it lay in a bed of fake snow, bright mittens and a snarky coffee cup completing the display. I shouldn't have. It would be smart to let this thing with Kate die a natural death. Enjoy it until I left and then cut communication, go our separate ways. The thought of doing that physically hurts me; like a gut punch, it knocks the wind right out of me.

"You want to keep shopping or—"

"Yeah. I, uh"—Kate paints a tight smile across her face—"I need to find something for Gracyn."

I'm pretty sure that's her roommate, but since I haven't met any of these people, it's hard for me to be positive.

Words can't do a fucking thing to fix this, make it better, so I wrap my arm around Kate's shoulders. Pulling her into me, I plant a kiss at her temple and guide her down the sidewalk, seeking the next shop, the next little thing that will turn her smile from forced to full and real.

We wander in and out of stores as the sun dims behind clouds, the temperature drops, and the wind swirls snow flurries around us. I make damn sure to ignore my phone and the constant buzz of it in my pocket. I don't give a shit what Jessica is trying to orchestrate. I have Kate here within my reach, and that's all that matters. Live in the moment; tomorrow is never a guarantee—or something like that.

"That should do it," Kate says as a cashier hands back her card and gift bag stuffed full of tissue paper and what Kate claims is the perfect gift for her roommate.

Seemingly more relaxed than she was earlier, Kate tucks her wallet back in her tote, and I take the bag. As soon as I'm able, I wrap her other hand in mine and bring her knuckles up, pressing them to my lips. So soft. Her lotion hints at something clean and powdery. Something I can't quite pinpoint.

"What kind of lotion is this?" I breathe it in, committing the scent to memory, allowing it to seep into me so that I can carry it with me when I go.

"Mine?"

"Yes, Kate. Yours," I tell her.

She rolls her eyes, and as innocent or annoyed as that little movement is, all I can think of is how, when she comes, she does the same damn thing.

"It's called Au Lait. You like it?"

"I do." I inhale another hit of it, like it's a drug I can no longer live without.

Snow blows across the road as we climb back up the mountain to our cabin. Kate softly sings along with Sinatra, her voice sultry and deep, like she's a lounge singer from back in the day. Nothing is better than a whiskey-tainted voice— or, in Kate's case, tequila-tainted. Just one more damn thing about this woman that has me falling when I have no right to. No time for it. This isn't what I wanted. It's exactly what I was running from when I left Montana for West Point, New York.

I'm more than happy to play the bachelor uncle to Jake. I don't need anything more than that. The demands and expectations that my parents put on me to marry and stay on the ranch were fucking ridiculous. Sure, I'm their only son, but my older sisters married a few years prior, and their husbands liked ranching. Wanted to do it. I found my way out, and for some dumbass reason, I thought my family would be happy for me. Not what happened.

Instead of pride and congratulations, I got guilt and a fuck-ton of pressure to pass up the opportunity of a lifetime. Honestly, earning an appointment to the military academy is one of the highest honors I can think of.

"What are you thinking on so hard over there?" Kate asks.

I didn't notice that she'd stopped singing with Frankie and Dean Martin.

"Nothing worth my time. You have fun today? Get every-thing set for Christmas?"

She hums her agreement as I pull into the drive for the cabin. The quiet shush of snow falling surrounds us. The flakes landing on Kate's bright red coat as we step out into the night is like a dusting of sugar. She looks good enough to eat.

I toss her a wolfish grin, trapping her in my arms as I reach around her to grab her shopping bags. "You want these inside, right?"

"I do." Kate reaches for the small bag partially hidden under the seat. "You want to take this in, too?"

I take it from her and tuck it back on the floorboard. "Nah, that can stay out. Nothing breakable in there." I don't know when I'll give it to her—hell, I'm not entirely positive that I will give it to her—but something about the way her eyes had lingered, like it was an extravagance, made me want to buy the thing.

"You found something for your mama then? For Christmas?" she asks, stomping the snow from her boots on the welcome mat.

I shift the bags to one hand and tap in the four-digit code, unlocking the door. "Meh, it's just a little something I didn't think I could pass up." I set the bags on the table and go straight to the fireplace, lighting the kindling, adding some logs. Coaxing some warmth into the room while steering her away from that line of questions.

The microwave dings, and Kate pulls out leftovers from last night, dividing the steaming pasta between a couple of bowls. "Is this good?" she asks, tucking forks and napkins into her hand and bringing it all to the rug in front of the fire.

"Perfect." I grab a bottle of wine from the grocery order I had delivered and pour us each a glass.

Kate twirls some pasta around her fork, shakes it off, and starts over again. "What's it like? Your job?" she clarifies when my brows pinch together, confused. "Can you even talk about it? Is that allowed?" She pops the pasta into her mouth, lips sliding the spaghetti from the fork.

"I can—"

"But you'd have to kill me," she teases.

"Yep. And that would be a waste." I swallow down some wine before continuing, "It's not very exciting until it is, and then time passes in perfectly choreographed chaos. Most of what I can talk about is the stuff you see on the news. Beyond that, I really can't." And I don't actually want to. I'll be back in the thick of it soon enough, and I took my leave stateside for an escape.

Kate nods, staring into the fire. "I don't know how Chloe and Jake do it. Do they get to talk to Dallas at all when he's deployed?" she asks quietly.

And this is why I can't do the family thing while I'm serving in this capacity. I know all too well how hard it is on the family left behind. "Not much. An occasional e-mail, maybe a call if the time zones and the mission starts line up just right, but when we're deep ..." I trail off, letting her make the natural conclusion.

"Wow. She's so strong, so stoic. Keeps Jake from losing his shit. She must not have the news on much around him, huh?"

"Probably not. Jake's a tough kid. This life is all he knows, so I think he pretty much rolls with it. Tripp has been popping in and leaving since he and Chloe got married. Hell, he missed most of Chloe's pregnancy. Almost missed Jake's birth, but that kid held out and waited for his dad to get home. He was a week late. Chloe said she was miserable, but I think, deep down, she was thrilled that Tripp was there for it."

We eat quietly for a bit, fork tines scraping against the plates.

"Y'all have been gone a lot then," Kate says, her accent coming out a bit.

"Mmhmm. But, when Jake was born, we were just out on an FTX—sorry, field training exercise—so it wasn't quite like it is now. Chloe called the CO's wife when she went into labor, and that woman was a teacup terrorist." I chuckle, thinking about how mighty my commanding officer's tiny wife was.

She sure as shit didn't let Army bureaucracy get in the

way of what needed to be done. If she had an important message to get to her husband, she found a way.

"She made sure the colonel knew that Tripp needed to be fast-tracked home, and he fucking made it. There are some truly amazing people in the world."

Kate smirks over her wineglass. "Kind of makes up for the assholes causing trouble across the globe."

If only. I have seen some things. Things that sour my stomach and make my blood boil. Make me question whether God exists. I don't tell her any of that. What's the point? I deal with the bogeymen and the bad guys, so the rest of the world can rest easy.

THIRTEEN

Kate

WE SPENT TWO DAYS skiing in what I guess was a rare powder event in the Catskills and two nights wrapped up in each other. Drinking wine and eating dinner in front of a roaring fire. The only thing that could have possibly made the weekend better was a promise of a tomorrow. The possibility of a future even if that future was as simple as a date next week. A phone call next month. But, no, not here, not with us.

This weekend was good-bye. Tomorrow, I go back to work, and by the end of the week, we'll each be tucked in with our families, celebrating Christmas.

Not once have I had a desire to be anywhere but home for the holidays—until now. Snowy horse rides, crackling fires, wool socks, and mountains of blankets. That's how I picture Christmas in Montana. I'll be home in Hattiesburg, pretending it's downright chilly out and anything less than a puffy coat, scarf, and fingerless gloves is just asking for pneumonia. Meanwhile, I'll be tapping the AC a few degrees just so I can survive the heat. At some point over the past three years, I became a Northerner. Or at the very least, my blood's gotten thicker.

Jack's voice pulls me out of my thoughts as we approach Beekman Hills. "When do you head out? You are flying to Mississippi, not driving, right?" Taking his eyes from the road, he glances over at me.

"Flying, for sure. Wednesday afternoon. What about you?" I ask, wondering if we'll see each other even one more time before this is all over.

"Out of Newark on Wednesday morning."

"I'm out of LaGuardia."

The awkward tap dance, the back-and-forth of how to end things. Maybe it would be best to say good-bye today. A kiss at the door. *Thank you for a lovely weekend*, and leave it at that.

"I have a date tomorrow night with Jake, for dude time. It's tradition. But Tuesday? Can I see you then? Dinner maybe?" he asks, guiding his truck into a parking spot in front of my building, one that seems impossibly small.

I nod, biting at the inside corner of my lip. "Yeah, I can do that." The streetlights glow in the cold night, a haze illuminating out from antique-style fixtures.

"Good," Jack says quietly, stepping out of the truck.

Cold air invades the warm interior, and I pull my gloves on as he comes around to open my door. The manners on him. I'm sad. I hate that what we have is so short-term, but dear God, if I got nothing else out of the past month, I got my recalibration. I will not be wasting my time on any more trolls from this point on. My standards have been elevated.

Jack grabs my suitcase and a handful of shopping bags, leaving me with just my tote and a few smaller bags to carry. We climb the stairs in silence, and after unlocking my apartment door, I hold it open for him.

"Where do you want these?" he asks, slightly lifting my bags.

"Anywhere. By the hallway maybe? Can I get you a drink? Do you want to stay for a bit?" I need to get unpacked and ready for the last two days of school before Christmas break, but I don't want him to leave.

"Thanks, probably not though. I have some stuff to take care of"—he sets my things down—"and I would imagine you've got to get organized, too, yeah?"

He walks toward me until he's right there. A breath away. If I were to lean forward, I could bury my nose in the warm hollow of his neck.

Instead, I close my eyes and breathe in the scent that is all Jack—spicy citrus, a hint of leather. He slides his hands along my neck, thumbs lifting my chin so that my lips meet his. The kiss is soft, full of reverence. And over far too soon.

"Thank you for spending the weekend with me, Kate. I needed that more than you know." His lips brush against mine as he speaks. "I'll call and let you know what the plan is for dinner." Tilting my head, he presses his lips to my forehead; it's sweet, tender, so much more intimate than the chaste action should be. And he goes.

This is not good. Completely and totally bad actually. My heart is not going to come out unscathed; that's for damn sure.

I text Gracyn, wondering where the hell she is at ten on a Sunday night.

Gracyn: Working late. My boss is an ass.

Me: You work for your dad …

Gracyn: Yep. Don't wait up. You have school in the morning. See you tomorrow maybe?

I send a kissy face emoji and pull my bottle of Casamigos Blanco from the cabinet above the fridge. Three fingers of oak-aged tequila will make doing laundry and organizing myself a little less painful. My playlists all feel just *too* much for my mood, so I browse through the categories, finally settling on something entirely *Jack*. Old-school Rat Pack. Crooners with voices rich and deep to balance the smoky caramel and vanilla notes of my drink and the melancholy that has descended on me.

I connect to my Bose speaker and let the music surround me, the tequila warming me, and I just start going through the motions of doing what needs to be done. I haven't been home much, not nearly as much as I normally am since hooking up with Jack. Gracyn, God love her, is not the neatest roommate in the world, but I guess the only other one I've spent a significant amount of time with was gay and ridiculously fastidious with his clothes and home decor. It's not a stereotype if it's true.

By the time I fall into bed, laundry done, apartment mostly cleaned, and supplies organized for two wild days in kindergarten, I think I should fall right to sleep. Sad to say, that's not how it works. Gracyn still isn't home, and I'm lonely. The apartment feels empty, my bed far too lonesome. I roll to my side and flop to my stomach, stretching out, reaching for the comfort of the person who's not there.

. . .

TWO DAYS OF TEACHING kindergarten is a walk in the park. Unless it's the two days before the biggest holiday in these little kiddos' worlds. Add to that the disruption of having a substitute on Friday while I was off sexing it up in the mountains, and even the most seasoned teacher would be considering a career change right about now.

"Miss Beard, were you sick?"

"Miss Beard, that other lady didn't read the story right."

"Miss Beard, I missed you so much."

I knew I'd get a full rundown from these kiddos on the injustices of having a substitute change their routine.

What I didn't plan for was Jake.

"Miss Beard, Daddy said Uncle Jack went away with a pretty lady this weekend. Did you go away with Uncle Jack?" Jake pipes up just as I think the complaints, questions, and commentaries are winding down.

Laughing to try to cover the uncomfortable feeling of getting called out by a five-year-old, I ask, "Why would you think your daddy was talking about me?" *Sweet Jesus in a manger at Christmas.*

"'Cause, besides my mom, you're the prettiest lady I know," he responds, eyes wide and earnest.

"Aw, thank you, Jake. That was a really nice compliment. Hey, I have an idea." I sit down in my story-time chair. "Come sit on the floor for me, and how about we take a minute to go round the circle and give a little compliment to our friends?"

Nothing like thinking on my feet and finding a way not to lie to the little bugger. I know I can do it, but since we're pretty much guaranteed to not get a whole lot of book learning done today anyway, why not work on life skills? And saying something nice is never a bad idea.

Sitting and listening to these sweet children tell their friend to the left of them what they like, what makes them smile, what they're good at, it makes my heart happy. Some of the best teaching moments happen spontaneously, and all the planning in the world just can't compete.

The rest of the day and much of the next are spent on fun—giving crafts and activities for the kids with lots of time to share their thoughts and excitement for the coming break —and all the packing and organizing for me once school is out.

On Tuesday though, the last hour of school is dedicated to the winter party. Pin the Nose on the Snowman, Snowball Scoop with oven mitts and small white balloons. Sugar cookies and gifts galore. Books and coloring books for the kiddos. And so many thoughtful gift cards and coffee mugs and goodies for me.

And I finally get to meet Jake's dad.

"Miss Beard," Jake says in his playground voice, bouncing on his toes. He grabs my hand and wiggles it, trying to get my attention while I thank Cecelia's mom for all her help with the party. "Miss Beard—" Jake whines, all patience gone.

"Jacob Triplett, you simmer down and use your manners, sir," a deep voice commands.

Jake stops bouncing and shaking my hand but doesn't let go for a minute. "Yes, sir. Excuse me, Miss Beard, this is real important."

He turns his puppy-dog eyes to me, and I'm lost. An

absolute goner. I squeeze his little hand and thank my party helper one more time before giving my full attention to Jake.

"Thank you for finding your manners, friend. What can I help you with?" I calmly ask him.

Jake smiles proudly and sweeps his free hand toward the giant of a man behind him. The one with the deep voice, soft eyes, and arm wrapped solidly around Chloe Triplett. "This is my dad. He and Uncle Jack are best friends, and they are soldiers and fight the bad guys."

I can totally see where Jake gets his sandy-brown curls.

Offering my hand, I say, "It's so nice to finally meet you, Mr. Triplett. Thank you for your service."

He takes my hand, firmly shaking it. "And thank you for yours," he says sincerely. "Jake talks about you all the time. All good things." He smiles broadly and winks at his boy.

"Ditto."

"Yeah, no need to sugarcoat anything. I'm sure he talks about Jack way more than me. Serious hero worship there."

"Maybe it's a phase?" I offer.

"It's all good. If I had to handpick someone for Jake to look up to, it would be Jack, all the way."

Jake beams up at his parents.

"Anyway, it was great to meet you. Enjoy your break. You've earned it with these heathens."

"Thanks so much, and y'all do the same. Merry Christmas."

I turn my attention to the class in general and get them ready to go. The class turtle is going home with Aubrey, the care instructions tucked into his food carrier. Flipping the chairs and shutting off the lights, I turn before locking my classroom door.

I couldn't be more ready for this little break, but I still have a few things to take care of once I get out of here. Most of my gifts were shipped home last week, but the ones I bought up in that little mountain town for my mama, I need to pad and pack, so they make it through the flight in one piece. And I want to make sure all of that is done and that my bags are ready to go before Jack picks me up in a couple of hours.

FOURTEEN

Jack

FINALLY, ON THE THIRD try, the lock clicks, and I push open the door to my room. Streetlight filters through the window, casting the room in a soft glow. It would be romantic as fuck if, for the life of me, I could think straight. But let's be honest; my blood has all gone south, and I can't process much more than getting to where I want to be. Where I need to be.

Kate drops her purse to the ground with a decided thud.

"You have enough shit in there?" I ask, chuckling.

She bites her lip and steps farther into the room, pulling at the belt tie on her ruby-red coat. Lord God, help a poor soldier. This woman is sexy as sin, even in the way she takes off her fucking coat. She might just be the death of me.

"Mmhmm, make fun all you want, but I do believe in being prepared, and you know, if we need it, I probably have it in that bag," she states, dead fucking serious.

"I have everything we need right here." I toss my wallet

to the table by the bed and slide the coat the rest of the way down her arms, dropping it to the floor.

And there she is. Standing in front of me in nothing fancier than jeans and a sweater, but damn the way her curves are hinted at beneath the bulky layers. I slide my hands along the sides of her neck, twining my fingers through her hair, and pull her in for a kiss. To savor or devour? Take my time and make this last, or rip her clothes off and ravage her until we're nothing but a sweaty mess in tangled sheets? This is it, and I'll be fucked if I'm not going to soak her in.

While my brain is trying to function on short rations, Kate's hands get busy, taking over. Working the buttons on my shirt, pulling it loose from my jeans. Shoving the material aside, she tickles and dances her fingertips down my torso, straight to my belt. She struggles with the buckle, getting nowhere fast, growling her frustration.

"You gonna laugh at me or help me with this?" she murmurs against my lips. "Why is this so hard?"

I try—really, I do—but I'm a guy, so pressing her hand over my hard dick, I snort out a laugh and tell her with all the honesty I possess, "You did that, sweetheart. That's all because of you." I shrug my shirt off the rest of the way and step into her. "Tit for tat, how 'bout you lose your sweater, so we keep things even?"

Before the words are fully out of my mouth, her sweater hits the growing pile of clothes on the floor. I flick open my belt buckle but catch her hands as they reach for me. I'm a grown-ass man, and I've got all kinds of control, but Kate makes me feel like a horny teenager, and one errant touch could have me coming in my jeans. And that's just not going to happen tonight. Hell no.

Holding her hands, I pull her toward me and kiss her again, parting her lips with my tongue, tasting her. Distracting her just enough to get myself back under control. Releasing her hands, I cup her tits, the lace straining over her tight nipples. The buds hardening against my thumbs while I hook my fingers into the cups, pushing the straps down off her shoulders. I kiss a trail from her lips, along her jaw and across her delicate collarbone. Dip my head and suck her nipple into my mouth, nipping at her through the lace.

Kate reaches behind herself, arching her back as she does, and pops the clasp, allowing her bra to drop away. Dear God, she takes my breath away. All that pale, creamy skin right there. Just for me. I guide her toward the bed and crawl up her body until she is splayed out, her chest to mine, touching everywhere we need to be touching.

Almost.

I push myself up and pop the button on her jeans, sliding them and her panties down those mile-long legs. I stand and grab hold of her boot-clad foot, unzipping one and then the other, peeling her jeans off and adding them to the mess.

"Katelyn, look at you. Fuck me," I mumble, working myself out of my briefs.

"That is the plan, right?" she asks, running her hands up to her breasts, pushing them together, toying with her nipples.

"It is. You good with that plan?"

I pick up her foot, kiss the arch, her ankle, behind her knee, settling it on my shoulder. I repeat the sequence on the other side and slide down until I am face-to-pussy and give her a long, slow lick before circling her clit with my tongue. Kate's hips buck off the bed, a moan escaping from her lips as she grabs at my hair. I drag a finger through her slick heat and curl one and then two fingers into her pussy, pumping and sucking and flicking and stroking her to orgasm.

That's one, just to get her ready.

"Jack," she breathes my name on a shuddering sigh.

"You good?" I ask, reaching for one of the condoms in my wallet.

Kate hums her satisfaction as I rip open the black square and roll the condom down my length. I lean over, grasping my cock and rubbing it against her, slicking it up. Nudging her entrance, I push in partway and drop my forehead to hers. And that little hum that Kate had kicking a second ago turns to a moan as she adjusts. With small pulses, I thrust in deeper and deeper each time, gritting my teeth so that I don't fucking lose it. Her moan turns into a gasp as I push in that last bit until I'm fully seated, my balls tight up against her. Her eyes blown fucking wide.

"You still good?" I grit out—pausing not just for her, but for me, too, because my dick is being strangled right now. The life squeezed out of it in the best possible way. "Fuck, Kate. Tell me you're okay." I fight to keep my eyes open as her walls flutter around me. I want to know, see it in her eyes that she's ready to go.

"Gawd, yes. Oh my ... yes," she pants, rocking her hips. "Yes, Jack. *Oh-ma-Gawd*, yes." And she rolls back into me, stroking me. Fucking me.

And far be it from me to make this gorgeous woman do all the work. Retreating until just my tip is nestled in her tight heat, I thrust back in, moving her up the mattress. God, I could fuck her through time, forever. She makes me forget to breathe, forget my name. She almost makes me forget that I'm getting on a plane to hell in a few short hours.

She's the first woman who's made me want to miss a flight and stay right here, wrapped up in her.

But that can't happen.

"Jack?" she whispers, pulling me out of my head. "Are you ... what happened? Where'd you go?"

I shake all thoughts of leaving from my mind and focus on the woman who's breached my walls and crept inside my heart. "Right here. 'M right here," I tell her, punctuating each word with a kiss down her throat and a thrust of my hips. Each thrust ending with an extra push to get closer, deeper, etching the feel of her permanently on my soul.

Her nails dig deep, piercing the skin on my back, marking my ass as she pulls me tighter still.

"Jack ..." she gasps.

I curl down on the next thrust and take her nipple into my mouth, sucking hard, cutting off her words. Biting just the way she likes, and she comes. Hard. Body shaking, muscles pulsing, head thrown back, arching into me. Eyes rolling back, lashes fluttering against her pink cheeks. I thrust two, three, four times, wanting to wring out every ounce of her pleasure before I explode.

And I do. A blinding fire races up my spine, and all I can think of is Kate. Beneath me, around me, consuming me.

"Jesus, how did you do it?" I ask before my brain completely comes back online. I push myself up, trying not to crush her, but she firmly holds me in place. "I don't want to crush you."

"You're not. I love feeling your weight on me. So solid, so ... you make me feel safe, secure." She runs her fingers through the hair at the back of my head. "How did I do what?"

"Huh?"

"You asked how I did it ... what did I do?" she hums, wrapping her legs around mine, hooking her feet under my calves.

Fuck. I'm pretty fucking sure I can't tell Kate I'm falling for her. Not now. Not when I'm leaving in a matter of hours, and I have never dropped into a mission with a girlfriend back home, counting on me to make it out alive. There are too damn many unknowns. All the messy complications that I've worked so hard to avoid.

"Swear I blacked out for a minute." I slide out of bed and take care of the condom before curling myself around Kate's relaxed, sated body.

And, as I drift off to sleep, I hear her whisper, "Thank you" and feel the press of her lips to the palm of my hand.

After a few hours of the best sleep I think I've ever had, I shower and throw on my clothes. I dropped my truck off at Tripp and Chloe's yesterday afternoon, swapping it for a rental to get to the airport. I'm fucking hard-pressed to find any desire to walk out of here though.

Light from the partially opened bathroom door slants across the room, highlighting Kate's sleeping form. Her creamy skin glows in the soft light, calling to me, begging to be tasted and caressed one last time.

If I wake her to say good-bye, it'll just be hard on her. On me. So, I do what any cowardly piece of shit would do. I sweep her hair aside and kiss the back of her neck, lingering for an extra beat. Inhaling the scent of her skin, committing it to memory before stealing away.

Her overstuffed tote bag is still where she dropped it after dinner last night, the top gaping open. I pull the wrapped journal from my ruck and tuck it into her bag. Fuck knows when she'll actually find it with all the shit she carries around in the name of preparedness. Hopefully, she takes the granny shears out before she tries to go through TSA.

My eyes dart over to her one last time as I reluctantly ease out the door.

FIFTEEN

Kate

MY PLANE TOUCHES DOWN in Hattiesburg, and the minute we get the go-ahead from the flight crew, I turn my phone back on. Desperate for a text from Jack and hating myself for it. The only new texts I have are from Gracyn, gushing about the Christmas present that I left on her bed and bitching about her asshole client. Her daddy runs the family accounting firm and seems to think he's got the right to hand-pick a douche-bag husband for her. According to Gracyn, he's nothing but a highbrow asshat, cheating on her mama and alienating his kids at every turn.

My mama and daddy, on the other hand, couldn't be any sweeter on each other.

I shuffle off the plane, stopping in the restroom on the way to baggage claim. The slash of red marring my panties has never been more welcome after the unfortunate condom debacle. Along with a deep sigh of relief and tension flooding from low in my belly, it's entirely possible that I do a little happy dance in my stall after putting myself back together.

On the short walk to grab my checked bag, I send a quick note to Jack.

Me: Have a fantastic visit home. Also … got the all-clear from Aunt Flo. No mishap from the ill-fitting oops!

I drop my phone in my tote, next to the pretty wrapped present that magically appeared in there overnight. Part of me wanted to open it the minute I saw it, but mostly, I wanted to wait. For what, I don't know, but it's still wrapped, still in my bag. Still a symbol of mysterious possibilities.

Naturally, my suitcase is just about the last one off the plane, but the minute I have it, I pull my phone back out and call my daddy, letting him know I'm ready. As I end the call, I check my messages and see dots bouncing from Jack. They start and stop several times, finally ghosting and disappearing entirely.

I shove down my disappointment and roll my bag to the curb where my daddy pulls his shiny red truck to a stop in the middle of God and everybody.

"Hey, sunshine," he calls, hopping out, rounding the front side and giving me a big bear hug. "Good to see you again." He holds me at arm's length, smile stretching his mouth wide.

"Hey, Daddy." I plant a quick kiss on his cheek and look to the line of cars stacking up behind where he stopped, essentially blocking traffic. Bless his heart. Airport security is for everyone but him. "Think we should load these up and head on out?" I collapse the handle of my big rolling suitcase.

He looks to the left, taking in the annoyed faces peering

at us through windshields. Smirking, he nods, and then grabs my bags and setting them in the back seat.

Yep, my daddy, Dennison Beard, with his brown hair streaked with bits of silver and tortoise-shell glasses drives a big ole truck. The man is president of a bank. A pretty sedan or lush SUV would fit him so much better, but he's a Southern boy through and through. Pickup truck and business suit.

We climb in and head into town, passing familiar landmarks.

"Gonna have to drop you home and head on back to work for an hour or so. Your mama's in there, baking, I think." He spins the steering wheel, bouncing us up the drive, stopping next to the house I grew up in. "You go give your mama some love, and I'll carry your bags up to your room and see y'all for supper." He gets my door and pulls my bag from the back seat in quick succession. Then, he bounds into the house.

This is the man who set my expectations so high. How did I fall so far? Being with Jack for the past month has reminded me of my worth. That it's good to have high standards because, if I don't have them for myself, no one else is going to have them for me.

"There she is," Mama says brightly as I push through the kitchen door.

"Hey, Mama." I wrap my arms around her, feeling like I just stepped back in time. This house, this kitchen, the smells —it all brings me back to the very best childhood I could've asked for.

"My God, I have missed you," she drawls, squeezing me

extra tight. "When are you coming back home? There's plenty of teaching jobs here, you know."

I do know. Maggie Hays Beard reminds me of that fact every time we talk.

"Maybe you and Daddy should come visit me in New York. Y'all just might like it."

The front door bangs shut, and my father's truck roars to life, the rumble fading as he takes off down the street. It doesn't escape my notice that my invite to visit has gone unacknowledged. Sometimes, I think my parents purposely stay away from New York, avoid visiting me because they might just like it up there the same way that I do. They've wanted me to come back home since Chance and I broke up. They still don't know the reason behind that shitshow, and if they acknowledge how beautiful it is up north, they might just have to give up their campaign for my return.

"Well, let's get to it, baby. We've got cookies to make and pies to bake," Mama says instead. "Tell me about those little darlings you have this year. Who had to take the damn turtle home this break?" She rummages around the cabinet under the island, pulling bowls and cookie sheets out for a full evening of baking.

"It's a coveted honor to take Dash home." Yeah, I didn't name the turtle Dash for his dashing looks. He actually moves pretty quickly for a turtle. Early on, when I was cleaning his cage, I about lost him as he scurried across the floor, heading straight for the kindergarten commons. "And it's a highly selective process. Grades, good behavior—"

"Willing parents," she finishes for me.

And I just laugh because it's absolutely true. So many

families travel over the break, so it's sometimes hard to find anyone willing to pull turtle duty.

"Who's your favorite this year? Still that one little boy, Jackson?"

My heart stutters at her mistake. "Jake, yeah. His daddy came home for leave. I don't know how he and his mom do it, being apart all the time, but Jake was so happy and proud when he introduced us yesterday. He was absolutely beaming."

"Bless them." There's more than one meaning to that phrase in the South, but this time, Mama is full of sincerity.

My family holds service to the country in the highest regard. My great-grandpa served during World War II, and the stories I've heard about what he saw would send chills down your spine and turn your hair white.

The rest of the evening passes in a whirl of food, conversation, and catching up. My brother, Sam, even stops by for a hot minute with my three-year-old niece, Harper, in tow.

"Y'all leave your mama home alone, Harp?" I ask, tugging on one of her curly brown pigtails.

Harper wiggles in my arms, trying to get to the rack of cookies cooling on the counter.

"Yeah, Jules isn't feeling so great right now," Sam says, snagging a cookie and breaking it in half. He blows on one piece before handing it to his daughter.

"Uh-oh. She caught a bug or somethin'? You tell her not to worry about bringing a thing to Christmas dinner. Kate can help me with everything." My mother pours some milk into a sippy cup, handing it to Harper. "Here ya go, darlin'."

Sam mumbles, "Something," and snags a couple of more cookies, smirking at me from across the kitchen.

I open my mouth, but he shakes his head and cuts his eyes to Super-Mimi, his nickname for our mother when she's in full grandma mode. Looks like we're going to have another baby to spoil next Christmas.

"All righty, Harper, let's hit it. Auntie Kate needs her beauty sleep, so she can hang with us cool kids." He quickly hugs me, whispering his plea to keep the surprise under wraps.

He plucks Harper from my arms and tosses her in the air. Harper squeals with delight, and Mama admonishes Sam with a smack of a kitchen towel even though he never actually breaks contact with his precious baby girl.

SLOWLY BLINKING AWAKE, I roll over and swipe my phone off the nightstand. Still nothing from Jack. Not a word. I guess he wasn't as concerned about our blowout as I thought he was.

Tossing my phone aside, I take a quick shower and throw on jeans and a super-lightweight sweater. It's significantly warmer than I'm used to, but if I go out in just a T-shirt, the winter-minded people of Mississippi might just shiver in their UGGS. And that just won't do.

"Morning, baby," Mama greets, handing me a cup of coffee in a hand-thrown mug. She does love her pottery. "After you eat, I'm gonna need you to run out to the grocery store for me." She fills a plate, setting it on the island in front of me with a napkin and fork.

"Jesus, are you trying to fatten me up?" I ask, looking at the homemade biscuits swimming in a pool of creamy gravy.

As a silent response, she plops a heaping spoonful of

sausage crumbles on top and starts writing up her shopping list.

"Sam's dropping Harper by on his way to work. I hope whatever Jules has isn't contagious," Mama muses.

I hide my chuckle behind my napkin. God, she's going to lose her shit when Sam and Jules tell her they're expecting again.

Any complaints I had about my huge breakfast are nothing but lies. My plate all but licked clean, I shove my feet into my Chucks and grab my purse, Mama's list, and the keys to her Lexus. "Call me if you think of anything else while I'm out," I toss over my shoulder.

I check my phone before pulling out onto the street. I check it again when I park at the store. I hate that I'm checking it again as I push my buggy past the refrigerated cases to the whipping cream. Disappointment settles in my heart at the lack of any new messages.

"Well, hey there, Katie. You lookin' for a text from me?" There's only one person that voice could possibly belong to, and I'll be fucked if it's the last person I feel like dealing with.

I place my carton of cream in the buggy and straighten, pasting a fake-as-shit smile on my face. "Chance, hey." I skate my eyes over his shoulder, scanning the area. "You finally bring your boyfriend home to meet the family?" I ask.

He stiffens and swings his head around, checking to see if anyone overheard me. "Would you hush?"

Oh Jesus.

"You still haven't told them? Bless your heart," I say, pushing down the aisle to the cheese case. And, yeah, this is the other kind of *bless your heart*—the *fuck you* version.

Chance wraps his hand around my arm, halting me. "I haven't," he whispers. "You know how my daddy is. He'd just die. And that would break my mama's heart, and you know it."

It's true. All of it, but I just can't really find it in me to care. I peel his hand from my bicep and cross my arms over my chest. I owe him nothing. Not a damn thing, but he's shifting on his feet and bouncing his hip, his tells for having some favor to ask. How did I not notice in all the years we dated that Chance acted like one of my girlfriends? Am I just now noticing this after all the time I spent with Jack over the past month?

"So, do you want to hang out while you're home? Maybe come by for dessert after y'all have Christmas dinner tomorrow?"

Blink. Blink. Blink. "Are you—"

"Kate, help me. Just this once. I swear, I'm going to tell them soon. Just ... just help me get through the holidays, and then I swear to God, I'll come out," he pleads.

Really? Really?

"Go to Hell, Chance." I shake my head in disgust and walk away.

"Kate?" he calls, still not seeing how fucked up what he's asking me to do is.

Hastily, I grab the last few things I need from my list and wave over my shoulder. "Say hey to your mama and them. Merry Christmas, Chance." I pay and haul ass to the car, cranking the AC once I'm settled in the driver's seat. And, because I really am a desperate fool, I check my phone one last time—I promise.

Jack: Check. Merry Christmas. Thanks for everything.

Thanks for everything? That nothing of a response takes the wind right out of my sails. Right or wrong, I wanted more. I could call him. Fake that I never received his text and tell him again that we're in the clear, but suddenly, all I want to do is go home and take a nap. I'm tired. I'm sad.

I just want to crawl into my bed and nurse my serious case of the blues.

SIXTEEN

Jack

"You're home."

That voice, almost as much as the question itself, causes tension to coil under my skin. This is one of the many reasons I don't like coming back home. So many damn people tried to keep me here, thinking they had my best interests at heart. In fact, they all had their own agenda at the forefront of their minds.

I turn to face my ex-girlfriend and take a step back when I see she's not alone. "Jess." It's curt, maybe too curt, but I sure as fuck am not thrilled to see her. I just want to grab the handful of things my sister asked me to pick up in town and get my ass out to the ranch. Face the next round of interactions that will confirm the wisdom of my decision to leave Montana and choose a completely different life. My skin feels too tight here, constricted.

Jess takes half a step toward me, a tentative smile painted across her face. "It's so good to see you again, Wyatt."

I bristle at the use of my first name. It's something I primarily associate with negativity. With home. With the need to run.

"You look good. Really good," she continues, her hand fluttering from the shoulder of the young girl standing with her to the base of her throat. A simple gold band on her left ring finger.

There is so much wrong with this picture. So fucking much, and I'm not sure if I don't know what to say or if I just don't care to say anything at all.

Jess stills, following the line of my gaze, and makes a fist, shoving her wedding-banded hand into the pocket of her parka.

Shaking my head, I step to the side, essentially putting her daughter between us before replying, "Nice to see you, too, Jess."

And the poor kid, twelve years old now—or she will be soon at least—has her head on a swivel, looking from her mother to me, probably wondering what the fuck is happening.

You and me both, kid.

I offer my hand, introducing myself, "I'm Jack. Went to school with your mom a million years ago."

"Charlie." The girl shakes my hand and screws up her face. "Jack or Wyatt? Which is it?" Charlie looks at me with all the attitude of a self-centered kid with nothing more than popularity on her mind.

The apple doesn't fall far from the tree.

"Wyatt Jackson. My friends call me Jack," I tell her.

"So, why'd my mom call you Wyatt?"

Why fucking indeed? Because she's a backstabbing, manipulative liar.

Obviously, that story isn't one that gets shared on the regular, but I don't need to be an asshole. Not at this given moment anyway and sure as shit not to a kid.

"Ancient history. You have a merry Christmas." I nod and walk purposefully away, gathering the list of shit Dana requested.

I didn't even make it out to the ranch before my past started rearing its ugly head. File this under reasons I don't come home.

Thank God I stopped for a bottle of tequila before leaving Missoula. I'm gonna fucking need all the help I can get to make it through this visit if this is how it's getting started.

I make it through the aisles, manage to pay, and escape to the parking lot, plastic grocery bags hanging from my left hand. Relief is sweet but fleeting as I pop the trunk of my rental car, and Jess sidles up, leaning against the truck in the next spot over. She stares as I place the bags next to my duffel.

"What is it, Jess?" I ask, patience gone.

"I want to see you while you're home. Spend some time with you, reconnect."

I glance around the lot, her daughter nowhere in sight.

"Yeah? Not gonna happen," I tell her, slamming the trunk closed. "I told you last week, I'm not interested. And I'm pretty sure your husband wouldn't be all that thrilled at the idea."

She's blocking my access to the driver's side of the car, arms crossed, looking a little more brazen with Charlie out of the direct line of fire. "I've never loved him, Wyatt. You were the one I wanted."

A huff pushes out of my nose. "Got a fucked-up way of showing it. You get Charlie's father to marry you? Or did you trick some other poor bastard into thinking he knocked you up?"

"I married her father right after graduation but only because—"

"Because your father found out who was really responsible," I finish, cutting off whatever bullshit excuse she was about to spew at me.

"I didn't have any other choice," she yells, her arms swinging out before they slap down at her sides.

"In what? Getting pregnant or trying to pin it on me?" Disgust drips off of my words. "Doesn't fucking matter, honestly. You knew I didn't want this life, that all I wanted was to get out of here, and you tried to sabotage the only way it could happen. I didn't want anything to do with having a family, Jess. And you tried to rip all of that out from under me."

I don't know how many times we've had this argument in the past decade, but I'm over it. So fucking over it.

"And now?" she asks, sniffling. It could be the cold, but everything about this whole interaction screams devious posturing.

"Nothing's changed, Jess. I'm happy with my life and not moving back here, so it doesn't matter." Manipulation or not, I soften my features, relaxing my stance. Mixing things up, putting Jess at ease, might be just enough to throw her off her game. Switch up the balance of power.

Jess visibly relaxes, moving with me as I saunter around

the side of the car. With each of my steps forward, she takes one back until she's far enough past the door that, when I click the lock button and pull at the handle, the door is a physical barrier between us.

"Go home to your husband, Jess. Raise your daughter with a good sense of right and wrong. Google that shit if you need to. But you and me? We're done. Don't contact me again. I'm not fucking interested." I close the car door, her face a mask of shock at my dismissal. I think I was really damn clear, leaving no room for doubt.

And, as I drive out of the parking lot, a middle finger in the air and Jessica's back are all the confirmation I need that this mess is finally done.

I feel for the kid. Hope she gets a fighting chance because her mother is batshit fucking crazy.

SNOW-COVERED FIELDS WITH PRAIRIE grass peeking through the crust line my drive out to the ranch, giving me a chance to refocus and prep for the next round of guilt and pressure to move back home. But not even that serenity is enough to temper the passive-aggressive bullshit that's thrown at me the minute I walk through the door.

"You ready to do some real work for a change, boy? Got fences need fixed and ..." my father bellows as soon as I breach the doorway.

The only reason he's here at the house at this time of day is to give me shit and lay me low for walking away. For the love of fucks, you'd think I left to go pursue fashion design in the big city. And that thought does nothing but land Kate front and center in my mind.

I set the grocery bags down on the kitchen table, gritting my teeth to hold back a smart-ass comment that will get me nowhere. I've fought with enough crazy today; it's safer in the desert.

"Thanks," my sister Sophie says, looking way too tired to be bustling around the kitchen. "Heard you ran into Jess at the store. How'd that go?" She unloads the bags, sorting items Dana asked for as she does.

"You coming, Wyatt? Time you pitch in around here for a change," Wyatt Senior throws at me.

Yeah, there's not a damn thing wrong with the name Wyatt. I just hate the bastard I share it with.

Sophie looks up at me and shrugs before going back to her task. I don't know why I expected any help from her. My entire family is on board with wanting me to come home. More hands make for lighter work.

"Give me a minute to change," I huff out.

The fight is not worth it.

I grab my duffel and take it up to my old room. Not a damn thing has changed there in all the time I've been away. Well, almost nothing. Every single thing that came home from West Point with me is gone. My annuals, pictures, my cadet uniforms, and even my saber—all gone. The life I wanted, the things I accomplished with blood, sweat, tears, and determination have so little meaning to those who can't see beyond their own front door. I pray that I can find my things later—when I have time to sift through the closet, through boxes in the attic. For now, I bite my tongue, change into jeans, and shove my feet into my old work boots, noting that they're still here. The worn leather cleaned and conditioned.

Because ranch work has value. Being a soldier, not so much.

My old man is outside in the warm cab of his truck, smoking and glaring. Not at anything in particular. It's just his version of resting bitch face. Reluctantly, I climb in next to him. We ride in silence out to a remote line of fence that's needed to be fixed for years, my brothers-in-law nowhere in sight.

Throwing the truck into park and cutting the engine, my father barely glances my way. "Gloves and work coat're in the back," he grunts before he swings himself out and starts pulling supplies from the bed.

I lock down my anger and grab my work gloves and beanie, swapping out my jacket only because the one I brought really isn't for ranch work. But who the hell thought I'd be running fence wire before even saying hello and merry Christmas to my mother? If this is the game my old man wants to play, I'll fucking win.

Trudging through the snow, I get as far away from him as I can manage. Jaw clenched, not a single motherfucking curse passes my lips as I set to work, my mind churning over the shit day this has already been.

I work for hours, silently pulling and securing wire, ignoring the big fucking elephant that has parked his ass on the prairie between us. I've got nothing to say to the bastard. Not a goddamn word.

As the light fades, my phone pings, pulling me from my almost-meditative state. I drop my gloves and swipe the screen to see a message from Kate.

Kate: Have a fantastic visit home. Also ... got the all-clear from Aunt Flo. No mishap from the ill-fitting oops!

Thank Christ she's not pregnant. I'm not sure what I would have done with that. I tap out a quick reply and shove my phone back into my pocket because I swear on all that is good and holy, I will finish this job. Get well beyond the meet-in-the-middle point and show the old bastard that I can not only just hold my own, but I can also kick his ass while doing it. Fuck him and his claims of old-man strength.

The sky darkens as I fix the last of the wire and load the remaining supplies and tools in the back of the farm truck. I climb into the warm cab, debating on the benefits of riding back to the house, cradled in warmth but subjected to more stony silence, or freezing my ass off in the bed with the tools, blanketed under the stars twinkling in the clear sky. I don't hate Montana. I just never wanted to be forced into staying here.

When I'm back at the house, the night passes in a flurry of passive-aggressive bullshit, though the meal is good, evoking some of the few good memories of living here. Farm work makes a man a different kind of tired, and though I've humped my ass in and out of some hairy shit overseas, I fall into bed, exhausted.

It's not until well into the next morning that I realize that I forgot to hit Send. And, the minute I do, all hell breaks loose, and any thoughts of texting Kate fly out the window.

SEVENTEEN

Kate

A CASE OF THE blues, my ass.

Gracyn might have the blues, pining after the one who got away. But I'm thinking I could be coming down with something. You know that feeling when you're on the edge of having a stomach bug, and you just want it to kick in, so you eat like shit in hopes of getting it started, so you can just get over it? Yeah, I'm there.

Absences from school are always up this time of year, but we seem to be on the front edge of a stomach virus, and I am exhausted from sanitizing all the surfaces in my classroom. Add to that my genius idea of having a student of the week. Not a bad thing in and of itself, but this week's student was so excited that he didn't want to miss anything, so he didn't run to the restroom before reading time, and he peed all over the upholstered bench I'd brought into school this semester.

Needless to say, story time was cut short, and I need a damn beverage. I pull my phone from my desk drawer and about have my SOS text fully typed when one comes through from Gracyn, thinking she's had a week already. Bless her heart—and that one is totally of the bullshit variety. It's only Monday. I feel like I haven't seen my girls in forever, and let's face it; I really need that drink, so I hit her back, telling her I'm in, and thankfully, Lis can make it, too.

Lis is already set up at the bar when I walk into McBride's at four thirty. Her auburn hair twisted up in a messy bun, a pint of beer in her hand.

"Hey, sugar," I say, leaning in to give her a hug.

Finn reaches for my bottle of Patrón, but I wave him off.

"I think I'll just stick with beer today. Thank you though."

"Where've you been? I feel like I haven't seen you in forever," Lis says.

And it has been a while. I take a big pull of my pint and press my palm to my chest.

"You okay?"

I squinch up my mouth like I just sucked on a lemon and respond, "Yeah, mostly. Just a little icky in my tummy."

It'd be just my luck to get the stomach bug that runs through the elementary school about this time every damn year.

The door to the pub opens, letting in a blast of cold air. Finn tosses a coaster on the bar beside me and has a full pint ready to go by the time Gracyn dumps her jacket on the back of the barstool. And, even though she drains half of the glass in one shot, she declares that it's a whiskey night for her. We chat for a hot minute, laying out all the badness of the Monday-est of all Mondays. Lis, a nurse, got puked on by a patient; I share the love of my story-time adventures; and Gracyn mumbles about her bad week.

Then, Gracyn turns to me, saying, "How's it going with your mystery man? I feel like I haven't seen you since that night you were on your way out to meet him."

It's true; we have been kind of missing each other. A wave of longing washes over me, and I know that, if I don't lighten the mood, I might just let a tear escape. And that would be a whole lot more talking than I feel like doing just now. So, I go for funny and lewd because that's certain to keep the deeper questions at bay. I'm just not ready to go there yet. "Mmm ... he's good. Really fucking good." I let my accent out to play, and the words come out, all kinds of Southern-fried.

"Yeah?" Gracyn asks. Her side-eye game is strong tonight. She has a tendency to do that when she's avoiding her own mess. "Is he the one to break your bad luck?"

Has he ever. My stomach lurches when she asks if they'll get to meet him soon. Every cell in my body is yearning for him again, to feel his touch, to have him near. To know that he's safe.

I call to Finn and order a platter of whatever they have that's deep fried.

"Not gonna happen, darlin'," I tell her. "He's gone already. He, um ... he was here, visitin' between deployments. Took off back to one of the 'Stans—Kyrgyzstan, Kazakhstan—something like that. But it was lovely while it lasted."

Both Lis and Gracyn stare at me, dumbfounded, glasses paused midair.

Gracyn sets hers back on the bar and asks, "How did this happen? Where did you even meet him?"

"Y'all know how you were asking me about parent conferences? And if I met any hot, divorced dads?" I launch into talking about Jake and his enthusiasm for his uncle, and though I try to hide it, it's obvious they both know that Jake's my favorite student. I would make him student of the week every week if I thought I could get away with it.

Lis smiles at me, and Gracyn shakes her head as I talk.

"Uncle Jack came and had lunch with Jake, and, Gawd, the way he squished that big ole body of his into the kindergarten lunch table ... y'all just don't even know."

Thankfully, Finn interrupts, setting the food in front of us. "Gracyn, give us the deets on the shite at your office. I couldn't believe I missed the lead-up," he says, surveying the bar area for glasses in need of refilling.

I dig into the deep-fried carbs, dragging a chicken finger through the various dips before popping it into my mouth. According to Finn and Gracyn, there was a knock-down, drag-out fight at the accounting firm that Gracyn's dad owns.

Lis and Gracyn nibble on the platter of snacks, but it seems as though I'm the only one really putting the food down. And, thankfully, that's not too unusual for me.

Finn nods to a customer and pulls a fresh pint for him. When he settles back in front of us, he crosses his arms over his chest and jumps back into his story about the fight. "The bougie little prat started the whole thing," he says, absolutely incensed.

While I'm only half-listening, my stomach rolls again, and I have to concentrate on making sure it stays put. For a girl who can put away some serious alcohol, I am not a good puker. If I'm going to get sick, the last place I want it to happen is here at the pub. No, I'd much rather be home, in my clean bathroom where no one can hear me.

I'm considering leaving, just in case, when Gracyn swallows hard and grips the edge of the bar.

"You're sure?" she asks. "It was Gavin Keller? *The* Gavin Keller?"

Color drains from Gracyn's face, and I meet Lis's eye. I might be the queen of dating disasters, but Gracyn's been messing around for almost two years, trying to fight what's turned out to be true love with this guy. She's been busting her ass at work to get a couple of days off, so she can go see him in LA before his band, The UnBroken, leaves on their European tour. They've spent so little time actually with each other, and now, with his tour starting, it's going to be even more of a struggle.

I pull my phone out at the same time as Lis and type Gavin's name into the search bar, perusing the headlines.

"Holy shit, he missed the first show. *Tour musician stands in for Keller. Will this be a permanent change?*" I scan down the seemingly endless hits on Google, stopping on a blurb from gossip site, theBuzz. "Oh my Lawd, listen. *Gavin Keller was arrested and detained stateside on assault charges. Speculation is that Keller is taking after bandmate Kane Newton and tapping that which can be tapped.*" I look up at Gracyn's stricken face. "Sorry, probably should have stopped before I hit that last part." I shrug, but I have a feeling this is bad.

Gracyn stutters, starting and stopping a million questions to no one in particular. She pauses and almost looks like she might pass out for a minute. Out of nowhere, she screeches,

"That fucking bastard! He knew. He sat at that dinner, knowing full well how pissed I would be."

The grease-laden food suddenly too much for me, I lean back from the bar while Gracyn calls her slimy client every name in the book.

"I'm gonna have to tell my dad, and—"

Finn cuts her off, looking uncomfortable, "Gracyn, love, your da was there. He called the cops."

Lis flashes us a picture on Instagram from the client dinner Gracyn attended on Friday. It's bad. To anyone who hasn't been around Gracyn and heard the stories of this client, the fucking bastard, it looks like nothing short of an engagement photo. Her hand on his chest, face tilted to his smiling one, the two of them surrounded by their parents.

"Well, shit. That sure looks bad," I say.

I should have bitten my tongue instead because Gracyn drops her tumbler, glass shattering across the floor. Shards jump up and bite at my ankles, skittering off the leather of my boots.

Lis jumps from her seat as Gracyn sways on wobbly legs. I reach for her arm, wanting to steady her, offer support of some kind, but Gracyn braces her hands on the edge of the bar and shakes her head.

"Gracyn? Are you okay?" Lis asks.

I mean, we all *know* she's not okay. Who would be if your father had the man you loved thrown in jail for not being the one he'd chosen for you?

But my roommate doesn't say a word. She just stands there, knuckles turning white as she grips the scarred, lacquered oak. It takes Finn and a broom to finally drive her away from the spot she's anchored to.

I slide out of my seat and shrug on my coat, leaving the belt untied. The greasy food might have seriously done its thing because my stomach is rocking and rolling. But Gracyn needs me, so I shove those nasty feelings down, swallow hard, and vow not to let it get in the way of helping my friend.

"Let's go home," I say, handing Gracyn her jacket. "We have ice cream, vodka ..." *A clean bathroom in case I need to puke.*

Lis tucks some bills under her pint glass, and we somehow manage to get Gracyn out to my car.

"Gracyn, give me your keys," Lis says, her hand extended, palm up. "Aidan and I can get my car later." Her boyfriend is the stuff that romance novels are made of.

EIGHTEEN

Kate

THIS IS NOT LIKE any stomach bug I've ever had before. Sick but not. There but not really.

Queasy.

Icky.

Some days are worse than others, but none of them are ever really *great*.

"Sugar, you doing okay? You don't sound so good," Mama says on an early morning call.

Soft down pillows cradle my head and one foot rests on top of the comforter while the rest of me snuggles deep into the fluffy warmth. If I lie perfectly still, I might be okay. "I'm fine, Mama. Just tired," I croak, my throat dry from sleep.

My mother *tsks* at me. "I hope you didn't catch something from those babies in your class. Drink some juice, take your vitamins, and all that. We can't have you sick when you come home in a couple of weeks."

She's right. My sister-in-law has just stopped puking her

guts up from growing baby *número dos*. If I descend on all them and bring any kind of sickness with me, she just might kill me.

"I'll be healthy, I promise," I tell her. "I need to get up and shower, Mama. I'll talk to you later." I end the call and toss my phone to the middle of my bed. *Lord have mercy, I don't feel well.* I roll to my side and breathe through my mouth until the roiling subsides.

As I contemplate making the move to a sitting position, I run through my class roster, making mental notes on who has been sick lately and whether or not they wiped their hands on me or sneezed on me. Anything. I am nothing if not religious with the hand sanitizer for this very reason. I hate being sick.

I push myself up and count to ten. So far, so good. When I stand though, my stomach revolts, and I run to the bathroom, wrapping myself around the cool porcelain just in time to heave. And heave. And heave again.

"Kate, you okay?" Gracyn calls.

She's the second person to ask me that today, and the sun's not even up yet.

"Yep. 'M fine." Actually, I'm seriously starting to question whether or not I really am. I lean back against the tub, the tiled floor cold on my legs.

I tilt my head back and try to relax all the muscles in my core. Breathing carefully. Moving as little as possible. Stillness has become my new best friend. Finally, I pull myself up from the floor and rinse my mouth out, splashing some cool water on my face. I open the cabinet door to pull out a fresh towel and see an array of pads, tampons, all unused since ...

Since when? Christmas? Meh, I was in Mississippi for Christmas and used what I had there.

Side-eyeing myself in the mirror above the sink, I count the weeks since my last period and come up the same each time. It doesn't make sense. Period at Christmas, no sexy times since then, so I can't be ...

Lord, I can't even think the word.

"Coffee's made," Gracyn yells from the hallway.

I'm having a crisis here, and my roommate is yelling about coffee. The faint odor of it invades my senses, and I lurch for the toilet, retching one last time.

No. Nope. No.

I rinse my mouth again and start the shower, hoping the now offensive smell will have dissipated enough by the time I finish up in here to grab a piece of toast from the kitchen. Or a cracker. I don't know.

I know. I totally know.

By the grace of God, I manage to get myself together for work. Opting for a bottle of green tea and a sleeve of plain crackers to get me through the day.

I search my symptoms during rest time, and for the love of all that is good, I don't like what Dr. Google is telling me.

I can't be.

According to my newest enemy, it's entirely possible to have a period early in pregnancy, which would mean ... I'm—

Nope. I can't be.

I close my laptop and put my head down for a rest, too. Denial and avoidance are my two new best friends. I'm totally ostriching this thing I have going on. This is such a foreign feeling for me. After what went down with Chance, I've made a big damn effort to not stick my head in the sand anymore, to face everything head-on. That saying about leaving nothing to chance, I normally take that shit pretty seriously. But the prospect of this, this situation, scares the shit out of me.

By the time I get home, bypassing McBride's for some much-needed quiet and solitude, my nerves are frayed. I make my way through the apartment, putting things away as I go. My lunch bag in the kitchen, laptop on the coffee table. The peace and sense of order that these simple things usually bring me are nowhere to be found.

Shuffling into my room, I sink down onto my bed and heave out what should be a deep, cleansing breath. Instead, it comes out shakier than I wanted and does nothing to calm me. Not a damn thing.

The need to process—*I can't even bring myself to think the word*—this p-p-predicament without actually talking to someone is overwhelming. And the only person I really want to talk to about any of this is the one person I can't reach. The person who deserves to know before anyone else.

I could text him. But, with his Merry Christmas text being the impersonal brush-off it was, I'm pretty damn sure that, even if I could reach him, this news wouldn't really excite him. Instead, I pull a thick sheet of paper from the stationery box my mama gave me for my last birthday and settle it on the surface, lining it up perfectly parallel with the bottom edge. I run a finger along the slightly bumpy surface, noting the imperfect pattern of fibers in the handmade paper. Anything to avoid what will undoubtedly be a difficult letter for me to write.

Jack,

Lord, how do I even begin this? Remember when I told you we were good, nothing to worry about on the exploding-condom front? Turns out, that might have been a bit premature. I haven't taken a test yet. I'll be honest, I'm not sure I can. I need to sit with it, make peace, process the reality of this ... change in direction. I sure as hell did not think this would happen. I really want you to know that.

You were clear on the fact that a family was not something you planned on having. Your job is your focus, and I get that; I do. But, as scared as I am about being solely responsible for another human being, I'm going to do this. I want to do this. And, when you get back, if you want to share in this little surprise gift, I —we—will scoot on over and make room for you.

Be safe.

—Kate

I STARE at the simple words I scratched onto the paper, wondering what Jack will think when he reads them. If he reads them.

Fully aware that I'm not ready for Gracyn to stumble across this little nugget of information, I carefully fold it and look around my room. My gaze lands on the pile of untouched journals stacked on my bookshelf, the pretty red one from Jack solidly in the middle of the grouping. I ease it from where it sits, realigning the others so that they're centered in size order.

The soft, buttery red leather feels decadent beneath my fingertips. The gift both unexpected and absolutely cherished. I open the cover, careful not to abuse the spine. The cream-colored paper, lightly lined, beckons for words. Pleading to perform a special service. *How can I have seven beautiful journals and no words in them? Is it really marring the pages, to fill them?*

Decision made, I pick up my pen from where I tossed it moments ago and date the top of the first page.

Oops. Such a simple word, but all the holy cows can it be powerful, too! Only by one of the definitions, are you an oops though. A surprise? You know it. But I will never apologize for your existence, nor am I dismayed. I haven't confirmed that you're really there. I'm not quite ready to share you with the world in any capacity just yet. I want to keep you close, just the two of us, since your father isn't here. Lord, your father. I wish I could predict how he'd react to this whole thing, but, baby, I don't know. Whether he's with us or not, you and I are going to have an amazing adventure.

I TUCK my letter to Jack between the pages and set my pen aside. This might possibly be the only way my baby will ever know his or her daddy. The weight of that thought forces me into the stack of pillows at the top of my bed. I clutch the journal to my chest and stare out my window, streetlights casting small pools of light below.

It'll be okay.

I'll be okay.

We ... we'll be okay.

"HEY, WHAT'RE YOU DOING?" Gracyn asks, pulling me from a dream that ghosts as soon as my eyes flutter open. "You still not feeling well?" She leans against the doorframe, not venturing into what could be a sick room.

I don't feel great, but it's not like I'm contagious. "I'm fine, really. Just tired from the little darlings." I tuck my journal under the rumpled blanket on my bed, praying that the cranberry-red cover is somehow hidden under the snowy sea of white linens.

"Mmm, they hit their slump?" she asks, taking a seat in the chair by the window. "Are they acting up?"

Pushing myself up so that I can lean against the head-board, I tilt my head back and forth before answering. "They're somewhere between lawless heathens and full-out riot. The snow days aren't helping much either," I lament. "They need some damn consistency."

Gracyn purses her lips, nodding slowly, but avoids meeting my eyes. "I used to live for snow days," she says softly.

Something's up with her. Or maybe I should say something *more* is up with her.

After the bullshit with her accounting client and the cozy, completely misleading family picture he posted, she has been dealing with misunderstandings, bad timing, and more fallout than a person should ever have to. I know it's hard, with Gavin and his band touring Europe, but her world has completely been thrown ass end up.

"Has Gavin responded to any of your messages?" I ask gently.

Her lip pinched between her thumb and forefinger, she shakes her head.

"You givin' up on him?"

Gracyn snaps her head up, tears sparkling in the corners of her eyes. Her nostrils flare as she tries her best not to fall apart.

NINETEEN

Kate

"Nope. I'm going to do it," Gracyn says beaming.

I love her, but I'm worried about her. "Gracyn, he hasn't returned a single message. Hasn't texted, sent an e-mail. He hasn't called again. Nothing."

Is this a maternal-instinct kind of thing? When did I become the voice of reason around here?

I drop into my chair and hoist my feet up onto the edge of my bed, sinking low into the cushions. Reflexively, my hands settle low on my belly, and my eyes drift shut. I'm so damn tired.

"Tell me again what you're gettin' inked," I say.

She wants to talk for the first time in a long time, finally opening up a bit again after essentially mourning the loss of her job, walking away from her overbearing asshole of a father, and hearing nothing from Gavin while he was on tour. In fact, it's been a couple of weeks since our last chat, and nothing's really changed except Gracyn is decidedly less weepy and sprawled comfortably across my bed.

"Are you still feeling like shit?" Gracyn asks, eyes taking in where my hands are splayed.

"Nope," I lie. "Just relaxing." I twist the hem of my shirt in my hands, hoping that looks more natural, more chill.

She hums at me, her tell that she thinks I'm lying, but whatever. We're talking about her right now, not me.

"Right. So, you know how Lis went to the last show of the tour? When Aidan took her to Dublin to see his family? She recorded the last song that the band played, the one that hasn't been released."

She's watching me, her gaze skating over me while she talks. I stuff down an after-school yawn and try hard to look like I'm not about to pass out.

"Yep."

"The recording isn't the best, but I'm pretty sure it's the song he was working on in Central Park when he was serenading me." Gracyn shifts forward, pushing off of the headboard and scooting her ass to the center of my bed. Thankfully, the more she talks, the more distracted she gets, folding and creasing the fabric of my duvet, making small fan shapes and then smoothing them out again.

"But the words, Kate," she sighs. "The lyrics of that song absolutely speak to my soul. I know how badly I screwed this thing up with Gavin. Every step, right from the very start. That whole twenty-twenty hindsight is making me its bitch, but I want this. It's a way to always have a piece of him close to my heart, you know?"

Do I fucking ever.

"It's the last line of the song. *One kiss, and I was done.*

Baby, you're my one. In a simple script, maybe along my rib cage." She sits up straight, running her fingers just underneath her left boob.

Boobs. Mine are popping, big-time. I'm almost exclusively wearing sports bras at this point because it just feels better to have them locked in tight to me. No bounce, no movement. Nothing brushing against them.

"Kate? Did you hear me?" Gracyn asks, head cocked to the side and her eyebrow raised up high. Just the left one.

There's no use in trying to lie. She wants an answer to something, and I have no idea what she asked.

So, I suck it up and admit, "I didn't, sorry. I kind of blanked somewhere after you showed me where you want this permanently etched into your skin. But think about it, G. Tattoos are forever. What if he never speaks to you again? What if there is no forward for the two of you, and then you have to explain having the lyrics of what's inevitably going to be a wildly popular song inked by your heart to some other guy? That's going to be an awkward conversation. I'm just sayin'."

Gracyn's jaw tightens a bit as my words settle between us. "You don't understand, Kate. Your dude was here and gone again. Hell, you didn't even tell us that you were seeing him until well after he was gone." She shakes her head at me, annoyed. "You just enjoyed him and let him go. I know you want more. I know you do. But, until you've met someone and you can't imagine *not* having something of them to hold on to when they're gone, you're just not going to understand."

She pushes herself up off my bed and stalks out of my room. I'm tired and cranky, and I know it, but that was pretty bitchy for someone who has been moping around and making life around her miserable for the past several weeks.

Silence echoes through the apartment after Gracyn leaves, probably heading for McBride's for a shift behind the bar. I'm not sure how much longer she's going to be able to make her half of our rent. Since she walked away from her job, she's been trying to drum up small businesses to do their accounting and working whatever shifts she can get at the Irish pub, but I know money is tight for her. And, now, she's apparently dead set on dropping a chunk of change on a tattoo.

I wouldn't care, but I'm pretty fucking sure I'm going to have some big expenses coming up. I really can't deny it anymore and should probably make an appointment before my belly pops out for real and takes over my silhouette. So much to do. So many things to think about.

Hoisting myself out of the chair, I take my red journal from the drawer beside my bed and grab a pen. The letter to Jack marks the next blank page, about a quarter of the journal filled with everything I want this baby to know about his daddy. With thoughts and concerns about how I'm going to take care of him ... or her and the adventures we'll have. Lists of what I need to buy.

My sweet little Oops.

I'm guessing that, today, you're about the size of a fig. And I still haven't taken an actual test to confirm your existence. You're there though. Changing things up, making yourself known, if only to me still.

Auntie G is maybe losing her mind, but you'll see, when you meet her, that's pretty normal at times. I love her dearly, but today, I just want to string her up by her toes. I've about had enough of her thinking she's the only one dealing with heartbreak and troubles. We've all been there, and maybe—just maybe—she needs to open her eyes and really see what's happening around her. She's going through some things at the moment, so I'm trying to give her some grace.

So, here's your nugget of life advice. Be aware, baby. Your daddy is so good at that. Paying attention to the things going on around him. Observing things, reading people. I don't know if it's something just quintessentially him or if he cultivated it for his job, but he watches, sees things. He's a good man. You've got good genes, baby cakes. Seriously good genes.

EACH ENTRY in the journal reminds me again of all the things that drew me to Jack. All the reasons I took that chance on someone I had known was short-term. The fact that I got a lifelong souvenir from that carnival ride is just a surprise little bonus. One I'll have to tell the world about soon.

Tonight though, I plan on crawling into my fluffy bed with a big bowl of oatmeal for dinner and a book. I don't have the energy for much of anything else.

In the kitchen, I scroll through Twitter while my oatmeal

bubbles and cooks. There's nothing much there aside from the gossip and speculation on how The UnBroken's tour ended. Maybe Gracyn does have reason to be touchy about the shit in her life. There's no escape. No way for her to get away from it since Gavin's disappearance after the last show is all over entertainment news and Twitter.

My issues? I just have to stay away from the world news. And newspapers. And pray that one of my student's family members doesn't run into any problems. Because, if Jake's daddy finds himself in trouble, Jack will be right there in the thick of it as well.

I scoop my steaming oatmeal into a big bowl, sprinkling brown sugar and raisins on top and putting in a dash of cream and shake of cinnamon, and take it to my bedroom. I change into jammies and crawl under the covers. I try to read while eating, but juggling the bowl and holding my Kindle leaves me frustrated, so I give up my book. Not that it was holding my attention, but escaping into another world gives me a much-appreciated reprieve from my thoughts. I seem to be completely stuck on those.

Maybe, instead of grace, I need to give Gracyn some actual space. I have a couple of long weekends coming up, and while I'd still love nothing more than to just skip telling my mama and daddy that I got knocked up, it's something I need to do in person. Face-to-face so that they know I'm really okay and so that I can just face the music and be done.

I stir my dinner and scoop bite after bite into my mouth, savoring the sweetness of the toppings, praying that the starchy goodness will help calm my roiling stomach when morning comes. The spoon clatters in the empty bowl, and though I know it'll be a bitch to clean tomorrow, I set it on my bedside table to deal with in the morning. I make a mental to-do list for tomorrow while checking available flights home for the end of February.

BECAUSE I'VE ADJUSTED MY schedule over the past month or so to accommodate my new, less than fun morning routine, I'm out of the apartment bright and early the next morning. I woke up feeling better than I have in ages and only puked once. Who knew the day would come when I considered that such a win?

Gracyn is still asleep after working until closing at the pub, and that's probably a good thing. I need more than a minute to get myself past the things she said last night. The attitude and shit she's been throwing my way lately.

If I go straight to school though, I'll be crazy early. With a deep, bracing breath, I stop at the drugstore. It's time. I stroll down each aisle, putting an odd collection of items into my basket. Saltines, ginger ale, lemon drops, a pretty new nail polish. Anything to avoid having *just* a pregnancy test as my only purchase.

I pick a box, not giving too much thought to which one I grab. I sure as shit don't need one of the early detection tests. The results are pretty much written in stone, but as I move down the aisle toward the front of the store, I pass through the section of baby things. There are only the basics here, nothing cute and adorable, just the stuff you might grab in an emergency. Diapers, wipes, pacifiers. Teething gel, baby ibuprofen, thermometers. And a rattle.

I pause. A fuzzy lamb with the cutest little face, attached to a minty-blue plastic teething ring, catches my eye. It's absolutely silly, but looking at the items in my basket, it's not like there's any doubt about what's going on in my world. On a whim, I toss the lambikins in with the rest of my crap and get in line to pay. As if the cashier will give a shit.

When I get to school, I tuck the crackers and ginger ale into my lunch bag and the lemon drops and test in my tote. Not a soul is paying attention to me as I waltz through the door as nonchalant as can be. My secret mission, stuffed deep down in the center section of my Mary Poppins bag. I stop in the teachers' lounge on the way to my classroom, thanking God the restroom is completely empty—small favors for being so damn early.

There're no real nerves. No big anticipation. No counting the minutes or fear of turning the test over to read the results.

I know.

I've known for weeks. But seeing those two bright blue lines pop out mere seconds after I cap the end of the stick warms my belly and puts a big-ass smile on my face.

It's official. I'm pregnant.

TWENTY

Kate

__You know when you__ do something, thinking you have your poop in a group? And then, at some point in the middle of the whole thing, when it's too late to turn back, you realize you might have made a mistake? Like, maybe I should have made a doctor's appointment before getting on the plane to tell your grandparents about you. Okay, I made the appointment, and I asked if it was okay to fly, but it's not like the doctor has seen us. So, even though the nurse said it was fine, how do I really know that it is? What if I'm ruining you? Lord, I'm already the worst mama in the history of the world.

I bite at the end of my pen as the plane hits a bubble of turbulence and say a little prayer. I'm such a fool. Such an idiot. Barely contained panic pushes me to flip to a fresh page in my journal and apologize to Jack for screwing up our kid. This was so dumb. I should have at least asked Lis; she's a nurse, for Pete's sake. I have a nurse as one of my best friends and didn't ask her a simple question because I'm a fucking idiot.

"Ma'am? Can I get you anything?" A flight attendant crouches down next to my seat.

She hands me a small packet of tissues, and it's only then that I realize I have tears spilling down my face. These hormones are stupid. Because that's got to be the reason for this ridiculous show of emotion.

"Thank you," I say, pulling a tissue from the plastic package. "I'm—I'll be fine. It's just a little ..."

The plane dips again, and my hand drops protectively to my stomach. I haven't puked in almost a week, and it would be a huge step backward if I started again now.

"Maybe a couple of packets of pretzels and some ginger ale," she suggests. "It helped me when I was pregnant." She pats my arm and hurries to the galley at the front of the plane. When she returns a few minutes later, it's with a glass of ice and a green aluminum can in one hand and several packages of pretzels in the other.

"How did you know?" I ask, tearing open one of the tiny snack packs. My stomach churns, but I'm not sure if it's hormones, emotions, or flat-out fear.

What if my father takes one look at me and knows? I need to be able to tell them in my own way. To make them understand that it was nothing but a slip-up and one that I'm already so in love with.

The flight attendant sets the full plastic cup in front of me and says, "I had to work through my pregnancy, and, honey, that turbulence can be a bitch. That look on your face was a permanent fixture on mine for a long time." She taps a nail on my tray next to my cup. "Sip at this while you can. We'll be landing shortly."

"KATELYN, DARLING, YOU LOOK different. Can't tell if you look like you've been sick or if you're filling out a little," my mother says over dinner later.

Neither option makes me feel all that good about myself.

"Thanks, Mama."

"I think you look good with a little meat on you," my father says, patting my hand.

Setting my fork down, I fold my hands in my lap. Now is the time to tell them. "Since y'all seem to be all over how I look and whether I'm sick or not—"

"Hey, we make it in time for dessert?" my brother calls, busting through the back door.

Harper flings herself into my arms, crushing me in her sweet little hug.

"Auntie Kate, I missed you." She kneels on my lap, squishing my face between her palms.

Sam and Jules settle in at the kitchen table, and for a brief moment, I relax, getting lost in catching up with them and all the things going on in their lives.

"It's not convenient with your teaching schedule, but we would love for you to come down if you can. The baby's due in the middle of September. Maybe, if I go early, it could be Labor Day weekend," Jules says.

"Oh, wild horses couldn't keep Katelyn from being here for that baby's birth. Isn't that right?" Mama smiles from the side of her mouth and reaches for my hand. Her gaze finally reaches me, taking in what I'm sure is pure guilt carved across my features. "Kate, baby, are you okay?"

"Darlin'?" The endearment rolls off my daddy's tongue, concern lacing his voice.

And all I can do is nod at my parents. Press my lips together and nod my head like the fool I am for thinking this is all going to be okay.

How am I going to do this? How am I going to have a baby all by myself? How the hell am I going to tell my family that I'm pregnant and the baby's father not only isn't in my life, but I also can't reach him? That I don't know if I'll ever see him again?

"I, um ... I promise I'll do my best but ..." My heart slams against my ribs, and for the first time in my entire life, I'm truly afraid of my family's reaction to my news. Fucking petrified.

How the hell am I going to make this okay? I'm sure my grandma Rose is fixin' to roll over in her grave.

"Auntie Kate, Mimi says you can say anything here 'cause family gonna love you, no matter what." Harper dispensing advice handed down to her from my mama with all the seriousness she can muster shifts my heart right back where it needs to be to get the words out.

"You're right, Harper," I say, smoothing back her curls and pressing my lips to her sweet little forehead. Her lotion, the baby shampoo Jules still uses on her, fills my senses and sets me right. "I might not be able to travel then because, uh ... I have found myself in a similar situation." For some damn reason, talking around the matter and not coming right out and saying it feels like maybe I'm not just talking over Harper's head, but my parents' heads as well.

Sam and Jules are fine. I'm not worried about any kind of judgment from them in the least, but my daddy ...

"What now?" Daddy asks, chin tucked to his chest, eyebrows high as a kite.

"What are you sayin'?" Mama sits straight up in her chair, hands fluttering, twisting her wedding ring around her finger.

Sam snorts, his shoulders shaking with laughter. That boy is always giddy at the slightest possibility of me being the kid in trouble with our 'rents.

Pointing my finger right at Sam, I say, "Just you stop it, you ass."

A giggle bubbles up inside me, threatening to break free regardless of how serious this stupid moment is. Sam's face is bright red, eyes squeezed shut, hands clutching the edge of the kitchen table. It's like time has rolled right on back to when we were kids, and I tried to talk my way out of whatever trouble was coming my way for "washing" Daddy's truck with a steel wool scrubber so that it would be extra clean. I'm in trouble, and my stupid brother can't stop laughing at me.

"Katelyn Hays Beard, you watch your mouth, young lady," Mama admonishes.

Sam and Daddy both mumble, "Brought you into this world, and I can take you out," and all the stress over telling everybody my news flies away.

My family has never *not* been there for me. Never. There's no way my worst fears will come true. It's another grandbaby, and there is nothing but love in the Beard household for sweet little babies.

"Are you trying to tell us you're ..." Mama nods her head and rolls her hand through the air, not saying the word.

But I can totally understand that because I haven't said it out loud yet either. I sit up straight and fold my hands on the table in front of me. "Actually, Mama, I'm doing my honest best *not* to tell you. But it is true." There's no point in pretending any longer. This is what I came home to do.

"You and Chance are back together?" she asks, looking at me over the top of her glasses. It's her signature *are you tellin' stories* look.

Another laugh surfaces, bubbling up from my toes this time. "Chance is gay," I tell them matter-of-factly. "He was supposed to have told y'all by now. In fact, he told me he was bringing his boyfriend home to meet his parents over Valentine's Day. I take it, that didn't happen?"

My mother looks stunned, but Daddy and Sam just nod, like they've known all along.

"But—"

"He asked me to keep his secret until he broke it to his mama and daddy, but that was supposed to happen ages ago. So, no, Mama, it's not Chance's baby."

"Whose is it?" Daddy grumbles, and I swear, he's shifting his weight to go grab his shotgun. "Where the hell is this new guy, and why haven't we heard anything about him besides the fact that he knocked up my baby girl and isn't man enough to come here with you to tell us about it?" Yeah, his hand is itching to sift through his ammo boxes.

On a deep, bracing breath, I explain that I met him through school.

"So, he's another teacher. What grade?" My mother jumps up, clearing dishes from the table.

I eye the fudge cake she made, hoping she doesn't try to send me to bed without dessert.

"Actually, he was having lunch with one of my kiddos." The cake knife clatters to the counter as my mother whips her head up to gawk at me. "No, no, no. Don't give me that look, Mama. He was home, visiting his nephew—kind of nephew—between deployments and—"

"Deployment? So, he's in the service," my father interrupts, respect lacing his words.

"Yes, sir. Special Forces," I offer. Because, though I know that's impressive, it's really the extent of what I know about his job. "He's in the desert for a couple of more months. I don't know where he'll be after that. He doesn't know about … this. I can't really reach him," I mumble.

Now that it's out there, now that people know, I wish more than anything that I could talk to Jack. Why didn't we exchange e-mail addresses? At the very least, I could have e-mailed. But how is that any different from texting him? Either way, it's just a message that he'll get, or maybe he won't. Hell, I couldn't even conceive of telling my parents over the phone. I'm a face-to-face girl, for sure. And I'm right back to wondering what I would even say.

The silence in the kitchen is deafening. Even Harper has muffled her usual chattiness, giving me the toddler version of the same appraising look gracing everyone else's faces.

Time stretches interminably, achingly slow.

My heart sinks, and I just want to crawl into bed and cry.

The hormone flip that goes along with being pregnant is a bitch. Now that I'm not puking at random moments, I feel like I'm always on the verge of breaking down and crying. Tears burn behind my eyes, and I pull in a shaky breath.

Jules leans over, reaching for my hand. "Are you gonna find out what you're havin', or do you want to be surprised?" she asks.

"You mean, more surprised?" my brother blurts.

And, finally, it's like everyone just resets and comes back to what's important.

"We're going to have two new babies for Christmas," Mama says, a big cheesy grin stretching across her face.

At this, Harper bounces up, running to her mimi. "I gettin' two babies?" she asks, her thumb pressing down on her pinkie.

Mama tucks Harper's ring finger down for her, showing her what two looks like. "Sampson, you need to work with your daughter on her numbers."

After the initial shock wears off and I talk my daddy out of trying to call up Fort Bragg, we get kind of excited.

MAMA, JULES, AND I spend the rest of my long weekend shopping, looking at all the cutest baby things.

"Well, I think you should find out what you're havin'," Mama declares. "You're a planner, Kate. And, being that you're doing this on your own, you need to be organized. We can't be buyin' pink if we're havin' blue, and Lord knows, we've got to get your nursery goin'." She does that looking-over-the-top-of-her-glasses thing again. I've been getting more than my fair share of that nonsense, but the real issue?

"And, honestly, you should just move home, sweetie. There's no better time."

"Not making that decision right now. I've told you that."

New York has become my home, and I really don't want to think about not being able to watch my students grow up and progress. One of my favorite things is having my kiddos from my first year teaching there come in and be reading buddies to the current class. This is the first time that's happened, and it's been just amazing.

"You can still teach here, and I'll get to snuggle both of my new grandbabies. Harper can be my helper. We'll just have a grand ole time."

Lord have mercy, I love my mother, but I'm not sure I can live in the same town as her anymore. Next thing you know, she'll have me moving into my old room.

Like she was reading my thoughts, she continues, "And we can make Sam's old room into the nursery, so the baby is good and close to you."

"Not happenin'. *If* I come back to Hattiesburg, I won't be movin' back in with you and Daddy," I tell her, flipping through a rack of sleepers. "But that's a big *if*."

Mama tries several more times, dropping hints, pinning nursery ideas to her Pinterest board, and even leaning on my father for an extra kick of guilt. By the time I get on my plane to head back north, I'm exhausted but feeling more at peace than I have in weeks. Now, I need to spill my shit to Lis and Gracyn.

TWENTY-ONE

Kate

A LOT CAN HAPPEN in four days. A person can go from being petrified of breaking news to family to making plans for matching monogrammed onesies for Christmas pictures. And your roommate can go from forlorn and downright depressed to getting a tattoo under her boob of lyrics to a song to hooking back up with the man of her dreams.

"And he even said he'd play at McBride's for St. Patrick's Day as long as we don't advertise that it's him. God, he's just so—"

"Not-your-typical rock star," I finish for Gracyn as she flops back on our couch.

"So true." She rolls her head to the side as a yawn rips from my body. "You gonna be there?"

There's no way I can go to the Irish pub on St. Patrick's Day and *not* drink and have it go unnoticed. "Maybe. I'll try, but I feel pretty behind at school, so—"

Gracyn hits me with a look. I've blown my friends off far

too many times in the past couple of weeks; if she didn't have her own hot mess of shit to deal with, she'd be up my butt, demanding to know what was going on with me. As it is, she just seems perplexed, like maybe she's missing something.

"Mmhmm. Hey, did I tell you the potter you fell in love with on your pre-Christmas mountain trip contacted me to do his accounting?"

Thank God for the change of subject. "You didn't. How did he find you?"

Gracyn pushes herself up off the couch and skips across the room toward the hallway. "I guess he's doing the whole small-business thing, rebranding or something. He had Addie do a website, and she referred him on to me. That girl has been a really good addition. We should hang out with her more."

"We should," I agree.

Finn stepped in it when he convinced Addie to give him a chance, not that he didn't have to work damn hard to convince her. But there are no two people more suited for each other.

"You going to bed already?"

It's early for Gracyn, but I feel like I could pass out in a heartbeat.

Not even trying to hide her giddy excitement, Gracyn twirls—freaking twirls—as she inches farther away. "Sort of. Gavin's in LA for one more night, so we're going to"—she waves her hands in the air—"chat for a bit."

Her thousand-watt smile lights up the room, and I couldn't be happier for her. From what she's told me, she and Gavin have finally found a way to be together. All their mess is getting worked out, and they are for reals dating now, actually dating as opposed to the running-away and then long-distance crap they did.

"Have fun, sweetie. Make good choices," I call.

"*Pffft*. What could happen? Not like we're having reckless sex all over the place."

Sometimes, the unexpected just kicks you in the ass.

AND, A MERE HANDFUL of days later, the truth of that thought darkens the doorstep of McBride's Public House. The pub owner's death took everyone by surprise. Francie, the man who selflessly took care of so many, making a small family of misfits, evidently didn't want to burden anyone with his illness. Sneaking off for a rest late in the evening on St. Patrick's Day, he went into his office by the stockroom. Gracyn was devastated when she found him hours later, splayed across the floor, already gone.

Francie was known for taking in strays and giving them a purpose. In fact, until Gracyn walked away from her family's accounting firm and offered to lend him a hand, Francie only employed young men from Ireland who'd found themselves wandering, in need of a soft place to land. His business model of hot men with a brogue kept the bar full, the beer flowing, and the drama low. Not that Gracyn amped up any drama when she started tending bar. That was just a matter of Francie's health failing and him needing another set of hands before his favorite holiday. The fact that he passed on the day he did, knowing that he had helped one of his surrogate kids, just made the whole thing even harder.

Aidan might have known Francie the longest, but Finn, Lis, and Gracyn were hit the hardest. Francie was the father each of them had seemed to be missing in life. I didn't have the same relationship with Francie as the others, but they say funerals are not for the dead, but for the living. My friends here have made me feel more welcome, more a part of their tight-knit family than the group I grew up with or even my sorority sisters ever could, and I thought we were close.

"Gracyn, you ready?" I ask softly.

"Not in the least," she replies, sniffling.

The last three tissues pull free at the same time, leaving the box itself to tumble to the counter. I set the empty box in our recycling bin, replacing it with a fresh one.

With my tote bag on the counter, I sift through the contents, adding several travel packs of tissues, mints, and a water bottle. "It's time, G. We need to get going."

"How am I going to do this? I can't say good-bye to him. I just can't," she says, fresh tears thickening her words. "He was more of a father to me in the last couple of months than mine was in the twenty-four years he had. God, Francie was always there for us. How ..."

"I know, babe. Come on. Let's go honor him."

I reach for her hand, pulling her into a hug. Gracyn squeezes me and shuffles out the door of our apartment while I throw on my raincoat, grab one for Gracyn, and sling my tote bag over my arm. I push down the wooziness that seems to be lurking just on the fringe today and slip into the car waiting at the curb.

Gavin turns, extending his hand through the front seats. "Kate, right? Good to finally meet you. Wish it were under different circumstances though."

I shake his hand, noting the way his eyes soften when he glances at Gracyn.

At the cemetery, he hops out of the car and gathers his golden hair back into a perfectly messy bun, one I wish I could accomplish on the regular. The lead guitarist for The UnBroken is gritty and gorgeous onstage, but in a dark suit, he's on an entirely different level. I wonder what Jack would look like in his uniform, rumpled, coming back from a mission. The formal one reserved for special occasions. More and more, I find myself wishing he were really a part of my life and not just a fleeting thing.

We gather at the graveside, each of my friends supported by their person—Gracyn and Gavin, Lis and Aidan, Finn and Addie. And then there's me. I tuck my hands into the pockets of my coat, using the fabric to mask how I splay them across my belly, the need to feel Jack close to me in this moment almost overwhelming.

I've been camouflaging my changing figure. Big sweaters and A-line shirts, leggings and jeans with the top button popped. Hell, I'm a little surprised I was able to get my black dress closed, though I'm sure this will be the last time I can wear it for a while. Thank God funerals are not a common thing in my world. I should be done cooking this kiddo and back to my normal size before I have to do this again.

Thoughts like this—clothes, random things—distract me from the cold, from the sadness. From my utter loneliness.

The world tilts and spins, the ground threatening to rush up at me. I should've eaten something this morning, I know better than to trust the relative newness of not leaving the house with an empty stomach.

Father Callahan lifts his head, meeting my eye as the final strains of "Amazing Grace" float off into the wind, and I can't help feeling like I've been caught doing something wrong. I was raised in the church, not Catholic, but still, I know I should've had my head down, eyes closed. But, the minute I took that stance, I felt ill. Sick and more than a little woozy, but I shoved that shit down because this is not about me. My friends, the family that I've found far from my own, are grieving today. This is their good-bye.

My heart breaks at the loss of Francie McBride, but there is no way—no fucking way—I'm going to steal from him in this moment. Francie was like a father to my friends Lis and Gracyn and especially Finn.

Swallowing my misery, I brace as my stomach does another untimely flip and roll. *Deep breath in, slowly blow it out. Deep inhale, slow release. I'm okay. I can make it through the service, and then I'll go home to bed.*

With tears tracking down her face, Gracyn reaches a hand toward me. I quickly grasp it, giving her a squeeze, thankful for the grounding contact. Caretaker tendencies and distraction come together in that moment, and I dig into my bag, passing out packages of tissues. Anything to keep myself from falling apart as unbidden tears flood my cheeks. I'm not a crier. Never. Not at sad movies, not when I read. I just don't, and today, they just won't stop.

"You okay?" Gracyn asks, leaning in close.

I just nod, afraid to open my mouth because, at this stage, I'm either going to bawl my eyes out—and I'm without a doubt not a pretty crier—or I'm going to hurl. And no one appreciates it when someone pukes at a funeral. That's just bad manners.

"Kate? Honey, you don't look good. Are you going to ..." Lis, a nurse, leans in from my other side, assessing me as the priest continues his homily. Her hands flutter over me, taking my pulse, checking for a fever. "G, get the water bottle from her bag," she directs.

Gracyn rummages through my Mary Poppins bag and pulls out my water bottle, twisting off the lid. I reach for it, taking a tentative sip, praying silently that my nausea doesn't choose this solemn moment to rear its ugly head again.

A chair appears, seemingly out of nowhere, and I sink into it, dropping my head into my hands. "I'm sorry," I mumble, sipping at the water bottle Gracyn thrust into my hands.

Bagpipes keen and groan, their sad melody echoing across green hills. The remnants of an early spring shower chill the air as it swirls around the small crowd gathered on the hillside. When the service is done, when handfuls of dirt have been tossed into the open grave, and the cemetery is all but empty, Lis and Gracyn turn to me.

"You going to make a doctor's appointment, or am I going to drag you in?" Gracyn demands. "I know I've been kind of preoccupied lately, but I haven't missed you still feeling like shit. The way it comes and goes, how long has this been going on? Either the kids in your class really are cesspools of germs or you need a little boost to get over this and get healthy again."

"I made one. I'm going in tomorrow—in the morning, I think." In fact, it's at precisely nine in the morning. I prepped my substitute plan as soon as I made the appointment and am finally ready to do this and face the facts.

"Who's the doctor? Do you want me to try to get you in sooner with someone else?" Lis offers. "Or I can go with you. I have the day off."

We've all been so scattered, wrapped up in our own lives lately. I've missed my girls.

I brush more of the never-ending tears away and smile tightly. "I'll be okay, really. You need to sleep in once in a while, loll in bed with your sweet man." I squeeze Lis's hand and nod toward Aidan. "Let him take care of you. I'll let y'all know when I'm done."

I hug Gracyn and say, "I'm going to go. I'll grab an Uber and crawl into bed. Please raise a glass to Francie for me, okay?"

"We will, but let us drop you at home. And I'll bring you a plate from the pub later," she insists. "Gavin, will you grab the car, babe?" She pulls my hand through her elbow, and we walk slowly toward the tree-covered lane that snakes through the cemetery grounds.

AS SOON AS MY zipper releases and my dress falls to the floor, all the ickiness I was feeling earlier dissipates. Like the minor constriction around my middle was just way too much. I pull Jack's big, soft T-shirt over my head and slide on flannel PJ pants that are so soft and cozy it's like wearing nothing at all.

It's only late afternoon, but with all the emotion of the day, I crawl into bed, not even bothering with my journal. I'll have all the details tomorrow after my appointment.

TWENTY-TWO

Kate

I'VE KNOWN DEEP DOWN inside. Of course I've known, but I didn't want to face it because, once you acknowledge something like that, say it out loud, it's real. And this just became all kinds of real.

"Let's just see what we've got here," the nurse says as she moves the wand around on my belly. "We should get good heart sounds since you're thinking maybe your first trimester is up." She poses the statement like there's no question, or maybe it's a touch of judgment. That's not something I'm going to worry about at the moment. I have enough on my plate as it is.

The room fills with a rhythmic whooshing, and there's no question that it's my baby's heartbeat I'm hearing. That's my little Oops, thrumming away. I smile at the nurse, expecting to get the same right back, but as she moves the wand and tilts her head, a bad feeling washes over me.

"That's it, right? That's my baby's heartbeat?" I ask, worry seeping into my voice.

She hums a noncommittal sound and sets the wand on the counter, her mouth a tight line. "I'll just go get the doctor, so she can chat with you." And she's out the door before I have a chance to ask anything further.

Tears sting the backs of my eyes. This is my fault. I drank wine and tequila in the mountains with Jack. I flew home for Christmas and drank my fill there. I have drowned this child in alcohol and bad decisions before it—he? she maybe?—ever had a chance. I should have come in as soon as I suspected I was pregnant. I should have had some kind of maternal inkling that made me make better choices. I should have *something*.

Dr. Delaney walks in, all smiles, and rests a calming hand on my shoulder. "Hey, Kate. Isn't this a surprise?"

"Yeah." I swipe at the gathering tears. "Is everything okay though? We were listening to the heartbeat, and the nurse got real quiet and then didn't say anything other than she was going to get you. Oh my God, did I ruin it? Is my baby okay?" My words come out in a rush, desperation crawling up my spine.

"Let's take a peek, okay?" She pulls over a sonogram machine and squeezes a glob of warm gel on my stomach.

I close my eyes, afraid to look. Petrified by what I'll see, of what she'll say. The same whoosh that I found so exciting a few minutes ago now fills me with dread. There's an echo and a skip, not the solid thump-thump of a well-defined beat.

"Well, there we are," Dr. Delaney singsongs. She chuckles softly, moving the wand, clicking at the attached keyboard. "Looking good, Mama. You're gonna have your hands full in a couple of months. Oh, Kate, honey, open your eyes. Look at your babies."

Babies?

I pop one eye open, afraid to commit fully to looking at the screen. "Oh ..." Hot tears tumble down my face. Babies. Two of them. "There're two?" And that's just proof that there is such a thing as dumb questions because I'm lying here, looking at the tiny little aliens bouncing on the screen.

"Two. Can't tell yet whether they're going to be pink or blue yet, but you've got two healthy-looking babies measuring in right around fifteen weeks, give or take a couple of days." She prints off a stack of pictures and wipes the goo off me, handing me extra paper towels to finish the job.

I put myself back together, only half-listening to what the doctor is saying. *What the hell am I going to do? I can't do twins on my own, can I? Since Gracyn's moving in with Gavin, I'll have the room, but there is so much more to consider, to plan for. I need my planner. I need to sit down and see the schedule for the rest of the school year, figure out what needs to happen when. I need to tell my friends. And I need to cry. Holy shit, what am I going to do?*

"Any other questions?" Dr. Delaney asks, drying her hands and chucking the paper towel into the garbage can.

I look around the room, realizing how much I've missed in the past few minutes. The exam room is tidied up; the nurse has come and gone, leaving a gift bag on the counter by the sonogram pictures; and evidently, I missed an entire conversation as well. My heart sinks when I think that this is why there is supposed to be two parents at these things.

Holy fuck. I'm knocked up. With twins.

Blowing out a deep breath, I blink a few times and say, "I

have so many. But I think I need to process this, let it settle in my brain. Can I call the office in a day or so? I, uh … this wasn't planned."

"Absolutely. We'll see you in a month, but call us anytime." She reassuringly squeezes my hand and adds, "Congratulations, Kate. It's going to be fine."

I manage to hold my tears at bay until I'm tucked into my car, the heater running at full blast. Only as I touch the heart of Baby A and then Baby B on the sonogram image do I let the tears fall freely. Once again, life has thrown me for a loop, smacked me upside the head. There is no way past this, but through it. So, I dry my eyes, blow my nose, and send an SOS text, asking Gracyn and Lis to meet me. Gracyn responds that they are both at McBride's.

"HEY." Lis hugs me tight. "What did the doctor say? You went today, right?" She holds me at arm's length, taking note of my puffy eyes and red nose. "Oh, Kate, what is it?"

Lis pulls me to a barstool, and Gracyn reaches for my bottle of tequila, setting it on the bar in front of me. I reach out and place my hands on either side of the bottle.

"It's going to be more than a minute before Mr. Patrón and I spend any quality time together again," I say quietly. If I had my shit together, I'd have done something super Pinteresty to tell these girls that they're going to be aunties. Instead, I release the bottle, bidding it a silent farewell, and reach into my bag.

"Kate"—Gracyn pulls the bottle away from me—"did your sailor knock you up while he was ashore?" Her brows are high, eyes wide.

"He's in the Army," I remind her and set the stack of black-and-white photos on top of the bar.

Gracyn scoops them up, sifting through, handing each one to Lis as she goes. "Oh my God, he did. You're having a baby," she exclaims, cheeks pulled up in a cheesy grin.

"She's having two." Lis looks from the last sonogram picture to me and back again. Sifting through the photos a second time, she sets them down on the bar. "How long have you known?" She fixes me with the same kind of glare that the OB nurse gave me. The one that's assessing and a touch judgy. The one I've been dreading.

"A bit." I spread the pictures apart, pausing on each. Those are my babies.

"Totally makes sense," Gracyn says, placing a glass of water in front of me. "You've been weird, didn't come in for ..." Her voice trails off as she looks to the framed black-and-white photo on the wall behind the bar. She sniffs and continues, "I still can't believe he's gone."

I reach for her hand. "Gracyn, I'm so sorry—"

"Nope, not going there right now. We're celebrating babies." She stills and looks at me—like, looks at me hard. Then, slapping both palms on the bar, Gracyn cackles. "Holy shit, you're pregnant."

No shit.

"Have you told ..."

"Jack," I offer Lis, feeling bad that my best friends don't know anything about the man who changed my world. I shrug, continuing, "I can't. He's deployed."

"FaceTime? E-mail? He doesn't have an international phone?" Gracyn asks. "Gavin called from somewhere over there when he was on tour."

"It was a fling, short-term. Surely, you of all people understand that." I look pointedly at Gracyn.

Gavin was her spring break fling. And they went their separate ways, no contact until they ran into each other a year and a half later.

"But you met him at school, right?" Lis pipes in. "His nephew? Or friend's kiddo is in your class? Can you get ahold of him that way?"

I pick up the picture with both babies, the one that has their little alien bodies in profile. "They're Special Forces. Communication isn't really an option. Jake and his mom hardly ever get to talk to Tripp. God, and the last thing I want to do is have his best friend's wife know before he does. That's just too much drama and shit."

Gracyn pushes my water glass toward me. "You're not going to be hiding that for long. Especially not if there're two in there."

She's right. She's totally right, but I don't even know if Jack told Jake's dad that we were seeing each other. I asked him not to, to keep things quiet, and I just assumed he would. Why, if this was just a hookup while he was on leave, would Jack have told anyone?

"I don't know. I can't think about that right now. I need to process this. Go home and figure out what to do. Are you staying with Gavin tonight, G?"

"I don't have to. Do you want me to come home?"

I shake my head. "No, you're good. Spend time licking your man's tattoos. I'm going to bed early anyway, I apparently am growing a couple of humans." *Jesus, that sounds ridiculous when I say it out loud.* "Thanks, y'all. I, um ... I don't know what I'd do without you." I hug Lis and lean over the bar for Hollywood cheek kisses with Gracyn. "Love you."

I slide off the barstool and safely tuck the stack of pictures into my bag. As I toss a wave over my shoulder, the exhaustion hits. I drag my ass home, and as soon as I can, I crawl under the covers.

I click on the television and flip through the channels before turning it off again. There is no joy in reality TV, cooking shows, or watching people hunt for their dream homes. And I absolutely can't watch the news. Past attempts had me hyperventilating at the slightest mention of American troops.

Instead, I pull out my journal and smooth it across my bended knees. I hope that Jack will want to experience this pregnancy with me, but for now, this is the best I can do.

Flipping the creamy red leather cover open, I find the next blank page and grab a colored pen—dark purple for today's entry. Nothing like color-coding my feelings.

I wasn't just a little bit wrong. Darlin', I was way wrong. Went to the doctor today because Lis had insisted, and really, it was time. Hell, I wasn't even fooling myself anymore. And surprise, surprise, I'm pregnant. Yeah, that's on me.

Itty-bitty condoms were no use with your big, stupid dick, but I'm telling you, Jack, I sure as shit didn't see this coming. Twins, friend. Twins. Did they hit you with radiation or something to give you super sperm? Is that a government secret? Super-soldier stuff? You're my very own Captain America.

Lis thinks I should try to reach you through Chloe, but ... I don't know ... it feels wrong. Like a breach of trust or something.

I have pictures, Jack. Two little alien babies. The doctor marked them Baby A and Baby B. Since I've been calling the possibility of one Oops, I'm just going to go ahead and bless the extra with the name Uh-Oh. Next visit, they should be able to tell me whether they are pink or blue.

Sweet baby Jesus, we're having twins.

TWENTY-THREE

Kate

I'm doing things out of order, and that bugs the shit out of me. But I guess I've done this whole thing backward, and Mrs. Altman, my school's principal, was nothing but supportive when I told her what was going on. I mean, I did skate around plenty of the finer details, but those stories really are best kept quiet, shared only with my closest friends, if at all. Poor Lis would probably be horrified if she heard about trying to get that busted condom off of Jack. No, that's probably a story not to tell.

"What's the news? It feels like it's been forever since we chatted. You doing okay?" Jenny asks as I shut Mrs. Altman's office door behind me.

Suddenly, I feel the weight of the world on my shoulders, and I slump into the plush office chair usually reserved for the moms who volunteer in the front office. "It has been a while, more than a minute." I pause, knowing I'll confide at least a little bit in Jenny. The question is, how much do I tell her?

She's one of the few people in my life who has actually met Jack. And, because she's got her finger on the pulse of everything that happens in this school, she also knows that he's tied to Jake and his family.

"As far as news is concerned—"

"I'm so sorry, Kate. I heard about that nice man who owned the pub you and your friends hang out at." Jenny pats my knee, continuing, "My aunt Louise and her friends go there after they do their thing at the community center—some computer class or tai chi or something. For a while, I thought one of the ladies might have had a thing for the owner, but turns out, they all had a bit of a crush on one of the bartenders."

I chuckle, thinking on all the ladies, young and not, who have had a crush on that bartender because, really, it can only be one to whom she's referring. "Mmm, Finn has quite the following, but, yeah, Francie was a shock. One of many in the past month or so."

Jenny pushes back from her desk and cocks her head, brows drawn together as she waits for me to continue.

"I just told Mrs. Altman, so it's, um, not really a secret anymore, but ..."

"Oh, Kate, you're not leaving us, are you?" she asks, palm pressed to her chest.

There's time to make that decision, so I don't really have an answer for her question. "I don't think so. But ..." I pause, feeling all kinds of self-conscious once again. "Well, I'm, uh ... pregnant," I say quietly, bracing for her reaction.

And bless her, Jenny shows no shock, no judgment.

Nothing other than a genuinely excited smile lights up her features. "Oh, sweet girl. Well, that is exciting news. Maybe a bit unexpected?" she asks.

"Yeah, it is. For such a planner, I didn't really see this coming."

"A baby is wonderful. You'll do great, I'm sure. When are you due? Do I know the lucky man?"

And isn't that the million-dollar question?

I heave out a sigh and flop back into the chair, poking lightly at my pooch. "Actually, it's twins, double trouble, so early September but probably more likely to be August. It's going to be a big, hot summer." I huff out a laugh. "Bathing suit season might just be a no-go for me this year."

"Didn't answer my other question." Jenny side-eyes me, eyebrows raised. If she tilted her chin down just a little bit, she'd have my mama's look down to a T.

"You might have met him," I tell her, biting at the inside of my cheek. "It's Jack, little Jake Triplett's uncle. But, Jenny, I have no way of reaching him. I don't think Jake's mom knows we were seeing each other, so that would really be oversteppin' the whole parent-teacher relationship. God, imagine me asking her to let Jack know that I'm knocked up. I just can't."

She nods because, really, that conversation would be awkward as fuck. "He's coming back here though, right? You're going to see each other when he gets back home again?"

I push myself up out of the chair and round the counter that acts as her command post. "I don't know. We didn't really make plans. Sure as hell didn't expect to *have* to see each other. So, I've got to be ready to do this parenting thing on my own. Even if he does show up back here, this"—I sweep my hands up and down myself—"might not be what he wants. You know what I mean?"

Jenny purses her lips, sympathy written all over her face.

I smile weakly making my way to the door leading out to the hallway. "I've gotta get to class now. See you later, gator."

GRACYN: **McBride's tonight. Dinner and I'll buy you a Shirley Temple.**

Me: Sweet of you to offer. I'm tired though.

Gracyn: You're always tired. We have plans to make, things to discuss.

I am tired all the time. Apparently, growing multiple humans takes a lot out of a person. Who knew? My lesson plans for the rest of the month are done, and the framework for what we need to do through the end of the school year is in place. I really have no reason to use work as an excuse not to go.

Gracyn: Stop running through your to-do list, looking for a reason to just go home, and come meet us. Please?

Gracyn: Chicken tenders with hot sauce and extra ranch ...

Gracyn: You know how the babies feel about hot sauce.

Me: Fine.

Watery late afternoon sun filters through the blinds, casting shadows across the pages of my journal. It seems like things are moving superfast now that my pregnancy is out in the open and everyone knows. Everyone, except the man who should. I stare at the page, not quite halfway through the book, where my words hang, mid-thought. For someone who never wanted to mar the inside of a pristine journal so full of promise, I have poured my heart out over these pages. Thoughts and feelings. And my fears, so damn many fears. If Jack comes back and wants the play-by-play of the months he was gone, I've got them. If he decides not to be part of our lives, then my babies will at the very least have a glimpse into who their father was and why I found myself falling for him.

How did that even happen? Do I even know him well enough to have fallen?

Suddenly annoyed with myself and my melancholy thoughts, I close the leather book and tuck it into my tote, locking my classroom as I go.

"SO, WHAT ARE WE discussing and planning?" I ask, hanging my tote from the hook underneath the bar at McBride's. "And shouldn't my food be waiting for me already? These kids are demanding little boogers," I tease, hoisting myself into the seat next to Gracyn.

She's set up at the corner of the bar. A notebook in front of her, laptop open as she scrolls through Pinterest.

Kieran sets a coaster on the scarred wooden surface in front of me and reaches for a shot glass and well tequila, not saying a word. He was Francie's last hired McBride's boy, and none of us can quite figure him out. He's the least talkative bartender, and he never really seems to be fully aware of what's going on around him.

"Shit, Kieran, stop with that. She's pregnant," Gracyn says, putting her hand over the shot glasses.

He looks up, wild blond curls tumbling into his eyes as

his gaze bounces back and forth between the two of us. "Is she? So, the whiskey then?"

I can't help but laugh at his cluelessness. "No, just soda water and a couple of orange slices, thanks."

He shrugs and makes my drink before walking to the other end of the bar, his attention fully focused on his phone.

"I'm not sure I want to eat here if he's the one doing the cooking," I whisper, leaning into Gracyn.

"No shit." She angles her laptop toward me. "You look through this, and I'll go make us some food. Lis and Addie should be here in a little bit." She hops off her barstool, bussing tables as she makes her way to the kitchen.

Images of baby shower themes fill the screen of her computer, her Pinterest board ranging from extravagant Paris and Eiffel Tower–themed parties to sweet and simple. She even pinned an over-the-top Army theme that looks more like the birthday party of any little boy's dreams.

"She's got you picking your party decor?" Addie asks, perching on the seat just around the bar's corner. Her green hair, a St. Patrick's Day tradition since she and Finn started dating, is tied back from her face, all 1940s pinup style, purple cat-eye glasses perched on the bridge of her nose.

"Apparently. How are you doing?"

I lean over to greet her before remembering she's not a hugger. She gives me a tight smile, lips quirked up in an uncomfortable smirk.

"Sorry, I forgot," I offer.

"You're fine." Her eyes drop to my belly and then dart back up to mine. "What was that?"

"You can see it?" I ask, my fingers drawing lazy circles over where I felt a kick and a push.

Addie pulls her glasses off, setting them on the bar. "I thought I saw something, but ... holy shit," she exclaims, her mouth hanging open in surprise.

This is kind of new, like the next stage of an adventure. And Addie—who is normally so reserved, so closed off—has her fingers twitching, almost reaching toward the side of my belly.

"Wanna see if you can feel 'em?" I press in where somebody just pushed out to see if it'll happen again.

Casting off her reserve, Addie scoots closer and tentatively places her small hand near my bump. I pull her in, and seconds later, we're both rewarded with a strong thump, followed by a skittering push.

Addie lifts her head and takes her hand away. "That's just crazy kinds of weird," she says, sliding back into her seat.

"Let me feel." Gracyn comes dancing across the room, hands out, fingers wiggling.

Lis comes in through the back door of the pub, baskets of food clutched in her hands and balanced precariously along her arm. "They're moving?" she asks, hastily dropping the plastic baskets to the bartop.

And, suddenly, hands are all over me, pushing, pressing. Promises and bribes whispered, begging for just one feel.

"Come on, babies. Auntie G will buy you all the pretty pink things that your mama says no to. A pony. The biggest dollhouse ever," Gracyn cajoles.

"No to the pony unless you keep that at your house. Y'all have room for it out there," I say, trying to mimic my mother's mom look. "But I happen to think there's nothing more handsome than men who wear pink."

Don't I know how to throw a hush over a room? I have

had a lot of practice with it lately, but I swear, the entire pub goes silent, not just our little group of belly-gropers.

"Did you say men?"

"You're having boys?" Lis and Gracyn ask simultaneously. Eyes wide and bright.

A laugh rips from me as these two crazy girls pull money from their pockets and toss five-dollar bills at Addie.

"Y'all bet on my babies' sex?" I ask, pushing at whichever baby is on my right, shifting him into a better spot. "Assholes." I sit up straight, grabbing for the basket piled highest with food. I load hot sauce and ranch on a piece of chicken because, when my boys decide they're hungry, they mean it.

Gracyn spins her laptop to face her and deletes more than half of the pictures she had pinned. "That narrows down our party options," she mutters. "How are we decorating our nursery? All kinds of blue, whales and sailboats—how cute would that be?" She taps away at the keyboard, probably making a new board for nurseries.

"Slow your roll, G. We've got time." I push back, needing another drink and to visit the restroom, all at the same time. Pregnancy really is weird.

Lis looks up from her phone where she's been texting almost nonstop since tossing her money across the bar at Addie. "You think that, but it's going to go fast. Those boys'll be here before you know it."

TWENTY-FOUR

Kate

SPRING CONFERENCES ARE ANOTHER round of baring my soul and putting myself out there for the world. But the judgment and questions I expected are nowhere to be found. Every single parent of my students is nothing but supportive and genuinely excited for me. More than a few voice concerns that I'll be done with teaching and choose to stay at home with my boys. But the conference I'm most worried about is with Chloe Triplett.

Of course, she walks in, wearing a bright smile and carrying a blue gift bag. "Hey, I hear we have some exciting news," she trills. "Amelia's mom called me last night and told me you're having twin boys. I hope that's all right."

"Absolutely, we do. Well, I'm excited at the very least." I smile tentatively because this is usually the make-or-break moment with the parents. Although, with the way Chloe is practically pulling books and goodies out of her gift bag, I think we'll be okay.

"Look at you! God, I'd hoped when Tripp was home over Christmas ..." She pauses, letting her wish go unsaid. "But we've got time. He'll be home this summer, and then maybe Jake'll get a sibling. He's been begging for one, but I don't think he gets that he won't be the main man then."

Guilt bites at my heart. She's married, and she was trying, wanting to get pregnant while her husband was home, but it didn't happen. I had a couple of wild nights of sex with a man I hardly knew, and I've got more than I can handle. *Maybe.*

I shove my thoughts away and reach across, squeezing Chloe's hand. "He'll make a great big brother."

"He will, right? Such a little helper. Oh, do the kids know? Jake hasn't said anything to me, and he's usually all over anything that has to do with your happenings."

"Oh my word, no. I wanted to make sure all the parents were informed first and answer any questions. Make sure that we're all on the same page. So, if there is anything you want to ask me, now's the time." My words tumble from my mouth just as they have for every other conference I've had with the parents of my students.

And, when Chloe purses her lips and looks up to the left, I brace myself.

She starts and stops her inquiry, her mouth doing the fish thing over and over again. Finally, Chloe asks, "Do I ... is it ..." She laughs and shakes her head before continuing, "You'll let me know if you need anything, right? Help in the classroom, anything?"

It doesn't take a rocket scientist to figure out that that's not what she wanted to ask. I think the same thing has happened in more than half of my meetings, and I get it.

Everyone loves a bit of gossip, information that's pointless but a tad bit illicit. But, when it's Chloe—someone with close ties to Jack—hinting at asking who the baby daddy is, it feels different. Like I'm straddling the line of lying by omission.

Lis's suggestion of getting a message to Jack through Chloe rattles around the edge of my mind as Chloe and I discuss Jake and his classroom performance. That little boy is so ready for advancement to first grade.

Should I ask her about Jack? Ask her to have him contact me when or if he can? It would be wrong. I know in my heart that it would be wrong to ask her to relay a message like this.

I'm stuck though. If she tells her husband and he gossips to Jack, the results could be disastrous. He could think I lied to him at Christmas about being in the clear. He could think I'm somehow trying to trap him. He could just not give a shit, and that might be the hardest option for me to consider. That he just wouldn't care.

"So, don't say anything to Jake, but there's a chance his dad will be able to make it to kindergarten graduation," Chloe shares.

My eyes about pop out of my head, and there's no hiding my shock. At least, I think there isn't, but Chloe rolls right on, ignoring my freak-out.

"You're kidding. Really? That's amazing. I'm so happy for y'all," I gush. "Their deployment'll be done and all?" More than anything in this moment, I want to ask a million and one questions. Beg her for details and if Jack is coming, too.

Beaming wildly, Chloe nods, her face alight. "Should be. I'm just keeping my fingers crossed and saying all my prayers that everything works out. With any luck, Jake's uncle might be convinced to come, too. Lord, that little boy's head would about explode."

His and mine both.

Later, when I'm settled into my bed, the need to talk to Jack is strong. So, I do the only thing I can in the moment and flip my journal open to the next blank page and pour out my thoughts and emotions.

Jack,

Please know that my heart is torn on what I should've done today. Part of me wanted so badly to ask Chloe to have you call me as soon as you were able. Part of me wanted to beg her not to say a word to her husband because I can only imagine how news like this might be received.

Now ... now it's just a matter of waiting and seeing. Will you come home with Tripp again? I know Jake and his parents are a huge part of your life —like family—but Lord, I would love to be the one to tell you face-to-face. To introduce you to your boys— or at least, the idea of them.

Be safe until you're back on US soil.

"KATE, I've invited your mother and sister-in-law to your shower, but I haven't heard back from them. Do you know if they're planning on coming?" Lis asks. "Maybe we should have held off until after the school year was done? Everyone seems so busy right now." Her brows push together, concern pinching at her features.

"Are you serious? I know Jules hates that she can't make it, but Mama hasn't responded yet?" I'm shocked at her avoidance.

"Nope," Gracyn says, popping that P.

"Hang on and let me call her." I dial my mama and count as the rings stack up.

When I'm about ready to give up and call the house phone, she answers, "Kate, baby, you doin' all right? Everything okay with my grandbabies?" She's out of breath, and I can hear Harper singing in the background.

"We're fine, but Lis and Gracyn just told me they haven't gotten your RSVP yet. So, I guess I need to ask you if you're doing okay." I don't bother to hide any of the sass in my tone.

"Well, I'm not sure what bee has gotten in your bonnet, but I certainly don't appreciate that—"

"I know, but I've got your attention now, so how about you tell me why you're not coming to my shower?" I might never perfect her mom look, but I sure as hell can rock the teacher voice, even with my own mother.

Silence stretches between us, and I check the screen of my phone, concerned that I've lost her.

"Mama?"

"Is it too much to ask, wanting my baby girl to come home? To have my grandbabies here by family?" Tears touch the edges of her words.

"Of course not, Mama. There's no harm in asking and wanting, but just come to my party. Come meet my friends, see where I live. See my life outside of Mississippi. I promise you won't have to give up your Southern roots if you cross the Mason-Dixon Line for a visit." I hold my breath, replaying the words I just uttered. Hoping and wanting for her to give New York a chance.

Mama concedes.

Two weeks later, when she finally comes to New York for the babies' shower, the chatter begins almost the minute she gets off the plane.

"Now, your daddy and I are buying your cribs, but we'll just have them delivered down home. Don't want to have to pay to move those if we don't have to. And I brought an extra suitcase with me, so I can just pack that full of gifts and take them home with me instead of botherin' with shippin'."

I'm fighting a losing battle with her, but I calmly remind her, "I'm not positive I'm leaving New York, Mama."

She laughs at the idea. "Don't be silly, Kate. You're gonna need help and a lot of it. You think you can schedule and organize these babies into submission? I don't think so, darlin'."

I let her prattle on, not interested in starting anything with her. I'll just let her know—along with everyone else—when I've made up my mind. In the meantime, I take her to as many places as I can that show her why I love it here so much. And how hard of a decision staying or going will be for me to make.

TWENTY-FIVE

Jack

I'M GOING TO BE late. I knew it was a long shot when I changed my flight at the last minute, but I just couldn't miss out on Jake's kindergarten graduation. Tripp had talked nonstop for the past two weeks about nothing but getting to make it back in time for the big ceremony. I'd had no plans to go back to Beekman Hills. None, but after rolling around in the desert for another six months, spending a few days with my favorite kid sounds pretty good. And the possibility of seeing his favorite teacher and mine doesn't suck in the least.

I throw my rental into one of the only available parking spaces in the elementary school's lot and hustle for the front door at a brisk jog. Once in the building, I follow the little mortarboard clings lining the floor to the cafeteria. Gone are the cramped torture device tables that I squeezed my ass into back in November, and in their place are row upon row of folding chairs.

Parents and grandparents corral squirmy siblings,

claiming as much real estate as they can get away with. I search the sea of spectators for Chloe's curly black hair and Tripp's all-too-familiar head. I've been staring at the back of his block head for fucking months. I should be able to immediately find it, but Chloe is alone, an empty seat next to her.

I settle against the back wall, and before long, the principal climbs the steps to the stage.

"Welcome, family and friends. Thank you for joining us this evening as we celebrate the advancement of this year's kindergarten class to first grade. The entire class will perform two musical numbers that they've worked very hard on. Then, each teacher will present their students in turn. Refreshments will be available in the commons afterward. Please allow me to present you with this year's kindergarten class."

One by one, the kids file into the cafeteria and up onto risers set up on the stage. The teachers arrange and adjust them, grouping them by class. I run a hand over my stubble, eyes trained on the entrance. Waiting for a glimpse of blonde waves and a bright smile leading in the final class. I can practically see the sway of her hips as she led the kids down to her classroom that first day, hear the staccato click of those sexy-as-shit heels she was wearing.

The wavy hair and brilliant smile are there, but when Kate lumbers up the stairs, my breath slams out of my lungs in a whoosh. *Fuck me.* Gone is her hourglass figure. In its place is more of a Violet Beauregarde—after she turned into a blueberry in *Willy Wonka.*

Pregnant. Really fucking pregnant. Honest to God, she looks like she's ready to burst.

My nostrils flare as air forces its way in and out of my

lungs. Because I'm no expert, but if she's that fucking pregnant, that means she was already knocked up when we were together. And she likely knew it.

I push off the wall and stalk toward the exit, escape my singular focus. The need to get away driving me out of this place.

"Uncle Jack!" Jake screeches.

The excitement in his voice is the only thing that can stop me in this moment.

Every face in the room turns to look at me. Every single one. Kate leans in, whispering to Jake and getting him settled back into his spot onstage. But, as she descends the stairs, she finds me. Eyes wide, one hand supporting her protruding belly. She's white as a ghost, and she sways slightly as she joins the other teachers kneeling—fucking kneeling—on the hard floor in front of the stage.

Jaw tight, I survey the room, and Chloe pins me with a glare, waving to me.

"Get over here," she whisper-shouts, insisting that I take the empty seat I know is for Tripp.

My head is spinning. My heart pounding against my ribs. *How the fuck did this happen to me again?* I must be a fucking magnet for crazy women looking to start a family. I don't want that shit. Fine for others, but this fucking mess is not for me.

The music starts, and kids begin to sing.

Chloe leans into me again. "Where's Tripp? He said he was getting in before you and—hell, I didn't even know until yesterday that you were thinking of coming to this," she whispers.

"Last-minute decision. He should be here. Flight got in

almost an hour before mine," I tell her, getting shushed by the lady behind us. I lower my voice, biting out, "Jake's teacher's changed since fall."

"You met her?"

"Had lunch with Jake a time or two. Sure as fuck didn't know she was knocked up," I grumble.

A hand lands on my shoulder with a hissed admonishment from the dad behind us. "Hey, watch it. There are kids around."

He's right. I mumble my apology and turn back to Chloe, who's using her all-knowing mom stare on me. My phone buzzes in my pocket, giving me the perfect excuse to break eye contact. It's not a number I recognize, and no one knows I'm stateside yet, so I decline the call and focus on the kids singing—shouting—mostly off tune.

"Was it just lunch?" Chloe asks, digging at shit I'm not discussing.

I nod toward the front of the room. "Your kid is doing big things. Stop gossiping."

Chloe settles back in her seat with a huff but side-eyes me every so often. Fully focused on the end of the last song, I lock it down and ignore her. Maybe Jake'll run to us after this shit is done, and we can shuffle out the back. Not sure that I want to come face-to-face with Miss Katelyn Beard. The conversation we need to have sure as fuck is not appropriate for any kind of audience, let alone with kids around.

My phone buzzes again, and I silence it. There's still no text from Tripp. No call, nothing telling me he got delayed somehow. *Did he miss his connection? Get held up in customs?* Another buzz that is not my friend calling with excuses, so I decline again and turn off notifications for the next hour, sliding my phone back into my pocket. I'm here to see Jake graduate from kindergarten and maybe take him out for ice cream, so when his father finally gets his ass to town, Tripp and Chloe can have a few quiet moments. Yeah, totally gonna run interference with my little wingman, so my buddy can get reacquainted with his wife. My plans of hooking up with the hot teacher are obviously going nowhere.

My ass falls asleep as the eighty-plus kids wearing blue paper mortarboards make their way across the stage to shake hands with their teacher and the school principal. No doubt the scrolls they're handed will end up creased, twisted messes, probably forgotten under their chairs. And, through the whole thing, I can't take my eyes off Kate.

Much as I'm pissed at being played, I can't deny that she looks amazing like that, all swollen, round belly. You'd think, with her so close to dropping the kid, the dude who knocked her up would at least be here in case all this excitement sent her into labor. But I don't see that. No one sitting with her, no one looking concerned. No one to help her up the four steps to the stage when it's her turn to shake little hands.

"She looks like she could have that kid any minute now. Should she even be here?" I ask Chloe, forgetting my earlier avoidance of the subject.

Chloe pulls her phone out, ready to take pictures when we get a little further into the class roster. "Three more months," is all she says, scooting out of her seat and duck-walking toward the front of the room to capture the big moment.

Three more months?

I'm not a doctor by any means, and I have shit for med

training beyond basic field first aid, but there's no way in hell Kate's got another three months. She's huge.

Jake walks across the stage, getting his diploma, shaking hands like a boss. But, like the sensitive little dude he is, he places a hand on Kate's protruding stomach and gasps suddenly.

It almost sounds like he said, "They moved!"

Kate laughs and tousles his hair, sending him on his way. And, now, every kid after him wants to feel what he did. Six more hands stop on her belly, and by the time her class is done, she looks relieved to lower herself into the principal's chair onstage for the closing remarks.

Chloe slips back into the seat beside me, sliding her phone back into her bag. "How sweet was that? He's been asking for a little brother or sister again ever since Miss Beard started showing." A smile pulls at her lips, and she adds, winking, "Glad you guys are home for a bit. Tripp's got some work to do." Chloe stands with every other person in the room and claps as the kids are led out in barely contained chaos.

"Where's he going?" I ask, sure that we would just be able to grab Jake and run.

"Refreshments, Jack. Come on. You can't deny that boy the spoils of his accomplishments. Those are special Oreos out there in the commons. Not at all like the ones we have sitting in the pantry at home."

She pulls me up and drags me with her as we fight our way out to the open area just inside the front doors of the school. Tables with bowls of punch and platters of cookies have magically appeared while we were enjoying the ceremony.

"Good to see you again, Captain Jackson," a familiar woman says, squeezing my forearm.

Pretty sure she works in the office, but ...

"Jenny Simpson. I work up front. Kept hoping to see you pop in to have lunch with Miss Beard again, but she said you work with Jake Triplett's dad. So, I figured it might be a while before we saw you again. Welcome back."

She scurries off to help serve punch, and Chloe pins me with a hard look.

"Just lunch?" she asks, snorting out a little huff of judgment.

"Don't start with me," I tell her. "Can we just get Jake and go? I'll buy ten packages of Oreos and all the fruit punch he can handle if we can bolt." I'm not ready to deal with the questions, the looks from Chloe, and I sure as shit am not ready to talk to Kate.

But the universe is not on my side tonight.

Jake worms his way to us, breaking away from his little friends and runs straight for me. "Uncle Jack, you made it! I didn't know you were gonna be here. Did you bring my dad? Mom, where's Daddy? I thought he was coming. Uncle Jack, come on." His words all run together, questions melding into statements, as he grabs my hand and pulls me toward where his classmates are all sitting on the floor with their treats. Straight toward his ridiculously pregnant teacher. "Miss Beard, look. It's my uncle Jack." He bounces on his toes. "Uncle Jack, she has babies in her tummy."

"I see that." Because what the fuck else am I supposed to say?

Here I was, feeling like shit while out on mission, thinking about her and wondering for the first time in forever if maybe I could give the relationship thing a shot. See if it wouldn't be so terrible to have someone to come home to after deployments. Entertaining the idea of love because that was what I'd thought was happening when I left. That I was falling in love with her. And, all the time we were fucking, she was already knocked up.

Fuck my life.

Kate offers me a tight smile and says, "Hey. How are you?"

Yeah, she's displaying all the textbook signs of lying and withholding information. Shifting her weight and fidgeting, unable to hold eye contact.

I shake my head and answer, "I'm good. You, uh ... you've changed."

I take her in from head to toe, dick move on my part because, obviously, she's changed, and I'm just being an ass about it. But, for fuck's sake, maybe I've earned the right to be a little bit of a dick right now.

"Yeah, um ... maybe this isn't the best time, but I'd like to talk to you soon. Maybe we can grab lunch this week if you're around?"

I don't get the chance to answer her.

"Jack." Chloe's voice wobbles from beside me. All the color has drained from her face, tears gathering in her eyes, phone clutched tightly in her hand. "He's gone. Jack, he's gone. The police ... they were calling you, but ..."

"Can you—" I ask Kate, darting my eyes to Jake.

Hand over her mouth, she nods quickly, and I guide Chloe out the front doors of the school.

"What happened, Chloe?"

She trembles, tears finally tumbling down her cheeks.

"He stopped at a gas station, walked into a robbery. They stabbed him, took his wallet, and left. Crashed the car. Rental papers. Tried to call you. Why did they call you and not me? Why didn't they call me? He's dead. Oh my God, why?" Chloe crumbles, and I have to lunge to catch her before she hits the ground.

Motherfucker.

TWENTY-SIX

Kate

"Miss Beard? Why's my mom crying?" Jake asks softly, slipping his hand into mine.

I take a deep breath—at least as deep as I can with these two monsters taking up way too much space in my body. "I don't know, buddy. But I'm wondering if you'd like to be my helper for a little bit. Think you can keep an eye on this very important basket for me while I go get a chair?"

"Are the babies making you tired?" He places his small hand on the side of my belly and waits.

The kiddos love it when the babies are giving high fives, and it seems like that's been happening nonstop these days.

Another deep-ish breath because, if truth be told, growing babies is hard work, and I really am exhausted. "They are wearing me out, Jake. I'll be right back with a chair and—"

Just then, Jenny Simpson rolls one of the office chairs over, a smile brightening her already-cheery face.

"Thank you, Jenny."

"You know it. Got to take care of you, though it'll calm down a bit with school out for the summer. You know what your plans are yet for next year?" she asks. Lowering her voice, she adds, "I did see that Captain Jackson is back in town."

So did I, Jenny. So did I.

"Where'd he go? I thought I saw him heading this way."

"He stepped out with Jake's mom for a minute." I lean in, whispering, "I think something's happened. She looked like someone stepped on her grave. Do you think you could pop outside and see if they need anything?"

Jenny glances at Jake and then back to me. Plastering on her *it's all going to be fine* smile, she nods once. "I'll be back in a jiff. You go sit down though. You look like you could collapse."

I'm starting to feel like I could, too. I lower myself into the chair with an *oomph*, grateful for the plush office chair as opposed to the hard plastic one I was going to grab from the cafeteria.

Little by little, parents come by to collect their kiddos and thank me for the year. Jake helps me hand out certificates and small gifts to each of the kids. They grow up so much in kindergarten. Not just learning to read and write, but also how to be in a classroom and work with others. Their little minds are like sponges, soaking up every experience, every nugget of knowledge.

"Is one of those for me?" Jake asks, yawning as he hands over another little bags of goodies.

"Absolutely. Are you getting tired, buddy?"

Jack and Chloe have been gone for well more than a hot

minute, and Jenny has yet to come back from checking on them. In fact, the last of my parents have come for their kids, and when I look up, the commons area is just about empty. Only a handful of teachers, volunteers, and the custodial staff.

Jake leans hard on my chair and rests his head on my shoulder. "When is my mom coming back for me?" he whines.

I have never once heard this child whine in the nine months that I've had him in my class. Whatever happened, it must be serious because Chloe Triplett is always here for her kiddo. *Always.*

I run through the short list of things that I planned to do tonight before leaving and decide that I can push them all off to tomorrow or the next day. "Let's go lock up our classroom, and then we'll see about finding your mama for you, okay?" I run my hand over Jake's soft sandy-brown curls.

Needing a bit of space, I nudge Jake up and awkwardly push myself to standing. *Lord, I'm huge.*

Jake picks up the basket, empty now but for his gift bag and certificate, and carries it down the hall to our classroom. I still haven't decided whether I'm going to try and stay here, raising these babies on my own, or if I'm going home. Time is getting short, and I really need to make a decision soon, but my head and my heart are pulling me in two very different directions. I love it here, but twins might just be too much for me to handle without another set of hands.

I take the basket from Jake, handing him his gift bag. I'll keep hold of his certificate, so it doesn't go the way of the fake ones we handed them during the ceremony. Those were smashed to nothing, and you only graduate from kindergarten once. Best to have a little something to remember the day.

"Hey, bud. You about ready to go home?" Jack's voice drifts through the doorway, startling me.

"Where's my mom?" Jake asks shakily.

"She wasn't feeling well, so I took her home real quick. You want me to carry anything for you?" Jack asks both of us, I think.

Jack scoops Jake into his arms after the little guy mumbles, "Me," lifting his hands.

Sleepy Jake might just be my new favorite version of this kid because the way he's curled into Jack—head resting on broad shoulder, arms tucked up between them—melts my heart.

Moisture gathers in my eyes, and I curse the stupid hormones wreaking havoc with my emotions. I sling my bag over my shoulder, grab my keys and the rest of my stuff, and follow Jack out into the hall, locking the door behind us. We silently walk out of the building, and Jack clicks the locks on a small SUV, tucking Jake into the booster seat in the back.

"There you go," he says, snapping the seat belt into place. He shuts the door and turns to me, running a hand down his face. He looks exhausted, almost defeated.

I shift my bag to the other arm and hoist my free hand under my belly to support the weight, hoping for some relief to my back. "What happened?" I ask softly.

Jack presses his lips into a tight line, the muscles of his jaw jumping as he clenches and releases it. "I have to get Jake home. It's ... it's not good. Thank you for your help," he says stiffly. He drops his eyes to my stomach and shakes his head, mumbling, "Fucking hell," as he pulls open the car door and climbs in.

Fucking hell is right. I walk the short distance to my car—it's more of a waddle really—but since the principal gave me her parking spot for the last couple of weeks of school, I don't have far to go. When I've wedged myself behind the steering wheel, I look up and meet Jack's shadowed gaze. I'm glad he came tonight. I know it means the world to Jake, and with whatever went down with Chloe, it's good he's here to help. He nods once and pulls out of the lot but pauses before making it all the way to the intersection. My brain cells are dropping like flies, and I can't even begin to guess what he's doing. Instead, I start my car, turning in the opposite direction to head home.

This time last year, I was celebrating the end of another successful school year, slamming shots of Patrón at McBride's with my friends. Now, I can't wait to drop some cucumber slices in a big glass of water and crawl into bed. How times have changed, y'all.

As I turn the corner, I check my rearview mirror, and Jack's taillights are gone. It would be so like him to wait and make sure that I was safely on my way before taking off himself.

I SLEEP FITFULLY, even for me at this stage, constantly waking, wondering about what happened with Chloe Triplett last night. The text I sent Jack late last night, asking what had happened, remains unanswered. Nothing. So, when my phone rings as I'm pulling up to the school, I grab it and answer without even looking to see who's calling.

"Hey, how're my grandbabies this fine mornin'?" my mother's voice trills over the miles.

"Mornin', Mama," I answer, trying to stuff down my disappointment. "They're good, just wrestling before breakfast." Car parked, I grunt, pushing and shoving my way out of my Kia. It's not as easy as it used to be.

"You haven't eaten yet? Katelyn, go get you some breakfast. Those babies need calories, darlin' ..."

She carries on as I schlep myself across the drive and tap my ID card to the reader, gaining access to the school. I hightail it to the restroom because these two kiddos are not just wrestling; they're full-on tap-dancing on my bladder now.

"Mama, I have breakfast in my bag, but I've got to go. And, as much as I love you, I'm not chatting in the restroom. I'll call you later. Bye."

Lord have mercy, I'm not going to make it three more months. Really, a little bit less than that, but still, it seems impossible.

I finish up and wave to Jenny as I pass the front office, determined to clean up my classroom—not just for the summer, but also in case I decide not to come back. If Mama would just come up and help me for a couple of weeks—maybe a month—I'm sure I could get us on a schedule and make my life up here work. It'd be hard, but I know I could do it. Maybe.

But, with my sister-in-law delivering about the same time, I know—I just *know*—it would kill Mama to have to choose. To miss out on time with one grandbaby in exchange for others. She'd feel like she was picking favorites.

I look around at the classroom I love, knowing in my

heart that, unless some kind of miracle happens, I'm most likely kissing Beekman Hills good-bye.

The morning flies by with a million and one potty breaks, tons of boxes packed up, and more than a few tears shed. I really don't want to go back to Mississippi. Lord, the gossip over my return would about kill me.

Somehow, during the course of packing this particular box, my tape has rolled just out of reach. I need it. I'm starving, I have to pee again, and my damn tape is about three inches too far away. Why the hell did I think it was a good idea to sit on the floor to do this anyway? Right, because standing means bending over, and sitting in a chair is just not as practical.

I lean back against my pretty pink reading chair and close my eyes for just a minute's rest. One of the babies stretches, a small lump forming under my ribs. With two fingers, I push back, smiling as we start what I swear has become one of my favorite games. Push and shove. Hand-to-hand—or maybe foot—I play this little game, wondering which baby is my opponent in this round, guessing at the body part he's playing with.

"That's pretty amazing."

My eyes fly open to find Jack leaning in the doorway, a to-go bag from McBride's in his hand, the smell of something deep fried tickling my senses.

"It is," I agree. "Come on in and have a seat. I'd get up, but that could take a while." My heart skitters in my chest, not sure whether to beat harder or stop all together.

Jack showing up here today was about the last thing I expected, and Lord knows, there's no way of telling how this conversation'll go.

Jack walks into the room, filling the space somehow. The tan he had in the fall is deeper now, his skin a golden bronze. He plucks my water cup off my desk and then hands it to me, lowering himself to the floor.

"How're Chloe and Jake?" I ask, still only guessing about last night's events.

"Not good." He clears his throat and pulls black containers of chicken tenders and fries from the bag, setting them on the floor between us. "I took a chance that you'd be here getting shit organized today. Is this okay?" he asks.

"It's perfect, thank you." I pop the lid and snag a couple of fries, shoving them in my mouth. "Mmm, God, that's good," I practically moan.

"Yeah, I went to that Irish pub you used to talk about. I probably should have gotten something healthy for you, but this just sounded good. Comfort food, I guess." I'm fixing to ask who was working when he continues, "The girl behind the bar insisted on giving me extra tubs of ranch and hot sauce. She seemed pretty committed to the idea, so ..."

"Yeah, that was Gracyn then. My old roommate," I say. "And this is exactly the way they should be eaten." I dip a chicken finger in the hot sauce and then dunk it in ranch, licking the extra sauce off my fingers. "So good."

Jack

I HAD A SNEAKING suspicion that the girl behind the bar was Kate's roommate, but former?

"She moved out?"

Kate nods while she chews. "Yeah, her boyfriend bought a house, and she moved right in," she says, dabbing at a dot of ranch that dribbled onto her belly.

Passing her a napkin, I say, "That was quick. Did she even know him when we were ..." When we were what? Dating, fucking? And fast? Jesus, Kate fucking jumped into bed with me while pregnant.

She snorts a laugh through her nose and shoves another bunch of fries in her mouth. She bobs her head from side to side. "Sorry, I didn't realize I was so hungry. Um, it seems quick, but they met more than two years ago, kind of lost touch, and then reconnected right before we met, so"—she shrugs and pushes at the side of her belly—"it's all good."

She wipes her hands and grabs another piece of chicken,

mixing hot sauce into the ranch as she does her dipping thing. "Tell me what happened last night. I thought Jake's dad was going to be there."

I can't. It hasn't even really settled in yet, so I sure as shit can't say the words out loud. I shake my head and look at her —really look at her—not holding back or hiding where my focus is. "Tell me about this first. I think you should have told me you were pregnant when we were together. I kinda feel like that's not something you just hide." Maybe I'm being a little bit of a dick. "Christ, especially after the condom obliterated. You should have come clean about being with someone, unprotected, before. Do you have any idea of the risk you threw at me?" Totally being a dick.

"Wow. Okay, I guess we're doing this now," she says, dropping the chicken back in the box and laying both hands on her—what's bigger than a basketball? Because that bump is huge.

"And should you even still be working this far along? You look like you could drop that kid any minute." I should keep my mouth shut. Should bite my fucking tongue, but I've started it now, so I might as well finish. "And where the fuck is the father? He's okay with you working like this? Packing boxes and moving shit around? What kind of asshole is he?"

I don't lose my cool—ever—but the past eighteen hours have me so wound up that I can hardly see straight.

Kate's shock? I see that.

The hurt that clouds her expression? Can't miss it.

The flip to anger? That starts with a heated red flush at the top of her decidedly bigger tits and rises straight up her neck until I'm wondering if I just pissed her off enough to start labor.

"You tell me," she says, way too calm for anything good to be coming.

If I were a smarter man, I'd be catching on to what she just said, but no, I'm still stupid kinds of fired up.

"Why? Should I know him? That douche-bag doctor you were dating? Is that who it is?" I snort, honestly disgusted with my lack of control and rational thinking as much as the idea of that asshat knocking her up.

"You know him better than you think. But I'm blown away by how little you think of me." She struggles, shifting her legs so that one is out straight and the other is tucked in tight, her foot resting on the side of her thigh.

Kate pulls a deep breath into her lungs, blowing it out like the adjustment to her position took a lot out of her. *Why the hell is she still at work?*

She purses her lips, the dimple on her left cheek popping a little. "I'm due at the end of the summer." She runs one hand down the side of her stomach and then pushes gently, like she's repositioning the baby. "And the father doesn't entirely know," she says quietly.

"How does that work, Kate? You've either told him or you haven't. Which is it?"

She pins me in place and screws up her mouth again. Tilting her head to the side, she says, "I had no way of getting in contact with him—until now. And, yes, I look like a beached whale, like I'm ready to explode, because there are two babies in there."

Wait.

"They're yours, Jack. The condom ..." She shakes her head.

No.

"You sent me a text. Said you got your period, that we were clear," I throw back at her.

How the fuck did this happen?

"The doctor said that happens sometimes, that there's some spotting when they attach, nestle in there. I didn't lie, Jack. I didn't set out to do this on purpose, any of it. It happened. And you were gone."

Fuck my life.

"Two? Twins? Are you sure?" My brain is not firing on all cylinders because then I add my death knell, "You're sure they're mine?"

Kate stares at me like I'm stupid because I *abso-fucking-lutely* am.

"Yes, Jack. I'm fucking sure that there are two little aliens in there, dancing on my bladder, keeping me awake at night, wrestlin' and fightin' already like little boys do. Can I prove that they're yours? Sweet Jesus, not at this God-given moment. But there's no need to worry your pretty little head about it. You don't want to be a part of their lives? I won't make you. We'll be fine on our own. Made it this far without any help ..."

Wow. I mean, wow.

In less than a day, I went from a happy fucking bachelor —living my life, thinking about a repeat performance of the last time I had been here—to having not just one family to take care of, but two.

It took some time, but I finally pieced together the story from last night. Tripp had taken a knife to the chest. Totally a freak thing because I know—*I know*—the man can fight. I've seen him in a knife fight—trained with him, for fuck's sake— and if it wasn't for some stupid fucking luck, Tripp would've had the two guys subdued or in body bags without breaking a sweat. But some punk got the jump on him. I can *guaran-damn-tee,* though that, in his final seconds, when he realized he was done, Tripp fought his ass off and did some serious damage to the kid.

Doesn't matter that it was in a gas station just across the New York–New Jersey state line and not in the desert. He died, looking out for someone who couldn't help themselves. He died, protecting someone who needed it. Tripp died a hero.

And the calls? Tripp had me listed in his phone as his emergency contact. Thought shit news to Chloe would be better coming from me than a stranger. So, that stream of calls I ignored last night was nothing more than me failing in my duty to my brother. I fucking let him down, and now, I have to pay for that. Step up and take care of Chloe and Jake.

This, with Kate? I don't know. I just don't fucking know. I need a bottle of añejo tequila. I need some time to think. I need to process some serious shit and wrap my head around this mess.

She's sitting as still as can be, the picture of absolute calm in the storm of my emotions. Waiting to see what she's going to get from me. And I'm not proud of what I give her, not in the least.

No, I stand up, easy as you please because the only body I have to move is my own. And I walk to the door of Kate's classroom. When I get there, I pause because she asked me a question, and I owe her an answer. And, while the answer to that particular question should be given with some kind of compassion, that's not something I can find in my shattered heart. It's out of reach along with my rapidly retreating sanity.

Since I have nothing left today, compassion or sanity, I turn and take in every last detail of Kate. The tendrils of hair escaping her messy bun. The dark smudges of exhaustion under her eyes. The stain from the ranch she dripped on the rolling waves of her stomach. Her hands splayed across her belly, our babies safely nestled in there.

And then I tell her, "Tripp's dead. He was stabbed in a gas station when he stopped to grab a cup of coffee on his way home from the airport."

And then I walk away.

Kate

I KNEW JAKE HAD lost his daddy, that Chloe Triplett had lost her husband. Deep down in my heart, I knew, but it was the last thing I wanted to deal with. And how selfish is that? Chloe and Jake don't get to choose whether they want to face it or not. They're stuck with it for the rest of their lives.

Rocking from side to side, I get my hands up on the seat of my reading chair and wedge my feet as close to my butt as I can get them. With a deep-ish, bracing breath, I hoist myself off the floor and slide into the chair. Not my most graceful moment, but I'm up. Mostly. And, now, I need to move. I can't sit here any longer today—not because of the babies, but because people are hurting. People who mean a lot to me.

Tears gather in my eyes, and I brush them away, taking in the mess around me. I clean up the food and trash, sling my bag over my shoulder, and head out. My pace is already slow, but I take it down another notch, praying I don't see Jack as I go. I'm not sure I can go another round with him.

"You okay, doll?" Jenny asks as I pass through the office, checking my mail.

"You heard about Jake's dad?"

She smiles a sad smile. "I did. When I went out last night, I caught a bit of it. That poor, precious boy."

I nod because the tears are making another appearance. I just can't imagine what Chloe is going through, her family broken, her hopes dashed. Maybe it's better for Jack to not be a part of our lives. I don't know if I could handle having that love, that partnership, and then have it ripped away. Maybe it's better to just do this thing on my own.

Jenny hands me a tissue. "Life is messy, Kate. But missing out on the good things because you're afraid of what might happen is no way to go through it. Sometimes, you have to jump, have faith, and put your heart on the line. The risk can be scary, but oh, the reward." She gives my hand a couple of quick squeezes. "Go on, sweetie. Get on out of here."

She's right. In fact, her simple words of wisdom sound a lot like the little speech I gave Gracyn when she was struggling over what to do about her relationship with Gavin. Lord, it is so much easier to see the trees in someone else's forest than it is when it's in your own backyard.

I whisper a, "Thank you," and give Jenny an awkward hug before going.

She's been mothering me since I started teaching here, almost like she knew I needed a soft place every now and again.

If I go, I'm going to miss her something fierce.

TWENTY-EIGHT

Kate

"YOU READY, HOT MAMA?" Gracyn calls as she pushes through my apartment door.

The hot part is right. Even for the end of June, it feels beastly hot out.

"Just about." *Nope. Not in the least.* How ready can you ever be for a funeral, let alone one for a young father and husband? "Be honest, Gracyn. How bad do I look?"

I've been living in stretchy pants for months, my options dwindling every day, and even the biggest of my maternity clothes are stretched to their limits at this point. I'm desperately afraid of a wardrobe malfunction at any given time these days.

"Um, you look fine." Gracyn doesn't sound all that sure. "Is that the dress you just got last month?" She leans back, her eyes assessing the black ruched monstrosity.

"Yep. It's bad, isn't it?" I pull at the gathered fabric stretched around my massive bump.

She shakes her head and smiles. "No, but damn, you're—"

"Don't," I warn, cutting her off before she says something that I'll have to hate her for.

"It's just—"

"Gracyn, please stop," I plead. "I'm about as uncomfortable as I can be. It's hot out, and this whole thing is gonna suck bad, so just lie to me. Tell me I look pretty, and let's go."

Because she's one of my very best friends, she does just that. "You look gorgeous, Kate. Absolutely perfect. Come on. Lis is out front, waiting on us." She carries my tote bag for me, running ahead to push the elevator button. "You have your water bottle in here? Tissues?"

"Mmhmm. Not much point in bringing it unless it's stuffed full of all the shit we could possibly ever need," I say, huffing and puffing to catch up to her. *When did the elevator get so far from my front door?*

Hot, humid air about knocks the breath from me when we step outside of my building. This used to be my favorite time of year, but now, it's just miserable.

Grateful that Lis has the air-conditioning pumping, I wedge myself into her front passenger seat, muttering, "Fucking hell."

Lis reaches a hand over, smoothing my seat belt where it twisted as I clicked it. "Kate, I'm so sorry. I know what Jake means to you, and to lose his father so soon, it breaks my heart. Is there anything we can do for him and his mom?"

Blinking rapidly, I shift my gaze to the ceiling of her car and try to will my tears away. "I don't know. I can't even begin to imagine where to start, what to do."

Gracyn settles her hand on my shoulder and asks, "How did she sound when you talked to her?"

"I didn't. I, uh ... Jack told me about the accident, and I Googled to find the funeral arrangements." I sigh, leaning my head against the headrest.

"Jack? You didn't tell us he was here. How did that go? Is he ..." Gracyn stops mid-question, searching for the right words.

I slide my seat belt in my hand, holding it away from my body. "He showed up at graduation. Thank God he was there to take care of Chloe and get her settled before coming back for Jake. But seeing him like this was beyond awkward." I shift in my seat, glancing over my shoulder to look at Gracyn. "And he brought me lunch the next day from McBride's. You met him, G."

"Holy shit. Tall? Dark hair? A body you could climb? That was him?" She's far too excited for where this shitshow is going to end up.

"Mmhmm. Brought me my favorite lunch and—"

"And you told him about the babies. I mean, obviously, he could see, but you *told* him that they're his. How'd that go?" Lis prods.

I don't know whether to laugh or cry, so I manage both. "He asked me if I was sure they were his."

"No," Lis gasps.

"And he stormed out of my classroom after telling me that Mr. Triplett was dead. So, I'm thinking it's a pretty safe bet that he wasn't too excited to hear the news." I shrug, batting at the tears rolling down my cheeks.

Just because the logical part of me had expected that

exact reaction from him doesn't mean there wasn't hope for a fairy-tale ending.

THE SERVICE IS AWFUL in the way that all funerals are.

Jake and his mama softly sobbing in the very front, closest to the casket holding their daddy and husband. Jack next to them, his posture braced and rigid. Parents, siblings, aunts, and uncles are all around them. Men in uniform dot the pews.

To the side of the flag-draped coffin sits a pair of combat boots with a rifle standing upright, a helmet and dog tags completing the battlefield cross. Chills run across my shoulders and down my spine. This is so much worse than I anticipated.

A hush falls over the chapel, and the national anthem plays. The chaplain gives the invocation, and then Jack stands, making his way to the podium, face pale. Jaw tight. The freewheeling and fun man I met in the fall is gone, replaced with one I hardly recognize. Detached, stoic, and somber, his expression unreadable.

"On behalf of the Triplett and Franks families, I would like to thank you all for attending," he begins.

"Today ..." Jack's voice succumbs to the finality of this moment, catching as he chokes down his emotions. He clears his throat, bracing his hands on the podium, taking a beat to compose himself. "We've gathered today to say farewell to Sergeant Dallas Henry Triplett, father, husband, son, brother, and friend. The world is a lesser place without him.

"George S. Patton is quoted as saying, 'It is foolish and wrong to mourn the men who have died. Rather we should thank God that such men existed.' I thank God that I had Tripp in my life. To have been included in his. To have served with him, learned with him, laughed with him, and cried with him. He was my best friend, my brother in arms. The man I entrusted with my life."

Hot tears blur my vision, silently cascading down my cheeks. As Jack speaks about Tripp, my heart crumbles. Chloe's head drops forward, her shoulders shaking with grief.

The future they planned together, their entire life, is gone. Their course forever changed. Jake will be the only child Tripp and Chloe have, and that little boy is clinging to his grandpa, his body wrung out from tears.

Jack talks about Tripp's accomplishments in the service and how they met. The things he learned from Tripp and what he admired most. The way Tripp was able to set aside the hardships and demands of his job, a job that he loved and believed in, and be the very best father and husband when he was at home. How he seemed to flip a switch, not contaminating the sanctity of his family with the ugliness of war.

"Finally, an unknown author wrote, *The brave may not live forever, but the cautious do not live at all.* Tripp lived every day to its fullest." Jack pauses, looking toward his best friend's casket. "And he was the bravest man I knew."

The scripture is read; the hymn is played. A moment of silence is offered, but the room echoes with the sound of sniffles and sobs. Death sucks, but a senseless loss like this is so, so much worse. The boys who killed Tripp stole his rental car and crashed it after a joy ride. They got fifty dollars in cash from the register and a ride in the back of a police car. So damn stupid.

After the chaplain delivers the benediction, I breathe a little sigh of relief.

"The service will continue at Beekman Hills Memorial Cemetery. We ask that you join us, if you're able, to pay your final respects there." He nods, and with crisp precision, six of the men in blue uniforms carry the flag-draped casket up the center aisle.

Jack escorts Chloe, her arm through his, his hand wrapped around hers. His eyes staring straight ahead.

My tears start up all over again, watching the show that not one of us wants to attend.

"Kate, you okay?" Lis asks softly, her hand gently rubbing my shoulder.

"I'm good," I whisper.

Because, if nothing else, a funeral puts everything back in perspective, acts as a reminder not to get caught up in the little things but to look deep within, holding close the things that are important and casting off the rest among the tombstones.

The pews empty, faces downcast, tissues dabbing at bloodshot eyes. Gracyn steps out into the aisle and reaches out for my hand. Feeling more than a little off-balance, I take her hand and maneuver my bulk out of the pew. My best friends walk with me, out of the cool chapel and into the blazing heat. How can the sun deign to shine at a time like this?

The graveside service is what does me in though. A handful of chairs set up on the side of the hill. The plot is shaded, thank God, a light breeze stirring the leaves of the trees overhead.

We're not far from where Francie is buried, and Gracyn and Lis each glance in the direction of his grave.

"Y'all can go visit him," I say softly. "I'll be fine right here."

"I'm good," Gracyn says, squeezing my hand.

Lis adds, "I just came by yesterday."

I hit the jackpot when I stumbled on these two. They walk with me, our progress slow, up the slight incline to the sun-dappled gravesite.

A hush falls over the gathering as the hearse doors are opened. Chloe and Jack walk quietly behind the casket, her hand periodically reaching out. Reaching for her husband, not ready to let him go. The family settles in the chairs—Chloe and Jake, her parents and Tripp's. His sister and Chloe's brothers. Tripp's granddad, bless him, offers me his chair. Him leaning on his cane, me with this belly.

"Thank you, sir, but I'm just fine," I whisper.

I can't take his chair. I just can't stand the idea of getting any closer, like this whole thing is contagious and I could somehow be next if I got too close.

After the chaplain says a few words, all the uniformed service members shift, standing tall, hands held in loose fists that are precisely lined up with the yellow stripes down their legs. One of them, his uniform slightly different from Jack's, moves to stand next to the casket.

"Staff Sergeant Riojas," he calls in a booming voice.

"Here, Team Sergeant," comes the response.

"Sergeant First Class Baker."

"Here, Team Sergeant."

"Sergeant Vance."

"Here, Team Sergeant."

"Sergeant Triplett."

Silence. Of course, because Tripp is dead.

"Sergeant Dallas Triplett."

Why is he doing this? It's cruel.

"Sergeant Dallas H. Triplett."

The only sound is a gasped sob from Chloe as she pitches forward in her folding chair, her hand shaking over her mouth. Jack wraps an arm around her shoulders, pulling her to him. Supporting her because without him holding her up, holding her back, she looks like she could throw herself across her husband's casket.

I sway forward with her as she tries again to reach for Tripp.

Lis grabs me, pulling me back to balance. "Gracyn, get her water bottle," she hisses. "Kate, take a drink."

"I'm fine," I insist. I'm fine. I'm okay. This is not about me.

Gracyn shoves my water bottle into my hand anyway, lifting it toward my mouth. I don't have the energy to fight about this right now, so I take a sip, only to drop the bottle to the ground at the sound of rifle fire.

The retort echoes across the hill again.

And once more as Chloe weeps.

Jake startles, crying out, "My daddy. I want my daddy."

Lis and Gracyn move quickly as my knees buckle slightly, and I reach for the large maple tree behind me. As heartbreaking as Francie's funeral was this spring, this one is so much worse. So much.

The chilling strains of "Taps" rise up, sunlight glinting off the bugle.

"Kate, let's get you to the car," Gracyn says.

I shake my head, unwilling to try to form words.

"It's okay. We'll just—"

"No," I croak out. "Not yet." I cling to my friends as the flag is removed from the casket, folded precisely, smoothed, and presented to Chloe with three brass shell casings resting on top.

With a heavy heart, I nod finally. The flag clutched to Chloe's chest, Jake sobbing, and Jack tending to them is enough for me.

My heart breaks as I turn away, whispering, "Take me home."

TWENTY-NINE

Jack

I watch through a haze of grief as Kate and her friends arrive at the memorial. My eyes drawn to her at every opportunity. Her teary gaze dragging from the casket of my fucking hero to the wife and child he left behind while I delivered the eulogy.

Useless fucking words—that's all they were. There's no way to capture the things that made Tripp the man he was or even come close to doing him justice.

Tripp entrusted me with taking care of his family when he was no longer able. It's the kind of conversation you have when you've waded through hell and made it back out the other side. A promise made that never in your wildest dreams do you think you'll have to fulfill because the person you make that vow to is nothing short of invincible.

That was Tripp—invincible until he wasn't.

Every gasp that Chloe made, every sob from Jake

wrenched at my heart. My focus needs to be one hundred percent on Tripp's family.

So, I brace as rigidly as I can, practically holding Chloe up as she follows her husband down the aisle of the chapel. Eyes forward, hand covering hers where her fingers dig into my arm, guiding her down this hellish gauntlet to the car that will ferry us to a final good-bye.

Compartmentalization is my saving grace. I've had so much thrown at me in such a short amount of time; it's the only way I'm able to keep my shit together.

Give me a mission and an objective, and I'm fine. I can analyze the fuck out of what needs to happen—communications, transportation, the desired outcome—and choreograph the steps it takes to see it through. It's ingrained in me. Pounded into me by the very best of the best—my team, my friends, my brothers.

I've trained for that. I can dissect the situation, find our marks, and make shit happen.

Burying Tripp was never part of that mission.

And, now, there's Kate. Every shift, every sway of her body pulls at me, making me want to go to her. Wrap her in my arms and make up for everything I missed, and at the same time, I want to run fucking far and fast.

The news that she's pregnant hasn't even settled in yet, and twins ... twins are a fucking shock. But there is no denying that the belly she's got is home to some crazy, active boys. My active boys. Jesus Christ, this is not what I planned, not for an instant.

A million times, it's run through my head that Tripp had a gift for making this shit work, the job and a family. Most of the guys do and do it well. I don't think I have that skill, and

I've never fucking wanted it. Maybe that's the missing piece. Maybe that's my failure.

Kate's retreating form is surrounded and supported by her friends, each holding tight to her. Guiding her down the hill to a small sedan. When she is tucked into the passenger seat, I squint into the blazing sun, looking for the shift of her body, the glint of metal showing that she's buckled in safely.

"Go. You need to talk to her." Chloe's voice is hoarse, thick with all the tears she's shed and the ones still to come.

"I'm good."

"I know. You're fine. You know the definition of fine, right?"

Everyone knows the stupid definition. "Freaked out. Insecure. Neurotic. And Emotional. Yeah, but you and Jake are my priority. Tripp—"

"He'd want you to go take care of *your* family," Chloe rasps, her breath catching on her words. "You know he would, Jack. I know you didn't plan for any of this to happen, but Ms. Beard is the nicest, sweetest ... well, I'm guessing you actually know all of that already. Otherwise, there wouldn't be two sweet baby boys getting ready to join the world. You know your heart, Jack. And, however you feel about balancing a family with your career, that doesn't change the fact that you have a family now. Babies, Jack. Boys who need their father—for whatever time God sees fit to give you with each other.

"My parents are here, Tripp's parents. Jake and I are covered, really. And, God, all I want to do is go home and crawl into bed. I want to close my eyes and pretend for just one more day that he's going to be there when I wake up. That Jake'll have just one more day with his dad."

My molars grind against each other; the muscles in my jaw clench and tighten. It actually feels like every muscle in my body is contracted, locked down, and ready to explode. "I know. I will. I'll take care of things. But I need to see things through with this. Get you and Jake settled, make sure you're squared away."

"Okay," Chloe concedes. "But then I'm kicking your ass out, Jack."

Shaking my head, I allow the corners of my mouth to lift into the briefest of smiles because, damn, after all the time they've been married, Tripp is alive in Chloe. "You sound just like him."

TRUE TO HER WORD, Chloe granted me the honor of escorting her and her family home. Seeing that they had everything they needed.

And then she pushed me out the door. "You promised. Just go take care of your own business."

On the way back to my hotel—the same damn one down to the motherfucking room that I stayed in last time I was here—I stop by the Irish pub. Honestly, I'm shocked to see the blonde chick who was with Kate earlier behind the bar. The redhead sitting across from her turns to face me, my beret clasped between my hands.

"Is Kate ... *shit.*"

The looks from these two are enough to stop me in my tracks. I don't know why I thought for even a minute that Kate wouldn't have told her best friends about how I handled the news.

"Sorry. I'm Jack. We've not had the pleasure of meeting yet." I offer my hand, fully expecting to be blown off.

The blonde glares, scrubbing at the pristine bartop in front of her. "Because you were too busy fucking our friend last time you were in port," she spits the words like daggers.

"For the love of God, Gracyn, you don't have to be such an ass." The redhead shakes my hand, offering, "I'm Lis. It's good to meet you."

"Is it though? Really?" the blonde mutters.

"And this is Gracyn, but she seems to be struggling with manners today." Lis pops a side-eye at Gracyn, the former roommate.

And then, with a blink and a sigh, her demeanor changes, throwing me into a different kind of discomfort. "I'm so sorry for your loss. How's his family doing? Kate loves that little boy."

Emotions reach up, clawing at my throat, and I have to swallow them down to speak. "Thank you. They're doing as well as can be expected. Family is with them right now, and the team"—I clear my throat because the team will never be the same without Tripp—"will look out for Chloe and Jake."

"And you?" Gracyn asks.

"They're family. That won't ever change."

"What about your other family? What about your responsibilities to Kate and those babies? What about them?" She pulls a bottle of Patrón from the top shelf behind the bar and pours herself a healthy glass, two fingers easy. Maybe three.

Sliding a twenty across the bar, I nod at the tequila, and after a contemplative sip, she concedes, pouring a splash for me and then topping off her own.

"I appreciate your concern"—I lift my glass to this fierce friend—"but I believe that's between Kate and me." I swallow a paltry amount of tequila and set the glass back on the bar. "Is she at home?"

Lis doesn't have half the attitude that Gracyn is sporting and nods. "She is. Today took a lot out of her, I think."

"Thank you. Is there anything you can think of that she needs? I'm happy to stop on the way."

Silently, Lis shakes her head. And, with a final nod, I turn, the crisp click of my dress shoes matching the beat of my heart as I cross to the door.

"Why'd you come here first?" Gracyn's question pulls me to a stop.

I wondered which one of the women would ask, if they would ask.

"Because you're important to Kate. You've been here for her while I wasn't, and I owe you an introduction and my heartfelt thanks." Pushing out the door, I put my beret on, arranging the flash above my left eye, and hope that answer was enough.

THREE SHARP RAPS on her door get me nothing. Three more and a small bit of patience get me some slow shuffling and a call to hang on. When the door finally opens, something deep in my chest cracks wide open. Gone is the black dress from earlier in the day, the swaths of fabric that wrapped her up, accentuating her curves. Now, a T-shirt I haven't seen since our weekend in the mountains strains across her belly and pale gray pajama pants end just below her knees. Eyes puffy with tears.

And she has never looked more beautiful.

"What do you want, Jack?" Kate shifts her weight, one hand supporting our boys, the other pushing at her lower back. Light from the late afternoon sun glows through her hair. Beautiful. She shifts again and huffs a lock of hair out of her face.

"I came to apologize. Talk to you and figure this out, I guess. Can I come in?"

Beautiful, yes, but the way she's shifting her weight and pushing at her back, she's got to be massively uncomfortable.

Kate steps back into her apartment, waves toward the couch, and continues down the hall. "Make yourself comfortable. I'll be right back."

When she lowers herself down onto the gray velvet cushions several minutes later, she says, "Sorry, one of them was tap-dancin' on my bladder. And I should have offered you somethin' to drink before I sat down."

"Stop," I say, holding my hand out at her. "Let me. What do you need?"

"Water would be great. Help yourself to whatever you want. I think there's a beer in the fridge—maybe. The good stuff is in the cabinet above."

I sift through the cabinets, finding what I need and, sweet mother of God, there's a half-full bottle of Casamigos Blanco in her liquor cabinet. I grab the bottle, tucking it under my arm, while balancing Kate's water and a glass of ice in my hand.

"You mind if I grab the bag of chips?"

"Have at it. Salsa's in the fridge."

I settle everything on the coffee table, handing Kate her water and splashing tequila into my glass. "Mind if I take off my jacket? I've, uh ... it'd be nice to relax a little." I push the polished brass buttons through, releasing the form-fitting jacket.

She waves her hand at me, tearing into the bag of tortilla chips instead. *"Oh-ma-Gawd,"* she moans around a mouthful of chips.

I missed that moan. Although last time I heard it was under much different circumstances. The first time I'd heard it was evidently what got us here.

Kate rocks, pushing herself forward, reaching for the salsa.

"Here." I pop the top and hand the jar to her. "Do you need something more? Have you eaten today?"

"Jack, I eat constantly. All the time. These boys are already wreaking havoc." Kate snorts, dripping salsa on her shirt. My shirt. "Damn it. Every single time." She swipes at the dab of tomato resting on the swell of her breast. "So, what did you want to say? Thought you were crystal clear when you stormed out of my classroom, and that's fine. Really."

"It's not. Jesus, Kate, I was surprised. This past week— losing Tripp, finding out about this." I nod at her.

A corner of a chip tumbles from her lips, coming to rest on top of her belly. The chip moves, lifting and then settling again. Moved by what? One of our kids?

"Why didn't you contact me? Tell me you were—"

"How would you have had me do that? Send a text that you'd get at some point when you landed? Last text I sent was that we were in the clear, and you hardly responded to that. Thought you'd have been all kinds of receptive, gettin' an *oops, guess I was wrong 'bout that* text. Or should I have gone to my student's mother and asked her to let you know I was knocked up? That woulda been real professional. And did they, either of them, even know we were—"

"Tripp figured it out. That we were seeing each other, but he never said anything about ..." I wave at the big bump between us, a lump pushing out at an odd angle. "What is that?" I ask.

Kate reaches for my hand, placing it over the hard alien lump. Pushing against it. "A butt probably. Maybe a head. I don't really know."

The baby rolls, shifting away from the pressure, shoving his brother, so a different ass or body part rolls down the other side of Kate's belly.

"This happen all the time?" I ask, enthralled by the wrestling match taking place.

Laughing, Kate nods. "All the damn time. You have no idea. If they're not fighting each other, they're beating on me." She splays her hands, running them in lazy circles over her abdomen, humming softly, and her belly—our babies seem to relax before my eyes.

"Jesus, you're amazing." The words leave me on a reverent hush.

THIRTY

Kate

THE JACK SITTING IN my apartment is not the same one who walked out of my classroom days ago. The one who spit condescension and judgment at me as he stonily walked away. This one is much more like the Jack I spent a month wrapped up in, falling for.

"You're right; it would have been awkward, putting Chloe in the middle of things. I just wish I had known." He runs his hand down his face, his scruffy beard no longer there.

He looks so different with his face smooth, hair cropped short, and in that uniform. Even half-undone, his jacket and tie neatly folded over the back of a chair, his bearing is entirely something else. Familiar and, at the same time, new.

"I wrote to you," I softly tell him. "Made sure to tell you every little thing—doctor's appointments, when I first felt them move. All of it. God, I have pictures from the sonograms. Let me—"

"Stop, Kate." He stops my struggle to stand once again. "You need something, just tell me where it is. I'm here now."

He pushes himself off the couch with so much grace and ease, not like the lumbering whale I've become, having to roll to the side and heave myself up. There is nothing graceful or attractive about that. Nothing at all.

"I have to get up anyway."

But, instead of having to struggle up on my own, Jack is there. A strong hand, a firm grip. Someone to steady me as I make it to my feet. I hurry down the hall as fast as I can manage. I grab my journal, not sure that I can make it back to the living room with it before I have to pee, but Jack's right there. Silently filling my room.

"Here, I have to pee." I push past him to the bathroom, thrusting the journal into his hands, careful not to let the pictures flutter out.

"Not sure whether to laugh or—"

"Probably not the best idea right now. No one likes the guy who makes fun of the fat kid," I call through the door.

Instead of an empty room, I walk out of the bathroom to find Jack propped up against my headboard, sifting through grainy black-and-white pictures, his jaw working tightly. Fingers dancing over the images of our babies. Watching him process in mere moments all that I've had months to wrap my head around is sobering. I have no idea what those months of his life held. The things he did, the decisions he had to make, the lives he saw come and go.

But I do know what he came home to.

Jack tilts his head, his eyes drifting from the pictures clutched in his hand, the most recent ones, showing our babies' profiles, to where they're pushing on each other, fighting for space inside me. "They're really real, aren't they?" His gaze meets mine, eyes wide.

"Yeah." I chuckle. "There's no pretending going on here. Contrary to popular opinion, I did not go on a binge and just get super huge for kicks."

He jerks his head, looking totally offended. "Who said that?"

I pull my salsa-stained T-shirt over my head, my camisole underneath hiding next to nothing. "No one. Just feels that way sometimes. Not as much now. I mean, I'm for sure knocked up, but ... I don't know."

He leans forward, scanning me from head to toe, eyes lingering on my boobs, my belly. Just as he opens his mouth to say something overly nice, I'm sure, his phone chirps with an incoming call. Checking the screen, he nods briefly. "I have to take this. I'm sorry."

"It's all good. Stay here. I'll go pee. Again."

Jack finishes his phone call, his voice the only indication that he's moving through my apartment. "Are you okay?" he asks, stepping into the kitchen, his warm hand heavy on my back.

"Lower. Put your hand lower on my back. God, yes, right there." I manage to barely suppress a moan at the relief his hand gives me as I sway my hips from side to side, elbows resting on the kitchen island.

Jack makes a strangled noise deep in his throat.

"Sorry. I'm sure this is a sight, but there're times when leaning on the counter like this is the only thing that feels good. It's like all the pressure is off my organs for a hot minute."

I straighten my legs and push back, looking to deepen the

stretch in my hips, but what I find is Jack. His free hand shoots to my hip, fingers digging in, holding me against him. My body lights up at the feel of him hard behind me.

"You have any idea what you're doing to me?" he rasps, his hard cock trapped between us.

He leans over me, chest to my back, and presses his lips to the back of my neck. It tingles down my spine. I push back into him again, rubbing my ass against his length.

Maybe it's just the hormonal hornies, but pent-up desire ignites as his hands roam and caress. Sliding up my sides, over my belly. Cupping my swollen breasts. The way he touches me is reverent, like he's worshipping the changes in my body.

"Mercy," he huffs, lips trailing electric kisses along down my spine, hips grinding into me. "Tell me you want this, Kate. God, tell me this is okay."

"Please ..." I gasp, my mind clouded with the need to feel more. To connect with Jack, to feel him in me, around me. With me. "I don't know how ... logistics ..." I start nervously.

Teeth sink into my hip as Jack steps away, his belt clattering open. The hiss of his zipper.

His wallet hits the counter beside me, and he fumbles it open, searching for a condom but coming up empty. Kind of a moot point at this stage anyway, but maybe he's had opportunities that I haven't. Maybe this isn't a good idea.

"Fuck." His head falls, forehead on my back as he dips his hand down the front of my jammie pants. "I swear, Kate, I haven't been with anyone since you, but"—his finger strums my clit, circling maddeningly—"I can still take care of you."

Moaning as he thrusts one thick finger and then two into

my pussy, I rock shamelessly against him. "Mmm-mmm. I need you, Jack. Please," I gasp. "Need you."

Shoving my PJs and panties to the floor, Jack frees his cock, and achingly slow, he fills me. Almost immediately, my legs start to tremble.

"God, yes," he grunts, thrusting gently, hitting *that spot*, the one that makes my eyes roll back and all my inner muscles clench.

Pleasure rolls through me, exploding in delicious waves. Jack stills, breathing hard, and pulls away, hissing as his hard cock leaves my still-pulsing vag.

"Why did you stop?" I stand and face him.

"I didn't want to hurt them." He makes a sad attempt at stuffing his dick away, pain and determination written across his face.

Using my toes, I fling my panties and PJs up into my hand and shove Jack out of the kitchen and toward the bedroom. "Nope. You're big, but that's not a thing. You're not poking anyone in the eye, not causing brain damage, none of that. If you changed your mind and don't want to do this"—I drop my gaze to his groin—"just say so. But we both know you're lying."

Lord, I hope he's lying. I can't say that, at this stage of pregnancy, I feel all that attractive, just bloated and huge, more like a sumo wrestler than anything. But Jack's caressing hands wandering over my body, feeling what I thought was his genuine excitement, made me feel sexy for the first time in months. The other moms in my prenatal yoga class all talk about how their husbands make them feel amazing and confident, sexy and beautiful. Today with Jack is the first time I've come close to feeling anything like that.

And I want more. Even if it's just for as long as he's here. Again.

But why would he want me like this? We're nothing more than two people who broke a condom. Spectacularly.

"Wait, why are you walking away from me?" Jack asks. "Are you crying? Did I hurt you?" He clutches my face between his palms, thumbs swiping at the tears under my eyes.

I shake my head, feeling overwhelmingly stupid. Hating that, once again, I can't seem to control my tears.

"Kate, talk to me."

"It's nothing. I'm fine."

Jack chuckles softly and kisses me slowly. Thoroughly, deeply. "Freaked out, insecure, neurotic, and emotional. That's what *fine* stands for. What're you thinking about?"

"This hasn't been easy for me. Everyone I know who's pregnant has support, all kinds of support. Gracyn and Lis have been tremendously helpful, but this is ... it's hard. The small hint just now of what it would be like to have a partner in this. To not be alone. To feel like I'm still a person, a woman, and not just a breeding factory. Because it's hard to feel attractive for a minute, let alone sexy. And I felt that out there."

I have lost my damn mind. I know it with every fiber of my being. Words are tumbling from my mouth, emotional vomit spewing across the room, thrown at the nearest target. "I shouldn't fuss. Thank you. That connection, however brief, is what I needed. Or maybe it was the orgasm that I needed, but really, I'll be okay, and you've been more than gracious. You don't need to feel pressured into doing that again or anything."

Jack sits on the edge of my bed, pulling me toward him. "Katelyn, I assure you, I was not being gracious. Not in the least. A little scared? Yep, absolutely, but that was not a pity fuck or whatever." He slides his hands under my camisole, exposing my burgeoning belly. "Take this off. Let me see you. Feel you. Worship you. How can you think you're not attractive?"

Before my cami hits the floor, Jack's face is in my tits, licking at where they overflow the cups of my bra. Swiping his tongue between them where they're smashed together. With the flick of his fingers, the clasps are unhooked, and my breasts spill free.

"Everything about you is ripe and gorgeous. And there is nothing sexier than seeing you filled up with our babies. Makes me want to keep you like this forever," he murmurs, sucking a sensitive nipple into his mouth.

I arch into him, digging my fingers into his shoulders until he pulls away, letting my nipple fall from his mouth with a gentle bite.

Jack pops the buttons on his dress shirt until it's free enough to pull over his head. Triceps flexing as he tosses it to the floor. He shimmies back into the middle of the bed, toeing off his shoes, shedding his thin blue pants and boxer briefs. "Come here. If you're in control, I won't feel like I'm gonna hurt you. Or them. But, sweet cheeks, I promise you, there is nothing I want more than to feel you sink down onto my dick and run my hands over every single one of your curves."

He holds his hand out for me, helping me to climb onto the bed and straddle his hips.

Never before in my life have I felt this exposed, this self-conscious. I wrap one arm across my chest, the other slanting down, futilely trying to cover up as much of my mass as I can.

"Don't you hide from me." He takes my hands, gently placing them on my thighs. "We did this amazing, unintentional thing. Neither of us saw this coming, but, Jesus, I can't stop thinking about the fact that we did this." His big hands spread across my belly, sliding up over the top, turning to cup my full breasts before roaming back down again. "How can you think you are anything other than sexy as fuck?"

Slowly rocking his hips, Jack lifts me, guiding me until he slides into me, and then he lets me take control of how much, how deep. And those sexy, confident feelings all come flooding back to me. His teeth sinking into his lip. His eyes caressing me, hands everywhere at once. Curses and prayers mumbled along with words of beauty.

The only thing missing is love.

THIRTY-ONE

Jack

I'M NOT A FOOL. I don't honestly think I have a magic dick that makes everything shiny in the world, but the change in Kate after we ... well, the word *fucked* isn't right. *Made love* feels closer to the truth, but goddamn, just thinking it makes me feel like I need to turn in my man card. I've done enough self-reflection, enough psych evaluations, to know that—for me at least—actions speak louder than words.

But the change in Kate pulled hard at my heart. That shit about not being attractive? Fuck no. She is stunning. I meant what I said to her about keeping her pregnant. All it took was Chloe's verbal slap upside the head and the reality of loss to bring me clarity, to confirm that I can do this. That I want this. The idea of being suckered did not sit well with me. Not at all. But ironing out those details in my mind, skimming through the journal she's been keeping, and seeing them—our boys had a bigger impact on me than I ever thought possible. How the fuck can seeing grainy black-and-white pictures of tiny humans twist something so drastically inside me?

Kate fell asleep almost immediately after she came. Well, after cleaning up our mess and pissing yet again. She crawled right into bed, nestling into me, her ass tucked in tight. How she sleeps with these two heathens pushing and kicking is beyond me. I rub my thumb across a bump—an elbow, maybe a knee—and chuckle at the push back from within. I get why her students were all about giving the babies high fives.

"They won't stop," Kate mumbles into the pillow. "They've got to be the most active kids ever."

"Probably how they were made, all rambunctious and with gusto."

"Gusto? What the hell with that word? Who talks like that?" She rubs her belly and laughs softly. "You know when they didn't move?"

"When I was bopping them on the head. So, now, we know how to get them to sleep once they're evicted." The kisses I trail across her shoulders are brought up short when she tenses. "What?"

"You're talking like you're going to be here, in our lives." She shakes her head and hides her face in her hands. "Don't do that if this isn't what you really want. You were super clear on not wanting to be stuck, Jack."

"The last thing I feel is stuck. I thought about you constantly. Talked to Tripp a lot, picked his brain. Team Sergeant has four kids, and they're good ones. Manners, smart. Not at all entitled, belligerent hellions."

It takes a lot of effort, but Kate rolls toward me, our babies tucked between us. "If that were all it took, Jake would've been proof enough that Army brats weren't necessarily brats. What about the other stuff? Your family, the girl who tried to keep you in Montana?" Her eyes are wide, her expression completely open, and all the Southern drawl this girl possesses is out for the world to hear.

"I saw Jess when I was home for Christmas, met her daughter, too. She's still manipulative. Asked me to spend time with her while I was there. Pretty sure her husband wouldn't have appreciated that too much. And my family ..." *What the hell do I say about them?* "My dad worked me hard, fixing fences and tending to the ranch. Told the town and the entire family that I was done playing soldier and was coming home to take over the ranch—do real work."

"Seriously? What would make him do that?"

"Purely selfish. He thinks I should be there, so that's all he can see. What he didn't expect were my twin sisters and their husbands taking exception to that."

"You have twin sisters? Really? You couldn't have mentioned that?"

"Yeah. Didn't exactly plan on all this." I trail my fingers down her side, tickling her as I get low on her bump.

"So, did they set your dad straight or what?"

"We all did. My brothers-in-law were ready to walk away. Ironically, they're brothers, not twins, but close enough—"

"Irish twins? That's what Francie used to call them, when he was still alive. Just nine months or so apart."

"That's about right. Who's Francie?" I ask.

"He owned the pub before." Kate sighs, looking like tears'll come any minute. "Before he passed away on St. Patrick's Day. He was an amazing man, a father when you needed one, a businessman who knew when to break the rules and how to take risks. He was the kindest, fiercest friend with a ready smile, a bad joke, and bit of wisdom. His only drawback was that he was a whiskey drinker and not a fan of tequila at all. But he did order a bottle of Patrón for the bar just for me."

I swipe at the tears gathering in her eyes. "I'm so sorry."

"He didn't want to bother any of us—Lis and Gracyn mostly and Finn—with the fact that he had cancer. So, he kept it hidden, put things in place so that the pub and the family he'd collected would all be taken care of. He was a good man. He's buried not far from Tripp." She takes a deep, cleansing breath, expelling sadness, painting a watery smile on her face. "Sorry. Tell me more about your brothers-in-law."

"Jesus, Kate, I'm so sorry. I would've liked to have met him and maybe ... I don't know ... shared a whiskey with him." I tuck a lock of hair behind her ear, the strand like silk between my fingers. Hating even more that she was hurting and I missed it, all of it. I huff out my frustration and continue, "Anyway, their grandfather died, left them some money and some land. Told my pops that, after all they'd done for him, for the ranch, that he'd best not push them aside for someone who didn't even want to be there. The guys at least talk with me once in a while and know full well that I don't want that life. There is nothing but respect in both directions, but relations are strained, to say the least. Despite all of that, I was headed there post-deployment to help with calving, but Tripp made a better argument for coming back here instead, and thank God for that." I brush my lips across her forehead.

. . .

"WHEN DID THEY GO from Baby A and Baby B to M and D?" I shuffle through the pictures of the babies again as Kate brings a basket of baby clothes to the kitchen island. "And what's with *Oops* and *Uh-oh* in your journal?"

A deep, sexy laugh bubbles up out of Kate, shaking her tits, distracting me. "*Oops*—well, I think that's self-explanatory. And, once the doctor told me there were two, *Uh-oh* seemed the perfect fit until I could decide on names."

"We're coming back to the name thing in a minute, but why did you wait so long to go to the doctor?" I ask. Little by little, piece by piece, we've spent the past couple of weeks reliving the six months we were apart. Kate sharing the details of what she went through alone, and me trying to make up for not being here for her.

"I was scared to face reality. Wanted to hide from it for as long as I could. It was stupid, not a good choice, but I'm human. And I was alone."

I can't argue with her, not with the way I ran when she told me the boys were mine. "Fair enough. And the names? What did you decide?"

"Mason and Dixon Beard. Thus the switch on the sonogram pics." She quirks her mouth and looks at me out of the corner of her eye. "Unless you have a really strong objection," she adds.

And do I fucking ever.

"Mason and Dixon are fine. I like the North-South thing you've got going on, but—"

"It's less to do with that than you think. My great-granddaddy was a mason—a bricklayer really. And I thought you'd told me you grew up near Dixon. Is that right? I thought I'd honor both of our families in some way." She smiles and rolls her eyes before adding, "And these two are probably the only reason my mama crossed the Mason-Dixon Line at all, so—"

Mesmerized, I watch as Kate folds tiny little T-shirts with the snap things at the bottom, each one ending up in a precise rectangle. She'd make any drill sergeant proud.

"I like it. Mind if I make a suggestion though?"

She tosses me a shirt to fold and leans over the counter, ass out, back flat, braced on her forearms. She's told me it feels good, relieving pressure, but I'll be damned if I have any kind of capacity to think when she does that. She sways her ass from side to side and eyes me like she's waiting on me to speak.

"Right." I clear my throat. "Mason Triplett *Jackson* and Dixon—"

"Dixon Wyatt Jackson?" she asks.

I hate that I share a name with my asshole father, but maybe between the two of us, Dixon and I—and Jake—can do the name proud.

Adding my rectangle of baby undershirt to the pile, I smirk. "I like that. Just one more thing we need to change."

I reach for the box I'd tucked away in the back of the liquor cabinet last week, just waiting for the right moment. I knew the night of Tripp's funeral, when she let me in, that this day was on the horizon, I just needed to get things in place for it.

"Are you going to show off, drinking the good tequila in front of me again? Makes you more of an ass than the sweet man you know you should be around a ridiculously pregnant woman," she says snarkily. "Think you'd know better by now.

Is there even going to be any of that left by the time I can drink it? I swear to God, you're doing this just to get under my skin." With her forehead resting on her folded arms, Kate's voice echoes hollowly against the countertop. She's officially hit the miserable stage from what her doctor said at last week's appointment.

The black box makes a quiet *shoosh* as I slide it across the granite counter until it rests right in front of her arms. "What's this?" she asks, plucking at the gray and gold bow. Finally, the ribbon falls free, and Kate lifts the tight-fitting lid to reveal two pint-sized black hoodies with the USMA cadet crest emblazoned on the fronts—one in gray, the other in gold.

"Oh, Jack, they're adorable," Kate exclaims, pulling the sweatshirts out one at a time and holding them up for inspection. "Shit, I think they left the sensor on this one." She reaches her fingers into the pocket on the front of the hoodie, practically turning it inside out to get to what is most definitely *not* a store-theft sensor.

"Oh my God." Kate slowly lifts her head, her gaze meeting mine.

I take the diamond ring from her trembling fingers, clasping her left hand in mine. "Kate, somehow, someway, you've done what no one has ever been able to do. From your disastrous history of dating pencil-dicked douche bags to the scariest busted condom removal ever. From one month of a good time to six months of stress and worry. From tombstones to bassinets, you've shown me that we can not just survive in the face of strife, but also thrive. I love you from the desert to the mountains, from the city to the country, across thousands of miles, and just across the room. I want the chance to prove that to you every single day. I love you more than anything in the world. Marry me? Please?" I drop to my knee in front of her and wait.

And wait.

"Yes," she whispers, tears rolling down her face.

"Yes?" I ask because she did not sound really sure about that answer.

"Yes, yes. Absolutely yes."

As delicately as I can, I slide the ring onto her finger. Her hands are kind of swollen, and the fit is tight, but that seems to be our thing.

EPILOGUE

Jack

Christmas in Mississippi

"I'll go." I push up off the floor, pressing Mason's bare feet to my lips.

He doesn't just giggle, but he full-on belly-laughs at the raspberry I blow on them. Dix stares at me, judgment in his big brown eyes. Daring me to do the same to him, but I know better.

My boys are as identical as twins can be, but that doesn't mean they don't have different personalities. Where Mason is a foot man, Dixon is a belly boy.

I walk my fingers up the red-and-white stripes covering his chubby thighs, and little gasps start puffing out of him. Anticipation. The second my face makes contact with his belly, he howls. Laughing and snorting. Gasping, arms flailing. Fat, little fists pulling at what strands of hair they can grasp.

"Uncle Jack, do me. Gickle me," Harper pleads, flopping on the floor next to the boys.

While Kate's niece and the rest of her family have made me feel more than a part of the family, I'm still working on her old man. For a Southern gentleman with a clean-hands banking job, the man is scary as fuck when it comes to his daughter. Granted, I know I did things ass backward and need to earn his respect, but I'm at a loss here. Bourbon, cigars, hunting. I've tried everything, and there's still a chasm that screams to be bridged.

But Harper? Yep, I've got that girl on my side.

Before I can even get my fingers near her neck, she's squealing and laughing, sliding herself across the floor to escape.

"Christ, I hope that never changes," Sam mutters as his older daughter finds her feet and runs to the kitchen.

I pop to standing, the sudden movement startling Mason and Dix, their arms flinging out to the sides, eyes wide.

Sam pulls the bottle from his baby girl's mouth, slack with sleep. "You teach her to run away from boys, and Daddy'll have no choice but to come around and welcome you into the fold."

Glancing over my shoulder toward the study—because, of course, Mr. Beard has a study—I huff out a laugh. "Won't hold my breath on that. Need me to grab anything for you from the store? You wanna go with?" I offer, knowing full well the answer is a resounding—

"Hell no. You have fun with hitting that madhouse on

Christmas." Shaking his head, Sam adds, "But I wouldn't say no to some beef jerky since you're going out anyway."

"Right. Didn't Jules say she didn't put any of that shit in your stocking for a reason? And what the hell makes you think you need jerky? They're in there, getting dessert ready." I slide my feet into flip-flops because Mississippi is a hell of a lot warmer than New York this time of year.

"You offered."

"That I did. Keep an eye on them, will you?" I nod at where my boys are lying on their blanket, eyes drifting closed.

Who knew I was missing a piece of my heart before they arrived? I shake the memory of that shitshow away as I lean into the kitchen. Kate, her mom, Jules, and Harper are all bustling around, getting dishes put away and desserts pulled out. Well, Harper's eating a cookie, but that's probably a strategic move to keep her occupied for a minute.

"Anything else I can grab? Diapers, for sure, but—"

Maggie pats my arm, guiding me to the door. "You just hurry on up and get those. And an extra can of whipped cream." She hands me her car keys and goes back to rearrange the platter of cookies Kate just finished making.

My wife looks exhausted, circles under the big brown eyes she shares with our boys. Lids heavy. Her smile pinched. But she couldn't be more beautiful.

I take three strides to her, unable to leave without kissing her first. "You okay?" I whisper, loving the way she sags against me, melting into my embrace.

"I'm fine"—she rubs her face and pushes her smile higher—"just tired. Hurry back, 'kay?"

I drop a kiss to her upturned lips and haul ass.

The drugstore is far busier than I thought it'd be, and grumbling, I stalk to the back of the store, praying that the refrigerator cases aren't wiped out. I grab the last can of whipped cream and scan the beer selections. Nothing worth my time, so I weave my way through the aisles to all the baby crap. I scan the shelves, zeroing in on the purple packages until I find the size to house my boys' asses. My phone buzzes with a text from Kate, asking me to get the green diapers in the same size for her littlest niece as well as a couple of bibs.

Me: Anything else?

After several seconds, there's no response, so I pick up the extra items and dump everything into a plastic basket before heading to the front of the store to check out. The line is a fucking mile long. I throw a couple of packages of jerky in the basket and settle in to wait my turn.

It's like those questions you see online. *What three things do you purchase that make the cashier wonder what's up?* Sure, my haul is tame, and I'm sitting at four items, but I chuckle at how my life has changed over the past year. Confirmed bachelor to happily married with two kids. Tense, uncomfortable Christmas at home to being welcomed with open arms by my wife's family—mostly. I'll win her dad over somehow.

My phone buzzes again, this time with a call.

"Hey, sweet cheeks. What else did you think of?" I hate to do it, but I'll step out of line, not that it's moved much.

"Jack, don't freak on me, okay?"

"What is it? What's wrong?"

"Nothing's wrong, but I just need you to stay calm and go to the back of the store. The aisle next to the baby stuff." Kate's using her teacher voice on me, and of course, it makes me want to do exactly what she asked me not to—freak out.

I stop at the head of the baby aisle and look to my right and then to my left. "Tampons or Seen on TV? Which aisle?" My heart rate slows to normal when I see the options, waiting for her reply.

"Tampon aisle, but ..."

I walk down the row, waiting for further instructions. I have no problem buying this shit, but for the life of me, I don't know what she needs. Hell, it's not like this has been a part of our relationship with pregnancy and nursing the boys.

"What do you need?"

"Um, the middle of the aisle, between the pads and the condoms," she whispers, her voice echoing like she's closed herself into a small space.

I nod to the dude standing in front of the condoms but avoid making eye contact because that's just weird. Another guy joins the first, standing closer than strictly necessary. No judgment, but damn if things don't feel a little strained all of a sudden. I turn away from them, offering some privacy, refocusing on what my wife is whispering in my ear.

"Start over, Kate. What kind do you need me to get?"

The last thing I expect is exactly what she says. "The brand doesn't matter. Just get a damn test, Jack. I'm panicking here."

My heart swells, and I swear, my chest puffs out with pride. "Katelyn, what are you saying? Are you ... are we ..." I set the basket full of diapers on the floor and shove my hand through my hair. "How did this happen, baby? The twins are only four …" Jesus, I can't even think. "Four months old. How? Your father's going to kill me, isn't he? I'm never getting past calling him Mr. Beard at this rate."

Kate barks out a husky laugh. "That's your big concern? That my daddy's gonna kick your ass? We're married, Jack, and at least he's not wondering if you're gay."

I pluck two different tests from the shelf, dropping them into the basket. "Yeah, no *chance* of that," I huff, putting a little emphasis on her ex's name.

A gasp shoots out of the dude with the condoms, his hand flying to his mouth. I turn to face him, wondering what the chances are that this is Chance. The *Chance*. I stare straight at him, shit-eating grin firmly in place.

"I love you more than anything in the world, Kate. Best Christmas gift, two years running. We gonna make this a thing?"

After calling me an asshole, Kate ends the call, leaving me standing between tampons and condoms, beaming like a fool.

Thank you for spending time in Beekman Hills with Jack and Kate. I would love to know what you think of these two! If you can, please drop a quick review on your favorite retailer for me!

To stay up on releases and happenings, make sure you're signed up for my newsletter *at* www.kcenderswrites.com

...now, jump into **Tattered Hearts: Fire Born Security** (formerly **Broken: a Salvation Society novel**) for the rest of Chloe Triplett's story.

PLAYLIST FOR TOMBSTONES

Hymn for the Missing - Red
Troubled Souls - Kail Baxley
Hero - Shaman's Harvest
Hail to the King - Avenged Sevenfold
Black Soul - Shinedown
Go to War - Nothing More
All of Me - Frank Sinatra
Into the Nothing - Breaking Benjamin
'Til the Casket Drops - ZZ Ward
The Time is Now – Atreyu

ACKNOWLEDGMENTS

ACKNOWLEDGMENTS HAVE NEVER BEEN all that difficult to write. This one, though is tough. Really tough and I have avoided it for longer than was practical or wise. This book, Tombstones, was planned a long time ago. Really since the idea that maybe, just maybe I could write a book—make that three—and if all went well, a handful of people might read it/them. Well, you all have gone above and beyond my wildest imagination in your kind words, recommendations and general excitement for my words. Honestly...what have I done to deserve this? The timing with this one is where things get tricky and emotional.

I started writing Tombstones, back in late September... early October and by the end of October learned that a family member was diagnosed with an aggressive cancer. He fought hard, but cancer sucks and just this morning he passed away. He was a bit of a Francie McBride, Irish as the day is long and always giving and caring for others. He left this world a better place for having been in it

I'd like to thank the amazing family I have. Typically, I dedicate my books to *My Fiends* — my husband and boys who support me like crazy in this writing thing. But family is so much more, and I have been blessed with the best of the best. Thank you.

Deedy, thank you for more than I can even say; keeping

my Pinterest boards fresh, brainstorming the funniest damn scenes, including one that ended up being absolutely pivotal to the story! You keep me motivated and sane and on track and all of that! Thank you from the bottom of my heart.

McKinzee, Robin, Alamea, Jenn, and Mel—much love for reading this and helping me to make it better.

Aerin for naming Jess. Stacy for the memes, check ins and word count reminders.

The bloggers who took time to post and promote this book. My ARC team for all your excitement and spreading the word. Your reviews and recommendations touch my heart and fill my soul. Thank you.

And then there are all the 'patrons' at McBride's on Main—my reader group. I can't tell you how much I enjoy each and every one of you! I'm thankful you've found me and can't imagine the place without you!! Thank you.

Prologue
Chloe

A hush falls over the cemetery as the doors of the hearse creak open.

My husband's best friend, Jack, walks with me behind Dallas's casket, quietly supporting me. I reach out, searching for one last moment with my dead husband. I'm not ready to let him go. I'll never be ready to let him go.

Jack escorts me to the chairs set in two precise rows, occupied by my son, my parents, and my brothers. Dallas's parents, his sister. Even Dallas's granddad—God bless him— is here, refusing a seat, instead leaning on his cane.

"Thank you," I whisper as Jack lowers himself into the chair next to me.

The chaplain speaks, his voice ringing out sad and clear, but nothing he says registers. How can it? My husband is dead, lying in the flag-draped box in front of me. It's too soon. We had too many things left undone in our lives for him to be ripped away from us now.

How am I going to do this on my own?

The air changes as the uniformed service members shift, standing at attention, tall and proud. Jesse Dennison, the team sergeant for Dallas's unit, moves into position next to the casket. Even though I know what's coming, I flinch as he starts the final roll call.

"Staff Sergeant Riojas," he calls in a booming voice.

"Here, Team Sergeant," comes the response.

"Sergeant First Class Baker."

"Here, Team Sergeant."

The crack in my chest deepens.

"Sergeant Vance."

"Here, Team Sergeant."

"Sergeant Triplett."

Silence. And my heart stalls in my chest.

"Sergeant Dallas Triplett."

Crippling pain sears through me, ripping me apart.

"Sergeant Dallas H. Triplett."

My life is in tatters, my love lying broken at my feet.

The only sound is my gasped sob. Jack wraps an arm around me, pulling me back from the brink. Back from where I was reaching out for Dallas, my hand grasping at nothing but air. I'm only barely aware that Jack is supporting me, holding me up. Holding me back because, without him, I think I could throw myself across Dallas's casket.

I don't know how much more I can take.

I don't know how I can live without him.

The crisp report of rifle fire echoes across the hill.

Once.

Twice.

Three times.

Jake startles next to me, crying out, "My daddy. I want my daddy."

Tears stream down my face, unbidden and unwelcome.

The chilling strains of "Taps" rise up. Sunlight glints off the bugle as the flag is removed from Dallas's casket, precisely folded, and carefully smoothed. Three brass shell casings rest on top.

With my husband's flag clutched tightly to my chest and Jake sobbing as Jack tends to us, I say my final good-bye to the only man I've ever loved.

Chapter One
Chloe

five years later

Deep breath in, slowly exhale. Deep breath in, slowly exhale.

Anxiety pulls at every cell in my body, panic looming, staring me down. My gaze darts around the inside of the gas station as I try to commit each face to memory, looking for a sign that one of them is harboring a secret. Searching for a tell, a flash of metal, a nervous twitch that comes just before the strike.

"Mom, can I get a soda?" Jake asks.

I scan the faces again, and with a terse nod, my hand clamped firmly on his shoulder, I guide my son to the wall lined with cups and fountain drinks.

"You're doing it again, jeez. I can get it," he whines, shrugging against my hand.

I miss my sweet, polite, respectful little boy and wonder for a hot minute who replaced him with this prepubescent Jekyll. Or is it Hyde? It doesn't really matter at the moment because we just need to get out of here—and fast.

"Quickly, please," I tell him, paying more attention to the bodies filtering in and out of the store than I am to Jake.

Concerned about what is taking so long, I dart a glance to Jake, only to see it's not just a soda he's getting. The biggest cup they have is nearly overflowing with the sugariest, most caffeinated bright red beverage available.

"Jacob Wyatt Triplett, what are you thinking?" I scold.

He, of course, rolls his eyes and gives me a frustrated sigh that would test the patience of Mother Teresa. There are only so many things I can concentrate on at once, and right now, I need to focus on our safety.

"Put a lid on it, and let's go," I say through gritted teeth.

I steer him to the register, already holding my debit card and hating that I have my back to the room. I feel exposed. Vulnerable. Scared.

Jake stands next to me, the ridiculous vat of soda clutched possessively in both of his hands. And with each step we take toward the register, he takes a half-step to the side, putting distance between us.

I swallow, trying to push down the lump that's formed in my throat.

"That's three dollars and twenty-two cents," the cashier says, sounding tinny and far away, already ringing up the next customer on the register to her left.

I shove my card into the slot, and the sun glints off something shiny, reflecting a burst of light into my eyes. I flinch, reaching blindly for Jake but he's not there. He's just out of reach, at the end of the counter, looking at brightly colored candies, oblivious to the world.

With a metallic flash, panic surges through me in a way it hasn't in a very long time. I bend my knees, lowering into a crouch, and step toward Jake. As my fingers brush against the sandy-brown hair curling behind his ear, what sounds like a gunshot slices through my heart, and the feel of shrapnel bites through the backs of my legs.

My only thought is of getting to my son, keeping him safe.

Another flash, and a hand latches on to my shoulder, pulling me back, away from Jake. Away from the object of my singular focus.

My heart thrashes in my chest, my blood like lead in my veins.

My lungs contract, pulling in tiny bursts of air, but I can't breathe. There's no in and out right now. Just in.

My eyes are wide, but I see nothing as black dots fill my vision, tunneling and then finally closing in on me.

I'm dying.

My eleven-year-old son is going to be all alone. How long will it take his uncle Jack to find him? At least he'll have a real family again. Jack will step into the dad role, and Kate will treat him like one of her own. Siblings. Jake will finally have the siblings he so desperately wanted before his dad died. He already fights with their twin boys like he is the older brother, and God knows he watches over their daughter, Hays, like it's his mission in life.

He'll be okay. He'll be okay. He has to be okay.

***

Jake's voice is the first to filter through my fuzzy head. Not so much the words, just the sound of him chatting—but to whom? I don't recognize the deep rumble asking Jake questions, but instead of pumping up my anxiety, the deep timbre soothes me.

Awareness slowly comes back to me in drips and pieces, and I take stock of myself. My head is killing me, and the tiles of the floor pressed to my back are cold.

The buzz and chattering of conversation between Jake and the stranger take form.

"Her name is Chloe Triplett. I'm Jake. We just moved here, so we don't really know anybody yet," Jake says.

A loud slurp through the straw tells me I've been out long enough for him to finish most of his drink.

Three warm fingers wrap around my arm and press into my wrist below the meat of my thumb. I don't know if it's actually possible, but I feel each heartbeat thrum against that pressure. And each thump seems to be stronger, more electrified than the last. Pushing harder, beating sturdier. Like my heart is grasping at something just out of reach. Something exciting but safe. Something new yet soothingly familiar at the same time.

My eyes flutter open, and I immediately seek out my son. When I find him safe, totally okay, breath whooshes from my lungs.

"Hey, buddy," I croak, my voice raspy and quiet.

What I get in return is a dramatic eye roll and a look of absolute disgust from my almost teenager.

"Why do you do that? Can we just go now?"

My thoughts jump from concern for my precious boy—the last link I have to his father—to the obnoxious reminder of why tigers sometimes eat their young. I push myself up to sitting and try to shake off the big hand still firmly wrapped around my arm.

"Slow down, ma'am." The deep voice only registers in my brain in that it's connected to the man holding me in place. Or maybe he's holding me up.

"Jake." The warning in my voice is clear to everyone standing, gawking, except my kid, if facial expressions are any indication.

I shove my feet underneath me and push myself up with my free hand, barely acknowledging that the stranger next to me is in fact helping me to stand. Panic bleeds through when I call to Jake again, and he turns and bolts out the door. I scoop my wristlet from the floor near my feet and search for my keys, but they're nowhere to be seen, and I can't let Jake be out there alone. I can't trust him to make good choices, even for an eleven-year-old. His shitty judgment, which gets him into trouble, is half the reason we're here in Virginia. The other half ... I just can't go there right now.

With as much dignity as I can muster, I mumble, "Thank you," to the kind stranger next to me and hurry out of the convenience store.

I close my eyes and blow out a sigh of relief at the sight of my kid, pouty and sulking, standing with his back against the side of my car.

"Hey, you've got to stick with me, Jake. I know you were embarrassed, but you can't just take off like that. Especially now, in a new place, right?" I keep my voice low and calm because fear is a close friend of embarrassment, and neither party is particularly welcome at the moment.

My friend, Kate, refers to it as the teacher voice. As a kindergarten teacher, hers is way different from mine, though there are times that I think her students are more mature than the ones I deal with in high school.

"This is stupid," Jake mumbles. "What if somebody saw you? What if they recognize me in school on Monday? I'll literally die of ... of ..." He screws up his face as he searches for the right word.

"Mortification," I offer, leaning against the side of the car next to him, reveling in the bright winter sun. January in Virginia is a stark contrast from what New York would feel like now.

"Yeah, that," he says, focusing on the scuffed, frayed toes of his sneakers.

I reach over and take a quick sip from the last of his soda, handing it back before the scowl fully settles on his face.

"The good news is, anyone your age is in school right now, so they missed the entire thing. You're safe from humiliation for at least another couple of days." I manage to let only a half-smile find its way to my face.

"And the bad news?" he asks, pushing his hair out of his face.

I nod toward the store. "We have to go back in there together and find my keys. I dropped them when I went down."

His face scrunches up, and for a brief moment, I have a glimpse of sweet Jake. My little boy shows his face at the strangest times—when I least expect it and, if I'm lucky, when I need it the most.

ALSO BY KC ENDERS

Sign up for my newsletter at www.kcenderswrites.com for release alerts

Beekman Hills Series

Troubles

Twist

Tombstones

Stand Alone Titles

Sweet on You

Tattered Hearts: Fire Born Security

The UnBroken Series

In Tune (*formerly Tunes*)

Off Bass

Beat Down

Coming Soon

Out Loud

ABOUT THE AUTHOR

Karin is a New York Girl living in a Midwest world. A connoisseur of great words, fine bourbon, and strong coffee, she's married to the love of her life and is mother to two grown men that she is proud to say can cook and clean up after themselves, and always open doors for the ladies thanks to the Rules of Being a Gentleman (you're welcome, world). Her one major vice is rescuing and adopting big dogs.
Tons of personality, not so good on manners.
She loves talking books, hearing from readers, and hosting the occasional virtual Happy Hour in her reading group.

www.kcenderswrites.com

 facebook.com/kcewrites
 instagram.com/authorkcenders

www.ingramcontent.com/pod-product-compliance
Lightning Source LLC
Chambersburg PA
CBHW060556300726
48975CB00005B/1345